ADVANCE PRAISE F

"*Mortal Coil*—unprecedented, visionary, compelling, affecting—transports the reader deep beneath the surface, where the forces that normally nudge our world along, unnoticed, emerge as vividly memorable characters with an agenda. The result is a story that charges through peril and passion with an edge-of-your-seat intensity. It's a parable, a thriller, a spiritual odyssey, a love story, and a novel for our time."
—PHILIP SHEPHERD, *New Self, New World*

"A rip-roaring story that closes the gap between imagination and reality, this novel of exploration into unknown realms introduces a new and breathtaking anatomy. You will cross the line into a deeper way of looking at the world without noticing, swept up in an extraordinary adventure."
—AMANDA HALE, *Sounding the Blood*

"Original, powerful, compelling, sometimes scary. This book contains many worlds, and takes the reader to all of them. Amazing and alive!"
—GALE ZOE GARNETT, *Visible Amazement*

"Buchbinder has created a shamanistic world in which elemental forces have been torn asunder. Vivid, thought-provoking, and startlingly beautiful in its contemplation. A battle cry to be fully alive."
—SHANDI MITCHELL, *Under this Unbroken Sky*

*For David
with gratitude ~ 2016
Revisioning Medicine*

MORTAL COIL

Amnon Buchbinder

(((resounding)))
media

Copyright © 2015 Amnon Buchbinder.

All rights reserved under International and Pan-American Copyright Conventions. No part of this book, except for brief passages in a review, may be reproduced in any form or by any electronic or mechanical means, including information storage and retrieval systems, without permission in writing from the publisher.

This is a work of fiction. Names, characters, places and incidents are either the product of the author's fertile imagination or are used fictitiously. Any resemblance to actual persons, living or dead, events, locales or other worlds is entirely coincidental.

ISBN   978-0-9940303-0-6
            978-0-9940303-2-0 (KINDLE)
            978-0-9940303-1-3 (E-PUB)

First published by
Resounding Media
139 – 260 Adelaide St. E.
Toronto, ON
Canada M5A 1N1

Cover Paintings by Deborah Koff-Chapin
www.touchdrawing.com

Cover and book design by www.go-word.com
Author photo by Chris Wiseman

for elyse

MORTAL COIL

I

I want
to do with you what spring does with the cherry trees.
—Pablo Neruda, *20 Love Poems and
a Song of Despair: Poem XIV*
Translated by W.S. Merwin

1

The motorcycle left the ground and Marti held her breath and slipped from the grasp of time. A new horizon blossomed; she was alone between earth and heaven, a thousand pounds of metal and burning gas propelling her across the threshold. The engine's roar opened out into silence. Silence swallowed everything.

She wasn't steering any more. Her arms wrapped around Rourke, her heart pressed against him from behind, she touched the back of his neck with her lips and felt his warmth flowing into her—alive again.

∞

She had known this ride was going to be different.

Once a year she saddled up the Commando, which she'd had completely rebuilt. Riding it she always felt close to Rourke, closeness that hardened her grief into stone.

Rourke had introduced her to the promise of speed, of leaving yourself behind; to the joy of daybreak on the canyon route, where they could be the only two in the world, the sun's climb over the horizon extended and reversed as the hills lifted and lowered the charging cycle. The climb upward made the sunrise last. Sunrise was something always happening, Rourke said, somewhere on earth. The only way to truly experience it was through movement. It wasn't the movement that killed Rourke. It was coming down to earth.

She remembered the moment they were torn apart. Why should their bodies, moving together, go in such separate directions? Then she was hobbling through the brush, bleeding but intact, believing for a moment that he and his beloved bike had simply disappeared.

She'd struggled for breath as the world around her expanded and contracted. When she found him he was still alive, waiting for her. His face was as beautiful and mysterious as she'd ever seen it, but it was no longer part of a fixed reality. His beauty went through her like a knife. She thought for a moment the pain was something torn inside her. But she recalled the first time she had seen his face, two years before at a friend's New Year's party. She'd felt the same pain then, a dread that, having seen it, she would have to live her life without that face. He'd reminded her of one of those saints by Caravaggio, all red cheeks and pale skin and black hair. His body had always seemed frail, and now it was hardly there, smashed under the bike. It seemed impossible that he was still alive, but his eyes were bright, and he was hyperventilating like a wild animal caught trembling in a snare.

Her first instinct was to pull the smoking bike off him, but the metal was impossibly tangled with his flesh. Instead she just sat with him, as close as she could get, their eyes locked together for a moment, before the light in him receded, and his body shivered and released a breath that seemed like it must have been the very first breath it had taken. And she was alone.

She had been alone ever since. Alone through that first sleepless year, in spite of the support of her friends, who eventually fell away in despair of reaching her. Alone through medical school, finding she could stay alive this way, in a world that gave her an intensity of purpose while protecting her from any obligations of the heart. Alone at the clinic, immersed in work that permitted no time for reflection.

On the first anniversary of Rourke's death she'd roared through the canyon at sunrise, alive, alone on the Commando. She hoped that the ride would free her. She was twenty-one and if she wasn't going to give up on life, she had to find a way to go on. When she eased the bike to a stop, her face wet with tears, she felt a joy she hadn't anticipated.

This time, ten years later, as she reached the canyon, she realized what she had really wanted. To be taken as well. And finally, it was happening.

She took a rise too fast, her bike lifting off the ground. She closed her eyes, still feeling her arms around Rourke. She could just stay like this, and she would be with him again.

Rourke was in front of her, but suddenly Marti felt something behind her. A line of people in the clinic waiting room, their faces tired and creased with worry. The image called her back. The clinic would open in a few hours. People were counting on her.

But the bike was hurtling away from the road. She had lost control. Adrenalin surged through her only to bring the realization that she was now a helpless passenger.

Then it was as if the air around the bike pushed back, correcting its trajectory. The bike returned to earth, skidding to a stop against a copse. Everything was still except the crashing of her heart.

Marti heaved for breath like a fish hauled out of water, then pulled herself off the bike and stumbled into the road. She half expected to find that she was a ghost, but her flesh seemed more solid than ever.

∞

The ride back to town was difficult. She was hemmed in, her body unwilling to press the machine between the lines of traffic as she always did, but plodding slowly, dutifully, within the rush hour's motorized, orderly stampede to another day on the job.

Something had brought Marti back down to earth at the same moment she was certain that she was being lifted away from life, toward reunion with Rourke. It seemed impossible that the bike had righted itself.

She approached the exit that would bring her home, and overcame the impulse to take it.

She passed industrial parks, blankets of pavement now cracked and torn, weeds invading. Expansive housing developments built two generations ago, still inhabited, but with a besieged look, the lawns brittle and shabby, with large, late-model pickups and SUVs in the driveways. A shopping mall, like a cubical space station orbited by a vast parking lot, already well-dotted with cars at this early hour. It occurred to her that she hadn't seen a single person, and for a moment she wondered if she was the only flesh and blood, exiled to a world of machines and concrete.

Finally, up ahead loomed the Park. Its towers gleamed coldly, the first to greet the sun.

The Park. The irony of the name was a given. Nobody called it by its full name, the Martin B. Mulroney Park. No one remembered that it had once been considered a desirable address, that the spaces between the nine towers had been green and open, as the name implied. This was back when there was an average occupancy of 1.4 in the mostly small units, which were being marketed to young office workers. Now the density was about five times that, with more than fifteen thousand human beings crammed into the small high-rise neighborhood, the highest population density on the continent.

Marti was amazed that the whole place didn't crash right into the earth—from the sheer weight of the humanity inside. Not the flesh, blood, and bones, not all the threadbare belongings, but the longings and disappointments. The stories.

As her bike pulled in toward the Park, she felt a surprising spark of pleasure to be back.

∞

The Bill Blake Clinic was built into the base of one of the nine towers, where a supermarket had been. To get there one passed through the more crowded areas of the Park: the tables where people sold one another scavenged or tattered goods that would be largely worthless anywhere else; the playground lit up by children's joy in spite of its crumbling and dangerous condition; the "free store" where charitable outsiders dropped off donations for residents of the Park; the aging picnic benches where teenagers clustered. Everywhere the ground was covered in concrete, pockets of grass mostly worn away, littered with slowly decaying trash. The only thing colorful in the Park was the skin of the residents.

Marti reflected darkly on the irony: people coming from all over the world to a place nobody wanted to live. Her own presence here, the presence of the clinic, had at first seemed like an anomaly, a concession to the medical needs of fifteen thousand humans, maybe a step toward making them part of the surrounding world. But after a time Marti came to feel that, like so many things, the truth was exactly the opposite of what it seemed. The purpose of the clinic was to keep the lid on, to keep these people out of the larger system, and to protect the more prosperous surrounding society by stemming the disease tide at its source. And while that image was offensive to her, there was no question that wherever a disease originated, the Park was a place it could come to multiply with a minimum of effort.

Marti climbed the metal steps to the staff entrance by the old loading dock. She looked around once, then pushed the buzzer and waved at one of the three security cameras. She could feel Mr. Ludovicu looking to make sure it was her, to make sure she was alone, then the lock clicked open.

Her second month at the clinic an addict had slipped in after her, grabbed her clumsily, and tried to throw her down. Her body reacted instantly, dropping into a defensive stance, allowing her assailant's momentum to throw him off balance. By the time Mr. Ludovicu had hustled down the hall, his hand on his holster, Marti was gracefully and with little effort flipping the surprised intruder off his feet and against the wall. Later Marti learned that her Jujutsu skills had become the subject of considerable office discussion.

The door clicked securely and, watched by another camera, Marti unzipped her leather jacket as she strode down the hall.

Alone beneath the locker room's crumbling, particle tile ceiling, Marti stripped and stepped into the shower. Within the blast of hot water the image of the bike hurtling irrevocably out of control and impossibly righting itself replayed in her mind. Marti turned the water up hotter, bringing her skin to the edge of pain.

Marti dressed in her uniform, watching in the mirror as she assumed the role of doctor. The mask was real because it was invested with reality by patients and colleagues. They were the ones who made her a doctor. And she was a good one.

The waiting room, papered with public health posters, was packed. Dozens of people sat, murmuring in their native tongues. They were perched on chairs, leaning against walls, a few children playing on the floor. Waiting.

Marti picked up a folder and called the name of her first patient of the day.

∞

By the time the morning was over, she was far enough behind that cannibalizing her lunch break was the only solution. This was hardly unusual. A combination of spending more time with some patients than the schedule allotted and squeezing in extra patients who lacked appointments insured that, for Marti, there were always more patients to see.

When she went out to the waiting room, she noticed a commotion. Two guards had confronted a waiting patient. The guards, dressed in the latest high-tech protective gear—bulletproof vests, truncheons, holstered weapons, tasers, and who knew what else—were not exactly under the control of the clinic, though they all had the same employer. Six months ago the city had transferred responsibility for the Park and everything in it to a private sector company, Harmon Logistics LLC, who were now responsible for all services within the Park. From garbage to security to the clinic, they managed it all with the ruthless efficiency that had made them into the top multinational provider of services to the public sector.

Marti sighed, then moved quickly across the waiting room, hoping it wasn't too late to intervene.

"Mr. Boujeyah," she called as she got close. She could see the guards had lost patience and were about to start hustling him out of the clinic. Emil Boujeyah was hardly a threat. He was, in fact, a poet—at least that's what he had told her. The regime in the country he had fled had, however, considered him a threat, and had broken his body in a failed attempt to break his spirit.

"Sorry, Dr. Powell," said one of the guards, evidently hoping to forestall a debate. "This one doesn't have a card. He knows he can't see the doctor without his ID."

Residents of the Park were all required to have an ID card provided by Harmon, and the guards made regular rounds at the clinic to make sure all those waiting were registered. But Emil Boujeyah did not believe in ID cards.

Seeing the stooped, gaunt frame, this gentle and kind

man—his damaged body covered in a poorly fitting suit and no shirt—in the gloved hands of the guards like some piece of refuse that had drifted in to the clinic, made her blood boil. But Marti knew it was not prudent to alienate the security personnel, or at least that's what the others, even Stef, kept telling her.

"Emil," she said, "have you not told these gentlemen that I asked you to come help me with organizing the papers?"

She hoped the guards didn't notice his momentary confusion, but he caught on quickly enough.

"I try, Dr. Powell, but maybe they listen to you better."

"Well, you heard me," she said to the guards. "He's not a patient, he's here to assist me. He's a volunteer and I need his help. In fact, he's now late."

One of the guards looked to the other for a cue as to how to respond. The senior guard wasn't quite ready to give up. "But Dr. Powell, he should still have an ID card, he shouldn't even be in the Park without—"

"Perhaps that could be dealt with later, officer? I have patients waiting, and I need Mr. Boujeyah's help right now. I'm sure you also have duties to attend to." The guards made regular sweeps of the clinic, checking appointments and IDs, but they were not assigned there exclusively.

The tense silence broke as the guard nodded. "Okay, then, I'll note in the log that you're taking responsibility for this, Dr. Powell."

"Of course," Marti said, her hands now on the patient. "Thank you for your help, officer."

As Marti led Emil back to the exam rooms, she noticed Rhea, the receptionist who ran the waiting room with firm hands, roll her eyes. Rhea, like the others, had to deal with considerable bureaucratic fallout from Marti's way of doing things.

In the exam room, Marti chastised Mr. Boujeyah. "I told

you, come in at the end of the day." She briefly wondered why she did this, why she accommodated this difficult man. It's not like he couldn't get an ID card. It just offended his sense of dignity. But when he took his clothes off, she was reminded that this was a man who had already suffered much worse. And as she attended to him, she realized that she was grateful for his stubbornness, his determination to be true to himself.

The appointment didn't take long. When it finished, others were returning from their lunch breaks in the staff room.

"I see another blow has been struck against 'Harming.'" Marti turned and saw Dave smiling at her. Why did Dave always catch her by surprise, make her feel like she was being watched? It wasn't an unpleasant feeling at all, more like being watched out for than watched, she supposed. Of the other three doctors her mentor and friend Stef had recruited along with her to staff the clinic, Dave was the one with whom she felt a sense of common purpose, in spite of their obvious differences. For him the crazy environs of the clinic actually represented something more stable after a decade spent as a doctor in an international relief organization. He was around forty, and sometimes his calm confidence made Marti feel like a pretender.

"We do what we can," Marti said. She wondered why it sounded like an admission of defeat.

"Are you okay?" Dave asked. The question took her by surprise, and even more so the steady concern of his gaze. She realized that, considering she saw him every day, she knew very little about Dave. And that was just fine. Dave was not her type. He was too sunny, with his sandy blond hair, freckled bronzed skin, crinkly eyes, and ready quips.

"I'm fantastic," she said, with the most sarcastic tone she could muster.

"I've got something that might help," Dave said. "Do

you have a moment?"

Marti was nonplussed. Didn't Dave understand that she wasn't interested in socializing? But he didn't wait for her answer, and she dutifully followed him to the staff locker room.

Dave was ahead of her, and by the time she got there he was pulling something out of a pack. A small brown bag. He opened the bag and brought out a jar, carefully, as though it contained something of great value. A thick amber liquid, which seemed warm and inviting in spite of the cold fluorescent illumination.

"My bees have had a good season," Dave said. "I'm sharing the bounty."

He held the jar out to Marti. She stood frozen for a moment, feeling reluctant to accept a gift, but unable to refuse. She had no idea he kept bees.

"It's okay," he said, "you'll be doing me a favor. I can only eat so much of the stuff. It's really good, though. Want a taste?"

"I'm fine," said Marti, cornered.

"I insist." He looked at his watch. "We still have two minutes before lunch is over. Not that you took lunch. So you could probably use some. It's medicinal, you know. Antibacterial. Well, don't get me started, just try some."

He had found a teaspoon and held it out to her, a tiny, glistening pool of golden honey hugging the edge.

He brought it toward her and Marti's mouth opened of its own accord, the spoon depositing its gift. The sweet, sticky nectar made her mouth tingle, filling her with a sensation of flowers and sun. She suddenly felt something open inside her, heat and a moisture that wanted to force itself out in tears, but she held it back, ashamed and bewildered by her fragility, and not wanting to know what Dave would think. She muttered a thank you, accepted the jar, and stuffed it in her locker.

"I have to get back," she said.

Marti's sudden charge out of the locker room led her to collide with two men. One was Stef, with his usual preoccupied look of trying to solve a math problem that no one else even knew existed. Goran J. Stefanovic, her mentor in medical school, was the founder and director of the Bill Blake Clinic. He had taken a few steps past her before he even noticed that his companion had been waylaid. The visitor was not someone Marti had seen before. He smiled humorlessly at their awkward encounter and picked up his dropped daypack, clasping it to his chest. The awkward silence stretched, neither Marti or Stef saying anything. Stef always thought outsiders in the clinic ought to be introduced. But now he just waited, impatiently and without a word to Marti, as the visitor collected himself and scurried after.

The hallway encounter unsettled Marti. She thought of the afternoon just a few weeks earlier when she had been returning to an exam room to prepare for her next appointment. Opening the door, she was surprised that the lights were off. She flipped the switch and the fluorescents burst into illumination. Someone was in the room.

Marti caught only a glimpse of the woman's face before she raised an arm to cover her eyes. It was a pale, long face. Old, Marti thought, ancient. But then it struck her that the skin was smooth, free of lines. The eyes were black pools that reflected nothing. Something frighteningly unnatural in them, but the glimpse had been too brief to see what. Marti felt a chill run through her, the hairs rising on the back of her neck.

Quickly she turned off the light and apologized.

She closed the door gently then jumped as someone came up behind her. She turned and was surprised to see Stef.

"It's okay," he said. "I've got a patient in here. You can

use room E." With a tired smile, he closed the door behind him.

Marti had still been thinking about the empty eyes when she got the file for her next appointment.

2

As she worked through her afternoon appointments, Marti felt depleted. Her patients kept her focused, but in the moments between appointments a disturbing sensation of unreality crept over her. It was a warning sign, but she only understood that later.

The old man was her last patient of the day. He'd been brought in by his daughter and son-in-law, who'd also brought along their two small children. They were indigenous people from an Indonesian island, refugees from land development or conflict. It seemed like some part of them had been left behind, and now they clung to one another.

She had conducted the examination in private, then invited the family back in to discuss the patient's condition: advancing dementia. The grandfather interrupted her with a rush of words in his language. His daughter began to comfort him but he only became more agitated, gesturing toward Marti, which suggested to her that she was the source of his alarm.

Suddenly, without any pause, the old man shifted into English.

"He is gone, gone, but you won't let it gone," he said. "All these years, we cry for you, you can stop to cry, you must stop."

"Who is gone?" Marti asked. She looked at the family members, who looked at one another, not understanding what she meant by the question. But the English words did not stop.

"You can't hold him, you must stop to try, you must stop."

Marti grabbed the old man with a roughness that surprised her, as if grabbing on to Rourke, flying across the universe. Then she realized he wasn't, and hadn't been, speaking in English at all. His eyes flashed with fear, a lick of spittle drooling out of his open mouth. The little girl began to cry and her father pulled Marti off the old man as his wife gathered up the kids.

Marti was unable to move for a long moment. Ashamed and terrified. A private world of grief, which she hadn't admitted the existence of even to herself, had exploded.

∞

Stef was preparing his pipe, puffing the flame through the tobacco. Marti sighed and dropped back on the couch. She had told Stef her version of what had happened with the Malaysian family. He sat close to her on one of the chairs. His silence began to gnaw at her.

The clinic was closed and everyone else had gone, except for the night security guard, quietly opening and closing doors.

Marti wondered how Stef kept at it with such an unflagging sense of purpose. If Stefanovic was one thing, he was a man of the big picture. She was here because he had recruited her, three years ago, out of medical school. She would have followed him anywhere, and however disillusioned she might be about the clinic's mission, she could feel no disillusion about Stef.

Stef was in his early sixties when she first met him. Marti's impression was of the classic absent-minded professor;

she had once seen him, in the course of a conversation, distractedly search for the pipe that was in his mouth. He always wore the same handsome, outdated linen suit, now getting threadbare at the elbows. Marti guessed he'd purchased it when he was first hired.

But no one who studied with him could make the mistake of thinking that this was merely some distracted old gent. Stef had a way of bringing the subject to life. He challenged his students, demanding they view medicine not as some sort of dead catalogue of knowledge about the body, but as a quest, a personal journey to grapple with all the mysteries of the cosmos, revealed in the human form. The relief of suffering, in Stef's view, was a direct outcome of this quest. His true vocation was medical research, so Marti was surprised when, soon after she completed her residency, he told her he was taking leadership of the new clinic, and invited her to become part of the team. He believed strongly in the clinic's mission. Indeed, the idea of Stef outside the lab, on the front lines of human need, made a lot of sense.

During the first course Marti took with him she had absorbed the principle that a good physician treated each patient as an individual human being, not simply a collection of symptoms. As Stef made rounds and talked to patients, his gift for making people comfortable elicited their stories. Patients would tell him things they hadn't realized until they spoke, as if the light of his attention invited self-discovery. So much of what Stef had to teach was simply Stef. But his example was so powerful Marti suspected this was what all great teachers did: they provided a model, allowed their passion to awaken their student's passion. In so doing, Stef threw Marti a lifeline. Without him, she felt, medical school would have been a process of forgetting why she wanted to do it in the first place.

In the clinic, Stef spent most of his time hunched over at

the large desk in his office. He was the director of the clinic, and no doubt had plenty of administration to attend to. No one ever saw Stef arrive in the morning, or leave in the evening; the rumor was that he actually lived inside the clinic, sleeping in one of the examination rooms and hiding all evidence of it. Marti knew otherwise, having on several occasions been to Stef's home, a small house that was as frayed and rumpled as his clothing. During one visit, he had gotten caught up in a phone conversation about funding politics and excused himself from the room. While she waited for him, she explored. Upstairs there was one room so different from the others Marti wondered if he had a tenant. While the rest of the house was a clutter of books, pictures, and old furniture, this room, which was filled with light from large, south-facing windows, was almost bare. Some pillows, a low table with a few framed things on it, and a subtle smell of fragrance. Marti only caught a glimpse before she heard Stef calling her and, mindful that she might be invading his privacy, quickly turned and went downstairs, too shy to ask him about the room. Marti didn't understand how a man who was so kind, and whose manner was so open, could at the same time be so mysterious.

Stef's office desk was a huge oak behemoth from another era. Two walls were lined floor to ceiling with shelves, crowded with as many art books as medical books. On the third wall, surrounding the doorway, were framed degrees and photographs of his family, his wife who had died many years ago, a grown son and daughter, his infant grandchildren. They lived across the country and he seldom saw them, but he spoke often of his intention to spend time with them.

The office's clutter was contradicted by the remaining wall, which held only a large framed painting. The piece baffled Marti. Translucent, layered with swirls of color, it seemed less like a work of art than some sort of natural phenomenon. It did not provoke thought or reflection, complacency or disturbance, but rather, invoked a mood that was never quite the same, as though it were a screen onto which one's own imagination could project itself. The swirls looked troubled today, like clouds massing for a storm.

"Was he right?" asked Stef.

The question startled Marti. "Who?"

"The old man."

Marti snorted. "The old man was talking in a language I don't understand, saying something that probably wouldn't have made sense even if I did."

"You know what I mean," Stef said.

"The point is, I'm hearing things, Stef. I see a patient and I can only hear my own mind. I've totally lost it."

Feeling too restless to be lying down, and too resistant to the psychiatric implications of it, Marti sat up abruptly. She opened a lush book of photographs lying among some medical journals and flipped through it. It was a book of doors. Doors of wood and bronze, even stone. Carved, chiseled, cast.

When she realized Stef was smiling as he watched her, she quickly let the book close, like a child caught out.

"Lost what?" he asked.

For a moment Marti didn't understand the question. "What did you lose?" he repeated. "You said, 'I've totally lost it.'"

"It's a figure of speech. I lost a grip on myself."

"Maybe the grip is the problem. At least it sure sounds like that's what you were trying to tell yourself." Stef sighed. "We resist growth, Marti, we all do. I don't know why. Something in us prefers things to stay the same." He leaned forward, pausing for emphasis. "But things never do."

Stef reached across and flipped the book open to a pair of magnificent copper doors, green with age. They were more than twice the size of a man, with fearsome dragons swirling across the surface.

"Imagine what it meant to a person to walk through these doors," he said. "Imagine the courage it took. Think about what she had to leave behind. What she had to let go of before she could find out what lay on the other side."

Marti felt like she had been stuck in a room for a long time, since Rourke had died. It was as if she believed she'd been condemned to this cell. And maybe she had been. But was it a life sentence? Was anyone keeping her there? Maybe the problem was she didn't know where the doors were.

And if she left, what would she be leaving behind? Everything in her life now, all the things that gave it meaning—her job, in particular—were things she had built while under sentence.

Marti looked up and saw the time: it was almost 8:00. She remembered that she'd agreed to have dinner at her sister's house. She was already a half hour late. She considered phoning Jane and begging off, but she knew what a big deal that would be.

Stef got up to see her out, and Marti surprised both of them by sweeping him into a hug. They'd never hugged before. At first she thought she embraced him because she wanted him to know how important his words had been. But the hug had a life of its own, it was as though there were many others joining them in it, and Marti felt a warmth that reached deep into her, felt some part of her loneliness releasing itself into that warmth. Maybe this is what letting go feels like, she thought.

3

Stef usually liked being in the clinic alone, late at night. He found that he could use the silent emptiness to work his way through particular problems, or simply to review the day and reflect on the condition of the clinic. He could then bring these reflections into his sleep, and be better prepared the next day for any decisions that needed to be made.

Tonight he had a lot to think about.

Mostly it was the young man from the lab, Adam. Fortunately, after describing the strange results, Adam had given him back the materials. Now the specimen and the test data were locked in his desk. He had spoken with no one about them.

There had been a moment when he believed Adam would refuse to give them to him. The man had clearly wanted to bargain for information on where to find the donor. But in the end Adam had settled for an assurance that Stef would get back in touch with him after he had reviewed the findings. Stef wondered how many others at Harmon already knew about it.

He himself would not have been so inclined to accept Adam's claims if he hadn't already had the bizarre experience of examining the woman, who called herself Violet. No last name. No reflexes. No dilatory response in her pupils.

No pulse. Clinically, she was dead. Yet she was walking, talking, responding. She'd said little, but a comment she had made had implied that she wasn't alone in her condition. He'd left the room with the specimens, and when he'd returned a moment later she was gone. Afterward, he thought his examination had been some sort of delusion, wondered if it was the beginning of Alzheimer's.

Nevertheless, when they'd sent the specimens to the lab, he'd included the note that the specimens, along with the test results, were to be returned to him directly. He wondered now if flagging it like that had been a mistake. Stef supposed he should be grateful that they hadn't been destroyed, now that he knew the contact information the patient had left was bogus and she might never come back.

Until Stef could feel an inner clarity about how to proceed, he would do nothing. If he had learned anything, it was that harm could be done by moving too quickly. Evil didn't always arise from a bad intention. Often it arose from a misjudged effort to help, forcing something into the world.

Stef glanced at the large painting, as if something had called his attention there. Ursula's painting. His ears began to ring. As he looked at the painting, he felt something shudder inside his chest, a searing pressure.

His heart. He had pills to take, but he couldn't move to get them. The pain quickly became a white-hot needle of fire, pushing deeper.

He tried only to breathe, but the needle was penetrating his heart, opening it up, and he could feel a balloon that surrounded him bursting in slow motion, an ocean rushing in and beginning to fill the space where his body had been. The pain subsided, he was thankful for that. But the gratitude turned to the realization that he was dying, and he felt a sting of regret.

Stef thought about Violet, the mystery of her. Why had

this been given to him now, when he wouldn't be able to do anything about it? He wondered if he should reach into the drawer with his last strength and break it, smash the specimen vial under his heel.

He could still feel the chair underneath him, could still feel the desk on which he was partly slumped. The room was becoming vague, and he could feel the connection to his body loosening, like a cork being gradually eased out of a bottle. The sensation was balanced on the knife edge between a searing pain and an exquisite pleasure, both equally nerve-shattering. As long as he stayed on the knife he would stay alive.

He felt no particular desire to stay alive. His whole life was coming toward him now like music, a chord so dense and complex it had needed a whole lifetime to express itself.

For a moment, Stef actually thought someone was playing a stereo in the clinic. But the music was within him, and he could see as well as hear it. It was music he himself had composed. His attention was drawn most by his failures, which appeared as flaws in the music. His early marriage to Nadia, his inability to love her as she needed, his betrayal. All the ways in which he wasn't there for his three children. All the damage done by a man whose work was more important to him than any human relationship.

Then he noticed the light, shining in the music, the light of love given and received, of important tasks completed. He knew that it was only in that light—a light, he could see now, shown to him and shared with him by others who had become part of the music—that he could learn what he needed to.

He was already far enough gone that thoughts were becoming different, concrete things outside of him that he could see and touch. He had a specific task to do, one that could only be done at this threshold between his earthly life and what lay beyond it, and the thought of it appeared to him as a looming edifice, deliberately constructed and reinforced through regular meditative work.

It felt like the most difficult thing he had ever done. Every part of Stef's being wanted to surrender itself to the music.

While the rest of physical reality grew dim, Ursula's painting gained vibrancy. He allowed the painting to become what it wanted to be: an image of the threshold upon which he was now perched.

As Stef focused on the painting, he felt something in his heart: a last moment of aching suction; a brief explosion of pain that his will carried him through, and then a freedom he had never felt before.

He was rushing upward. The loss of gravity gave him a shock, but gradually he was able to stop the upward fall.

Below him, his body slumped on the desk, torn and spindled, like a fully inscribed parchment that had been wadded up and discarded. He felt an intense sorrow and then the lightness of his new form. He was surprised that he still had a form. It seemed as though it were made of bubbles in an underwater world, yearning to rush upward to rejoin the world of air, but he was able to hold himself here for now.

When Ursula had taught him about thresholds, about the Guests, he came to understand the meaning that this moment would have, and then he began to prepare. He did not retreat from his worldly responsibilities, far from it. But he rose early every morning, and for an hour devoted himself to the practice she had given him. Anyone watching him during this time would have seen a man sitting quietly, his eyes closed, in a state of meditation. Inside himself he was creating an image, an image strong enough to withstand the shock of the body's end.

And now, having died, Stef invoked this image and found it was no longer inside him but in front of him, projected onto the surface of Ursula's painting. He looked forward to telling Ursula about this, and then wistfully realized that he would not have that opportunity.

The image was of a pair of magnificent doors. They were not doors that appeared in the book Marti had been looking at, nor that Stef had ever seen, nor that existed anywhere on earth. They were doors he had created, in painstaking detail, and with precise intent, in his imagination. There, they had been carved out of precious stone, drawn up from deep within the earth. This alone, the mining of the enormous stones, had taken Stef more than a year of meditation. Simply to "find" the mineral deposits had taken many mornings. And then to extract the deposit with the consciousness that would not disturb the surroundings had required almost as much care as if he had been physically engineering it.

Eventually the stones, massive in size and weight, clouded in the universal night of the underground world and attended by a vast retinue of beings that lived invisibly within the earth, had been presented to the sunlight.

Then the stones had been hewn into shape, and mounted. Finally, by far the most time-consuming task, they had been carved with intricate designs on both sides. On one side, the side now facing Stef, the designs were of life on earth, expressing the joys and sorrows of childhood, maturity, and old age. Eighteen such images formed the carving, each an image within an image, each with a vividness and detail that was the result of Stef's tireless inner work. He had not created the images whole, but had sculpted them blow by blow, no less than if he had held a chisel in his hand.

On the outward facing side was a single carved image, round in shape and taking up almost the entire stone canvas of the two doors. Stef could not see it now, but he knew it better than any part of the body he had lived inside for sixty-nine years: a sort of hieroglyph that Ursula had first drawn for him. She never explained its simple design. It was like a letter in an unknown alphabet, or more than that, a whole new language. He knew it was a call, a beacon.

The doors loomed over Stef. For a moment he thought: I cannot do what is required of me. Doubt enveloped him like a cloud. Some part of him wanted to surrender to it, be freed from the uncertainty of his task, but he summoned his will and his strength.

He moved himself closer to the doors, at first too abruptly, causing some of the bubbles to tear loose and pop. Stef felt a concussion deep inside himself as the bits of his being held in each of these bubbles were released completely from the last vestiges of earthly form. Each explosion burst him into the panoramic memory of a forgotten moment from his life. These memories toppled over one another as though happening at once, like the musical lines of a symphony, but he was able to hear each separately and experience them distinctly. Stef shivered with terror and wonder as each memory unlocked one more particle of his separate being. Soon Stef himself would be just a memory.

But not yet. He drew the expansion of himself inward, concentrating toward the greatest density he could. He placed himself right up against the doors, their surface polished, glistening as if wet. Experimentally at first, he willed his force against the door, not strong enough to move it, but as a test to see what the effect on him would be, whether he would simply be torn apart.

His form held. Where, floating in space, this temporary form had seemed wispy, against the stone of the doors he could feel a power beyond that of flesh and blood. His will would be sufficient to master the implacable surface of the doors he had created.

And so, Stef began, slowly, to push against the doors. They shifted, accompanied by a massive rumbling that seemed to have the entire earth as a resonating chamber. Stef wondered if those he had left behind could hear it at all, perhaps as distant thunder. This reminded him of why he was doing this, of what the good was, and he felt a surge of joy and strength.

As the doors parted, Stef could feel a warmth radiating toward him, reminding him of the ineffable security of the sun's love. The weight of the stones had diminished and he could feel two atmospheres blending in the open space between them.

Stef drew back and prepared himself for what would greet him on the other side. He saw that his office, with his life's rich residue, remained. He hadn't left earth, not yet, though he had certainly left his body, and that reassured him that his task had been properly conceived and the event was on course. It could be accomplished only by someone perched between worlds.

He felt a quiver of fear. Thoughts of what he would miss flickered across his mind. As the physical realm continued to dim, his scope of perception was widening, so that it was no longer anchored in a body but in an awareness that radiated around him in all directions. He was entering a world without shadow.

He shrank in the face of an onslaught, a storm of light and sound not meant to be confronted by such a limited being, and he realized that he was in pain. It was like staring into a thousand suns.

The last vestiges of Stef's sight burned away, and the last of his hearing. Yet he perceived still. The pain disappeared.

He felt something reaching toward him. A singular concentration within the vast nebulae, squeezing into something human in form. He used the still strong memory of his cellular, human body, and concentrated a hand with which to reach back.

Two beings faced one another across the threshold, two

hands joined. Stef felt, as his hand became more and more light, as he began to lose his integrity and the bubbles began to disperse, how the hand in his and became more and more solid and human. In the last moment he pulled on the hand. He could feel the presence and will of another being. The hand stayed firmly in his as he drew it across the space between worlds, pulling it through layer after layer of cellular membrane. And then Stef had his last thought: this was a good end to his story, and as he relaxed he felt himself surrender to the cascade of memories that carried him away.

4

Jane watched the blades of the blender tear the ice cubes to slush and told herself she would not give Marti a hard time for being late. She knew she was lucky her younger sister was coming at all, but that just made it all the more irritating. Marti spent all her time helping other people, but her own family apparently meant little. The fact that, unlike Jane, Marti had not started a family of her own didn't help. Jane would have liked her kids to have cousins to play with, as she and Marti had. Extended family took the edge off being a family, allowed for an experience of blood connection without the stress of living together day in and day out. Jane poured the margaritas into the salted glasses and sighed. Why dwell on it? Her kids were too old now, anyway. Carly was finishing eleventh grade in a few months, in a social orbit of her own that Jane couldn't penetrate. Trevor had no social orbit at all, spending all his time, when he wasn't busy barely passing ninth grade, glued to his computer.

Marti arrived, her cheeks flushed red. Jane hadn't seen this spark in her sister in a long time. She felt a familiar mixture of love and envy. Why should Marti be the beautiful one?

∞

Marti sipped the drink and it tasted unusually good, exactly what she needed. Normally, she felt Jane's showy affluence was in poor taste, but today she was grateful for it. Grateful that after a day in the Park's threadbare poverty, she could find a moment of refuge. She threw herself onto the impossibly comfortable leather couch and settled into it deeply. "I'm just glad to be done with work for the day," she said.

Jane grinned and joined Marti on the couch. "I'll drink to that!"

The women laughed and knocked back their drinks. Refilling their glasses, Jane said, "Dare I speculate on the reasons for this unusual exuberance?"

Marti looked at Jane. "Just because I'm in a good mood," she said, "doesn't mean I've met a guy."

"And would that be so terrible?" Jane said. "You don't want to be alone forever, do you?"

"Jane, please don't start."

"No, it's great to see you like this. This is not the Marti I was expecting tonight."

Marti smiled. "You and me both. I'm tired of that other Marti. Too fucking serious!"

Jane raised her glass. "To the new Marti!"

So this was the trick, Marti thought as the alcohol exploded into her bloodstream, and she relaxed in her sister's company for the first time in years.

Marti joined Jane in the gleaming, stainless steel kitchen and watched as she dished out the elements of a prepared meal from a gourmet takeaway. Jane's gestures were brittle, and it struck Marti that her sister's whole life was an effort to find a plateau of comfort. But the greater her efforts, the more it eluded her.

"Should I call everyone else?" Marti asked.

"Anyone you can find," said Jane.

She found Barry, Jane's husband, in their bedroom, sitting in an armchair watching the TV. Actually, the TV was watching him. Its eye was open, his closed, his bald head lolling. It shone in the television's phosphorescent glow, as if he weren't asleep but simply watching TV at a deeper level, taking it into his bloodstream directly through his skin.

"Barry," she said softly.

Barry stirred, as if surprised to find himself here.

"Hey, Marti," he said, weakly.

"Hey, Barry," Marti responded. "Jane's got supper on the table."

Trevor was also easy to find. His basement bedroom looked like it had been hit by one of the natural disasters from the news on Barry's TV. His face was puffier than the last time she had seen him, and she remembered that he was on antidepressants. "How's it going, Trev?" she asked. He nodded a little too eagerly, asking, "are we eating?"

Marti couldn't find Carly, but when she made her way back to the kitchen, she found the girl already there, along with the rest of the family. Carly's face lit up when she saw Marti, who folded her into a hug. Marti swept her niece's blond hair back, admiring the beautiful young woman Carly had become. Marti felt closer to her than anyone else in the family.

"I thought you were in such a hurry," Jane snapped at her daughter. Carly rolled her eyes at the sound of her mother's voice and spoke without looking at her.

"I haven't seen Aunt Marti in ages. Anyway, I'm going." She pulled a small purse onto her shoulder and checked her smartphone. Carly was dressed for going out, Marti realized with disappointment.

"I thought you and Neil split up?" Jane prodded.

"I'm not going out with Neil."

Before her parents could ask who she was going out with, the doorbell rang.

"Mom, Dad, this is Spencer." Marti watched as Jane and Barry shook the young man's hand. His golden looks matched their daughter's and he laid the parent-pleasing small-talk on thick. She remembered meeting Neil, who was more the moody artist type, which seemed to suit Carly. She stole a glance at Carly, and a look of shame flickered across the girl's face. Finally Carly interrupted, reminding Spencer that they would be late for the movie and ushering him out the door.

Marti watched as Jane, her jaw set hard, turned her attention to the food someone they didn't know had prepared.

5

Marti opened her eyes, uncertain where she was, and then remembered.

She had slept on a couch in her sister's basement family room. The room was dry, airless. It was still dark; she felt fuzzy and hollow, in the middle of a hundred-hour night. A bare fog of illumination entering through the high basement window shrouded the shapes surrounding her, just enough light to render them ominous.

What time was it? She rummaged beside the couch, found her pants, and pulled out her phone. She was dismayed to see it was only 4 a.m.

The weight of the room, the massive house, was crushing down on her, and it didn't take much longer to decide that sleep was a vain hope.

∞

Marti straddled her bike. She felt the new day was very far away, and unsure how to attain the newness she would need to face it. She felt disturbed, and it couldn't just be the effects of a few drinks and some gossip with her sister. If sleep wouldn't do it, there was only one solution, and here it was, right below her. Movement. She roared the motorcycle to life.

As the wind whipped her face, Marti was reminded that there was one damn good thing about 4 a.m., and that was the empty roads, especially out here in a place like Beulah Hills. She hoped the private security wasn't about. The machine's demand for attention tore off the sluggish carapace of alcohol, sleeplessness, and suburban basement; shredded away suffocating doubt and all her mind-forged manacles, and pulled her, naked in two sets of skin, into a future of ripe possibility.

The first time she rode a motorcycle was with Rourke, just after she turned eighteen. Petrified, when the bike turned she wanted to lean away to right herself; Rourke laughed and yelled, "lean into the curve," which seemed impossible. But she tightened her hold on him and allowed his body to show her. She'd held on for three years, never sitting up front on the Commando. Why would she? There were plenty of other places in their relationship where she had control.

In bed, she was the more experienced, though he was two years older. Rourke was like a puppy, enthusiastic as hell, but he hadn't begun to learn how to use his body for states of pleasure, nor how to give real pleasure to another. An electric chemistry sizzled when their bodies came together, they didn't even need to take their clothes off to feel it. For Marti this was a promise, a wrapped present she longed to tear open. Their early couplings were explosive enough to sustain the promise, but much too brief and generalized to begin to fulfill it.

Marti had been worried at first that if she fully took leadership of their lovemaking, turned it into the journey she wanted and showed him where they could go, he would reject her; even at eighteen, she knew how frightened men could be by female sexual appetite and power. So she had proceeded carefully at first, tolerated the clumsiness and wasted opportunities, while he exclaimed over how great it was. But she made herself a student of his body, paying attention to his responses, without seeming to do anything deliberate. Soon she understood his erotic affinities better than he did, and then she began to teach him.

Marti tilted herself forward, wishing for a moment that she could escape the sound of memory. The bike was all about the road, and the road was about leaving the past behind. Rourke had taught her to live in the moment, and yet it seemed she had failed to learn the lesson, and those long ago moments were now the only ones in which she had.

And she now knew with certainty that things had to change. It had been ten years. The parts of herself that had died with Rourke needed life again. She had been ready to choose death, but life had chosen her. It was time to live.

∞

Marti was almost to the Park when she realized her mistake. It wasn't even five in the morning. She was so buried in her thoughts she had automatically driven the bike in the direction of work, rather than home. She stopped on the side of the road. The streetlights glowed, the trucks whined past on a nearby freeway. Too many lights to be truly dark, too much noise to be really quiet. Something was pulling her toward the clinic. She felt a brush against her cheek, or thought she did, but there was nothing there. She shivered and wondered at the peculiar sensation, somewhere between peace and terror.

It took a long time for the night guard, Randall, to buzz her in. He was flushed and distressed.

"Oh, Dr. Powell. You know about it already? Dr. Stefanovic?"

"What about him?"

"No, sorry. How could you know? You better come with me. I just found him, I was about to call someone."

He was already moving. Marti followed, but it felt like moving underwater, as the implication of Randall's words hit. Wait, she wanted to cry, I'm not ready for this, I'm not ready. She had known about Stef's heart disease, in general terms, because she had seen the medicine he took, but they had never discussed it.

The door to Stef's office was closed. Randall stopped and looked at her before opening it. Marti took a deep breath. The strange disorientation subsided, and a new feeling washed over her. She felt that Stef needed her and, for a moment, she dared to hope that she had jumped to the wrong conclusion and he was alive.

But Randall opened the door and when she went inside she found him slumped on his desk, facing the large painting. Marti nodded to Randall and he backed away.

Marti believed in nothing beyond the body. But, seeing Stef's like this, she felt a swell of gratitude and reverence rather than grief. She was in a heightened state, as if in the presence of something great. Something holy.

Marti cleared space around Stef. His right arm was stretched out, as if reaching for something. She touched his hand, but it was cold. She gently removed his glasses.

"It's okay," she said. It was a whisper, but her voice seemed impossibly loud to her. She suddenly had the sensation of being watched, and turned to see if someone else had come into the room, but there was just her and Stef. She took his hand and held it.

"I wanted to tell you," she said. She wanted to say "I love you," but she couldn't get herself to say it aloud. As if he could hear it better in the silence.

She rolled back his sleeve to take his pulse, a formality. She'd have to be the one to fill out the death certificate.

6

The mortician removed Stef's body shortly before the staff started showing up for work. Word spread instantaneously as they arrived, and Marti called everyone together in the clinic's cluttered conference room, which doubled as a file storage area. She was the only person who wasn't crying.

Four doctors were gathered, including her, and eight other staff. She looked around at all their faces for a long moment, one by one, as gradually their attention shifted outward toward her from their own grief, and they waited hopefully for her to say something that would make things better.

"We all know what Stef would have wanted," was all she had to say. She looked around at her comrades as they nodded in agreement.

They had left the front door of the clinic locked, and it was now a little past time for the first appointments. Over a hundred patients, and often their families, would come to the clinic today to be seen—and they would be seen.

As the group broke up, people began to exchange hugs, giving and receiving warmth and comfort they knew they would need to get through the day. Dave suddenly held Marti tight, and then afterward looked surprised, even a little embarrassed.

Marti stepped out into the waiting room. Fifty faces looked at her expectantly. Waiting for her to say their name, to be beckoned from this public space into the examining rooms. Under examination, she encountered people and their problems, often with an intimacy her patients wouldn't share even with those closest to them, in which they willingly revealed the most private spaces of their bodies to her. So the moment after she quickly looked at the file of her incoming appointment, and spoke clearly and loudly the name of that next patient, was a sort of threshold that gave her day a rhythm.

Washing up after one of the patients, Marti was surprised when the antibacterial soap pumping mechanism broke off in her hand. It was one of those small rebellions of physical objects that she found so annoying. She threw the plastic bottle into the garbage and went to the supply room to get a replacement.

She heard the choked sounds of weeping before she saw who it was. Dr. Neville Hobbs. Reflected light flashed from a metal flask before he dropped it into his white coat, wiping his face as he looked at Marti in confusion. Hobbs was the oldest of the four staff doctors, and the one Marti knew the least well. That he drank did not come as a surprise. To see him an emotional ruin did.

"Neville? Are you okay?"

"Yes, yes. It's just, you know..."

"Stef?"

"What are we going to do, Marti? What are we going to do?"

∞

At the end of the morning, Marti came out for her next patient, but there was no folder in the file box. When Marti stepped into the glassed-in office, Rhea turned and held out a file.

"This one's a puzzle," she said. "Been here all morning. Naveen can't get him to explain what the problem is, wouldn't speak at all. Just pointed at you several times, quite insistently. You're running ahead, so why don't you give it a shot before going to lunch?"

Usually patients needed to convince Naveen, the intake nurse who spoke about eight languages, before they got an appointment. And he was no pushover. Marti looked over to Naveen, at the next station. He was interviewing a patient but he noticed her and shrugged helplessly. She rolled her eyes and looked down at the name on the file.

"Mr. Stride," Marti called out, looking around the room, wondering whom it was going to be.

For a moment, unusually, no one responded. She announced the name again.

No response. She glanced at Rhea and held up the file. Rhea pointed to a man, his hands folded in his lap, his eyes closed, head drooped. He looked like he had been born in that spot, had spent his whole life there, a point of stillness amid the crazy movement of the clinic. The ill-fitting clothes he was wearing looked exactly like the uniforms the clinic stocked for the janitorial and support staff.

For a moment she thought him dead, shrunken into himself in that way that corpses are. But then he returned, rising to the surface out of some deep pool. His head lifted, his eyes opened, and he was staring right back at her, as if it were her eyes and not her uttering his name that called him.

Marti's breath froze and her knees turned to water. The face staring back at her was Rourke's.

She placed a hand on the wall for support. Ten years of grief and loss rushed at her like a hailstorm. She wanted to turn and look again at the patient to prove to herself that her mind had conjured up a ghost, that this was just another unknown denizen of the Park. But she could not get herself to do it, too afraid that it would again be Rourke staring back at her. And just as afraid that it might not be him.

She consulted the folder again, to reassure herself that she had the name right, and there it was, "Stride." No first name. She summoned every bit of will she had and screamed at herself: Rourke is dead, let him go.

And then the man was standing very close to her.

Not Rourke.

His eyes seemed to carry their own, golden, light source. He was neither young nor old. His skin was olive, his race indeterminate.

A thirst opened up in her and she felt the urge to touch him. She needed something here. Disturbed, she shook off the feeling, but in restraining herself she was paralyzed.

Marti felt like time itself had slipped from her grasp, but finally she managed to say, "Come with me."

∞

Marti closed the door to the examining room and opened the folder to see Naveen's notes, but there weren't any. She took a breath to steel herself and turned to face this "Stride."

He was already looking at her. Where before his gaze had been one of the most unabashed intimacy, now he seemed to be sizing her up.

"What seems to be the problem?" she asked.

He cocked his head, then glanced down as if searching for something.

After a moment he began taking off his uniform, fumbling with the buttons.

Once his shirt was off, Marti had him lie back and began to palpate him. Everything felt normal, more than normal. He appeared to be in radiant health. She had him sit back up. She looked in his ears, checked his eyes, his reflexes. His body gave her the impression of a work of art, his health a summit of beauty and perfection.

She kept thinking she should be saying something. But her thoughts were unsettled, and his silence was contagious.

She put the stethoscope to her ears and then gently placed the bell against his bare chest. She listened, and it was as if she moved into him. The pulse of his heartbeat resounded more and more deeply inside her, and she found herself unable to stop listening. She began to hear her own heart beating as well, the two heartbeats joining.

Marti was desperate for solid ground. She pulled the stethoscope from her ears, but the sound only diminished, did not go away. She felt flushed, thought maybe she should have gone home today, wondered if this was all some symptom of grief, prompted by the loss of Stef. She looked to see if the man was reacting to the strangeness of her behavior, but she saw only acceptance.

As if in response to her thoughts, Stride said his first words, or tried to. All that came out was a rasp. He tried again.

Marti filled a paper cup with water and handed it to him. He looked at it for a moment, then slowly brought it to his mouth and drank it all. He took a breath, cleared his throat noisily.

"I—I'm s-sorry. About Stef." His voice was still rough, and the words took considerable effort to get out.

Marti nodded and sighed, and only then wondered what he knew and how he knew it.

"Please," he said, his words still halting and difficult. "Please." He looked at her as if he had asked a question and was awaiting a response.

Marti wondered if the source of his radiance was schizophrenia. "I'm here to help," she said. "But you haven't told me what the problem is."

"Problem," he said, chewing and swallowing the word, like a baby putting something in its mouth to map it.

He gestured with his hand, as if trying to summon a word he had lost.

"I'm going to have Dr. Pollack see you," she said, referring to her colleague who dealt with the psychiatric cases.

She was scribbling notes in his file when he gently took her hand in his and put the pen aside. She wanted to resist, but her hand ignored her. He clasped it between both his hands, and she felt warmth entering her.

"Trust," he said, nodding his head, pleased that he'd found the word. "Trust...me."

Marti was still for a long moment, not sure what to do. She felt the emotional exhaustion she had been keeping at bay, the wall of professional routine she had erected against it crumbling. But what was being offered felt like comfort, and she could not refuse it. She realized that she felt safe. She did trust him.

His body began to shiver, more and more convulsively, a seizure of some sort. She wanted to pull her hand away but something told her not to and she obeyed. In moments the convulsions subsided, and he collected himself. He looked at her. He worked his jaw, and then it was as though something engaged. He spoke, the voice the same but the speech now unconstrained.

"You are so patient. And understanding," he said. His eyes moistened, and he seemed surprised. He wiped them and looked at the moisture on his fingers for a long moment.

He looked up at her. "Things change. You've had more than your share. But—there is danger now."

"Danger?" she asked, although she was thinking about his eyes, not his words.

"I'll leave soon. Forget me, if you want. But they are coming soon."

"I don't understand," Marti said. She let go of his hand and stepped back. "Who are you talking about?"

She saw that breaking the physical contact made things more difficult for him. His body shuddered, and then settled.

"There is a package. In the top drawer of his desk. Stef's desk. He wanted you to take it before they come. He doesn't want them to have it."

He got off the examining table and began to button his shirt, before adding: "He loved you."

Marti felt her heart in her throat. She took a step toward him. "You knew Stef?"

Stride was already moving to the doorway. He turned to her with his hand on the doorknob.

"I will wait outdoors. At the fountain. If you want to see me." He added, "I hope you will come."

He was out the door in a heartbeat. Marti heard herself blurt out, "Wait—" but he was gone.

Whatever spell she'd been under broke with his departure. But, as angry as she was that she'd let him get under her skin, she found herself walking down the hall to Stef's office.

His body was gone and the room felt as though it had also died. She tried the drawers in his desk, opening them one by one. They contained only an assortment of office supplies and personal effects, nothing that looked like a "package." But the top drawer was locked.

Marti felt a blind desire to open it. She grabbed a ring with some small keys on it she'd noticed in one of the other drawers. Her hands were shaking as she tried fitting the keys in the lock. None of them worked. Some noise from the hallway jarred her and she jumped back, dropping the keys.

She forced herself to take a deep breath, trying to beat back the senseless panic.

Marti went down the hall to the utility room. The toolkit was where she'd seen it. A large screwdriver and a hammer should do the trick, she thought. She brought them back to Stef's office, half expecting someone to stop her.

Back in the office, she placed the tip of the screwdriver against the old lock. A few decisive blows against it with the hammer and the wood splintered, the old desk giving way with little protest.

Marti's heart was beating. She rifled, for a moment thinking she was on a fool's errand. Then she found a small metal case, the kind used to transport important lab specimens. She ran her hand across its surface, desperate to look inside, but thought twice.

She had made it to the locker room when all hell broke loose in the clinic.

7

The footsteps were the first thing Marti noticed. Instead of the staff's decisive, yet softly efficient steps, she heard a clump of people moving through the clinic with a heavy tread. She hesitated, and gently opened the door of the locker room.

There were eight of them. Seven of them were Harmon security guards—she'd never seen that many at one time before. The eighth wore a suit: a security executive with Harmon, who had been part of the delegation that visited after the company had taken over the clinic. What was his name? Gansrud, she remembered. He was issuing orders to his team as they spread into the clinic's warren of rooms. When she saw Gansrud himself head directly to Stef's office with a couple of others while the remainder branched off to wait outside the examining rooms, she felt certain she had to get out of the clinic as quickly as possible.

Marti pulled off her whites and dressed quickly. Her breathing was hard but steady.

Smooth inside her bike leathers, with her courier bag now containing the case over her shoulder, she opened the door again. The hall was empty and she headed toward the back entrance.

The clinic was clearing out through the front. She could

hear Pollack protesting and Gansrud placating him, assuring him that things would be back to normal tomorrow, but that certain security concerns necessitated closure for the rest of the day.

She could see that most of the activity of the Harmon team was centered on Stef's office. Stuff was being boxed up and piled up for removal. She was near the security desk when one of the Harmon staff came out of an examining room and took up a position in the hall. He noticed her with a quizzical look, but by now she was at the security desk, and she grabbed a package waiting there for pickup and acted like she was just a courier on the job, hoping the goon in the hall wouldn't know that the clinic used its own staff to drive lab materials back and forth.

Unsettled by her gambit, Ludovicu had a frightened look unbecoming a security guard. She winked at him, but he seemed to have turned to stone. She put her hand on the door, hoping he would buzz her out, and out of the corner of her eye noticed the Harmon guard moving toward her.

Marti looked back to Ludovicu. "Please," she said. "It's for Stef."

Without anything in his demeanor changing, Ludovicu pressed the door unlock buzzer. Marti got the door ajar, dropped the package discreetly back on the desk, and then pushed her way out the door without looking back.

She crossed the asphalt toward her bike, her heart beating, resisting the urge to run but terrified a hand would drop on her shoulder any moment. She noticed that there was a black van parked in the loading dock, with a driver in a Harmon security uniform standing beside it.

As she started her bike, she saw more of the Harmon team coming out, carrying boxes. They didn't notice her as she peeled away.

She passed the front of the clinic. The patients had been evacuated. The staff were communicating to them with placatory gestures. Dave caught her eye, a look of concern on his face. A moment later her phone rang.

Marti didn't answer; she wanted to put as much distance between herself and the clinic as she could. She hadn't had time to really think about what she was doing. It was possible that Harmon was looking for exactly the thing she had taken from Stef's desk; it was also possible there was a broader agenda at work, or something else altogether. Dave had been the one, before their meeting that morning, to raise the question of how Stef's death might impact Harmon's relationship to the clinic. They had been protected, kept at arm's length from Harmon primarily by the power of Stef's credibility and the degree to which the clinic was an extension of him. The more Marti thought about it, the more she figured this was a move by Harmon to assert a much tighter control of the clinic.

Marti uttered a curse. Stef had made something good in the clinic, something that raised the quality of life of people who really needed the help. She knew he must have fought a lot of battles to make it that way and keep it that way. Why did there always have to be bullshit?

Bullshit was not a good thing, but it wasn't a reason for her to flee. Her colleagues would certainly need her; it would take all of them working together to stake out and protect the clinic's independence, its mission.

She got off her bike and found a concealed spot beside some dumpsters, their stink repellent. She popped the clasps on the case. Inside, held securely in foam, was a specimen tube filled with some sort of serum, and a flash drive.

Marti had to find out what Stride knew, if he had known Stef, what this sample was, how he had known Harmon was coming, if he had known. First, though, she decided to call

Dave and see what he could tell her.

He said her name, his voice alert with concern.

"Can you talk?" she asked.

"Where are you?"

She ignored the question. "What the hell's going on?"

"Some sort of power play by Harmon. Stef must have really been keeping them at bay. They're cleaning out his office, acting like it's a matter of national security."

"Pricks."

"Are you okay? Where are you? He's been asking about you. Gansrud. What should I tell him?"

"Tell him to go fuck himself." Marti wanted to hang up, but Dave's concern touched her and she didn't want to insult him.

"I already did that." Dave chuckled. "You should have seen the look on his face." Marti laughed, glad to feel that she and Dave were still on the same team.

"Listen, Marti. I'm here if you need anything. You don't even have to tell me what's going on. Just—any help you need, you let me know."

Marti nodded, as if he could see her. "Thanks, Dave. Really. Thanks. I'd better go now." Marti took a deep breath then headed to the fountain.

8

The Fountain was one of the Park's landmarks. It hadn't had water flowing through it in some years, and was now merely a basin of cracked cement. When Marti arrived, she didn't see Stride right away. There was the usual assortment of flotsam: people with nowhere else to go, buyers and sellers of illegal substances. It wasn't a place you went to hang out unless you wanted to disappear.

She could feel eyes on her while she circled the perimeter and looked for the strange patient. Perhaps she had imagined the whole encounter. That would be less fantastical than the notion that it had really happened.

She paused, having completed her circle, and was just starting to wonder what to do, when a voice behind her spoke her name, startling her.

She turned, and there was that face, very close. His eyes golden pools, carrying a suggestion of the unknown, as if she could enter there and find a world more vast than the one she inhabited.

"You came," he said.

Marti was snapped back to awareness by his words. "What's this all about?" she asked. "How did you know that—"

He held a hand up in a gentle gesture for her to wait.

"Any answers I give you are going to beg for more questions. Do you think you can wait for understanding?"

Marti shrugged in exasperation. "I don't know. What do you want from me?"

The question made him smile. She blushed, realizing she couldn't help asking questions. "'Want,'" he repeated, musing on the word for a moment. "Were you able to get the package?"

She nodded. Questions piled on top of one another, but she bit her tongue.

He winced painfully, and she had the impression that his calm demeanor concealed some sort of tremendous act of will. His clothes—the janitorial uniform she now realized he must have stolen from the clinic—seemed more absurd here. His eyes had clouded over and he sat down weakly.

"I'm sorry," was all he said. His head was down, and he looked quite broken.

"Look," she said. "If you want this case of Stef's, you're going to have to tell me what it is and why I should give it to you. And why Harmon is after it."

He looked up at her. "Have you looked at it?"

"Now you're asking me questions," she pointed out.

"I don't want it," he said. "I want it destroyed. It's dangerous."

"Dangerous to whom?"

He looked at her, his expression haunted, then shrugged, as though it were hopeless. She didn't give a damn about the case, but if it really was what all the fuss was about, danger wasn't an implausible idea.

"Why does Harmon want it, then?" She could see he wasn't going to answer. "Or maybe I should go ask them?"

He looked up at her like he knew she was bluffing.

She turned and started walking away, as if she was going to do it, but then felt silly. She stopped but didn't turn around. Her phone began to ring. A number she didn't recognize.

"Get rid of it," he said in her ear. Again she hadn't heard him come up to her.

"What?"

"Your phone."

She held it helplessly in her hand. Stride grabbed it and did something with it before shoving it into an overflowing waste receptacle. She hoped he had torn out the SIM card.

"Come on. If you want some answers, follow me."

Stride was moving fast now, and she hurried to keep up. They rounded the corner of one of the apartment towers, and she followed him inside. Slipping through the door was easy, given the constant flow of people coming in and out. He led her down a stairway into a dingy basement corridor. She could hear the faint rumble of the building's aging furnace. She felt like she had been eaten by something, swallowed by a whale perhaps.

Stride leaned against the wall and slid to a crouch. When they were moving he had seemed energized, but now he looked positively sick.

"Are you okay?"

"We're safe here," he said. She wondered how he could know.

She opened her bag, got out the package, and held it toward him, but when he reached for it she held on. She opened it up and displayed the contents.

"We produce a hundred specimens like this a day. What's so special about this—and who is 'Violet' anyway?"

"This is different," he said.

She did not resist when he reached into the case and took out the tube. He held it up to the light for a moment, as if confirming something, though to the naked eye there was nothing to see but a yellowish fluid resembling blood plasma. But why would such a thing be unrefrigerated, and locked in Stef's desk?

He turned toward her and opened the tube, held it out to her, as if she would know what to do. He leaned over and mimed spitting into the tube, then held it out again with an expectant look on his face.

Hoping that it would all start to make sense, she did as he wanted, collecting as much saliva in her mouth as she could and then spitting it into the small laboratory tube.

He held it up so they could both see. At first the clear fluid from her body sat on top of the darker, thicker plasma or whatever it was. Then, slowly, an encounter began. The fluids mixed without blending, and it was the saliva that changed, beginning to bubble and turn black. Hairs rose on the back of Marti's neck, and a shiver rippled through her body, leaving in its wake a feeling of nausea. She took an involuntary step backward. She had naturally assumed that the specimen was from the body of a patient. But Marti knew of no human bodily fluids that could have such an effect. Was it an illness of some sort?

As if in response to her reaction, Stride dropped the tube to the concrete floor and ground it under his heel. Marti blurted a loud "No!" of protest but Stride ignored her, continuing to smear the fluid. Then he took the flash drive out of the case and stomped on it as well. He threw the now empty case off into the recesses of the basement.

He breathed a sigh of relief. After the momentary panic, Marti found herself sharing in his feeling.

She broke the awkward silence. "How did you know Stef?"

He looked at her for a long moment as if considering something. "He thought so highly of you, you know."

Marti's first reaction to this was anger, anger at everything: at losing Stef, at maybe losing the clinic, at this strange man who wouldn't explain anything. But his words, and somehow his presence, were bringing Stef back to her. He touched her arm gently, and she felt something enter her and begin to open.

She hadn't realized she was standing on ice until it broke. The tears that had held mercifully in abeyance arrived. The water coursed through her, into dry, cracked, closed places. To live had demanded all her strength, and strength had demanded that she banish tears, turning grief into hardness.

Her body was wracked with sobs that resounded in the cavernous basement. She wanted to fall over, to dig herself into the ground, but there was only the hard concrete floor. She became aware of Stride's arms around her, his body supporting her, and she allowed herself to fall into him. She no longer understood why she was crying. It was just something her body was doing, releasing everything it had held onto. It was an alchemy in which stone was turning to water. She became vaguely aware that her voice was joined by another, a baritone lament from another body. Two different sources joining as the air vibrated with sound.

Gradually, the storm subsided. Marti groaned as her body began to find a new equilibrium. She had sunk deeply into Stride's embrace. For a moment, ashamed of her vulnerability, the totality of her surrender, she couldn't bring herself to look at him. She thought this must be the most intimate moment she had ever shared with someone, and it had been with this man she barely knew. She supposed that intimacy could come more easily with a stranger. But she no longer felt there was anything strange about him.

When she caught a glimpse of his face, she was startled to see that his cheeks were wet, his eyes glistening with tears. His look to her was one of the most beautiful things she had ever seen. It was one of discovery, the look of someone who has had an utterly new experience, and through the experience has come to understand something; it was a look of compassion; it was a look of love, as though love was what remained after the storm washed everything else away.

Marti smiled and touched Stride's wet face. She felt a current of rapture flowing into her. What he had done had required a kind of strength she had never seen in a man.

His outpouring of grief had not been separate from hers, as if he had no grief of his own. He had an agenda, he hadn't pretended otherwise; he'd been telling her what to do from the moment he'd showed up at the clinic.

Some part of her mind was sounding an alarm, an old warning, a warning that had kept her solitary for many years. It was distant and weak, but it was enough to make her withdraw her hand and pull herself away from him a bit.

"I guess I really needed that," she said, her voice shaky.

Stride smiled at the obviousness of the statement. She dug in her bag for something to wipe her face. She found a tissue. She looked around at their dismal surroundings.

"This is crazy," she said. "I have to go back."

She looked at him, the whole question of the future suddenly asserting itself. Perhaps that's why she had avoided any relationships. It had been a long time since there had been any need to think about the future.

"You'll go back," Stride assured her. "But please, not yet. I still need your help."

She turned to him. "Then tell me what this is about," she demanded. "What was that stuff?"

He nodded. "I'll do more than tell you. I'll show you. But you have to come with me."

"Come with you where?"

"I promise. You will understand within the next day. It's the only way. Come with me, and I will show you everything."

She searched his face. He was a mystery, but he promised

her understanding and she believed him.

∞

He couldn't tell her where the place was that they needed to go, he said he didn't know the name and couldn't find it on a map, he could only direct their journey.

Marti straddled the bike and kicked the motor to life. She turned to Stride and motioned for him to get on. On his face she saw an inexplicable hesitation.

"I'm a safe driver," she said with a smile. He smiled back uneasily, and then mounted the machine behind her.

"Slowly," he said.

"Hold on," she said, and as soon as she felt his grip around her, she put the bike into gear and they took off.

He said he couldn't know the route in advance but could only recognize it as they proceeded, so they worked out a system for him to indicate directions to her—a tap on the left or right shoulder for an upcoming turn; on her back, when needed, for continuing straight.

It was close to dusk when they roared out through the Park gates, a trickle of pedestrians flowing in the opposite direction. Marti wasn't sure why, but she breathed a sigh of relief as they joined with the passing traffic.

At first, Stride's directions were clear. They were heading out of town, but he kept them on surface routes, avoiding the freeway; she assumed it was because they weren't going far, but they kept going. She realized they had been going straight for a while, at a gradually accelerating speed, with no signal from Stride, and she felt him starting to slump up against her.

Marti pulled into the parking lot of a strip mall. As she braked to a stop, Stride slumped off the bike and dropped to the pavement. His face was hideously bloody, a red river issuing from his nose. His body began to convulse. Marti dragged him to the side and sat him up against the wall. Another spasm racked his body, pumping a gout of blood out of his nose. Marti was stunned. This wasn't a nosebleed, this was like all the blood in his body trying to escape. She knew that more could be going into his stomach. For a moment she had the devastating thought that she was going to lose him too.

She pressed against his nose, staunching most of the flow, and held tight. She yelled at one of the teens standing around to get her some napkins from the convenience store behind them.

Blood. Covering her hands, Stride's face, shirt. A human body held about six quarts of it, not a lot in the scale of things. If it lost some, it could make more, but only up to a point.

She checked Stride's pupils carefully; they were widely dilated. But the seizure began to subside.

One of the teenagers handed her a wad of napkins. She removed her hand and rolled up the paper to make plugs that she placed in each nostril, damming up the blood that was still trickling out. Hopefully his body would take over, that amazing ability of the blood to stop its own flow.

His eyes were serene. "I'll be okay," he said. "Don't take me anywhere. To a hospital, I mean."

"Bullshit," she said, "you need a hospital."

He shook his head, and she could see that he continued to recover with what seemed impossible speed.

"What the hell was that?" Marti asked.

"Movement at high speed—my body can't handle it."

Marti was confused. The simple fact of a motorcycle ride had caused this seizure?

"Why didn't you say something?" she asked. "Does that mean you can only go where you can walk?"

He shook his head. "Cars, buses, things like that should be okay. They'll make me feel sick, but gravity disperses itself differently, my body won't take all the impact."

"But we don't have a car or a bus, we just have a motorcycle."

Marti sighed. A moment ago she was worried he might die, but he seemed fine now, and she felt irritation rising up in her. Resignedly she went over to lock her bike and retrieve her courier bag, which she had left in a side pouch.

The bag was gone.

9

The small tribe of teens that had been there when they arrived had dispersed and Marti and Stride were alone in the empty lot.

Marti angrily tallied up the losses. No viable mode of transport, no money, no phone. Her job probably in question. All exchanged for what?

Stride. She looked at him, his clothing caked with drying blood, and could not help feeling tenderness. She wondered again if he were mentally ill. But he looked back at her directly and she realized how much had already grown between them. The more everything that she'd believed constituted her life had been stripped away, the more this connection felt real and compelling, as though it had always been there.

"How are you doing?" Marti asked.

"Better," Stride said. He looked fine, if a little weak. She shook her head in disbelief; he should have been in shock.

"I know somewhere nearby where we may be able to borrow a car. Do you think you could handle going there on the bike, if we went really slowly...?"

Stride took a breath. She realized that what he had experienced had been painful. But he was summoning his forces, and he nodded his head.

Marti drove just quickly enough to keep the bike vertical. The ten-minute trip took more than an hour. She stopped periodically to check on her passenger's condition. She could see that even this slow movement was having a painful effect on him, but at least his body wasn't erupting anymore.

∞

The silence of the night in Jane's posh subdivision seemed artificial, as if everything had been wrapped in a blanket.

Marti helped Stride off the bike. He leaned on her without protest as they progressed up the walk.

It took a while for Jane to answer the door. Marti was glad that it was her sister and not Barry.

Jane, astonished, looked back and forth between Marti and the badly disheveled yet still undeniably handsome man whose body Marti seemed to be holding up.

"Can we come in?" said Marti, and she stepped forward with Stride, not waiting for an answer. A big smile bloomed on Jane's face as she moved aside to admit them.

The first thing Jane wanted to know, once Marti introduced Stride, was whether he had a first name. Marti realized she didn't know the answer to that. Before Jane could launch into more questions she couldn't answer, Marti quickly explained that they'd had a minor accident, and Stride needed to clean up.

Stride's presence had gotten Jane excited, and her face had yet to relax from a big, knowing grin. Jane dug up some old clothes of Barry's she had bagged for donation. Carly passed through and gave Marti a hug and Stride a strange look before heading into her room.

In the basement ensuite, Marti thought about how strange it was that she had ended up back where she had started the day. The sheets were still where she had left them, folded up at the end of the couch in the family room.

Marti gently let go of Stride, expecting him to sit down

on the closed toilet seat. But he remained standing, apparently able to support himself after all.

"The shower's good," Marti said. It was one of those fancy things with an array of jets that maintained a perfect temperature, no matter the number of toilets in the house's many bathrooms that were flushed at the same time.

Stride nodded and looked at the shower. Marti leaned in, turned it on, and showed him how to adjust the temperature.

He looked down at his clothes and began to peel them off. They were stiff, plastered to his skin, crusted with blood. He yanked up several layers exposing his midriff.. Marti realized she was staring.

"Good," she said, and then headed to the phone to cancel her credit cards.

∞

Jane was mixing some sort of hot drink when Marti got off the phone. She turned and thrust one into Marti's hand.

"Okay, sister, talk."

Marti took a sip and felt her body refuse the alcohol. She put it down.

"It's been a strange day," was the best Marti could do.

"Yes, and...?"

"What do you want to know?"

"Oh, come on. You show up at my door late at night with a handsome man of mystery, covered in blood. I think I deserve an explanation."

"I was hoping we could stay here tonight, and then borrow your car in the morning."

Jane coughed back the swig she had just taken.

Marti sighed. "Please, Jane. I know it's crazy, and I promise to explain it all to you. Right now I don't really even understand it myself."

Marti could see that Jane actually liked this, the romantic fantasy of it. So Marti fed Jane a mixture of truth and invention, uncertain herself where the dividing line lay.

Downstairs she found Stride asleep on the couch, the sheets thrown over him.

Marti sat down in an armchair and contemplated the man sleeping in front of her. The shower had transformed him. His body glowed in the moonlight like a statue. His beauty was making something move inside her. It wasn't love in the way she had experienced it before, but maybe she had simply forgotten what love was like.

∞

Marti awoke to the sound of her name. It was Stride, dressed in Barry's castoff clothing, which fit him reasonably well. The difference in him was startling. It wasn't only that he was clean;, but the night's rest seemed to have renewed him profoundly.

Marti had slept sitting up in the chair, and felt like she could still sleep a lot more.

"What time is it?" she asked.

Stride pointed to a clock that indicated just after 6 a.m. "We should get going," he said.

Soon they were on the road in Jane's Lexus. Marti hoped her sister wouldn't be too upset when she realized Marti had departed, taking the car with her. But she had left the Commando as security, even though she knew Jane wasn't about to use it to do her errands.

She looked over at Stride, still nervous that the car's motion might activate a seizure the way the motorcycle had. But he seemed alright; his eyes were closed as he concentrated on whatever inner perceptions were navigating their journey. Periodically he would indicate a turn and gradually they left suburbia, passing through several small towns.

Finally, they turned off onto a dirt driveway. The car headed slowly up the long, uneven path. Stride was sitting straight, his eyes alert.

The house was not like any Marti had ever seen. It wasn't large, but seemed to have been formed by hand directly out of the earth in an upward-spiraling movement. She had seen one or two buildings before using this kind of straw bale construction, but never one as bold as this. Wooden beams jutted out in a circling, geometric progression.

Off to the side was a garden of herbs and flowers. The garden gave an impression of wildness in its vigor and density. She could hear the resonating hum of a crowd of bees working their way through the nectar borne by the resplendent flowers. Not for the first time in the past day or two, she felt like her senses were sharper.

Stride, who had come up silently behind her, spoke softly.

"This is what we came here for."

Confused, she asked, "These bees?"

"'The kingdom of heaven is laid out before you, but you do not see it.'"

Marti turned away from the bees and looked at him. She distrusted religious quotations, and wanted to protest that what she saw was not heaven. But then, she had seen bees before, and what she was seeing now was different. The bees were more than insects. But perhaps it was she who was different.

Stride smiled. He gestured with his head toward the house.

∞

They rang the bell several times. No answer. Stride tried the door and found it unlocked.

Marti held back, uneasy.

"It's okay," Stride reassured her. "She won't mind. Come on."

Reluctantly she followed him inside, half expecting to barge in on some horribly private scene. People sometimes had good reasons for not answering the door.

But the house was empty, silent.

What Marti saw on the walls of the house made her forget all fear.

10

Marti stood awestruck before the painting. She had never asked where the painting in Stef's office had come from. Now here was another—several others. The pattern of colors in each was different, and each evoked a distinct feeling, but they could only have been painted by the same hand.

She gazed at the painting as she had gazed at the bees, and felt the same inexplicable longing she'd felt the night before while looking at Stride sleeping. Her body flushed with a warmth moving into all the places that had opened up when she had wept deeply in Stride's arms.

It was too intense. Marti turned away. Stride was just coming back into the room, having explored the house.

"She'll be back," he said.

Marti asked it gently. "Please. Tell me who."

Stride nodded. "Her name is Ursula. Ursula Sparrow. I know her from Stef."

"And how did you know Stef?" Marti was pleased she had finally gotten an answer to a question.

Stride looked into her eyes. It was as though he had been concealed before, as though she'd never fully seen him. She felt her knees go weak and he caught her before she fell. This is ridiculous, she thought. Falling in love.

She thought he would kiss her, but he didn't, so she brought her lips forward until they touched his. At first he didn't respond at all, but then, as if his lips were learning from hers, they came to life.

He stepped back, took her hand, and led her through the house. Ursula's paintings, and other art works from around the world, covered the walls. A bowl of fruit sat on a rough-hewn wood table, and she realized how hungry she was, having missed several meals.

"She won't mind," Stride said.

Marti opened the fridge and found the ingredients for a meal: steak wrapped in brown paper with the name of a local farmer on it, a range of vegetables.

It had been so long since Marti had cooked for someone. The meal she made for herself and Stride wasn't fancy, but the steak was done perfectly, the vegetables juicy and flavorful.

Marti found herself ridiculously grateful. As she chewed, she felt something she had never felt before. The gift of the animal's sacrifice, its weaving within its body the earth, the grass, the rain, together with its own breath and love for the one who cared for it, for the offspring it suckled, for its existence. She could feel all these elements nourishing her in incomprehensible but crucial ways. She looked at Stride's face and wondered if this new perception came from him, but she was certain they were sharing it. Sharing a sacrament.

∞

As Marti and Stride finished their meal, the house, which had been brightly lit by the sunlight pouring through its large windows, was becoming dusky. Few words had been spoken as they ate; words had not been needed. The communion that had graced Marti while she ate had also been a communion with Stride.

As she got up from the table, she felt a twinge of doubt.

She half-wondered if she had been drugged, or hypnotized. Stride had seemed so helpless, yet now she had the impression of enormous power surrounding him, and that the strange things she was feeling were some sort of effect of that power.

"I want you to show me," she said.

She watched as he arranged wood in the fireplace. His gestures were precise. He was laying down a path, making a home for fire. He lit a match and the fire began to move, feeding hungrily on the wood. The fire had been there all along within the wood, and all it took was the call of combustion for the fire to explode, energy releasing itself out of its temporary state and into its true purity of being. The size of the split wood suggested a tree of impressive girth, an old fir, much older than she was. Another sacrifice. All those years, drawing the sun's fire down into itself, into the earth's raiment. And now, releasing the treasure it had stored. All combustion was spontaneous, she thought. How remarkable that people weren't bursting into flame all the time. Perhaps she was now.

Stride turned to her and smiled, and again she felt that the depth of perception she was experiencing arose from being in his presence. She had arranged some pillows from the couch here on the floor, and they leaned against them and watched the fire dance. She felt the patterns of its movement massaging something deep inside her, something that had become rigid from living in a world where the fire was concealed.

Their bodies were side by side, not touching, but she felt his warmth. He was collecting his thoughts, and then he spoke while gazing into the fire.

"I have to thank you. First of all, for your help. Without it, I would be lying out there somewhere."

"It's my job..." she started, but then thought, no, my job is exactly what I haven't been doing.

"None of this can have been easy for you," he continued. "I know how many questions you have, and in spite of that, you've trusted me, and you have been willing."

She nodded, and he went on.

"Can you feel it? The threshold?"

His eyes searched hers; she knew nothing less than the deepest truth she could summon would do. She closed her eyes.

There was always a moment with others, a moment that marked a crossing into a relationship that would bring change. Innocence was lost, again and again, the price of admission to experience. She'd experienced a few one-night stands, but they repelled her, because they sought to satisfy a craving without any actual threshold crossing, without initiation.

Intimacy with him, just being near him, had already changed so much in her. They weren't lovers, but no coupling had ever felt to her so ineluctable. Now he was asking her to be conscious: to come to him not in surrender to an attraction, but with eyes open to what lay behind the attraction, for that is what one always, eventually, discovered. The result could be comedy or tragedy; sometimes it was even a love that endured.

With her eyes still closed, she saw the image of a great pair of doors. They were vivid and particular. She remembered where she had seen them before: in the book in Stef's office. She allowed the doors to grow more vivid in her imagination, and then she tried to sense what lay on the other side. Initially she felt only a void, but then the darkness began to fill with light.

The doors were metal and green with age, pocked with holes. The light radiated through every opening, and Marti felt it on her face. She thought about what lay behind her. Years of hard work and sadness.

She willed the doors to open, and slowly they did. The light that poured through was bright. It made her face tingle, and slowly her eyes adjusted. Within the light, she saw the bees she had seen earlier in Ursula's garden. Many more of them. Hard at work, moving with a resolute purpose. She saw a figure standing in this garden, and realized it was herself. She tried to see more, thinking that Stride must be there with her, but she could not see him. So she focused her attention on the version of herself that lay across the threshold. And to her surprise, she realized that she was still a physician, and as soon as she did she saw that she was ministering to people, with the same care and concern she had always brought to the task. The next thing she realized was that Stride was there; he was there in the bees. They were working together.

Then she was back beside him, staring into the fire while they trespassed in the home of this friend of Stef's. And now she understood why she hadn't been more distressed at their crazy flight. Her vision, even if it was nothing more than the contents of her own unconscious, suggested that this journey was not taking her away from her life, but toward it.

So she turned to Stride, and said aloud the easiest, deepest, most challenging thing she could: "Yes."

She was still silently saying the word as they began to make love.

11

Marti had begun discovering Stride's body first with her hands, reaching under his clothes, enjoying fighting against the restraint they imposed. She felt the strength of his chest, his nipples hard. She was straddling him and below her she felt the swelling in his groin.

He began slowly unbuttoning her shirt. She thought of how he had thrown another log on the fire, at once slowing it down and building it up. She looked into his eyes as he pulled her shirt off her shoulders. The longing she saw there suggested not lust, but reverence, a man who was seeing the face of something long hidden.

She wanted so much to feel his hands on her breasts that she groaned with it, closing her eyes. But his touch didn't come.

He stood up. She watched him as he stripped off his clothes. In the irregular light of the fire, his skin seemed to glisten like his gold eyes.

He reached out for her, and she took his hand. He pulled her up, standing beside him. Gently he removed the rest of her clothes and stepped back to admire her in the firelight.

Marti felt goose bumps appearing on her skin. She could swear she could physically feel the touch of his eyes, across her breasts, her lips, brushing her ears, stroking between the cheeks of her buttocks, down the inside of her thighs, curling in the hairs above the seat of her sex. She had the impression that it could continue like this, that they could have intercourse without ever really touching, that his eyes alone could drive her to heights and beyond.

So when he finally touched her, for the first time since they had disrobed, she gasped.

He had found some sort of oil. It had the fragrance of herbs. He rubbed it slowly in a small circle on her forehead with his fingers. This lasted only a few moments, but the sensation continued even when his fingers dropped away. She felt all of the sexual heat in her body being drawn upward toward that spot. She began to tremble.

"Lie down here," he said softly. She lay back against the pillows. He had poured more oil into his hands and he crouched in front of her, anointing her from the shoulders down with the oil. His hands were strong, but they seemed to be doing more than massaging her skin. Her awareness was expanding, and she felt as if he were drawing it up into his hands, while something of him was moving inside of her. They were flowing into one another.

Her eyes were half closed, and as he moved around her she caught glimpses of him, his dark hair, his round buttocks, the hairs on his thigh, his nipples. For moment she thought his body was hers, and she saw herself as he did. Her pale skin, her breasts rising and falling with her breath, her erect nipples, her full lips, the moist lips below, swelling apart in the desire to receive. His hands traversed all of these terrains, but with a kind of impersonal benediction. The flow of sexual energy, familiar from her past experiences, kept spreading out into something new. Where before her body had been the terminal point of the pleasure, it was now a coil, conducting a current that kept flowing beyond her.

She saw the seriousness of intent on his face. She was

amazed by his restraint. The flickering patterns of the fire's movement across their skin increased the impression that they were sharing one body, a body that was preparing to move beyond its condition of duality.

She wasn't sure if he moved her or she moved herself, but now she was facing away from the fire and he was massaging her from behind. His hands spread the oil across her shoulder blades, down her back, over the mounds below. Gently he slid his hand between her buttocks, his fingers pressed against her. Reflexively she tensed. His hand stayed there, not applying any pressure, and she felt the warmth spreading outward. Something in her let go, and then a jolt of pleasure drove right through her, and her groan turned into a cry. The orgasm deepened. Nothing was penetrating her, but his heat and light was bringing her into flame.

The orgasm became a plateau and she stayed there, even when he took his hand away. He fell back on his haunches and she turned around to face him. Her legs were spread apart, and he was kneeling between her thighs. She took the oil from him, poured it onto her own hands, and anointed his rigid sex.

She took hold of his wrist and pulled his hand down between her legs. His fingers slipped inside her, while with her hand she squeezed his thickness.

He brought his other hand to her mouth and she let his fingers slide between her lips, while she reached under him to massage right at his base.

The firelight had ebbed, but she had the impression that their bodies were beginning to glow, to give off light. She stroked up and down on his erection, her touch light, and felt a tremble run between them and magnify. His hand had found the right spot inside her and was caressing it with exquisite delicacy. She climbed toward a still higher plateau, sensing that the longer she could avoid convulsing in the release of orgasm, the higher she would go. The light glowed brighter; it was streaming up and out from his body, a channel of light arcing between his shoulders and the ceiling. She feared that reality itself was going to break.

He brought his mouth to hers and she surrendered the fear as the kiss took her, her eyes closing, and his hand dropped to her breasts. It took only the barest touch on her nipples to send her over the edge again, and she cried out as her whole body went into a spasm, and she felt the spasm pass through both of their bodies.

He wrapped both his arms behind her and urged her toward him. She lowered his cock and gasped as she felt it begin to move into her. As ready as she was, it had been many years since another body had entered hers: since Rourke's death.

She was the one controlling the progress of their union. She moved slowly, allowing the erection to open her. Their mouths were still joined, sharing tongues and breath. His hands cupped her buttocks, taking some of her weight, but allowing her to retain control.

He kept sliding deeper, impossibly deeper. And then, just when she thought it would never end, that there was nothing but this, going ever deeper, finally she felt her thighs all the way against his hips.

He withdrew his mouth from hers, breathing hard, and then from his depths a pure tone of sound rose. It seemed to her like a call, at once overjoyed and lamenting, its tone radiant and dense. Involuntarily, her own body responded. The intense pleasure continued to rise in her. It blossomed in her throat, and a noise unlike anything she had ever heard began to pour out from her, joining his song in a strange duet.

Her ability to distinguish between what was going on inside her and outside her had completely disappeared. The sound was all around them, and their movements seemed to be carried by it. She felt him rising beneath her. She fell back, and he moved over her.

Their bodies moved together, but not in a charge toward sexual release. Sex had been a platform they had jumped off from, into something far beyond it. They were joined and it felt like they had always been like that, the separation had been a temporary illusion, and she had returned to a native state of being.

He looked down at her with such love and tenderness that tears flowed from her eyes. She felt as if she'd known his face since before she'd been born, as if it were the face she'd been searching for. No wonder, the first time she had seen it, she had briefly thought it was Rourke's face. It must have been, in reality, that Rourke reminded her of this face she had not yet seen.

And then it wasn't Rourke's face she was looking at, it was her own, and she was seeing out of his eyes. She saw her strength, and her weakness. How hard she was on herself, how keenly she felt every shortcoming and never celebrated any accomplishment. How her need for approval allowed others to control and manipulate her, and the only way she found to deal with it was to finally separate herself from others. Her bitterness at losing Rourke and the vain pride involved in her refusal to love again.

She closed her eyes, and when she opened them Stride was above her still but they weren't in Ursula's living room anymore. They were inside a fountain of light. She knew somehow that this was the light that had been inside Stride's body, and the ritual they were performing had released it. She could see it flowing out from his shoulder blades, two great wings of light.

The wings rose and fell with palpable force over and over, like a great bellows, and she felt an explosion inside herself, as if every synapse and cell in her was having its own orgasm all at once. It was beyond pleasure, or pain. She wondered if she were dying.

And then she lost consciousness.

12

Marti opened her eyes, but the darkness persisted. Her other senses assured her of her wakefulness. She could hear her own breathing. Her mouth was parched. She wrapped her arms around her shoulders, holding on to herself.

She could sense the dilation of her pupils, that involuntary yearning for vision, for light. But there was no light.

Yet some other sense was also dilating. At first it was a sense of movement within the dark. An intricate, swirling pattern that gradually became more and more detailed. It was a movement of tiny shivering bodies. Inside them was a memory, the suffusion of remembered light. It churned within them until it overflowed, until they began to secrete it.

Bees! The small bodies were honey bees. In the darkness of their hive the light issued forth as the gold of honey, propolis, wax.

Some part of Marti felt concerned. How could she be inside a hive? And wouldn't the bees object to this? She'd had her share of bee stings as a child and still remembered the heat of it, a molten pinprick that spread through your body like a fire.

She shook off the concern. Reason didn't matter. Somehow she had been invited here, she was permitted here. Fascination held her. She felt a thirst, a need she hadn't ever noticed, that the golden, hidden light promised to satisfy. She would imbibe it through this organ of perception that was able to perceive the bees in their dark.

Something else was calling for her attention, but she shook it off and tightened her concentration on the bees. She began to glimpse, beyond the cascade of thrumming bodies, an entity that was singular, as though the hive were one being. She could hold her awareness on it for only a few moments before she slipped back to the perception of merely individual bees.

Again something tugged on her, and she realized that there was a hand in hers. Not now, she thought. She wanted to make a home here with the bees, and learn to see in their light.

But the hand was gently insistent. It reminded her of wings, of a light so intense that she had sought this darkness. He wasn't done with her. He had shown her the bees, and in doing so was showing her something of his own nature. And now he wanted her to follow.

Marti turned away from the bees and allowed Stride to lead.

They were climbing upward. She felt the earth under her feet, and although it was still dark, she could smell things now, moist earthy smells that held the memory of day and the promise of its return.

Stride had let go of her hand and she noticed that she could see his faint outline against the rising ground. Leading her on, up the hill. Dim silhouettes of trees slid past them as they moved. His form was that of a man, except from his shoulders where the great wings rose up. The wings were the source of the soft, glowing light around them.

She thought she must be awake now, but she tried to remember the moment she had woken up, tried to remember leaving the house. She could not.

Marti had stopped moving. She looked ahead and saw that Stride had reached the crest of the hill. He turned back now and beckoned, and in moments she was there beside him.

The place was a kind of overlook. It felt to Marti as if they were at the top of the world. The landscape below and around was now just barely visible, so dim it had no color, only shape. She could hear Stride breathing and she felt startled by the earthliness of it. His wings pulsed gently, rising and falling with each breath, while the world around them seemed to be holding its breath, waiting for something.

In the distance, the curved line of the horizon was beginning to emerge from darkness, like a crack between a dark earth and a shrouded heaven. A thin ribbon of dark red began to glow as the source of the light approached.

Marti knew there was a word for this, but she couldn't think what it was. Around and below her the trees and rocks waited patiently. She could feel thousands upon thousands, no, millions more lives waiting among them, the world holding its breath and waiting. Waiting and longing.

"Sunrise," said Stride.

The light was increasing. And now the first rays of molten orange swelled up over the horizon and swept over Marti like a wave of brilliance. She began to weep with the immensity of it.

She couldn't tell if this sunrise was some sort of new thing, or if she was just experiencing it for real for the first time. When was the last time she had actually seen the sun rise? She could not remember.

Marti's eyes were closed so that she could keep her face turned toward the sun. But its light was entering her through every pore, every cell that comprised her body experiencing a sunrise, an awakening from night to day, a coming into light. Suddenly she knew that she could open her eyes, and she did. She was staring at the sun, but there was no pain. She was the sun looking back at itself. She felt a moment of terror at all that was hidden in her coming into light.

She looked down and saw she was casting no shadow. Neither below her nor behind her. Stride was no longer beside her. Yet she felt his presence, even more strongly than before.

It was there inside her. In her gut, her sex, her head, her heart. Stride had slipped inside her, or perhaps that's where he had already been, and only now in this light could she see it. When she moved her arm, his arm moved too. She stepped back and felt his movement.

His touch was gentle, a question. She felt weightless, lifted up by his wings. Their movement a trembling joy.

The world around her was exploding in light, and so was she.

∞

Marti shuddered awake. She was lying alone in a bed. The light coming in the window suggested that it was late afternoon, turning toward dusk. The dream was already vanishing. Time was confused and she had no idea where she was, or whose house this was, or how she had gotten there.

A painting hung on the wall, reminding her: the house belonged to Ursula, whom she had never met. She remembered her journey with Stride. She remembered arriving at a house. But she could not clearly remember anything after that.

Marti moved, and was immediately assaulted by pain. She felt like she no longer fit in her own body, as if she had been torn out of it and stuffed back in the wrong way. Her joints were stiff, her head throbbed, her mouth was full of grit.

Had she been drugged? She vaguely recalled strange visions, but she pushed them from her mind, determined to regain a grip on reality. Something in her was telling her not to be afraid; to remember. But she pushed it away angrily. She was naked, but she did not remember removing her clothing.

Her hand went up to her clavicle and found something there, resting against her, small and hard, strung on a leather thong. She'd never seen it before, yet her hand had somehow known it was there. She pulled it off over her head and looked at it; a single, flat, undistinguished stone. She tossed it aside.

With great effort, she swung her legs out of bed. She had to get away from here. Her clothes were lying folded on the bed. She dressed quickly. Opened the door quietly. Saw no one, and padded down the hall.

A male figure was seated in the living room, facing away from her. Stride. In the dusky space her vision was strangely distorted; pale light was streaming up from his body to a pool of colors that swirled below the ceiling.

She crept past the doorway. Part of her wanted to stop, to go and join him, to wrap her arms around him. But she was also repulsed by the idea, as though it were something alien that had been implanted in her and that she needed to resist in order to recover her own reality.

At the last moment he turned and looked at her, rising from the couch. His face bore through her, carrying an inner gesture of great sadness and knowing. But she wanted neither.

She made it out the door and hurried down the driveway. For a moment, she was surprised to find her sister's Lexus parked there, but then remembered yesterday and also that dusk had fallen soon after they had arrived, and now it was falling again, meaning she had been here for at least twenty-four hours.

As she walked to the car, she reached for the keys in her pocket and felt relief when her fingers touched their cool, jagged edges. She turned back and saw that Stride was standing in the doorway now, the grief on his face even deeper. He said her name.

The car felt strange, like it had gotten much smaller. Her hand was shaking and she had to steady it to get the key into the ignition.

The engine roared to life, jangling her further. She shoved the transmission into reverse and began backing down the driveway as fast as she could. The car seemed to have a crazed mind of its own; she couldn't establish a connection between the movements of her body and the path she wanted the machine to take. The car shot back across the road and slammed into a mailbox. She yanked the shift into drive. The car fishtailed as it tore down the road.

When she was confident she was far enough away from the house that Stride could not catch up, Marti pulled over. She was breathing hard. She kept seeing Stride's face, stricken with the realization that she was leaving.

She felt a surge of anger, at him—what had he done to her?—and at herself—why had she gone there with him? What had she forgotten? Up ahead, she could see the evening sky, churning clouds that didn't look like any clouds she'd ever seen.

Enough. She had to return the car. Get her Commando. Go home. And go back to work to sort out the mess she'd left behind, which she could now only vaguely remember.

She pulled the car onto the highway, and quickly realized that she was out of her depth. The brightness of the lights from other cars turned her field of vision into geometric chaos. The noise assaulted her. She hunkered down, and cars behind her began to honk loudly as her speed dropped. The horns split her already aching head and made her want to scream. The trucks roaring past left a jet stream that threatened to sweep her away.

She looked up at a route sign and realized she wasn't

even on the right road. She must have taken the wrong merge a mile back; she hadn't even noticed the signs. She took the next exit.

The exit did not feed into a surface route, but was a huge truck stop: gas station for big rigs, diner, gift shop, motel. She pulled into the parking lot, thinking a cup of coffee might help restore her.

Just as she was about to get out of the car, Marti remembered that her wallet was gone. Well, she thought, coffee makes all things more possible. She dug around in the car and found a few dollars in coins.

Everything around Marti was an assault—the roar of the freeway, the fierce whine of air brakes as the trucks decelerated, the stink of petroleum, the bright lights. She was relieved to be out of the car and eager to be surrounded by people, people living normal lives, traveling predictable journeys between fixed points, remembering what had happened from one day to the next. But when Marti opened the door to the diner, she suddenly felt things would never again be so simple.

13

Marti stood still in the doorway, staring into the room. The diner was full of people, sitting at tables, eating, talking. But this commonplace reality had been blanketed by another, turning it into an overwhelming blur of color and movement. She had the impression of many additional beings in the room, hovering around those seated at the tables. She struggled to bring her eyes into focus, to force physical reality to conform to its expected dimensions.

The effort didn't make any difference. Her impulse was to flee, but she had been running continuously. She would sit down and make her coffee last as long as possible. While waiting for ordinary perception to return, she could figure out what to do next.

She walked discreetly to a table, trying to avoid staring at the strange apparitions around her.

After a little while she looked up from the table and realized that things were coming more clearly into focus, but not in the way she had wished.

It appeared that each person in the diner was tightly surrounded and interpenetrated by forms, colors, and textures that constituted a kind of second body. Less stable than the physical bodies, these second bodies were densely packed toward their centers, which reached down into their hosts' physical forms, but diffuse and swirling at the periphery.

She felt a blaze of curiosity, the scientist in her asserting herself. Even if this were a hallucination, perhaps it had something to tell her.

She looked at the several dozen people busily eating and drinking and saw that these second bodies were as particular and at least as varied as the physical bodies to which they apparently belonged.

"Know what you want, hon?" asked a waitress, interrupting her reverie. Marti turned to look at her: a pot of coffee in one hand, a name tag reading "Grace," fifty-something, thin, dyed blonde hair, her make-up a homage to the pretty looks that time had eroded.

Marti shook her head to the question, and Grace handed her a menu before moving off to refill the coffee of the four truck drivers at the next table. While Grace took a moment to banter with them, Marti had the opportunity to study Grace's second body more closely.

It was formed of hundreds of small individual, shapeless—things. It was impossible to tell how many, because you couldn't see to the bottom; the inner layers were more and more densely packed. The things—no, they were beings—were not solid in color, but most had a dominant hue, and taken together they formed a single overall impression. In Grace's case the predominant colors were a sludgy brown and a pale yellow, the latter not unlike the color she had dyed her hair. Marti was noticing some other details, including threads of black around her chest, when Grace returned to the kitchen and disappeared from view.

Marti saw a cup of coffee in front of her that she hadn't noticed the waitress pour. She focused her attention on it. The sight of the steaming black liquid comforted her. She took a sip and felt it spread almost instantly through her body, smoothing and soothing her nervous system. Her disorientation was receding, she thought. The crazy visions would as well, no doubt. She would drink the coffee slowly, as many coffees as it took—thank God for the bottomless cup—and then carefully drive herself back to Jane's and to her life.

She was on her second cup before she looked up again. It happened reflexively when a man at a nearby table cried out. A burly trucker jumped back with a yell of pain. A cup of hot coffee had spilled onto him. Grace began trying to dab at the spill while gushing apologies.

Marti was struck by the man's second body. It was dark, the layers of it consisting of various shades of black, some gleaming like an oil spill, some dull and flecked with a purulent yellow-white, the color of an infected wound. His rage, all out of proportion to the accident, heaved and swirled his second body like the surface of a stormy ocean. He let forth a stream of curses. When his anger was at its peak, Marti saw a cluster of forms free themselves, squeezing forcefully out of his second body. About a dozen of them; black, shot through with strains of bloody dark red. Separated from the coherence of the clustered body, they seemed shapeless, and they moved in a way that suggested a primitive consciousness, like single-celled organisms.

As they separated themselves from the still-enraged trucker, the vile-looking children of his rage went in different directions. Marti's impression was not that parts of his second body had come loose, but that they had actually been born in that moment and sent out into the world. Several simply floated upward, like helium balloons. The largest number dived at Grace, pressing against her own second body as if looking for ingress. One of them succeeded, and Marti watched as it wriggled into one of the black spots she had noticed earlier in Grace's second body, subtly enlarging that spot and sending a wave of its own particular color through Grace's second body. At the exact same moment, Grace's demeanor, which until then had been focused on desperately trying to make the situation better, suddenly shifted. Exasperated by the trucker's refusal to be placated, she finally registered the abusive stream of invective he was still hurling as he pushed away her efforts to help. Marti could see that Grace felt an urge to scream back at him, but she resisted it. In doing so she suppressed the ugly wave that had passed through her second body, while at the same time intensifying the vividness and hold of the parasite that had attached itself to her. Grace turned and stormed back to the kitchen, while the trucker shook his head and muttered to himself and the momentarily very quiet diner returned to its usual noisy distraction.

Marti watched as the rest of the trucker's progeny wandered around the room. One passed by her and she reflexively batted it away, which only succeeded in bringing it into contact with her hand, to which it briefly adhered. Marti couldn't see any indications of a second body attached to her own physical form, and wondered if this was proof it was all a hallucination, or further indication of a credible reality. The blob prodded at her like a mosquito before giving up and going elsewhere. Some of the others had more success, quietly infiltrating the second bodies of other customers. One person, Marti noticed, a thin and very sour-looking man whose second body was already encrusted with a great deal of similar colors, actually attracted a couple of them.

Two others floated by a heavy-set, gray-bearded man in his sixties, who looked like a regular. He wore an old leather vest and a stained, faded T-shirt. But shabby as his clothing was, his second body was something splendid; as with most of the others she was seeing, there were a range of colors and textures woven together. The dominant tone was golden, and the impression his second body made was of a simple, almost crude, but beautiful work of folk art.

The floating minions—the name that occurred to Marti for them—weren't attracted to this bearded man in the way the others had been to the sour man, as if to a good meal; rather they were sucked in, and themselves eaten, metabolizing into the benign substance of this man's second body.

Marti looked up to see what had happened to the minions that had floated upward. She saw that some had become part of a cloudy atmosphere hovering below the ceiling like old cigarette smoke.

Marti looked around the room again and allowed herself to think that what she was experiencing was real. What previously would have seemed to her a shabby and ordinary space, filled with ordinary people at a trivial, dreary, and forgettable moment, now seemed like a universe, a cosmos of universes, all engaged in some sort of vast exchange of darkness and light. She reeled with the scale of it.

A couple had just come in, sitting down at the nearest table to her. A man and a woman, around forty. Like most of the customers here they had the tough edge of people who did a lot of their living on the road, but Marti also saw something tender in them. They held hands when they sat down, spoke some words softly, and made each other giggle. The giggle sent out a few tiny minions from each of them, which quickly rushed toward, and buried themselves into, the second body of the other. Marti could see that their second bodies had much in common, but with different patterns. It was as though, over the years, each had gradually taken on some of the colors and textures of the other, like collaborative works of art.

The woman leaned over and whispered something to the man, with a look on her face that sent a spear of loss through Marti. It was a sensation with which she was all too familiar, triggered often over the years of her solitude by witnessing a moment of intimacy between a couple.

Marti intuited that the couple had just come in from the motel. They had the glow of sexual communion about them. Whatever the woman said to the man caused him to light up. He nodded, and his second body produced several more minions, delicately multicolored. These were larger, their birth more elaborate and protracted than the earlier ones. Most of them immediately moved into his partner's second body, but one of them floated away, and as Marti watched hypnotized, drifted toward her.

Part of her wanted to flee. But instead she turned toward it quite deliberately. It came up against her, nudged her gently in a few places, and then disappeared into the center of her chest.

A warmth spread out from this point of entry. She felt it grow, intensify with her attention. And then the heat caused something to crack and break open. And when it did, images began pouring out, filling her body from the inside.

A man's strong hand, rubbing oil on her forehead.

Stride. His eyes, looking down at her with such infinite compassion, love, joy, and sadness also, as if in finding her he was losing her.

Rising up from Stride's shoulder blades, twin fountains of light reaching to the heavens.

Her own body exploding with the same light, every cell irradiated with it.

Coming back to herself, she felt the wave that engulfed her subside, leaving behind an overpowering ache.

She knew only one thing: she wanted to be with Stride.

But she never made it back to the car.

14

Outside, Marti steadied herself against the column of one of the huge lights. As she'd left the diner the change in surroundings disoriented her again. If the interior had been defined by the human presence, out here there was only a world of noisy, smelly, bright machines. She gulped air, feeling faint, but the air was tainted with fumes that burned her throat.

As soon as she was confident she wouldn't fall over, she started toward the car. But it did not come into view. She stopped and turned, scanning the lot. A man was staggering between the cars. At first she assumed he was drunk, then that he might have a disability, cerebral palsy. She couldn't take her eyes off of him. He drew closer, but appeared lost in his own world.

Marti felt an uneasy burning in the pit of her stomach. Something was telling her to run away. But first she must find the car. She turned. Where was it?

Just as she spotted the car Marti felt someone behind her. She knew it was him, though it seemed impossible that he had covered the distance so quickly.

Marti spun around and was surprised to see he was still about ten feet away, heading toward her. His movements were wild and imprecise, inefficient, with the spasmodic jerkiness of a poorly assembled marionette. His face was immobile, frozen like a mask, devoid of awareness even though his eyes were open.

His second body was not like those she had seen in the diner. It appeared to have had a huge bite taken out of its center, leaving only a bleeding fringe. The empty space was filled by a black cloud, the edges of which trailed behind him like tentacles. It was like some sort of malign creature to which he was merely host.

Marti stood rooted to the spot, unable to move. She understood that she was being hypnotized by the vision of the second body, yet that only increased the fascination. The blackness suggested not a void, but something beyond color, something so bright that it was blotting out vision. She looked away for a moment and found that her eyesight was afflicted, as though she had been staring at the sun.

Horror still froze her in place and made her look back. The man stopped walking and tottered. Suddenly the tentacles snapped out toward her and lashed onto her ears. The rest of the black entity followed. Marti heard a piercing, high-pitched whistle and felt herself blanketed inside by something cold. The man's body dropped, his strings cut.

Then the shrill, burning blackness swallowed Marti up.

∞

In the blackness, there was no time.

In the blackness, space was torn apart.

After a void of feeling or sensation, Marti awoke to a yearning for re-membering, for the reassembly of the fragmented dimensions of her being, for the embracing unity of time and space.

Her life was but a distant memory. Could she be dead, then? Her condition was too sentient for the oblivion she associated with death, while too diminished for a supposed afterlife.

She tried to pull the vast distribution of her parts back

toward some embodied center, but the darkness would not relent.

An undertow of oblivion pulled at her awareness. She summoned an effort of resistance and felt the response of a remote presence, an image. It was benevolent, overseeing, yet too distant to be seen.

Then, a pinprick of light appeared. It had neither substance nor location; it was just a small tear in the enveloping dark. It responded to her yearning by moving toward her. Then there were others. Their movement reminded her of the bees, heavy with pollen, awakening space in their wake.

She felt a terrible needle of pain, like a bee sting. But in the cauterizing pain was a summoning of bodily awareness that released into a kind of pleasure. Another sting, and another, and finally a whole constellation of light enveloped her.

Each sting opened a pathway. The lights were entering her. And having entered, they moved out again. In and out the portals of her body: through the soles of her feet, the palms of her hands, her sex, anus, umbilicus, her throat, her nipples, her fingers. Embroidering her with light.

Gradually they were bringing her back to her self, to her body.

∞

Marti's senses were tangled and disordered. Gradually she sorted them out: a snarl of weeds and trash lit up in irregular glares of passing light, the smell of diesel fumes, the screaming of traffic.

She couldn't move at first; a million miles lay between her will and body. She concentrated her efforts and gradually managed to sit. The movement sickened her, and her stomach heaved up toward her throat, pitching her forward onto her hands and knees.

But her stomach was empty and she could only retch.

She wiped her mouth, breathing hard, her ears ringing, and leaned back on her haunches and looked around.

Her surroundings were a cruel mockery of the dawn plain she had visited with Stride. She was in a hollow beside a freeway exit ramp, stinking of trash and decay, lit by an eerie mixture of street lights and morning, though the sun was nowhere in evidence. It was an abandoned, bleary world, smeared with the toil of a million machine journeys. It had been made this way by humans, yet there was nothing human about it; her nausea the condition of one stranded on an alien planet. It was less a feeling of exile than one of a devastated return, and she wondered how one could do anything but mourn.

Only the living can mourn, and so she was alive. Her last memory returned, of being invaded by something that had plunged her into a pitiless void. She felt her body, wondering for a moment if anything had been lost in the gap of awareness, but beyond the feeling of nausea, everything seemed intact. Well, that's something at least, she told herself.

With considerable effort, Marti stood up. She hoped she would see the parking lot where she'd left the car. But she was surrounded by highway. She chose a direction and started walking. Only then did she realize that she wasn't wearing any shoes.

∞

The exit ramp did not lead to the truck stop where the diner was. The only thing here was a gas station and convenience store. Marti staggered toward the florescent oasis.

She came upon some human beings, though here they looked like mere appendages to the vehicles they were fueling. They seemed to avoid noticing her as she staggered across the road. Perhaps I'm a ghost now, she thought. But as she approached the station, a short black man pumping gas into a battered pickup truck registered her. He had thin gray hair, thick features, and the muscles of a lifetime spent at physical labor.

"You okay?" he asked.

Marti caught a glimpse of herself in the rear view mirror. A mess, a bag lady without any bags.

"I think so," she said.

He nodded, as unconvinced as she was. She noticed his second body. The colors lacked vibrancy, but there was a pleasing, well-ordered harmony to it.

"I need to call someone," she said. "Can I use your phone?"

"My phone?" She could tell he didn't like the idea. The gas pump clicked, indicating that his tank was full, and he replaced the nozzle.

"Please," she said.

He nodded, reached into his pocket, and held it out to her. As he did, she noticed a small minion, born in the moment of his generosity, pull loose and float upward.

Marti couldn't remember any phone numbers, but a name came into her head. Ursula, Ursula Sparrow.

"I just need to search for a number," she said.

∞

When the vehicle pulled up, Marti was just finishing the coffee Lionel had bought her after she gave him back his phone. She'd gotten Ursula's number, and the woman had answered almost on the first ring. Marti started to sputter a confused explanation, but Ursula cut her off to ask, "Where are you?" Lionel gave her the name of the location, and when Marti told Ursula, the woman said, "Stay there, we're coming to get you."

"Thank you," said Marti, but the woman had already hung up.

Amid the constant flow of vehicles at this busy refueling stop, somehow Marti knew that the white panel van had come for her, and she was heading out the door before it had even pulled to a stop.

The man who jumped out of the passenger side was in his mid-twenties, a look of worry creasing his scraggly-bearded face. He saw her right away.

"Marti?"

She nodded and he reached out his hand for her.

"Where's Ursula?"

"She's back at her place," he said. "We're going to take you there."

Marti felt a moment's hesitation, wondering if this was a good idea. Why hadn't she phoned Jane, or a friend, someone she knew?

"Please," he said. "I'm Ben. Ursula's nephew. She sent us for you. We need to hurry."

He was looking directly at her eyes with gravity and sincerity, and she took his hand. She glimpsed his second body, an inviting swirl of violet, orange, and blue.

Ben helped her into the passenger seat and then got in behind.

"This one with our life in her hands is Murdoch," he said, indicating the driver, who was flooring the gas even before the doors had closed. Murdoch, about Ben's age and of indeterminate gender, gave Marti an elfin wave from under a toque.

"We were relieved to hear from you," said Ben.

"How did you…"

"We'll let Ursula explain everything," he said. "We'll be there soon."

15

The van barreled up the driveway, branches scraping as it whipped past. Ben had the door open before they had reached a complete stop.

A woman sat framed in the door of the beautiful house, her posture an etching of defeat, long white hair cocooning her head and shoulders.

Ben hurried Marti out of the van, with Murdoch following behind. They stopped when they realized their host wasn't making a move.

Finally the seated figure slowly looked up, as though she hadn't noticed their noisy arrival. She made no move to stand, her eyes penetrating Marti with an indecipherable question.

"We're too late," Ben said.

"Too late," Ursula said, so blankly that Marti was unsure if she was affirming it or merely repeating the words.

Ben sat down next to Ursula and put his arm around her.

"I'm so sorry, Aunt," he said.

She patted Ben's hand gently, then extricated herself. She stood up tiredly and stepped toward Marti. She took both of Marti's hands in hers and looked her up and down. Marti noticed the masculine size and strength of her hands. The hands of a gardener, and an artist. Ursula appeared to be around seventy-five; later, Marti found out that she was well into her eighties. Her blue eyes had the sharp clarity of a bottomless mountain lake, and Marti felt exposed by their gaze.

"Stride...?" It was the only word Marti could get out. She was afraid to ask more.

"You left too soon, my dear," said Ursula, stating it gently as a fact and not an accusation.

"I was coming back," said Marti, too loud, suddenly angry at being on the defensive. But Ursula only gripped her hands tighter. "It's okay," she said, "I'm glad you're here now," and Marti felt herself drawn into a perception of Ursula's second body.

It was exquisite, unlike any Marti had seen in the diner. Instead of random patterns, Ursula's was harmonious, not symmetrical or obviously ordered, but a shimmering display of colors that fanned out from a deep emerald, resembling the paintings hanging inside on the wall. It was tall, ascending well above Ursula's head where it was crowned with a ring of gold and green, fountaining in a continuous movement and bathing the area around her.

Marti returned to the present as Ursula let go of her hands.

"I don't understand," said Ben. "She's here now. What was the point, if it was too late?"

Ursula sighed. "I don't know," she said softly. "But we know that there are no assurances. We serve the Partnership, but none of us knows the plan, if there is a plan."

"Never mind the talk, I want to see him," Murdoch said, voice trembling, stepping in front of Ursula. "Where is he?" She pulled off her toque, exposing a head of red hair, and multiple piercings in both ears.

"He's inside," said Ursula, gesturing with her head. "Well, what's left of him."

The house was as Marti remembered it, but it was like

the memory of a dream. It was just as beautiful, but somehow stark and empty in the morning light. Ben and Murdoch followed as Ursula led them to the living room. She approached the couch with trepidation, but then stopped. Marti came up beside her. The couch was empty.

"No...." Ursula's whispered word boomed in Marti's ears.

"This is where he was?" asked Ben.

Ursula sat down heavily on the couch and patted it. "I left his body here."

Suddenly Ben let out a laugh. "He's alive then. Don't you see? He must be alive."

Ben and Murdoch looked at one another and then quickly spread out and went through the house. Marti heard doors opening and closing.

They returned a few moments later. "Nowhere," Ben said.

"But he must have gone somewhere," said Murdoch.

"I held his hand while he took his last breath," said Ursula. "He departed from that body."

Ursula's words seemed to resound in the silence for a long time.

"Please," said Marti. "I think you'd better tell me what's going on."

Ursula gave her a strange, fearful glance. "We were hoping you would tell us what you know," she said.

"But I don't understand any of it," said Marti. "I don't even understand what he was." She shivered, as though the only explanation was below the surface of her skin, in the places where he had touched.

The others seemed to be alone in their thoughts, but Murdoch turned and looked at her with a strange tenderness, gently pulling Marti's hair back from her face as if to see her more clearly.

"A Guest," said Murdoch. "Angeloi. You know that much, don't you?"

"Angeloi? You mean, angel?" The term brought Marti up short. She hadn't even thought it. And yet she could still see his wings, beating above them to the throb of her heart. "But he was a man. He was flesh."

"Briefly," said Ursula. "Too brief."

"But we can't know, Aunt," said Ben. "You always say we can't know the results of our efforts."

Ursula smiled tiredly and caressed Ben's cheek. "You're right. Why don't you and Murdoch fix some breakfast for us all. I need to talk to Marti."

She motioned to Marti and they sat together in the living room.

Ursula unclasped something from her neck, and pulled a piece of jewelry out from underneath her clothing. She showed it to Marti. "Stride left this for you. He called it the Onoma."

"Onoma."

It was the thing Marti had been wearing when she woke up. At first, it just looked like a small, flat stone. With Ursula's encouragement, she took it in in her hand.

It felt heavy for its small size. As Marti turned it she saw a glint of color. Marti wondered how she could have cast it aside.

A single pattern was engraved on it, worn by time but still distinct. It compelled Marti's attention. Something was familiar about it. A letter in an unknown alphabet, from a forgotten language, perhaps even older than Sanskrit or Hebrew, those ancient languages in which letters were also images, invocations.

The periphery of her vision became indistinct, the coin and the letter or image on it growing more and more vivid. She had the impression that she was seeing everything from a great distance, a field of matter lit up from within by a letter. A name.

A name is a sound. We may write it down, but it is a sound first. The child hears her mother say her name long before she can read. Marti heard a sound echoing, and she recognized it immediately. It was the call that Stride had issued when they were making love, the sound that resonated through her until she didn't know whose voice it was. She allowed the sound to move through her body now, her vocal chords once again resonating with it.

It was almost too much. Suddenly the sound turned into grief and her throat closed against it. What had she done? Why had she cast aside this gift, cast aside Stride?

"I'm sorry," said Marti, but when she looked up at Ursula she saw a piercing look of compassion. Ursula gently took the Onoma from her hand and placed it around Marti's neck.

"He gave it to you to protect you," she said. "You mustn't take it off."

But she had taken it off. Taken it off and fled. Marti thought about the strange attack she'd experienced. The need for protection suddenly seemed very real.

"It will also help keep you connected to Stride," Ursula said.

"But I thought—"

"He's gone from here," Ursula said. "But he's not gone."

Marti wondered what that meant. She held the Onoma tightly in her hand, feeling the continued resonance of the name. Was he here in the sound?

"An angel," Marti said. She shook her head. She felt silly trying to grasp it. She hadn't believed in angels since her forced Sunday School classes.

"So you're telling me," she continued after a pause, "the world really is like some medieval stained glass window, us down here, God up there, angels between us, devils down below? And all the rest of it?"

"No," said Ursula. "No more than the world is a giant

machine, or a giant cauldron of chemicals. Those are human images. Each with a grain of truth. Each incomplete. What does the word angel mean to you?"

Marti shrugged. "Just the obvious. Winged messengers who live in heaven, soldiers in God's army, offering help and protection to humans. Something humans invented to help us deal with life's difficulties. Something for sentimental verses and kitschy paintings. That's the way I've always seen it."

"And you've been right," said Ursula. "Mostly when people say angels, that's what they mean. But have you ever played the game broken telephone?"

Marti nodded.

"Our concept of angels is like that. It's very hard for us to imagine what the experience of humans was like in other times. We think they simply understood less than we do. And that's certainly true, at least in some ways. But they also perceived things we aren't able to. The membrane between the physical realm, which we can see with our ordinary senses, and the realm of the angels, was much thinner."

"Membrane?"

"It's a strange image, I guess. A boundary, but a permeable one. A skin between worlds."

Skin. Marti thought about the body's largest sensory organ, the place where inside encountered outside. But Ursula was continuing.

"In those days, people had experiences of angels. Those were recounted in scripture and imagined in art, and the culture took the images and used them, as culture does, in ways that were useful. The result often seems naïve and childish, the product of wishful thinking. But that doesn't mean it isn't a pointer to something real.

"Today, we believe there are no more secrets. Yet even today, there are forms of knowledge and practice that remain guarded. Not, as in older times, by priesthoods, or decrees, or temple gates. Today, the only place to hide things is in plain sight. They are protected by peoples' inability to see."

Marti stood up and paced, feeling the weight of Ursula's words.

"That's all very interesting. Really, it is. But what about me? Why am I involved in this? Why did Stride come to me?"

"I wish I could give you an answer. Why does one person win the lottery, another get cancer? I do know that someone was needed, and you are the one that Stride chose. You will have to try to understand. Because the answer will lie in what you need to do."

"And where do you come into this? Why did Stride bring me to your house?"

"Goran and I were among those who undertook the task of learning to see these things. Part of a group of beings—humans and others—calling ourselves the Partnership. He and I both prepared for many years, for something that could only be accomplished at the moment of the death of our physical body.

"I won't get into all the specifics of how it's done," Ursula went on. "And we had no certain proof or knowledge that it had ever been done, only legends and stories. But legends and stories tell more of the true history of the world than we realize."

Ben's voice broke in. "Breakfast is ready."

∞

Over breakfast Marti heard bits and pieces of the life stories of the others, stories focused on how each had become involved in the Partnership. The name made Marti smile, as if this strange undertaking were some sort of law firm. A mixture of inexplicable experiences and disturbing and wonderful dreams had led to recognition and involvement, through a gradual process for each that took place over a lengthy period of time.

But their accounts raised more questions than they answered. Marti tried to hold back her urge to seek more explanations.

"I don't understand," she finally blurted. "You all seem to have a clear sense of why you are here. But I don't know anything."

Ursula gave an exaggerated sigh, as if Marti was a recalcitrant pupil. "It's not about what you know, my dear, or understand, it's about what you do."

"But doesn't what I know determine what I do?"

"Actually, it's the other way around."

Marti shook her head. For a moment she felt pinioned, trapped. The events of the past few days had divided her life neatly in two. She could not go back, and she had no idea how to go forward.

Suddenly she burst out into hearty laughter. The others watched with bemusement and a slight bit of concern.

"I've been fucked," said Marti, still laughing, trying to explain. "Fucked by an angel."

For a moment Ursula looked shocked, perhaps by the image, or the reference to an old TV show, but then began laughing too, her laughter high-pitched and trilling. The others were slower to join, but soon they were all laughing.

Marti could feel an enormous, charged accumulation of anxiety, hope, grief, being released as the laughter massaged her organs. Tears ran down her cheeks.

Gradually the laughter subsided. They wiped their eyes, which shone brightly, and breathed deeply. For a long moment no one spoke. Marti basked with the others in the renewed atmosphere.

16

After breakfast and a round of hugs infused by the irrational gift of laughter, Murdoch and Ben departed.

Marti and Ursula sat in the kitchen together, drinking more coffee.

As Ursula spoke, Marti noticed a minion forming slowly from her second body. She could see how much love and concern it expressed.

"The simplest way to think of Stride is as a traveler, a visitor from another place."

Marti nodded.

"So the question is, what is that place? Well, where do the angels live, according to popular belief?"

Marti shrugged. "Heaven."

"Right. So there's a name for the place. But what is it? We know that Stride was real, as real as you and I, maybe more so."

Again Marti nodded.

Ursula continued. "If heaven's defining characteristic is that it is not physical, then it isn't somewhere else, not separated from us by distance, but by condition. So that's the first principle to understand if you want to understand Stride.

"Now let's leave aside this word 'heaven,' which is loaded with far too many limiting associations. Do you want to know what Stride told me his kind call it?"

Marti nodded eagerly.

"They call it Home."

Marti felt let down by the obviousness of it. Everyone calls the place they are from "home."

But then Ursula explained that "Home" included the physical world as well. To them, it was actually all one continuum, comprising physical and non-physical realms.

Marti recalled the minions that had filled the diner, woven invisibly into the visible world. She felt a swell of regret rising for all that she and Stride hadn't shared. But then she thought, I'm just beginning to realize how much he did share with me.

Ursula continued. "Now that humans have, by separating our awareness from heaven, developed our individuality, the aim of the Partnership is to bring the two worlds of Home, the world of humans and that of angels, closer together. We are hungry for it but we don't even know it."

The dream she'd had after their lovemaking came back towards her, the climb with Stride from the dark of the beehive to see the glorious sunrise. There was something far greater here than a material event. The transformation in her own perception proved it.

"I was trying to come back, you know," said Marti. "And then, this thing..." She shivered as she remembered the black cloud, invading her. She wondered if it was still there.

Ursula refilled their tea. "It's not entirely a surprise that there are forces seeking to counter our efforts. That is a kind of law, it seems, of Home: growth only happens through overcoming resistance to change. Sometimes the resistance is within us, sometimes outside of us."

"That's pretty abstract. Someone...something...didn't want me back here, you're saying, because it wanted things to stay the way they are?"

"Or much worse."

"What does that mean? Worse how?"

"If heaven and earth can be brought closer together, they can also be driven apart."

Marti felt a creeping dread. "So I am now some sort of, I don't know, tool in this fight? I don't recall signing up for it!"

"Are you sure?"

Marti felt vexed by the question. How could she have chosen something she could even now barely comprehend? But before she could answer, she remembered the "yes" she had given Stride, and it had indeed felt like she was saying "yes" to more than she could imagine.

Ursula watched these thoughts flicker across Marti's face. Finally Marti nodded. "I did," she said, "I did consent."

Ursula nodded. "And you will find the need to renew this consent, and ample opportunity to withdraw it."

Marti nodded, filled with a terrible foreboding that was nothing like regret, but rather like the weight of a responsibility she still didn't understand.

Ursula gently touched her hand. "Why don't we sit outside?"

∞

The morning sun was pouring down on the garden.

Ursula positioned two garden chairs to face one another.

"Do you know, Stef and I had not been in the same room in over twenty years."

"Really? I thought you were close. You lived so nearby."

"It was a choice we made. We had to learn how to be together when we were physically apart. We would come here together," she gestured to the garden, "but only in our imaginations."

Marti looked around at the garden.

"After today, you and I must do the same."

"What do you mean?"

"Meet only in our imaginations."

Marti looked away. "I'm sorry, I just...I mean, what's the point in that? Either we meet or we don't. Why does it matter what we do in our imagination?"

But even as she said it she realized that she already knew better. She thought of the second bodies, wondering if that's what was meant by the word "imagination."

Ursula smiled, as if reading Marti's thoughts, and so confirming them. Marti blushed.

"I want to be able to help you," said Ursula.

"To do what?"

"I can't answer that."

"Can't or won't?"

"Questions are important, Marti. They invite experience. But answers can be deceptive, even when they are correct. I can't tell you what the path is. The path is made by walking. I can only tell you that I will try to walk with you, as much as I can."

Marti nodded. She was so accustomed to the solitude of her own inner life. Now here was this woman, offering help and, well, a kind of partnership.

"Did you know that the word 'paradise' means 'a walled garden?'"

"I think I've heard that."

"Well, imagine that garden is inside you. You are the wall, holding it in. No, don't close your eyes yet. Look out here, look at this garden, but imagine that what you are sensing out here is actually inside you."

Marti nodded at Ursula and turned her attention fully to the surrounding garden. Its perfection lay in the balance between the wild urge of growing things to propagate and the human will to order. The plants were arrayed in beds, mulched with cut grass, but mixed together in unexpected ways.

Marti didn't even notice the roses at first. They were embedded in a cloud of darker geraniums and other companions; shades of red and pink, the roses reached upward from the dark green tangle as though the whole community of plants had found its ultimate expression in their extravagance.

Their stillness was somehow deceptive, concealing a mystery that demanded attention. The sun was touching them, and in return they surrendered their fragrance, an intoxicating haze Marti could almost see.

She focused her attention on one of the roses in particular. It was at the peak of its flowering, quite glorious in its rich blush of color, the delicacy of its folds, the symmetry of its form. The other flowers surrounding it seemed either to be growing toward such perfect expression—their petals tightly arrayed—or aged beyond it, losing their form.

Thus the cluster of roses appeared as an image of past, present and future, all at once; and in that image Marti felt her sense of time slipping away, as if in the garden's sublime marriage of wildness and harmony all times were present. She felt herself pass through the still surface as if through the surface of a pond, and into the vast movement.

Or perhaps the movement was passing into her. Marti was felt a great swell in her chest, a marvelous ache that joined her and everything around her.

"Attention is the precondition for love," Ursula said, as if reading her thoughts. "Perhaps the only one."

Marti sighed at the truth of it. It often seemed that love was in short supply in the world, but really, it wasn't; the world we saw was merely the surface of an ocean of love. Yet without attention, we could not get beyond this outer layer, and attention was the thing in short supply. She'd merely had to place her attention on the rose for it to reveal the depths of its mystery, and you could not then help but fall into love.

It was so with a person. But a person was rarely so straightforward or self-confident as a flower. Many had grown in disturbed shapes, their petals impenetrably curled and folded. Yet the revelation of their beauty was merely waiting for the attention of some patient sun.

"Good." Ursula's voice brought Marti back from her thoughts. The woman was sitting very close beside her now, though Marti hadn't heard her move.

"Now, we close our eyes. But continue with the meditation."

Marti glanced at Ursula, and saw that the woman was looking at her. "Ready?" she asked. Marti nodded and closed her eyes.

∞

They spent much of the day in the garden, practicing the shared meditation to ever deeper effect. It was itself a kind of partnership, Marti realized, a merging first of inner and outer, and then of their inner worlds.

Afterward, they ate a dinner that Ursula pulled together quickly. Marti was surprised at the strength of her appetite. They hardly spoke, but their silence held a deep communion.

"Did you mean what you said before? That we can't continue to see one another?"

"We mustn't with the eyes. But with the heart, yes. Every day, for ten minutes. Wherever we each are, at exactly 7 a.m. We enter the walled garden, with one another."

Marti bridled. "Just like that? And what if, I don't know, I don't feel like it?"

Ursula cocked her head and sighed indulgently.

"Then you won't, I guess. But if you do this—if we do this—there is a chance we will see Stride again."

For a moment Marti was going to plead for an explanation, but instead she just attended to the hope Ursula was expressing. Maybe understanding wasn't what mattered.

II

.... For beauty is nothing
but the beginning of terror, which we still are just able to endure,
and we are so awed because it supremely disdains
to annihilate us.
—Rainer Maria Rilke, *Duino Elegies: The First Elegy*
Translated by Stephen Mitchell

17

At first, Marti had called in sick because she simply didn't feel ready to face the demands of the clinic. After such strange experiences, she needed time by herself, time to make sense of it all.

By the third day, she had to admit that she wasn't heading in that direction. Things were not making sense.

Even the empty apartment seemed more than she could handle. The space around her did not feel empty, but charged with fullness. She kept glimpsing movement within it, out of the corner of her eye.

She wondered if this was what babies and small children experienced. She found herself sitting on the floor, entranced by the dust motes in a stream of sunlight. She gazed at them and felt like she was looking not out into the world but into the core of her own being, as though the sun were shining outward from a center deep within her.

Several mornings she put on her coat and stood before the door, but she could not get herself to go through it.

She had food delivered, but ate little of it.

She kept seeing Stride's face, with the look of grief it had worn as she'd fled. In her dreams she searched for him. Every morning she awoke to a more harrowing loneliness.

Ursula's promise they would see Stride again now seemed a false comfort. Stride was gone. And it was Marti's fault.

She considered getting in touch with Ursula. But of course, she couldn't; Ursula had said they would communicate only through a daily meditation. But Marti made only one half-hearted attempt at the appointed time.

She felt someone, or something, trying to reach her. But she sensed the intention to comfort, and she didn't want comfort. All she wanted was oblivion.

Finally, Marti just stayed in bed.

She found herself wondering what would have happened if she hadn't fled Stride that night. The question was almost too much to contemplate, but she took a kind of pleasure in the familiar pain of love lost. She'd had another chance, a literally miraculous chance. And she had blown it. Now all she was left with was a kind of residue of sensitivity that promised to make her life more than she could handle.

She wanted it all to go away. She wanted to go back to the way things had been. She took the Onoma, the amulet, off from around her neck, hoping that the dreams would subside. But she only sank deeper into grief. She wept. And wept some more.

The condition was familiar to her. Ten years before, in the aftermath of Rourke's sudden death, she had taken to her bed, unable to stand beneath the crushing weight of loss. Now it seemed as though the time between had all been a dream; abandonment was the reality.

Darkness brought a promise of comfort. During her residency, when the long shifts had sent her home to sleep at odd hours, Marti had installed blackout shades on her bedroom windows. Now she kept them drawn and stayed in the dark, losing track of day and night.

When she first noticed the lights, she assumed they were phosphenes, those mischievous, abstract images produced by rubbing the closed eyes or spending too long in darkness. Three of them circled slowly, their narrow orbits interlacing with one another. But when she moved her head, they stayed where they were, suggesting some sort of independent existence.

She tried to see them more carefully. They were hovering some ten feet away. The fixed square walls and ceiling began to seem unreal next to the mysterious circular movement.

They were the same lights, she realized, that had come to her while she lay by the side of the highway, only now more defined. But she felt no comfort in the realization.

"No," Marti said aloud. She wanted no more hallucinations, or whatever these were. She wanted the hard, certain edges of the known space. Now, darkness and oblivion were relief.

She pulled the covers back over her head. But the lights were still visible through the fabric with no diminution.

She concentrated her will to make the lights go away. "Leave me alone." She spoke the words so softly that even if there had been another pair of ears in the room they wouldn't have heard. But as she repeated it, the lights began to recede.

Some hidden iris inside her began to shrink, and the searing pain of it made her gasp.

"Leave me alone," she repeated, but now it was the pain she meant. She had thought she was driving herself away from such torment, yet her own will was magnifying it. Maybe oblivion was pain and not relief.

The three lights, which had receded to about half of their former presence, hesitated, waiting.

Marti needed air. She sat up and pulled the covers back.

She remembered the "yes" she had given Stride. Was this all life wanted from her, to say "yes" again and again?

The question reminded her that she had a choice. She looked at the lights again in spite of herself, and she saw that their presence was comforting. Once more she saw that they were offering her something she needed.

The recognition brought the lights into sharper focus. She saw that each comprised many individual movements of light, shimmering with the same spiraling pattern. Again they reminded her of the bees she had seen with Stride, though now they didn't look like bees to her, but something for which bees might be a kind of allegory. Sparks of light, carrying within them a vast space. Atoms?

As Marti allowed her resistance to dissolve, they responded by moving closer. She understood now. The lights were there to comfort her, to heal her. They moved slowly and with a kind of gentle tentativeness that communicated respect for her wishes.

As they approached, the three bodies opened out, like slow-motion fireworks. The shimmering movements that defined them became more intense so that each of the thousands of particles now moved around its own center. The spiraling, orbital pattern remained constant, but multiplied.

They weren't merely light. Light was the medium, but what it carried was a presence of being, of beings. Surely these were also angels? Had it been three angels? Or three thousand?

What they wanted was to be closer to her. For her to be closer to them.

Now they seeped through her pores, moving in and out of millions of tiny openings, weaving a web of increasing density. Again she felt the pinprick ache of each entry, and she held on to the edge where pain released itself continuously into ecstasy. Then she let go, and there was no more pain.

With her surrender, the light magnified and opened up once more. It had been outside of her, and then it was inside her, and now she was inside of it. She recognized the landscape from the night she had spent with Stride, the place where she had followed the bees to the sunrise. Once again the place was on the cusp between night and day, lit by a soft glow.

A slight breeze caressed her. Goosebumps rose on her skin, and a trembling shook her at the root.

Stride's touch.

It turned her legs to water and she crouched down, brooding the feeling.

The touch lingered. It had taken her breath away. She looked to the ground. The dark soil was alive with movement, the familiar spiraling pattern. Her breath slowly returned.

"Again," she said. "Touch me again."

As if in response, she heard a distant, insistent banging. There was nothing in it of Stride's touch, and she willed it to go away.

The banging continued, pulling her toward something she didn't want.

Waking.

∞

The banging had stopped, but she'd heard a voice.

"Marti?"

She sat up abruptly. Two silhouetted figures were in the doorway to her darkened bedroom. She felt a stab of fear. She shrank back in her bed, trying to think if there was something she could use to defend herself.

One of the figures said her name again and stepped forward, and Marti recognized the face.

"Dave?"

What was her colleague doing here, in her bedroom?

He gestured to the other figure, who Marti realized was the building superintendent.

"Are you okay, Dr. Powell?" the man asked.

With a scratchy voice, and doubting her own words, she

assured him that she was fine. Uneasily the man backed out, leaving Dave alone with her.

∞

Dave was clearly surprised and relieved that Marti appeared to be well. He waited awkwardly while she had a quick shower.

Now they were sitting in her kitchen, sipping coffee with the consistency of sludge. Dave had found an old jar of instant and dumped most of it into her cup.

"I understand how you're feeling," Dave said. This seemed unlikely to Marti, but he continued. "I think we'd all like to just stay in bed. Everything in the clinic just seems like a reminder of Stef."

Stef. At first Marti felt the impulse to say, this has nothing to do with Stef. On the day of his death she had led the charge back to their posts, to their patients.

But then she realized that would require her to explain herself to Dave. She wasn't ready for that.

"Stef would be horrified to see me like this," she said, hoping that the acknowledgment would keep Dave from probing deeper. But the words were true, she thought, more true than she intended. She had wanted to find words to fend Dave off, to get him to go so she could climb back into bed. But now it wasn't just Dave getting in her face, it was Stef.

"You know, the first conversation I ever had with him, one on one..." Marti trailed off, suddenly worried that any narrative of her own experience would lead back to the strange events of recent days, which she felt entirely unready to disclose. But Dave nodded at her offer of a reminiscence.

"Go on."

Marti took hold of the memory that had presented itself to her.

"I'd already had him as a teacher for a full term. But I

hadn't spoken with him. I wasn't even sure he knew who I was. Frankly, I was scared of him."

Dave smiled. "That's not hard to imagine." His smile caught Marti off guard. She noticed his second body, distinguished by a skein of blue iridescence.

Marti forced herself to continue. "I'd had a really difficult first term in med school. I felt like I didn't belong there. It wasn't just that I was older by a few years than the others. It seemed none of them took it very seriously. I mean they studied, they were serious about doing well, about being successful at it. But the why of it didn't seem to be a question for them. And questions were all I had.

"Finally, I decided I had made a mistake. I was going to drop out. But without telling anyone. I let it slip out one day, kind of accidentally, when talking to some of the other students.

"One day, soon after, I was walking down the hall in the medical building and I heard someone say, 'Dr. Powell!' I thought there must be a doctor with the same last name as me, since I wasn't a doctor yet. But when I looked back, there was Stef, and he was leaning out of his office and staring right at me. He gestured and I followed him into his office and sat down.

"'So,' he said, 'we're not living up to your expectations?'

"I pretended I didn't know what he was talking about it. It seemed unlikely that he had heard about my intention, and impossible that he cared."

Dave snorted.

"I know, right?" said Marti. "As if Stef could ever not care. I don't even remember the rest of what he said. I just remember that he spoke to me like I was already what I wanted to be but now felt incapable of. He didn't coddle me, or offer some kind of reassurance. The message was just kind of, let's get on with it."

"Let's get on with it," said Dave, gently. Marti felt herself flush, and wondered what activity of her second body was bringing such heat to her face.

18

Marti's return to work at the clinic was both easier and far more difficult than she'd imagined. She'd been away for little more than a week, but it was as if she'd lived several lifetimes. She had left the clinic under such strange circumstances, fleeing with Stride with the specimen that Harmon might have been looking for.

She'd been welcomed back with a short, early-morning gathering, presided over by the new director. James Gillespie had been brought in to replace Stef. He wasn't much older than Marti, late thirties, but seemed to belong to a different generation, one that had accepted the world as it was and wanted only to make the trains run on time. He was prematurely balding, short of stature, and uncomfortable with eye contact. If Stef carried the disposition of a captain, combat-scarred and responsible for the soldiers in the field, Gillespie was more of a civil servant. His accustomed battlefield was the head office.

As they chatted over coffee, she found that her colleagues were optimistic. The general feeling among the staff was that it might be good for the clinic to have this "inside man" who would know how to handle the relationship with Harmon, upon which the clinic's survival would depend.

As the gathering broke up, Gillespie invited Marti into

his office, the office that no longer bore any traces of Stef. She couldn't help gawking around the room, looking for something that would reassure her Stef had once existed here. Even the old-fashioned oak desk had been replaced, by a catalogue item made of laminate.

"It must seem strange," Gillespie said. Marti looked at him, feeling caught out.

"A little..." Marti said, thinking: You don't know the meaning of strange, mister.

"Well, I want you to take your time. It's been a big loss, and if you feel some doubt about whether I can fill Dr. Stefanovic's shoes, I can understand that. I'm not so sure myself. But I do believe I can honor his legacy. The main thing is to protect what he—what you all have—built here."

Marti nodded, surprised by the tack he was taking.

"I've heard great things about you from your colleagues," he said. "You have a reputation for giving your all, and then some. Well, we're all glad you're back. But I want you to know: I don't want any burnouts on my watch."

"No, sir," Marti said, smiling.

Gillespie nodded. He reached forward and riffled through a tall stack of paper on his desk. "I get the impression that Dr. Stefanovic was something of a visionary. Alas, he wasn't that attentive to the tiresome functions so necessary to the successful running of the institution. I intend to rectify that, and reassure our benefactors at Harmon that resources are being well used. So if you have any ideas about how we can improve our delivery of services, anything at all—my door is always open."

As Gillespie spoke, she studied his second body. It was a typical mixture of light and dark, the colors tending toward the dull. But she did notice a kind of disconnect, the kind she imagined you would see in politicians, between his words and the interior flow of his second body.

Marti realized that he had stopped speaking and was waiting for her to reply.

"That's great," she said, standing up, "thank you, I guess I'll get back—"

"No, no, wait," he said. "Sorry, there's one more thing, someone else that wants to speak with you. Please." He motioned her to sit down again, and then he opened the door and nodded to someone outside.

Gansrud, Harmon's Head of Regional Security, strode in.

"Dr. Powell," he said, "we're glad to have you back," but she saw no gladness in him at all, and as she shook his hand she felt something in her shrink in fear.

He gestured for her to sit down again, but he remained standing, leaning against the desk, looming over her.

"There's just the one matter, of some company property that disappeared after Dr. Stefanovic's death."

So here it was. What she had been expecting.

"A specimen," she said. "I destroyed it on instructions from Stef. He had concerns about patient privacy."

Gansrud nodded. She was betting that he could not push the matter. Laboratory specimens, legally, did not belong to the clinic or to Harmon. They were disposed of as a matter of course once tests had been performed. She still did not know what the specimen was, where it had come from, but she remembered the primal surge of terror she had felt when Stride had showed her its response to her own body fluid.

Gansrud stared at her for a long moment. She wondered if he was deliberately intimidating her, or if this was just his manner. Suddenly he smiled a cold smile and said, "Well, then, we just needed to account for it."

"Is that all?" she asked.

"We'll see," said Gansrud, and tossed something casually onto the desk in front of her: her cell phone, which Stride had thrown in the garbage.

"I've got my eye on you," he said with a wink, sighting along his finger, the thumb cocked out like the hammer of a gun. Then he held out his hand, a gesture which somehow seemed even more threatening.

Outside the office she took a long, shuddering breath.

"Is everything okay?"

Startled, Marti turned to face the questioner.

Deep set, dark eyes below a stern brow. A wry, knowing smile. He looked familiar, but she couldn't place him.

But of course—it was her colleague, Dr. Neville Hobbs. Why hadn't she recognized him? She remembered the last time she'd seen him, a weeping, drunken ruin in the supply room. He looked far more composed now.

"Everything's fine," she said, unconvincingly.

He was looking at something, and she followed his gaze.

The Onoma. She never took it off, but she was careful to keep it hidden under her clothes. Somehow, though, it had gotten out, and was dangling free.

She quickly replaced it under her shirt.

"Quite unusual," said Hobbs. He looked up to her face, and she felt a chill run through her.

"My patients are waiting," she said.

He nodded. "Of course. I'll see you later."

∞

Tomor smiled as Marti came in to the examining room. Here was a patient who had tested her faith in her job. He was fifteen, but his small, delicate frame and unchanged voice belonged to a ten-year-old. As underdeveloped as his body was, his eyes were deep and reflective: an old soul in a body that refused to age. Marti had diagnosed his growth hormone deficiency, but the injections that should have kicked his system into forward drive had not worked.

Now, months later, Marti saw he was still locked inside

a shell of childhood, and there was a darkness to his ringed eyes that went beyond lack of sleep.

The boy stood patiently, his underwear clinging to his bony hips, while she studied his body from front and rear. She stepped toward him and touched his shoulder gently, while he looked shyly at the floor.

With that touch, what it meant for Marti Powell to be a doctor changed. Or rather, the change that had happened to her now brought itself to bear on her work.

Until this moment, the prospect of a return to work had meant a return to her life as it was. At least, that was the hope, and the prospect that it might not be possible was the fear. But now things rearranged themselves in her mind, and she saw that fear and hope had gotten mixed up.

More exactly, what she saw was Tomor's second body.

It surprised her, and made her realize that her practice of medicine must now become something very different.

Tomor's second body looked like a sky in which terrible storm clouds and rays of the most dazzling sunshine were struggling to claim the same day, with the sunshine decidedly on the losing side. She studied it carefully. It made an impression of grandeur, of strength and purpose, belied by his body's refusal to mature. But what good was this perception?

Second bodies could be much more dynamic and mutable than physical bodies, and as such highly responsive. Perhaps this awareness was what caused her to ask a question without even planning to. "Tomor," she said, "is it possible that you are afraid?"

For a moment, she saw something flash below the surface of his second body, like an underwater creature glimpsed within a lake, writhing toward a hiding place.

"Of what?" he asked.

"I don't know, maybe you could tell me. Have you thought about it?"

"I guess afraid I'll stay like this forever."

Marti nodded. "I can understand that. How about the opposite?"

Tomor looked at her curiously, his dark eyes unreadable. "The opposite?"

"Yes, is there anything that frightens you about not staying like this? About growing up."

Again, she saw movement. He seemed to genuinely be searching for an answer, but whatever she was glimpsing was far below his awareness. "I don't think so."

"How does your mother feel about it?" She knew that Tomor's father was out of the picture; the boy's mother had told her that he was a political prisoner in their country of origin. Unsafe, they had fled at his urging, also leaving behind Tomor's older brother who had disappeared into the political underground.

Tomor shrugged, deflecting the question. Marti had stepped back for their conversation, but again moved closer to the boy and placed her hands gently on his shoulders. She repeated the question, intuiting that she had located the source of the problem.

There she saw it: the same movement, the same attempt to hide. "How do you feel about your mother?" she asked.

"I love her," said Tomor. "I want to take care of her."

She could see that he was speaking the truth. A golden shimmer passed through the sky of his second body.

"Of course you do," she said, maintaining her focus on the slippery thing still hiding in the depths. "And what are you afraid will happen if your body changes, if you become a man?"

"I don't know," he began, but she could see he was struggling to find the answer, and this was good; she needed him to work with her. "A man might have to leave, like Jeton?" he asked, referring to his brother.

Was that it? It was almost too easy. The thing was wriggling now, but coming closer, being drawn toward the surface by her attention and his openness.

"You would have a choice, though, wouldn't you?"

"I couldn't leave my mother. She needs me." His words were not coming easily.

Now she could almost reach in and touch it. Not too soon. Marti could feel that there was more here. More than a mother and son, subjected to the trauma of displacement from home and the rest of their family, ending up halfway around the world among a sea of similarly dispossessed human beings; more than a mother whose world had shrunk down to the size of her small son; more than a boy who was willing to sacrifice his own growth to offer her a feeling of safety.

Buried even deeper was something else.

"How do feel yourself about leaving one day? When you're older?"

He couldn't answer, but she could see the fear there. It was something she was beginning to recognize: how human beings were most afraid of the challenge posed by whatever was great in them. Life, fully lived, was fundamentally heroic.

As she moved her imaginary hands closer to the hidden source of his disease, she felt how great his fear was. He was afraid of betraying his obligation to his family and of facing the tasks that might demand such a betrayal, afraid of failure.

"Do you think you can let go of it, Tomor? The fear? I want you to look at it, to feel it now, can you feel it?"

Tomor had his eyes closed, really concentrating, and now they were working together. As Tomor opened up its hiding place, Marti reached in with her "hands," feeling the layers of his second body give way until she could grab hold of the strange minion that had been hidden down in his depths. She worried that she would have only one chance; if the minion wasn't detached, its hold could become tighter. She held on.

His breathing had deepened until he was almost hyperventilating, his diaphragm heaving as his bony chest expanded and contracted.

"Okay, Tomor, are you willing to grow? To be a man? You'll be able to do so much more for your mother, for everyone. Is that what you want?"

Tomor nodded. "Say it, then," Marti encouraged him.

"I can't," he said, crying.

The thing was thrashing, trying to get away. Marti tightened her grip just as it began to plunge.

The floor seemed to give way beneath her, and she was pulled down into a watery depth below. The minion was mottled, dark brown, gray, with lines of silver. She could feel its clammy, moist surface, her whole body pressed against it now, determined to hold on. They were plunging into a bodily gorge, and she felt fear rising. What if it threw her off down here, what if she couldn't return to her own body? The fear was a scent invading her from the minion, but it was real. Had this creature been created by Tomor's fear, or was it the other way around?

Marti had lost all awareness of the examining room, of the outer physical dimension. The minion was in its own element, dragging her deeper, and it was not losing power, but gaining in fury. She was in over her head.

The minion circled down until it reached a rounded cavern. It rubbed itself against the membranous walls in an effort to dislodge Marti. She might have held on, but she felt an impulse to let go, that the creature would show her something. She was afraid that once she let go she would be pulled out of the vision, but she wasn't sure anyway that she had a choice; the thing was determined to dislodge her.

Marti let go. She found she was able to hover close by. The minion had curled compactly into the cavern. This was the place where it felt safe. A nest. Here it came to rest, curled around something protectively, like a dragon with its treasure.

The images Marti was seeing were coming through her own second body rather than her eyes, a sensory blur. But she tried to see what the minion was cradling. If this was its home, perhaps there was a key here to unlocking Tomor's prison.

Marti inched closer. She saw that the minion was curled around a thick protuberance rising from the smooth surface of the cavern. It was coated in a dingy sheen, as if it had taken on some of the coloring of the minion that guarded it. But as Marti stared at it she discerned its real color, a radiant gold.

Moving slowly, she was able to reach down and touch it without disturbing the minion.

For a long moment, nothing happened.

"What are you?" Marti asked silently.

She felt a dim, slumbering movement within it, a movement of images. The thing was like a womb of images. They pulsed deep within it, unborn. They were crisp, exact, like patterns waiting to be fulfilled. She could not see them clearly, only feel. What she felt in them was Tomor himself. As a purpose, a potential. A dream of the future.

She wanted to see more clearly and leaned in closer. But in doing so she brushed the minion. It stiffened with alarm and lashed at her, smashing her away. Reflexively she grabbed at it and held on as it shot out of the cavern.

Marti felt a thrum of remorse as she was dragged away from the golden tabernacle. But she knew she had to deal with the minion. She held tight, but its strength was undimmed.

She looked down and gaped with horror as it oozed into her palms. It was seeping into her, an invasion of burning cold, clammy, numbness. Having breached the membrane of her skin, it began invading her everywhere, and she shivered with revulsion as she felt herself penetrated.

There wasn't much time. The thing was going to swallow her up.

"Please," Marti whispered inwardly. "I need help. I can't do it myself." She said the words without thinking them first. It seemed a revelation: had she ever admitted that she couldn't do it all herself? Certainly she had often failed, and judged herself harshly. But she never exempted herself from the expectation.

The lights appeared, rippling as if on the surface of water far above her. The minion shrank away, pulling her with it. For a moment she thought they would simply watch her drown, be absorbed by this creature. What would happen then? Her body was still out there in the physical world, but the minion would be inside her.

She renewed her intention and directed her attention toward the lights. They were still far away, making no movement to help. "Come get me," she wanted to cry. The impulse only made them more distant.

What had they taught her in the previous encounter? To open. But everything in her, entangled with the minion, wanted to shut down! With great effort, she directed her attention toward them. "Hosts," she thought, "that's what you are."

They responded instantly. It wasn't that this brought them closer. The relationship was not, after all, defined by space. They brightened and, as she surrendered the clench she was holding within her and opened, she felt the ecstasy of their spiraling movement, felt a wave of consecrating warmth flowing, felt it flowing into her.

She knew this warmth. She had known it as love. Her heart trembled. The minion's tentacles shrank back, and she squeezed it tighter. But its ferocity did not diminish.

"Tomor," she whispered, hoping that her words would be audible. "Tomor, I need your help."

"How?" he asked.

"Are you ready to grow? No matter what? I need you to decide."

Tomor was still breathing hard, perched on the edge of the abyss she had opened. Marti channeled the loving radiance of the hosts. The light swept through him like a current, and she felt him respond with a firm resolve.

"I want to grow. I want to grow." His soft, heavily accented voice rising on a current of hidden strength.

His body began to shake in spasms, strangled sobs erupting from his throat. The impression was not one of pain, but of release.

"I want to grow!" he shouted, the constriction that had been there even in his speech tearing away.

Marti felt everything in him soften, she felt the oppressive minion begin to shrink as she squeezed it with her hands and maintained a commanding focus of intent: to free the boy. Like a beach toy that had lost its air seal, the dark thing lost its form, folding inward until it became smaller and smaller. Finally, she felt forces within his second body close in on it and dissolve the foreign body completely.

Marti gave Tomor's shoulder a reassuring squeeze. He opened his eyes, wiping away tears, as the intensity of emotion subsided.

Marti gave him a moment of privacy to collect himself while she instinctively washed her hands with cold water. She also needed the moment to regain her bearings and process what she had experienced.

She thought about her experiences in the birthing room,

during her rotation as a resident. Whatever had just happened with Tomor, she had midwifed; the healing, if that's what it was, had been accomplished only with his effort and consent. She doubted that every affliction was to this extent within the patient's power, that a cure could always be achieved.

She turned to him and asked how he felt.

"Different," he said.

She advised him to take it easy for a few days, and to pay attention to how he was feeling.

She had his mother come in and had Tomor translate for her as she gave them a simple daily physical exercise his mother needed to help him with. The specific content of the exercise was of little consequence; what mattered was the intent, which she defined clearly to them. It would engage them both, in a practical way, with the future, and fill the space that had previously been occupied by fear.

Marti checked her watch, and for a moment she thought it must have stopped. The appointment had only lasted fifteen minutes. She followed them out to the waiting room and asked Rhea to schedule what she expected would be a final follow-up appointment in six months. Then she grabbed the file for the day's next patient.

19

The next weeks went by with an intensity and purity of purpose Marti had seldom felt. While she'd always been deeply committed to her work as a doctor, she'd also been equally assailed by her doubts about herself and the whole institution of medicine. Now, such questions were irrelevant.

For many patients, things were the same. Their illnesses or injuries required straightforward treatment, with typically mixed results.

Yet other cases were remarkable. "Miracle" seemed too fanciful a word. And yet perhaps, miracles were really very practical things, achieved through hard work, by both doctor and patient. Perhaps the miraculous was the natural order of things.

Often enough, her patients resisted. There was Mrs. Lee, who kept returning with the same kind of self-created minion that was causing her arthritic condition. By then Marti was realizing it wasn't always enough to simply remove troublesome minions, it was sometimes necessary to convince her patients to shift the behavior or beliefs that might be attracting or sustaining the minions—in Mrs. Lee's case, a raging bitterness about the circumstances life had dealt her.

On other occasions, Marti only understood the source of the problem when she saw all the members of the family.

Some troubled people generated minions that afflicted only others; she noticed how a particular family member could become saddled with the work of bearing the others' minions.

Just as often, the source of the illness wasn't so clear. Mr. Narayan was cured of his longtime insulin resistance when Marti gave him placebo pills to cultivate his expectation of success, and then, over the course of several visits, helped him shake loose the minion that was causing it. But she never figured out where it had come from.

She was astonished by the strange, unnoticed conditions of interconnection between people. She saw several patients, all living in the same building, whose second bodies each carried a similar minion of exceptional beauty and peace. These were otherwise ordinary people, and Marti saw that the minions were operating within them as sources of hope and growth. Later, passing by their building, Marti saw a hunched, elderly grandmother, dragging home her shopping buggy. She held the door for the slow-moving woman, and watched in astonishment as several of those familiar minions emerged from her second body and drifted gently. One entered Marti and brought with it a delicious sensation of expectancy, of impending goodness. She wondered how many quiet saints the world was filled with.

Perhaps the most breathtaking experiences were the pregnant women. In them she saw a kind of germinal form, a tightly wound spiral of light, slowly turning, like a galaxy. It wasn't part of the woman's second body the way minions were; Marti's saw it as a completely separate being, working on this woman's second body as if from a different dimension. She wondered if the physical pregnancy was something similar: not only the nourishment of a developing, embryonic being by a mature, adult body, but a more subtle, reciprocal maturation being initiated within the adult by the gestating entity, perhaps merely another form of angel, educating and preparing the mother.

Many complaints that brought people to see a doctor involved conditions that were ambiguous, or highly resistant to treatment. But the expectations of the doctor-patient transaction considered non-action as failure. You either treated—often, with prescribed pharmaceuticals—or you referred. Since Marti had been changed, she had stopped treating symptoms and started treating the unique constellations of heredity, chance, choice, and subjective being that were her patients.

But she had learned that the currents of cause and effect were far too subtle and complex for her to fully unravel. She could trace back from Mrs. Lee's joint pain to bilious yellow minions and then to a heart too full of bitterness to notice anything good in life. But what she couldn't do, at least not yet, was extract universal diagnostic principles. Each situation was, to some degree, unique.

And for every treatment she had given someone, she had given someone else its opposite. While Mrs. Lee needed to see life's gifts, to discover a capacity for gratitude, another patient needed to get in touch with anger; one to divorce, another to reconcile; one to take some pills and one simply to bear the disease but in a more meaningful way. It was as if you had to make the good out of the bad because there weren't any other raw materials available.

In college, Marti had filled one of her electives with a music appreciation course. The students had each been assigned a major classical composition. They were required to listen to a recording of it, repeatedly, with and without the score.

Marti had been given the adagio movement of Gustav Mahler's tenth symphony, the rest of which was still uncompleted upon the composer's death. When she first played it, she found it an overwhelming and somewhat disturbing cacophony, with occasional bursts of astonishing beauty. But as it became familiar through successive listenings, she found she was able to move inside the piece. And as she moved inside the piece, the piece moved inside her. She began to feel it. The feelings held a mixture of terror and beauty she couldn't name. Soon enough it was inexplicable that she had ever found it alien.

The process offered a tantalizing glimpse of something essential about life: attention was always repaid. Of course, Marti thought as she studied the musical score, a welter of black marks splayed across the white page, a work of art was designed by human beings specifically to repay attention. Could the same thing be expected of life?

Where the new world that had opened to Marti was concerned, it seemed that it could.

She kept a notebook in which she sketched the anatomy of this body she was discovering. While many specifics of the second bodies she treated were highly individual, she was accumulating an understanding of some universal anatomical principles.

The most expansive and immediately visible layer of people's second bodies was the diffuse, colorful and cloudy aura. Woven into and around it were the minions that normally began to emerge and attach during pubescence, gradually gaining in number, density and complexity as people aged.

Just as the physical body possessed a skeleton, the second body's third and innermost layer was a glowing pale white structure, smooth and curving. It formed the cavern where the minion had made its nest in Tomor's second body. She didn't always go so deep, but she had found that all second bodies had, buried deep in their folds, the mysterious protuberance she had discovered in Tomor. The size, the sense of fullness and power, varied. Sometimes, especially in older patients, it seemed like a forgotten piece of junk in the basement, buried in clutter. But it was never entirely inactive.

The word that had asserted itself originally was tabernacle, for she did sense it was the dwelling place of something mysterious and even holy. But when she first drew it in her notebooks she named it, without thinking, the Milgram Knot.

She called it a knot because she sensed that it secured the second body to something. Perhaps it was the point at which the second body was joined to the physical body.

Milgram had been the name of her kindergarten teacher, Miss Milgram. Sylvia, that was her first name. Marti hadn't thought about her in years, and at first she wasn't sure why the woman's name had asserted itself when she was drawing the knot in her anatomical notebook. Later she remembered that Miss Milgram had been the first one she'd heard talk about angels.

∞

If there was one person she wanted to tell about the strange, almost incomprehensible things that had happened to her, and the way they had changed her medical practice, it was Dave. She still felt grateful that he had come to find her in her apartment and bring her back to the clinic. But back at work together they had quickly found themselves in their old groove of professional cordiality and nothing more.

So she had not told him, or anyone, about her new approach. She figured that she would accomplish more if she didn't have to deal with the misunderstandings, fears, and outright obstructions that would arise once other people knew what she was doing. If any of her colleagues had noticed anything different, they gave no indication. The one exception was the increasingly mysterious Dr. Hobbs.

"Exhausting, isn't it?" he said. She hadn't heard him come up behind her in the lunch room.

"What?" she asked.

"Oh, all this helping people," he said. "There's no end to it, really."

Marti looked at him sharply, trying to discern the subtext. But he had become unreadable.

"It's what they pay us the big bucks for," she said.

"Right, yes. You're definitely getting maximum earning value out of that medical degree."

"Careful," she said. "Sarcasm is bad for your health."

"Mea culpa," he said. "I'm just concerned. I've seen people in your position overextend themselves. With tragic results."

"I don't know what you're talking about," she said.

"Don't worry," he said. "Your secret is safe with me." Then he was gone, leaving her to wonder if he had meant more by her "position" than her role as a doctor, as his reference to her "secret" suggested.

Many of Marti's patients knew there were strange, new things about her practice. But she explained nothing to them, only advised them that the effectiveness of her treatments relied upon their discretion about what she did. They did talk, of course, at least to exclaim to friends and family about the remarkable results—when there was a remarkable result, which certainly wasn't always the case—and they encouraged loved ones to seek her out.

∞

It was when her shift ended that the really hard work began. The events of the day, the encounters with patients, their illnesses, their powers and burdens visible in their second bodies, all came back to her.

Surrounded by people on the crowded streets, she felt overwhelmed by the intense perceptions of so much that had previously been invisible. She bought a pair of polarized sunglasses hoping they might reduce the effects, and was delighted to discover that through the glasses the world looked almost as it had before. Somehow the polarizing effect the glasses had on light obscured the otherwise vivid second bodies and their minions.

She'd had to abandon her cell phone. The use of it produced instant and agonizing headaches. She could no longer sleep under synthetic blankets—it had taken her weeks of bad sleep to figure that out. When she replaced her fleece covering with a woolen blanket that had belonged to her grandmother, the problem disappeared. She felt like the princess and the pea.

She wore the dark glasses whenever, outside the clinic, she wasn't alone. Let others think it some sort of affectation. Her steadily deepening perception of the nonphysical realm made it difficult to remain focused on the common realm of socially recognized reality. She felt alone enough already, and wary that if she wasn't careful, she'd cross a line and people would look at her the way she had seen them look at the mentally ill.

She was well aware that what she was experiencing could be diagnosed as a psychosis. In spite of that, she had accepted it for two reasons: One, it was a psychosis that actually worked. People were being healed. Two, she doubted she had a choice.

There lay the point of deepest disturbance. In bed at night she found herself following a trail in her mind, trying to understand what had brought her here. The encounter with Stride could easily be seen as an incomprehensible eruption of the paranormal that had turned her life upside down. But at a deeper level, her life seemed to her to have an integrity that belied such a meaningless scenario. This is apocalypse, she thought: not a bomb that devastates your life, but a revelation that brings you closer to reality. When you looked deeply enough, you began to see that control was an illusion, and so was randomness. Chance was merely the beauty of infinity, a pattern so vast in its coherence that it lay far beyond human comprehension, a paradox in which all free will boiled down to a choice between participation or refusal. No one got to set the terms of participation, and she was no exception.

Back home she stripped off her clothes, grateful to be alone. But then the solitude gave way to a prickly feeling that seemed to force its way out from her gut. No, from the space between her legs, burning just below her skin, needing a touch to free it. Needing Stride's touch.

She had taken a bath and now lay in bed, naked under the sheets, a candle burning. Her eyes were closed and she allowed her fingers to brush the skin of her arm, trying to imagine that it was his touch. But her body could not be fooled.

Experimentally, she moved her hand down and brushed it at the gate to her sex. There she felt more of a response, the uncoiling of a snake. The prickles under her skin intensified. She softened and opened to herself almost instantly.

Her fingers reached the place of greatest sensation and continued their movement. Gradually a wave arrived and she felt an aching spasm rush through her body, like lightning roaring down to earth. It was as if her body had learned, under Stride's touch, to go to a new place, and, while there was still an enormous difference of degree and intensity, she was finding her way back.

The first bolt of lightning cleared away the stagnant air, as if reversing ions in an explosion of pleasure. This became the threshold for a climb higher, toward the source of the lightning. The subtlest movements of her hand were taking her there, and then the rain broke. What she felt wasn't another orgasm; rather than being struck by lightning, she was becoming lightning, her body electrified in a continuous pulsing.

It was a vast inner movement swirling around her on some mountaintop, and she became as still as possible, lest she be completely swept away. The stillness brought her to the highest peak, and here she found that she was not alone.

She felt she was supposed to hold on to this awareness, but she could not. The great wave had reached its extremity. It crashed through her, wracking her body with a shuddering climax that took her by surprise.

Then the wave departed, leaving her collapsed, lying on a desolate beach. The electricity that had been burning beneath her skin was now fully discharged, every part of her was spent. But the discharge of pent-up energy had only revealed a deeper need. She knew of course what the need was, and if it no longer made her skin itch, it still made her heart ache, more than ever. Somewhere a woman was crying, an unreserved lament. It seemed to Marti like the voice of the abandoned earth itself, abandoned not by God but by its partner, the Human. Then she felt the wetness on her face. The grief was all hers, she thought, all hers.

But whatever loneliness she felt, at 7:00 every morning Marti sat quietly and imagined herself with Ursula among the roses and other plants. The first few attempts felt awkward and uncertain. Gradually, though, the sense of shared presence became more palpable, and her loneliness began to diminish.

∞

"Ah, Dr. Powell, we're glad you could make it," said Gansrud, who was sitting at one end of the table in the clinic's conference room.

The clinic's whole medical staff was in attendance. Marti had been the last to arrive, having as usual been involved with her patients beyond the appointed hours.

She felt a perverse gratitude for what she expected to be a boring meeting—no doubt another effort by Harmon to impose tighter controls on the clinic operation—because it would allow her thoughts to drift. She was curious only to better understand why the unsettling Gansrud was involved.

Gansrud was flanked by three unfamiliar faces. They introduced themselves as being from Harmon's medical research arm; early thirties, conservative dress.

As one of the team droned on about a drug approval study, Marti found her attention drifting to Hobbs. He was looking down at the paperwork in front of him, apparently as bored as she was. She willed herself to look away, certain he would look up at her any minute and catch her staring, and for some reason the thought terrified her. But she could not. She was trapped in his immobility. Yet she had the strange feeling at the same time that he was watching her. Smiling. Playing with her.

Marti felt her armpits becoming sticky. She was sweating with the effort of disentangling herself. She was able to move only one of her hands, but she took hold of the soft flesh between thumb and index finger of her other hand and squeezed, digging her nails in as harshly as she could. The sensation was dull.

A pitcher of water sat on the table and she poured herself a glass, her hands trembling, careful not to look back at Hobbs, though she felt a terrible urge pulling her.

She forced herself instead to pay attention to what was being said. The presentation was finished—how long had she been out of it?—and now they were answering questions.

Dave spoke. "But what if people don't want to participate?"

"Obviously," said one of the visitors, a woman with the kind of careful hairstyle that was a rarity in the park, "no one can be compelled to participate against their wishes. They have to sign the consent forms, of course. But we hope you and your staff will take the trouble to explain the benefits of participation."

"You mean, that they're being paid."

"That, and there's reason to believe they will experience benefits from the product, based on the stage one results."

"But you haven't shared those results with us," Dave said.

Another of the visitors chimed in. "At this point, you're going to have to trust us on that. We have all the necessary approvals in place—in spite of the unprecedented timeline. The potential benefits to health consumers are enormous."

"And to Harmon's bottom line, no doubt," Dave muttered.

"What's your point, Dr. Earle?" That was Evan Pollack, the fourth of the clinic staff doctors. "I think running the trial here in the Park is an opportunity for everyone."

"The point is," Dave said, "we don't really have a choice, do we? They've told us almost nothing. We don't know what this stuff is. I just thought we were more than a dispensary for Harmon's product trials. What would Stef have said?"

As he invoked Stef, Dave looked at Marti, clearly hoping she would back him. But she was too busy playing catch-up, and too uneasy after the experience with Hobbs, to intervene.

"Thank you for your input," Gansrud said. "Over to you, Dr. Gillespie."

"The trial will start next week," Gillespie said. "We just wanted to make sure you were all up to speed. I'm sure you all join me in thanking Mr. Gansrud and his colleagues for taking the time to explain things."

Before Marti could flee, Gillespie told her he wanted to see her in his office.

∞

"Do you mind if I share some statistics with you?"

Surprised, Marti nodded for him to continue. With evident pleasure at the grasp the calculations gave him over the messy human goings-on in the clinic, he recited an accounting of numbers of patients visiting the clinic, numbers of those who specifically asked to see a particular doctor, and how those numbers had changed over the past three months.

The startling change lay in the increase of patients appearing at the clinic specifically to see Marti. This reflected an overall increase in clinic visits.

"You've become our star attraction," he said, "and I'm wondering if you can explain why you think that is."

Marti shrugged. "I just know I squeeze in as many patients as I can. I'm sure we all do. Maybe we should ask Harmon to give us the fifth doctor we were supposed to get." She winced inwardly at the obviousness of her attempt to avoid answering his question.

"You're not hearing what I'm saying. Something is different."

"What do you want me to say, Jim? If my patients are having good experiences and telling others, why is that a concern? If you want to compare me to the others here, go ahead, but don't ask me to do it."

"I also noticed that there's also been an increase, albeit much smaller, in the number of patients on return visits who specifically ask not to see you. How do you account for that?"

Marti held her hands up in a gesture of helplessness. Gillespie stared at her for a long moment, a look of curiosity more than concern.

"Well. That's all, then. I just wanted to thank you for your devotion to our patients."

But it felt that a big part of him was behind a hunting blind.

20

It was a few days later when her niece Carly came to meet Marti at the clinic. Marti had forgotten about their plan, but as always she was happy to see the girl.

Carly herself looked less than happy. Something was going on with her, and it was a sense that the girl needed new experiences that had prompted Marti to suggest she might want to volunteer at the clinic. Jane had pooh-poohed the idea, remarking that Carly had to focus on her homework. Of course, Jane's discouraging comment had prompted Carly to accept the invitation immediately.

"How are you?" Marti asked, glancing at Carly as they walked through the clinic. "Fine." Carly shrugged. Marti stopped and looked at her. She did not look fine. Marti pulled her into an empty examining room.

"Is everything okay?" Marti asked.

"You mean, like normal?" Carly said. "Or do you mean good?"

Marti took her hand. Carly's second body looked volatile, like a new continent forming out of geothermal chaos, fairly typical of a teenager.

"Have you seen Neil lately?" asked Marti. She knew he wasn't Carly's boyfriend any more, but it occurred to her that the change in the once cheerful girl's moods had happened with their breakup.

Carly shook her head and then turned away for a long moment. When Carly looked back, Marti, noticed a few tears.

"I'm sorry," she said, wiping her eyes.

"Oh, honey," said Marti, and wrapped her arms around her. The girl seemed to tremble in the embrace.

A loud knock on the door broke the moment. Carly separated herself from Marti.

"It's okay," said Carly. "You need to get back to work."

"I suppose," said Marti, feeling an impulse to grab the girl, take off, go somewhere together, and just lie in the sun. "We'll talk about it later, okay?"

Carly nodded.

Marti passed Carly over to Rhea, who had prepared some tasks for her to help with in the office. By the time Marti sat down with her first patient, she had stopped thinking about Carly completely.

It was discouraging to learn at the end of the day that Carly had left without saying anything to her. In fact, no one seemed to know exactly when the girl had gone home.

Heading to the locker room to change out of her uniform, Marti was already feeling, as she often did, an anticipation of sleep. She would go home to her bungalow, have a light meal, and prepare to dream. She didn't even notice Dave in the room until he spoke to her.

"How did it go with Gillespie yesterday?"

Marti rolled her eyes. "The anti-Stef. Seems like it all boils down to numbers."

Dave nodded. He was already in his civvies.

"Did he say, 'I'm just here to help'?"

"I've heard that once or twice, yes. I almost believe it."

"I think he believes it," said Dave. "The question I'm asking is, 'Help whom?' Us and our patients? Or 'Harmin'?"

"You think we're at odds?" Marti asked, disingenuously.

Dave looked at her to see if she was being facetious, but her attention was on her clothes.

"Ultimately?" said Dave, "Of course. But maybe he hasn't had to decide yet."

Marti nodded and pulled on her boots. Speculating about what people might do was of little interest to her.

Dave stood in front of her. "I really feel like a good meal. I've got a tip on a great new restaurant, and I'd hate to have to go there alone. Do you have any plans right now?"

Taken aback, Marti looked up at him. "What about Holly?" she asked, referring to Dave's live-in girlfriend, whom she had met once.

Dave smiled ruefully. "We broke up a few months ago."

Marti felt embarrassed at how little she knew about Dave's life outside the clinic, how little she knew about any of her colleagues.

As her mind was organizing the best way to refuse his invitation so that it wouldn't sound too much like a rejection, her mouth just went ahead and accepted it. "That sounds great..."

Dave gave a puppyish nod, as surprised by her answer as she was. For a moment she wondered how long he'd been waiting to ask her.

"We can go in my car," he said.

∞

He was still feeling awkward in the new body. He needed to shake off his feeling of disgust to really make good use of the vehicle.

But it was such a small thing, puny, mortal. He had spent most of his existence in far vaster forms. And there was a risk involved. If anything happened to the body he could be badly compromised.

He reminded himself that it had been his choice. It was necessary to get close to the Coil.

The girl was just leaving the clinic when he struck up the conversation.

∞

"What happened with you and Holly?" Marti asked.

The glib answer Dave had used with his family and friends was already on his tongue when he looked up from his menu and saw Marti's face, saw that she wanted something more real than that. He took a breath.

"It wasn't really that anything happened, at least not outwardly. We'd only been living together nine months, going together for a few months before that. You know, you go into a relationship, and it's like there are all these things you ignore because if you paid attention to them, you wouldn't get together, and you want to get together. But then there's a moment when you have to admit what the relationship is, rather than what you want it to be."

"What weren't you paying attention to?"

"Well, I guess, that it was pretty much a recreational thing for me, and she believed it would become more than that."

Marti nodded and Dave wondered if he was being too frank.

Marti was enjoying seeing the consonance between Dave's words and the movements of his second body. Suddenly she realized the movement was a reaching toward her. And though she could not see her own second body, she felt a stirring within herself, a deeply pleasant one.

The waiter came for their order and they paused to give their menus the necessary attention, their conversation resuming once they were alone again.

"So you had a big fight?"

"No, that's what was different. We had the deepest moment of...intimacy...we ever experienced together. Holly and I never made love during the day, but suddenly there was just this incredible passion. It just blew away the pretense. And then, at the end of it, it was just, like, we both realized it had been a goodbye."

The waiter arrived to pour some wine, and they had a few sips, feeling the weight of the silence.

Marti saw how Dave's flushing was a physical outcome of his second body activity. Love, she had come to feel, was the medium of the second body, as what plasma is to blood, or calcium to bones. Or maybe love was the medium of everything. She felt heat rising inside her and realized again that some part of them was flowing together.

Dave took a much larger sip of wine. "You see, this all happened the day I came to your apartment. Something changed."

Marti was disconcerted. She seldom thought about the effect she might have on others, outside of her patients. She remembered the strange intimacy of Dave's unexpected visit.

"We were worried about you. You had phoned in sick at first, but the days kept passing. We couldn't reach you on the phone. When I knocked at your door, and there was no answer, I found myself wondering if I would ever see you again. Then, when I did..."

Dave looked away, embarrassed.

"You don't have to talk about it," Marti said.

"Would you rather I didn't?" he asked.

"No, actually," she said. "It means a lot to me."

"Well, there's not much more to it," he said.

Marti smiled at the paradox, knowing there was so much more, but also how hard it all was to put into words. Dave was surprised by her smile. He looked away awkwardly. When he looked at her again they both laughed, dispelling the tension.

After that, Dave talked about his three kids. She enjoyed seeing his face light up. His close-cropped blond beard softened his strong jaw line. He has the rugged kind of handsomeness, she thought, that improves with age. Marti was grateful to let him do most of the talking.

The wine they were drinking was good. The food was a kind of adventure. Dave had explained that the chef worked closely with a number of farmers, sourcing the meat and produce directly, and shaping his menu according to what was available from them in season. As she hadn't for a while, Marti felt her body absorbing much more than physical fuel from the food. The delicious tastes were, of course, part of it. But there was more.

Without planning to, they had each ordered the same dish. She could see how the food and wine were releasing more fully the currents now moving between them. Somewhere in her a voice squawked that she should be at home, in bed. That this was self-indulgent. For a moment, she felt herself contract inward as she weighed the possibility that this was not a good thing, this fraternizing with a colleague, tinged with intimacy, and the promise of intimacy.

What about Stride? Some part of her felt married, felt like the wife of a seagoing man, left behind on shore, a test of faith.

In the glow that followed the food, the wine and the smiles, as they sipped coffee, Dave told Marti about a dream he'd had when he was ten years old. In the dream, he'd been part of a group of kids journeying on foot over the countryside to an unknown destination. Among those on the journey was a younger girl. One night in the middle of the journey, he had found himself wide awake. He watched the beautiful girl sleep, feeling a reverence toward her he hadn't noticed before, and he realized that, without anyone knowing it, she was their guide, the only one who knew the purpose of their journey, its destination and the route they must follow. As he gazed at her sleeping countenance, lit by the moon, he made what felt like the first adult vow of his young life: to protect her, without revealing that he knew the secret.

"It's funny," said Dave, putting down his coffee. "When

I think about that dream now, the girl has your face. But I don't know if she really did, or if I've replaced her face with yours." He looked down for a moment. "I guess it doesn't really matter."

∞

When they were back in Dave's car, Marti could feel the question hanging in the air.

Part of her wanted to go home with Dave. The evening together, the mingling of their second bodies, had felt so good. Her body had been aching to be touched again.

But lovemaking with Stride was an initiation that had changed everything for her. If she made love with Dave, what would that do?

She wasn't ready to find out.

"Dave, this has been a fantastic evening. I didn't realize how badly I needed it."

He gave her a sober look. "It doesn't need to be over yet," he said gently.

"I know. And part of me, believe me, wants it to go on forever. Or at least until morning."

"But...?"

She struggled for words he would understand. "I'm not ready. It's as simple as that. But I'd like to get together outside work again soon," she said.

"That would be great."

"I'd love to meet all your kids."

Dave blinked with surprise and nodded. He gave Marti a hug and they parted.

∞

After saying good night to Dave, Marti found herself thinking about Carly. She tried calling the girl and got no answer. She sent a text message. She felt an impulse to go to her niece's house, make sure she was okay. But this she quickly dismissed as silly. Instead, she phoned Jane, who reassured her that yes, Carly was at home, safe and sound in her bedroom. When Marti hung up, she found that her unease had not dispelled.

21

Dave stayed in the shower for a long time. Hot water tingled against his skin. He thought about baby chicks that drowned in the rain, their mouths wide open; about people standing on dry land who are taken by a freak wave. About what it would feel like to be washed away, carried out of this world in a roaring current. He had always been a man standing firmly against the storm that surrounded him. He had chosen his work because, inside himself, he felt the keenest equilibrium in the roughest surroundings. But now everything was different.

He had finally done it, and yet, instead of feeling satisfied, he was uncertain.

Since Holly had moved out he had been aching to find a way to connect with Marti beyond the superficial and limited associations that took place at the clinic. Yet he had felt like a tongue-tied adolescent. He'd made a few efforts, but they were clumsy, easily deflected by her, leaving him feeling wounded and helpless.

Tonight, the door finally opened. He wasn't sure exactly what he'd been expecting on the other side, but he'd experienced a simple depth of connection that had left him feeling shaken. A sense of disturbance had always been a distant note in their relationship, becoming forcefully pronounced when he had visited her apartment, resonating like a tower bell through his carefully compartmentalized life, sending Holly away, leaving him lying awake at night, tying his tongue in knots in Marti's presence. It infected his whole life, leaving him distracted, restless.

All of this could perhaps be attributed to the state of mind of a lovesick individual, he thought, with a rueful smile, but it didn't stop there. Shortly after Holly left, he was blindsided by a letter from Becca, an old girlfriend, full of cold anger, accusing him of selfishness that had done permanent damage to her. He wondered how many other people he had hurt without even realizing it. Then, his cat, Schweitzer, a stray who had shown up on the day of his divorce six years earlier, adopting him with that feline noblesse oblige, and who had seldom left the house or yard since, had been hit by a car and killed. As he buried her in the yard he cried silent tears, overcome by a grief whose intensity amazed him. The cat was a companion, even a friend, but he had never expected her to stay as long as she had, and she probably didn't have that many years left in any case. Why would her death leave him feeling torn open and bleeding like this?

The apparently random series of events felt emotionally knit together, as though some reckoning had been set in motion when he had gotten the building super to let him into Marti's apartment.

He had begun to imagine that if he could overcome the space between them, become in some way intimate with her, this disturbance would be quelled, and he would not only regain his equilibrium but find a harmony he had never experienced.

He had moved toward her tonight, and she had moved toward him, and what he felt was not some sort of launch into romance as he had expected, but an intensified disturbance, as though he had simply moved much closer to its source.

Was this what love was, then? A disturbance?

As he dried himself off, Dave asked himself what he would give up for love. He had never thought of love as something that demanded sacrifice.

He'd be picking his kids up tomorrow for the weekend. He felt a sudden intake of gratitude.

∞

Carly wondered if she should phone Marti. She knew she couldn't talk to her parents about it. For some time she had been sick of living out their "good girl" idea of her.

At first she'd tried being as bad as she could instead. Alcohol and boys, it was so easy. That provided a thrill, but soon she realized that it too was a trap, and a punishing one. She still felt more shame and disgust than she wanted to admit over what had happened. She chose the first boy because he was so wrong for her in her parents' eyes. Darren was a high-school dropout with a shitty job and a fast car. On their first date they hadn't even gotten to the mall before the back seat was wet with sex. It was her first time—she and Neil, her one serious boyfriend, had done pretty much everything else with their bodies they knew of, but had never really fully shaken the sibling-like feeling of their relationship. She'd wondered if he was gay.

Disposing of her virginity was going to be one more way to separate from the childhood that bound her to her parents, but continuing onto the mall with Darren for a post-coital meal in the food court, she felt like nothing had changed for her; he, meanwhile, was incredibly pleased with himself. She'd stuck it out through two more dates, which included two more ritual fucks, through which she felt increasingly alienated.

She moved on to another boy, this one a grade ahead of her and on the football team, but with similar results. She didn't feel like an experienced woman, but rather a sullied virgin, a receptacle for helplessly thrusting attempts to reach the country of manhood.

Finally there was Greg, also on the football team. On their second date, they were already halfway through a fifth of tequila and well advanced in a two-person game of strip-Gears of War, when his friend Evan, or was it Ewan, had suddenly shown up inside the house without even ringing the bell. She'd gone along with what they wanted. They'd tried to make it seem spontaneous but their scheming had been obvious, the mere execution of a porn fantasy. Are there any boys, she briefly wondered when she realized their plan, for whom a girl is more than some sort of flesh doll?

There was a moment, with both of them inside her, when she'd felt the possibility of utterly losing herself, as if she were being erased.

When Greg had asked her afterward if she'd enjoyed it, she'd even said she had, because the thing she'd loathed had, in replacing the possibility of pleasure, become a twisted kind of pleasure.

She'd woken up the next day with a headache, and a desperate nausea. Over the next few days she began to feel a craving that scared her. She could feel that it could consume her, could lead to a darkness that had no exit. Greg kept calling, but she refused to answer, finally blocking him from her phone.

And now something so unexpected had happened.

She wasn't sure why she'd left the clinic that day. But suddenly she had the feeling that she could walk out and no one would notice, that she could leave the whole world and wouldn't be missed. She was in the middle of the thought when she had collided with the man.

Later, when he had touched her, she felt things change, felt a burden lifted. She removed no clothes, and his hands never went below her shoulders. It wasn't sexual, not at all, it may have been the least sexual thing she'd ever felt. It felt like what had been behind the sex, the thing she had been looking for all along.

∞

Carly didn't return to the clinic, and neither did she return Marti's messages. A few days later, Marti made a trip out to the suburbs to check on her niece. It was Carly who answered the door, and Marti had a shock. She had never seen her with short hair before; the girl's long, luxurious hair had been a lifelong signature.

Equally shocking was the girl's tone. "My parents aren't here," she said. Normally Carly was happy to see her, but she might as well have been a canvasser.

Marti could see an even bigger change in Carly's second body. The whole thing had been blanketed by a chilly, gray fog. Marti tried to penetrate it with her vision, but it seemed to deliberately resist her efforts. She felt a headache starting.

"Are you okay?" Marti blurted the question.

"Yes," said Carly, "why shouldn't I be?"

Marti went into the house and Carly followed her, looking impatient. Marti sat down on the couch in the living room, a formal space that was seldom used. Carly stood, her arms folded.

"How was the day at the clinic?" asked Marti. "I was hoping to see you afterward."

Carly looked away and shrugged.

"Rhea said you were a big help. Would you like to come back?"

Carly looked back at her. Now Marti had the distinct impression of a kind of sneer on the girl's face. But it quickly receded.

"I don't think so," she said. "It's not for me."

"Is everything okay, Carly? Are you angry about something?"

"I already told you. Everything's fine. I'm just thinking about other things now."

"School?"

It was the wrong thing to say. Carly laughed a frightening, arrogant laugh.

"I have to go," she said, "I was just on my way out when you came." She turned and headed for the door. "You can wait here for my parents if you want."

The door closed with a cold click, leaving Marti alone in the big house.

22

Marti sipped her coffee. The clinic wouldn't open its doors for more than hour. She liked being the first one here, silently broadcasting her intention into the empty space around her. The intention of a day filled with purposeful work.

Coffee brought a gift of wakefulness, but it couldn't entirely dispel the unease that was spreading through her life.

The change in Carly soon after the girl's visit to the clinic had shaken her. But what could she do about it?

When she crossed paths with Dave, she felt a weight of expectation she didn't know how to deal with. She couldn't move closer to him without letting him into her confidence. On several occasions, she tried silently rehearsing a speech that would explain it all to him. While she no longer doubted the reality of her experience, the words themselves sounded absurd. Perhaps there were some things that could only be experienced, not described. She felt Dave's hopeful glances turn to confusion and hurt as she avoided being alone with him.

In the past, her work had been the place where she escaped the messiness of life. However chaotic the clinic, however disordered and challenged the lives of her patients, it wasn't her life. To her patients, she was a force of order, of meaning, even of healing. At least some of the time.

But the meeting with Gillespie, with its implicit warning of scrutiny, left her feeling uneasy at work too, reminding her that she was now to some extent at odds with her own profession. She told herself she would have to be careful.

∞

The clinic's opening was normally greeted by a small line-up of people, and today was no exception. Typically, some of them would be parents who had become alarmed by a sick child during the night and showed up without an appointment. Naveen, the intake nurse, would make the determination of whether the attention of a doctor was needed.

Naveen was still working his way through this line when Marti picked up the folder for her first patient. Before she could call the name, her attention was drawn to some people standing at the back of the intake line. Two young parents, the mother clutching a three-year-old child, who lay in her arms like a bouquet of wilted flowers. They were standing quietly, but Marti could see a dreadful fear on their faces. The child's face—it was a girl, she saw now—was flecked with vomit. Her eyes were narrow slits, and she was breathing rapidly. As Marti approached, the parents surged toward her, their alarm overcoming the deference that had kept them waiting patiently in line. They had the small stature, coppery skin, and high cheek bones of indigenous Latin Americans.

Marti nodded at the parents and looked at the child. She didn't like what she saw. She put her hand on the child's forehead and examined her second body.

The little girl was under assault from within. Just as disturbances in the second body could affect people's physical conditions, physical illness produced symptoms Marti could read in the host's second body. She recognized the red storm of a bacterial infection in an advanced stage, saturating multiple bodily systems.

She probed the child's neck and elicited a pained yelp.

As she guided them into an examining room, she noticed a baffled glance from Naveen; the clinic had a rigorous protocol that patients had to be seen first by the intake nurse.

In the examining room, Marti gently pulled back the blanket the girl had been wrapped in. She saw a purplish rash on the girl's upper chest, and another across her thigh.

Meningococcemia, probably. The normal thing to do at this point would have been a lumbar puncture and, if it confirmed a diagnosis, a course of antibiotics. But Marti knew that, given the advanced stage of the infection, the girl could well be dead in twenty-four hours.

So with a reassuring nod to the parents, she put her hands on the girl's shoulders and set about seeing what she could do first.

Marti didn't hear the knock on the door, or notice when Naveen poked his head in to ask what was going on. By then she was deep into the child's second body.

It felt like a headfirst dive into a firestorm. Marti's eyes stung and her skin burned. The girl's defenses had clearly been overrun; the bacterium had total possession of her body. It might indeed be too late.

She tried to orient herself while she staggered through the storm.

What would happen if she was lost here, she wondered? Could you be lost and never return? Or perhaps she would herself be invaded by the same bacterium. It was a bacterium that could be found, at any given time, in ten percent of the population. Why did it flare up into this raging storm of illness in only a few?

She felt something drawing her forward, and she followed the feeling, hoping it was what was needed.

The heat was invading her. She wanted to lie down here, conserve her strength.

Marti crouched down. Just for a moment. She was sweating, feeling faint.

Three years, she thought. When a young child like this dies, it takes very little with it. Except the future. The faces of the girl's parents appeared to her.

It was enough to get her up again. She staggered forward with a final burst of determination.

And there it was. A few steps ahead in the whirling storm, a soft golden glow. It was like a beacon, only drawing her down, to the bottom of the child's second body.

The last few steps seemed to take forever. The storm pelting her, resisting, trying to drive her backward. Finally she fell to her knees, reached out, groping... and touched it.

The Milgram Knot.

She had never touched one before. Marti felt a current tear through her, an electrical jolt that crackled along the surface of her skin.

Before, Marti had thought the Knot was the place where the physical body and the second body were joined together.

But then why would a three-year-old child have one of such grandeur? The girl was tied to something here, something much larger than her own being. And its energy was pouring into her.

The Knot had a softness, a pliability she had never noticed. Before, it had seemed like a terminus. But she had not looked closely enough. It was an opening, a threshold.

Or was it she that was opening? The current of light continued pouring into her through the Knot and she felt things turning inside out.

Part of her wanted to pull back, to resist, but she sensed that if she did she would be torn apart. She had been captured in an undertow that was sucking her in. The power of it roared in her ears and the space it was dragging her into became more and more condensed. Her nervous system exploded in a fiery ball of pain. As she began to think that for sure she could not survive, she felt a sense of being pulled through to the other side and the pressure relented.

Here, she was no longer alone.

There were three of them. Their forms appeared human, but they were twice her size. They seemed to have been molded in more than three dimensions, out of something that was at once flesh and light, pulsing, expressive not merely in overall impression but in every particle. Their faces reminded her of religious icons, though not painted, or carved, but living. She somehow understood that this familiar appearance was something humans had created for them, that they wore to make a meeting possible.

"We welcome you, Coil."

"What did you call me?"

"Coil."

"I'm here for the girl," Marti told them. "Isabella," she added, remembering the name the parents had spoken.

"We know." The voice belonged to the one who was standing closest to her. "I am the girl's Guardian," he added.

"Where have you been?" she asked. She surprised herself with the challenge. She found herself angered by the aloofness of these creatures. "The girl is dying."

"I am the Guardian for many," he said. "And even so, life, sometimes, is lost. To you it is a tragedy. To us, it is simply the beginning of another chapter in the story."

"So you don't care," said Marti, spitting it out as an accusation.

"Your anger is righteous. But will you intervene for every dying child in the world?"

"I am a doctor," said Marti. "If they ask for my help, I give it."

"But there is a greater help you can give. You are more than a doctor now. You are a Coil."

"You said that. Am I supposed to know what it means?"

It was another one who answered. "Stride has made it so that you live in two worlds. The two worlds of Home."

The third continued. "Others have called them heaven and earth. But, as you are learning, they aren't entirely separate."

"What about the girl?"

"She will be saved by your intercession."

Relieved, Marti nodded. "Thank you." Then anger rose in her once more.

"But it's not enough," she said.

"What do you want, then?"

What did she want? She thought about all the suffering. Her own suffering. The words blurted themselves out: "I want heaven to care! What is the good of heaven otherwise?"

She was crying now. The catastrophes of history had, finally, rendered heaven a fantasy. Worse than that terrible loss would be the reality of a heaven that allowed such things to happen.

Her tears were another opening, and the beings had moved closer. The warmth that moved into her hurt was heaven's care. Everything softened inside her.

"What of us, Doctor?" the angel asked. "Are we worthy of your care? Of your help?"

Marti was nonplussed. "You?"

"We do not feel the ache of pain," said the angel. "But we do feel the ache of longing. As you long for the love of heaven, we long for the love of earth. The time of separation is coming to an end. We long for partnership. If we withhold our care it is only an invitation."

Partnership. A tangle of pain and joy, indeed, of longing, exploded in Marti's chest. How good it was to hear something named. The mysteries of the longing inside us were the most inscrutable. What else had she been longing for, since the first moment that Stride touched her, but partnership? Or indeed, maybe, for her whole life?

"But I don't understand," she said, "what you are asking of me?"

"The help that Stride needs. He has been badly weakened."

"Weakened? Then he's still alive? Where is he?"

"He's departed from your world, but even in ours his presence has suffered. He wagered on you and the outcome is not yet clear."

"Please, tell me what I can do."

She felt their compassion. "Do you understand what this is?" they asked, gesturing toward the Milgram Knot. She told them her name for it.

They smiled. "This is where heaven and earth are joined. In every human being. Beware those who would untie the knot."

"You mean those who deny heaven?"

"No," said the angel. "Belief matters not at all in this regard. Belief is human, and nothing purely human could ever untie heaven and earth. Though humans can play a role, unwitting or otherwise."

"And what would happen then? If the Knot is untied?"

"The work of eons is undone. Oceans of tears shed in vain. Just at the moment when we are so close to Sunrise. When the long night is almost over."

Why did every answer only produce more questions? But there was, Marti supposed, only one question that mattered:

"How can I help, then?"

Later, Marti would wonder if there would have been an answer, if things in the examining room hadn't happened the way they did.

23

Marti was still beyond the girl's second body, at the place where it was knotted to the dimension she now called heaven, when she felt them grab hold her. One moment, she was waiting for the angel to tell her what was expected of her. The next, two pairs of human arms had seized her, and her body was flailing like a trapped animal.

While she was treating the girl, there had been a knock at the door. It was Naveen, who wanted to find out what was going on. When nobody answered, he entered.

He saw the girl's parents sitting against the wall, watching, holding one another. The girl lay on the examining table. Marti sat in a chair, her hand on the girl's shoulders. There was a charged silence in the room. No, not silence. There were small noises. Grunts. Sighs.

Naveen took a step forward, waiting for Marti to look up. But she remained frozen. No, he realized, not frozen; her body was twitching, making the noises, which sounded little like anything he had heard before. The girl let out a soft moan.

Unnerved, Naveen cleared his throat. "Dr. Powell?"

But there was no reaction. He wondered if she was having some kind of seizure. He turned and left the room, returning moments later with Ludovicu, the security officer.

Naveen touched Marti's shoulder, gently at first. No response. He nodded to Ludovicu, and they each took hold of one of her arms and began to pry her away from the girl.

The result was unexpected. Like the proverbial awakened sleepwalker, Marti began to flail violently. She struck Naveen in the face with enough force to drive him back against the wall. He fled the room to get more help. Ludovicu grabbed her in a half nelson but her free arm resisted him and grabbed hold of his hair. Locked together like this, they stumbled wildly around the room, knocking over a tray of utensils that clattered noisily to the floor.

Marti's awareness had returned to her body, but she felt like a witness to its actions, as if, rather than awakening, she had fallen into a dream, or more exactly, a nightmare. The assault, the seemingly autonomous response of her own body, and the disorienting arousal from her trance, combined to force a rising spiral of panic. Yells of alarm and outrage from the girl's mother, now cradling her daughter, demanded that the men stop and leave Marti alone. The father grabbed on to Ludovicu and had almost separated him from Marti when Naveen returned with two other staff members.

Marti by now was getting her motor system under conscious control. But she was still entirely confused about what was going on. Naveen had gotten his arms wrapped tightly around her, genuinely wanting to protect her from hurt as the weight of three men brought her down to the floor, while the fourth placated the parents.

"Are you okay, Dr. Powell?" said Naveen. "Can we let go of you?"

Marti understood the question, but couldn't summon an answer. She was trying to figure out if there was some way of making this all go away, of returning to finish her conversation with the girl's Guardian. In the past, the transitions out of her trances had been graceful and quick. Now she seemed to be locked in the liminal space.

The mother pulled at the men, and feeling confused and embarrassed by what had happened, they peeled themselves off Marti.

Freed, Marti sat up.

Naveen tried to escort the patient and her parents out of the room, but the mother knelt down in front of Marti and looked deeply into her eyes. The woman's face, filled with maternal love and power, shook Marti back to reality. What Marti saw in those eyes was not only gratitude, but a kind of acknowledgment of her journey, of the risk she had taken, of a gift that somehow was even more than a little girl's life.

She showed Marti her daughter's face. The fever seemed to have broken. The purplish discolorations had receded. The mother pulled Marti into an embrace, squeezing her daughter in between them.

Abashed by the intimacy of the scene, which only added to their confusion about what had just happened, the men gave the women their space. Finally, with more nods of gratitude to Marti, the parents turned to go.

Marti's head was throbbing, and a dozen bruises were starting to ache.

Naveen was shooing away the other remaining bystanders, but Dave pushed through and knelt beside Marti.

"Are you okay?" he said. She looked at him, not sure how to answer, and then reached out and allowed him to help her up.

Later, Marti sat in the changing room, her head in her hands. Alone for the first moment since her convulsive awakening in the examining room, the words were returning. "The work of eons undone." Stride had wagered on her, and now he was not only lost to the earth, but maybe to heaven as well.

It was too much to process. The only question that mattered—what could she do?—had gone unanswered.

∞

He was feeling expectant. The girl herself meant little to him. She was a means to an end. She would help him remove the worrying obstacle of the Coil. But he knew he must not underestimate the woman.

His hands on her ears, he fully turned his attention to Carly.

It was a delicate balance. Humans were fragile organisms, like thin-shelled eggs. Rigid, and so, easily broken. Their self-definition was entirely wrapped up in the functioning of the membranes of perception that separated them from the world.

He thought about this as he reached, like a surgeon, inside Carly, and began to apply pressure. All the while he was asking her questions, but these were a simple distraction directed at the surface level of her awareness.

He fingered invisible forms, the riverbed of the current of life that ran in her. What he felt inside the tender, unborn caverns of this girl's inner life was the pattern of her own purposed growth yet to come. He sensed that this could not be altered or opposed by him—only by her own free will. That's what destiny was, that's all it was: the ground laid for a choice.

But he also offered a choice. "No" was easier to claim if it could be understood as a "Yes" to something else.

If to him the grand design was ugly and oppressive, he could still occasionally perceive the intricate beauty within its parts, such as this girl before him. He could still sometimes feel awe at the capacity of the earth to bring forth innocence. But slender threads of beauty or innocence were little compensation for the dreariness of his imprisonment. He didn't want consolation, he wanted release from this shabby domain.

How much simpler things would be if he could simply kill the Coil. But he suspected that would only, somehow, empower the Partnership further. No, he needed to turn her power against itself.

This Carly was not weak. He could see the being of her own destiny, its strength and majesty, curled inside her. Yet he knew it could not unfurl itself: she had to willingly open it, through outer trials. He would see that she never had the chance.

He turned his attention fully back to the inner folds of something the humans had been unable to name, a mystery they were terrified to explore. They wanted to mine it for pleasure, discharge the tensions it held, turn it to profit, make it serve their busy little plans. But understanding it: that, they resisted.

He had his hands where he wanted them, and he was pressing with his thumbs, gently. Too hard and he would break her completely, tear her mind open so that she could no longer function in the consensual illusion humans called reality.

Beyond here he could go only with her consent. He whispered, lulling her to surrender, to give up her destiny. Like all humans, as a child she had lived inside its growth pattern like a fish in a bag of water. Later she had begun to glimpse it in surges of consciousness that had not been possible for her as a child: moments of love for her parents or the world, moments of joy, of gratitude, of recognizing beauty.

These moments in which the soul celebrated its bodily existence persisted and remained as a residue he could feel now, coating this membrane he was touching inside her. At her age she hadn't experienced many such moments, but he could feel the powerful capacity and responsiveness of her soul.

Now he was almost ready to create the image of what he would have her do.

∞

In her dream, Carly felt a strange discomfort. Something held her tight, like a nightmare from which she could not awaken.

The boys she'd had came to mind. She'd offered her body to them to be opened, the sacrifice of a girl body for a woman identity, in desperate hope that womanhood would be a relief from the pain. It had not worked. Instead of giving her something, they had taken. If they had opened her, it was only to leave her feeling torn.

Now she felt this powerful being reaching inside her, probing. Under his fingers, feelings and thoughts lit up, as if she were a manuscript being read for the first time. What they were offering surprised her: a promise of relief.

"Lay down your burden." The words were forming in her mind, but spoken in his voice. "Come to me and lay down your burden."

"How do I do that?" she asked. She felt his fingers slip deeper inside her. She gasped, the sensations almost too intense. He proceeded gently but insistently.

"Allow me in," he said.

Wasn't she doing just that? But now she felt an ache, a kind of outward pressure that resisted him. It welled up in her like a sun trying but unable to rise.

She had the strangest thought, suddenly overwhelmed with gratitude for the sun's loyalty. Had she ever really looked at the sky? But then the ache brought her images, a few scattered moments. They were moments of love: her mother's crooked smile, an astonished look in her eyes; her brother standing up for her to some rude boys and getting thrashed for it; her father's arms.

Then there was Neil, her one real boyfriend. The one she shared secrets with and dreamed with, and ventured beyond childhood with. When she thought of him, the aching increased. Suddenly she was aware of how much their breakup—her rejection of him—had hurt him. She'd explained it away at the time as good for him in the long run. Yet when she had seen him at school, the light had gone from his eyes.

Now it felt like the hands were probing right into this sore spot, and the pain grew. Had she been carrying this all along, this guilt and regret? Why had she rejected Neil? She'd had the sense that the relationship was holding her back, but from what?

The pain kept increasing. "Don't resist," he said. She knew that he would take the pain away. But she felt she must resist. This guilt and regret was a weed in the same garden with the love. If she let him take any of it, he would take it all. She didn't know how she knew this, but she did.

She felt pinioned, like a butterfly with a needle going slowly through its body. Pain and pleasure, love and regret, were mingling in an incomprehensible weave. But life is not a trap, she thought! Life is beauty, life is a miracle, life is a necessary adventure. These words formed in her from somewhere beyond, and she felt a strength rally to them, against the strange comfort he was offering. She stiffened against him.

He said, "No. You came to me to escape the trap."

At the word "escape" she felt a thrill rise up in her. Yes. School was a trap. Her family was a trap. Boys were a trap. The future was a trap. Indeed, escape was what she had been seeking all along.

She gasped as his fingers, and now hands, slid deeper, the folds of her soul stretching to accommodate him, smoothing out, losing the intricacy of their hidden shape.

He watched as her minions departed, the dark and the light, like rats off a sinking ship, except she wasn't sinking. She was impaled and he was shaking out the last residue of her separateness, this terrible, beautiful, mingling of love and longing and sorrow.

She felt certain that she could still stop this; she just had to choose.

But as things fell away, she was filled and held by him, most of all by a coldness. As Carly gave herself over to that chill, it felt like comfort. Nothing rots or decays in the cold, everything stays pure and perfect. She wondered if she would miss what she had given up. She wondered if anyone would notice.

Carly left the room, but she had left something important behind, and now it was part of him. He felt relief. For a moment it had seemed that she would refuse him. But she had succumbed. He had opened up a void in her that would soon begin to fill with something dark.

∞

Carly felt like she wasn't even in her own body, though when she looked down, there it was. The rest of her, most of her, was somewhere else now, but she couldn't figure out where.

A car honked loudly and Carly jumped back, only then realizing she had been crossing against the light. She crouched down on the curb and breathed deeply, trying to come back to herself. Then she rejected that reflex. There was no going back.

24

In the parking lot, Marti stood by her motorcycle. She wasn't sure she was in a condition to drive. It had been awkward getting out of the clinic.

Her head was pounding still, and her dark glasses did not do enough to relieve her eyes. She heard a familiar voice behind her say her name. Dave had come out of the clinic to find her.

It had been two days since the evening they spent together. Dave had left a message for her on the first day, but she'd been too preoccupied to return it, even wondering if she should allow things to continue to develop with him, wondering if she really had space in her life for a relationship.

Now here he was before her, and she felt a surprising gratitude at being relieved from the burden of solitude.

"What happened in there?" he asked.

Marti didn't know how to answer. Her feelings of violation, at what had happened in the examining room, rose up in her. She felt her gut lurch and some hot tears squeezed out of her eyes.

"What's the matter?" asked Dave, alarmed, thinking it must have something to do with him.

"Why is it so hard, Dave?"

"Maybe if you told me what happened, I could help?"

"I don't know," said Marti. She remembered all the disturbed faces in the doorway of the clinic, looking at her. She wondered what Dave had heard.

"I think I may be in trouble," she said. "With Gillespie and them."

Dave flipped his hand cheerfully. "Oh, that comes under the heading of Illegitimi non carborundum," he said, "which is Latin for 'Let's go have a drink.'"

Marti smiled in spite of herself. "I'd like to, but I think a drink is the last thing I need right now."

"I understand," said Dave, though his expression belied his words.

∞

Jane opened the door when Marti rang the bell, then walked away without saying anything and resumed watching an inane TV program.

Marti came inside and closed the door behind her. She was content to let Jane ignore her; she had come to see Carly, after being unable to reach her on the phone. But there was no answer at the door to the girl's bedroom; she didn't seem to be in the house.

"You could have told me," said Jane. "What happened to Carly when she was at your clinic, anyway?"

"I don't understand," said Marti.

"Some doctor? She mentioned it once, and when I started asking questions she slammed shut like a clam. Now she's been gone for two days."

"What?" Marti tried to put it together. Something had happened to Carly at the clinic, but what? Marti felt a guilty shudder. She'd known something was wrong, but she hadn't spoken with Jane about it.

"Gone where?" she asked.

"You tell me," said Jane.

Marti didn't know what to say. Jane went to the bar and poured herself another drink, her body moving robotically. Marti took the opportunity to focus on her sister's second body. It was raw and inflamed, turbulent. As Jane drank, it softened toward a dull equilibrium, its inflammation still visible, the tormenting minions suppressed but not diminished. She drank vodka as though it were the only liquid available to put out a fire. But if she was drinking to insulate herself from minions of rage and resentment, the vodka was only feeding them.

"It's hard for Carly." Perhaps she could get Jane to think about her daughter as a person, not an extension of herself. "It's hard being young today," Marti said, though she knew there was more than that involved.

Jane barked, a sound that was intended as a laugh of derision. "Being young is a picnic. Try being old."

Impulsively, Marti reached out and gently took hold of Jane's hand and guided the bottle back to its place before she'd poured yet more into her glass. Jane's face snapped toward her, and she wanted to say something but no words came.

She put down the empty glass. "Let me show you what I found," she said with sudden energy, and she lurched out of the room.

A moment later Jane returned with a piece of paper.

"It's a poem she wrote when she was fourteen."

Jane started reading but stumbled over the words. She handed the piece of paper to Marti.

The writing was in pencil and had faded somewhat. The letters were in a girlish hand, all rounded curves, the words full with a virginal ripeness.

The poem was titled "The Place That No One Knows." It was an awkward, heartfelt paean to adolescent loneliness.

Marti had written poetry at that age as well, and indeed she could have written the same poem. The only thing wrong with it, she thought, is that it should have been called "The Place That Everyone Knows." To be fourteen was to separate for the first time, fallen from the innocent unity of childhood. Perhaps it was a condition no one ever recovered from.

"She's had everything she wanted," slurred Jane, wanting Marti to explain who had left the gate open, how this goblin of discontent had infected her daughter. The whole point of having a daughter was to create a space that was free of such shadows. But she had failed, and in failing she was pressed to confront the demons she had hoped to escape—first through parenthood, then through alcohol.

Marti grabbed hold of Jane, as if she could somehow pull her out of her own skin, detach her from the minions she was feeding with a grim diet of resentment and vodka. Everything feeds something, she thought, gives power to something.

For a moment, Marti's bold action had the intended effect, shaking Jane out of her self-involved trance, the glaze suddenly gone from her eyes.

Marti hadn't been planning to intervene. But for a moment, she couldn't help herself. She felt a surge of compassion, that willingness to share another's inner burden. This is the answer, it hit her, to "the place no one knows," the proof that we aren't alone.

Her hands on Jane's shoulders, she mustered as much calm and acceptance as she could, and allowed it to communicate itself through her touch. Marti could see the ugly minions rearing up, but helpless against the simple remedy she was offering. Jane sat immobile, as if caught between the familiar torment of her pet monsters and the peace Marti was offering. Why was this even a choice? The dark was a powerful thing. The monsters might take bites out of us now and then, but at least they offered the promise of protection from something worse. If only we knew what that was. Ourselves?

Marti felt Jane begin to open to her, her breath deepening. Emboldened by this encouraging response, Marti went further. She was probably driven partly by her own feelings of guilt, feelings she was almost as reluctant to face as Jane was about her own.

Perhaps that accounted for the clumsiness of Marti's inward lunge as she tried to gain purchase on the ugliest of Jane's minions, ready to pull it out. But she was forgetting, among other things, what she had already learned the hard way: that with an intoxicated patient there is little ground to stand on, even in ideal therapeutic circumstances, and these were far from ideal.

Jane cried out and reared back, pulling away from Marti violently, inadvertently smacking her across the face. The look in Jane's eyes was animal fear.

Marti stammered an apology, but had no idea what Jane would think had just happened.

Jane turned away and poured another drink, her hand shaking. Marti got up. She had begun to shake inside.

"I want to help, Jane," she said, disgusted with the sound of pleading in her voice.

"I am going to bed," Jane said. "You know the way out."

Taking the bottle with her, Jane left Marti standing there.

Riding home, the bike reminded Marti that peace in life had to be found through balance rather than stillness. Stride had torn some carapace from her being, leaving her naked and trembling before the infinite, and then he was gone. But maybe if he remained distant, it was only as a kind of call, a beckoning. The distance was in her, and she was the one who had to overcome it.

But how?

∞

Marti was unlocking the door to the apartment when she felt the hairs rise on the back of her neck. Her body reacted before her mind registered that someone was coming at her from behind.

She spun around and slammed the assailant back against the wall. She was surprised when she realized it was someone she knew.

"Carly?"

Marti quickly let go of her niece, who appeared not fazed at all by the rough handling.

"Why were you sneaking up on me like that?"

"I just...wanted to see you." Carly shrugged, her affect flat.

"Well, come inside," said Marti. "We've been worried about you."

Marti pushed the door open and gestured for Carly to enter. "I just saw your mother. She's really upset, you know." As soon as the words were out, she realized it was probably not the ideal subject.

But Carly's reaction was muted. "My mother..." she mumbled, almost as though she had no idea who that was.

"Where have you been?" asked Marti. She looked Carly up and down. The girl's second body was cloaked in an impenetrable gray cloud.

"Are you okay? Are you hungry?" That was more like it, she realized: stop asking for things, offer something.

"I'm really tired," said Carly. Perhaps that explained her condition, though it seemed unlikely. Marti had seen tired people, but she'd never seen a second body that looked so obscure.

Marti felt her own exhaustion crowding in. She had dragged herself home ready to fall into bed. If Carly had come to her to get a good night's sleep, that was a good thing. They could figure out the rest in the morning. She'd call Jane then too, once she saw whether she could convince her niece to return home.

She offered Carly some pajamas, set her up with some bedding on the couch, and brought her a cup of tea in spite of her listless claim that she didn't want anything.

Marti hoped the girl wasn't sick; her forehead was cool to the touch. Marti helped her under the covers.

"Did anything happen that you want to talk about?" The girl shook her head, her look still blank.

"You've got everything you need? You'll be okay?" Marti asked, not sure what else to do. Carly nodded. "See you in the morning, then?" Another nod. Marti kissed her on the forehead.

Marti's own transition into sleep came quickly. Later, she wondered if there had been any sound to wake her up. She'd left the door to her bedroom ajar, so she'd be available if Carly needed her. When she opened her eyes, she thought for a moment that almost no time had passed, but the clock claimed that she'd been asleep for hours.

Sitting up in bed, Marti couldn't shake the feeling that something had woken her. With the blackout shades down, the room was mostly dark, but there was some light spilling in through the open door. Marti became aware of the unmistakable sound of breathing not her own.

"Carly?"

At first, no reply, but the breathing was there, heavy and ragged. Marti shifted her feet to the floor, and that's when the scream came.

Carly came with it, hurtling out of the darkness. She blew into Marti like a feral cat, carried on her own unearthly shriek, her weight knocking Marti back on the bed.

Marti tried to throw her off, but Carly had a tight grip

on her hair and Marti felt a clump of it tear away in Carly's right hand as she was thrown back. But the left hand stayed attached.

With her now free hand, Carly pulled at something in her waistband and lifted it up. Marti recognized the large knife from her own kitchen. She reached up with both hands and grabbed Carly's extended arm. Carly had the advantage of gravity, and with her other arm hammered at Marti to defeat her grip.

Desperate, Marti drove her weight forward, piling her head into Carly while continuing to ward off the knife. Carly lost her balance and toppled backward off the bed, the knife flying out of her hand.

Marti threw herself on top of Carly and held her down. Now it seemed the girl was in the grip of a seizure. Her limbs flailed, but the exertions were no longer aggressively directed at Marti, they were simply out of control.

"Stop," Marti yelled, "Carly! It's me! Stop!"

Gradually, after struggling helplessly against Marti's restraint, Carly calmed down, a look of confusion settling on her face.

"Can I let you go now?" asked Marti.

Carly nodded, though her eyes betrayed no understanding.

Tentatively, ready for anything, Marti gingerly let go of the girl's limbs and climbed off her.

"What happened?" said Marti. Carly looked at her. Blank.

Marti touched for forehead. Cool. "Can I examine you?"

Carly shrugged. Marti thought her passivity was almost as frightening as the unmotivated hysteria of the attack. She guided Carly to sit in a chair, turned on a low light, and then put her hands on the girl's shoulders to see what she could learn from her second body. This time she persisted and was able to penetrate the gray cloud.

Marti recoiled in shock. She had seen this once before, in the zombie-like creature that had attacked her in the highway diner parking lot: her niece's second body had been completely gutted. It brought to mind a forest that had been clear-cut, transformed into something not merely dead, but alien. This, thought Marti, was the essence of the unholy: the negation not only of life, but of life's renewal. Only a bleeding fringe of Carly's second body remained. The rest was a void.

She willed herself to move in for a closer look. Normally, entering a patient's second body required a kind of subtle pressure on her part. But now she felt herself forcefully sucked in, as if by the void she had just seen, and her awareness disappeared instantly from the physical realm.

Inner space rushed past her. Normally her movements in the second body were dictated by her own will, but now some other force was pulling her down.

A cloud of white particles swirled around her, as if being pulled into the same vortex, thickening as she descended, so that soon she was falling through the pure white of a driving snowstorm. The ground suddenly appeared before her, a vast white expanse, rising up until it slammed into her and arrested her movement.

The impact was painless. The flakes continued to fall around her.

Something in this white expanse was deeply comforting. The flakes falling on her skin were cold, but they melted, the liquid seeping into her pores. She was becoming white inside as well. Purified.

But she wasn't here for herself. She was here for Carly. The girl was lost somewhere in the devastated wilds of her own being. Marti had to find her. As she had the thought, she looked up and saw, through the snowstorm, a hut. She made her way toward it, sensing that it held the answer.

It was a crude frontier dwelling, assembled from unmilled timber. Marti went inside.

She recognized the furnishings: this was Carly's room, or a jumbled and rearranged version of it. Someone sat here, turned away.

"Carly?" There was no response. Marti approached, a feeling of dread choking her.

She knelt down beside the figure, still unable to see its face. "Carly?"

The girl turned around now. It was Carly, but a much younger Carly, eight years old.

"Aunt Marti?" the girl said, and hugged her. "He told me you wouldn't come."

"Who told you?"

"I don't know his name. He said you didn't care about me."

"That's not true," said Marti.

The girl's eyes widened as they fell on the Onoma, resting against Marti's heart.

"What is that?"

"It's called the Onoma."

"Can I wear it?" Carly was already reaching for it.

"I'm not supposed to take it off," said Marti.

"Why not?"

"It's for protection."

"What about me? I need protection."

"I'll protect you," said Marti.

"You can't," said the girl. "Besides, you only care about them."

"'Them?'"

"The ones in the other world."

"I care about you, that's why I'm here."

"Then prove it to me. Give me the Onoma. Do it now."

"I can't."

The girl began to cry. "You will sacrifice me."

"Don't say that. I'm going to take you out of here. Come with me." Marti held out her hand, but Carly took a step back.

"And then how many more will you sacrifice to serve your new masters?"

"My new—? Carly, where are you getting this from?"

"It's the truth. You don't have any idea what they are. But you are doing their bidding."

The truth of the words suddenly brought Marti up short. It was true: who were they? How much were they expecting from her? And to what end?

Marti felt her grasp slipping. She had gone inside Carly's second body. She intended an act of retrieval, she needed to bring Carly back to herself.

"Will you come with me then? If I give you the Onoma?"

Carly nodded eagerly.

As she slipped it off, Marti told herself it was the only thing she could do. If she was going to sacrifice anyone, it had to be herself. What good was protecting herself if she couldn't protect Carly?

But as soon as the girl had the Onoma in her hand she fled, slipping out the door, and Marti realized she had made a mistake.

Marti charged after her, back out into the snowstorm, which was now roaring with gale force. Visibility was zero, there was only swirling white across a gray canvas, the gray of Carly's second body. But Carly was gone, and with her the Onoma.

Marti tried to will herself back to herself; she must still be sitting in her own apartment, the Onoma around her neck. But her intention yielded no effect. She remembered the strange feeling of her descent. Now she understood why it had seemed like she was being pulled in. A trap had been sprung.

Perhaps, back in physical reality, she and Carly had changed places; she was now the lost one.

She sensed that she wasn't alone. Someone, or something, was waiting for her here. But it wasn't ready to face her yet.

She trudged forward in the snow, unable even to keep her eyes open. The wind blew through her clothes, and she felt the cold piercing to her bones. She crouched down, seeking to concentrate her strength. But every bit of strength and body heat was being sucked out of her.

She curled up in the snow. The cold was smoothing out all feeling, like a blissful sleep. All she had to do was agree to it. The snowfall thickened as she surrendered, and she felt it covering her like blanket. He was waiting for her to sleep, then he would come. She wasn't afraid any more.

Her eyes were losing focus. Snow was falling on the back of her hand, resting on the ground in front of her face. Her skin gradually disappearing under the white.

She remembered as a child the first snowfall, sticking her tongue out, feeling the snowflakes, cold tickles on the tender sensory organ. Making snowflake cutouts in class. Her teacher, Mrs. Milgram again, telling them, no two snowflakes are alike. It had been her first encounter with infinity: trying to grasp the number of snowflakes in a snow-covered city, every one of them different.

The memory stuck to her like an irritating barb. It demanded that she look closer at the white flakes. They were melting in her palm but she held her gaze, increasingly sensing that something was wrong.

The effort required was enormous. Now she was doing what she hadn't yet had a chance to do—use her own will to compel the movement of her awareness. She had been pulled here, as if leaving her will behind, but she did not have to consent.

Why, though, why resist? To see the snowflakes. Just that, and then she would accept the sleep that wanted to overtake her.

Her vision moved in to the white particles, longing for their purity, endless variety run on a singular crystalline pattern.

But these weren't crystals. They weren't even white. And they certainly weren't unique.

The tiny bodies, hard and flat, each exactly the same, as if punched out of the same mold, were more like insects than snow crystals. The whiteness was an effect created by imprinted patterns on their backs and a shivering movement of their bodies, an illusion. And they weren't melting on her skin, but descending into it, like burrowing termites.

Marti tried shaking her head, as if to reset her vision, banish this malign hallucination. But the more she exerted her will, the more vivid it became.

Horror rose in her. As if in response, the storm of insects accelerated, a thickening crust of the wriggling creatures enveloping her, invading her. Each brought with it a sensation of cold, which somehow she had been perceiving as heat. They were consuming her; not her physical body, of course, but this was worse.

Movement was becoming impossible, and her panic was making her helpless. This is what drowning feels like, she thought, the moment when you realize you have lost the power to resist, and are now in the grip of something you will never escape. What surprised her was that the blade of grief that drove itself between her ribs carried the awareness that far more was being lost than her own life, a realization of many other beings that had been counting on her, counting on the Coil. Why hadn't she felt this before? Why had she been given a responsibility she couldn't hope to live up to?

She heard the footsteps approaching. She was helpless

now, the way it wanted her, and it would take her.

∞

Ursula had been lying on the daybed in her studio, drifting in a reverie. She was feeling the impulse to take up a brush and execute a painting. But her brushes were put away; it had been some time since she had done any painting. She would make the painting inside herself.

She closed her eyes. Just as painting was an act of discovery, a revelation with hand leading eye, so the meditative image drew her awareness along.

Within the image, Marti appeared. Deep shadows came with her. She was submerged in something dark, frightening.

Ursula concentrated herself and reached out.

It was not only skin that could touch. There was another way to touch as well, another organ that existed both for perception and encounter: and that was the heart.

The human heart, as an organ of touch—of perception and communication—was something very new and young, something that had barely begun to discover its capacities. Its development was a work in which all those bearing a heart were engaged. What work were future generations counting on us for, Ursula wondered, that could bring the heart to the fulfillment of its capacities?

Ursula felt her heart tremble. It was an ache of love. Love undertaken as a choice. Not merely because it made her feel good, or because it fulfilled a wish or fantasy, or any of the other, weak reasons that made love too small and perishable a thing.

In the image she was creating, the love became a flow of flower petals. Liquid color. She saw it soak into the younger woman like water into dry earth.

Then she understood that she was responding to a need. She felt a quiet joy that she might serve Marti like this, sensing that such help was badly needed.

And it was being received. Ursula felt, like Marti, bathed in its resplendence. As with all true gifts, there was an immediate, magnified, current of return.

∞

The sudden blaze of dark red brought Marti back to her eyes. Settling on the thickening crust of the white insect covering on her hand, the blood-red curve of a single rose petal. The incongruousness of it grabbed her attention, but the beauty of it brought a current of warmth she felt deep within. And then another one fell, and another, and flower petals of other kinds. The cascade of petals began to bury the synthetic flakes.

Marti didn't know where they had come from, but she could feel what they were: the evidence of love. And it was love that rose in her, love for Carly and for this unexpected grace.

As the warmth intensified, it began to slow down the great wave she had been drowning in. And then, the wave turned.

The flower petals were pouring into her now. The insects fled, slowly at first, then as from a house on fire, disappearing into the ground. In the distance, a sound echoed, a voice, a cry of rage.

With that, something snapped, and Marti found her awareness back in her body. She was shaken. Something had tried to use someone she loved against her. Because she was a Coil.

She felt like she was caught in someone else's war.

Carly was clutching the Onoma, its strap wrapped around her hand. Marti gently disentangled it and put it back around her own neck, feeling relief.

The sensation didn't last long. Carly was barely breathing.

∞

Ursula had registered the shift before she understood

what it was. First she felt the freeing of Marti from the darkness that had been crushing in on her. Ursula should have stopped there, closed off the channel, but she was too immersed in the delight of it to change direction.

By the time she realized the malign force, expelled from Marti, was following the flower petals back to their source, back to Ursula, it was too late: she was in its grip. It felt like something grabbing onto you from the inside, a fist wrapped around your viscera, and tightening. It was the last thing she felt before a black space swallowed her.

25

Jane was not taking it well. They were sitting together in Emergency and waiting fretfully to hear what was happening with Carly.

"You can go. I'll let you know what they say."

"Don't be silly," Marti said. "I'm not going anywhere." She put her hand tentatively on Jane's shoulder.

"I still don't understand."

"She seemed fine last night," Marti said, repeating what she had already told her sister. All she could do was stick to her story. "We agreed I'd get her up early so I could bring her back home. It was late when she showed up and I thought it better for her to sleep. But when I went to wake her up—"

"There was something wrong," said Jane, "just like that."

Marti shrugged helplessly. What could she say? "Your daughter inadvertently found herself caught in a battle between me and some sort of hostile, supernatural adversary?"

She tried to convince herself that it was unreasonable for Jane to blame her. But the truth was she blamed herself.

Who do you think you are? Playing with fire, and someone you love has just gotten very badly burned.

She had a bitter taste in her mouth. She thought about the little girl Carly, and about what she'd said: that the Partnership used people, was using her. And Carly was paying the price.

She looked up at the clock in the waiting room; it was a few minutes after seven. Past time for her daily meditation appointment with Ursula. She closed her eyes, tried to center herself in spite of her turbulent feelings. She felt nothing, no image of the garden, no presence of Ursula, nothing at all. It struck her that maybe she had been playing some sort of game, and now the shit had gotten real.

After a while an emergency room doctor who looked like he wasn't old enough to shave appeared and awkwardly reported on Carly's condition. She was on life support but appeared to be responding, and they were hopeful she'd soon be out of critical care. Jane wept with relief and allowed Marti to hold her. But Marti felt no comfort.

∞

"I don't understand," she said. "Why don't you just kill this doctor. The humans die easily."

He looked at the creature, enjoying her ugliness. How different from the beautiful girl he'd had to sully.

"The doctor will die when it is time," he said. "But you needn't concern yourself with the details of my plan."

"I just want to be sure you have one."

He glared at her. "Do you think I would be here, would subject myself to the conditions of this body, without a purpose?"

She made a wet rasping sound that rumbled out of her massive body. A laugh, he realized. Again, there was something that pleased him. She was disrespectful, true, but he relished the way her existence mocked the human undertaking.

But he couldn't help ask, with a scowl, "What's so funny?"

"Most of us didn't choose to be here."

"And I am going to help you with that. If you help me."

∞

By mid-afternoon, Marti was on her fourth coffee, and the caffeine's half-life seemed to have reached its vanishing point. She went to get her next patient folder, but the only thing in her box was a telephone message form on which someone had written, "Meeting in Dr. Gillespie's office."

When she knocked at his office, it wasn't Gillespie's voice that said "Come in."

Behind the desk, Gansrud sat heavily in the chair. Two of his security staff flanked him, one standing with his arms folded, the other sitting against the wall, a tablet in his lap poised for note-taking.

Gansrud asked her to sit.

"I suppose you know why we want to see you?"

"Where is Jim?" Marti asked.

"Do you know why we wanted to see you?" he repeated.

"Please," she said. "I can't take a guessing game right now. What is it that you want?"

Gansrud clenched his teeth. His second body, a riot of cold, steely minions, was that of a criminal.

"We want to know what it is you are doing with your patients."

"Pardon me?"

"Don't play dumb. We have known for some time that something strange was going on. Yesterday was only the most obvious example." Gansrud nodded at the standing associate, who swiveled the desktop monitor and pushed a button. A movie began to play. It was surveillance video, captured from the security cameras that were in all the exam rooms, of her sessions with patients. It was impossible to tell what was actually going on, but it was clear that it wasn't normal exam room procedure.

"I want to talk to Gillespie," said Marti. "He knows that whatever I've been doing, it's been working."

"First of all," said Gansrud, "not everyone feels that way."

"How many complaints have you had?"

"I am not here to answer your questions, but to ask my own. The point is not that patients were dissatisfied, the complaints simply alerted us to your professional misconduct. Do you deny that you have been using a range of..."—he groped for a word—"practices...with your patients that aren't in any way medically sanctioned?"

"If you mean that I've been doing what I can in an effort to heal their ailments, as I have always done, then no, I don't deny it."

"So you see no substantial difference between this sort of thing"—he gestured to the video footage that was still playing—"and accepted medical practice? Is this what Dr. Stefanovic taught you to do?"

Marti bit her tongue. She knew she would not be able to convince him of anything. A jolt of panic went through her that she was going to be deprived of her practice.

"Why didn't Gillespie just talk to me? You had no right to pursue a spying campaign like that."

"He did talk to you," interrupted the man who had been taking notes. He mentioned the date. "According to his notes, you denied you were doing anything out of the ordinary."

"We had every right," Gansrud said. "You are employed by us. You are required by your contract—not to mention the code of conduct of your professional organization—to abide by certain guidelines. We had reason to believe you were violating those guidelines. Do you deny that our suspicions were well founded?"

Marti felt a flash of hatred for Gansrud that took her by surprise. She realized that the most visible minions on his second body were hate minions. She watched as several angry red blobs came loose from him and floated toward her. Like fear, she thought, and maybe even more so, hate was contagious. Another one penetrated her, and it felt good, permission to unleash her own shadow, to free herself from the dark burden. But it also clouded her vision, leaving her queasy and disoriented.

Her unease must have registered on her face, for she saw a kind of gloating on Gansrud's. "You haven't answered," he said. "Do you deny our charges?"

Marti folded her hands and bit her tongue, sensing anything she said was likely to make things worse.

"No? Then you are suspended indefinitely," Gansrud said. "We will be completing our investigation and submitting our findings to the College of Physicians." Gansrud leaned forward as if he had something affectionate to say. "And we fully expect that they will strip you of your license."

Marti looked back at him. Suddenly she saw that there was something pitiful about him, something abjectly weak being revealed in his exercise of power. He was older than her by a decade, but she found herself looking at him as a mother might.

Such compassion felt forced; his smugness was repulsive and he was unrelated to her. But she kept herself focused on his second body, deepening her perception that his outer attitude was a mask over inner disorder and distress. How difficult it must be to go through life like that! Now compassion swelled within her.

In response, Gansrud's mask wavered. His gloating look of hatred was replaced momentarily by fear, and then a kind of childish panic, as though he felt himself losing control of the confrontation but couldn't understand how or why. He dropped his face down to his papers and pretended to look for something.

They ended the meeting as quickly as they could, stripping her of her swipe card and keys. As Marti realized that nothing she said mattered, that their course of action was fixed, she felt a gradual swell of outrage, on behalf of her patients as much as herself.

Gansrud's lackey escorted her to collect her things. The rest of the staff had already left and there was no one around to see Marti being marched out.

Alone in the parking lot, she experienced a long moment of disorientation. Her life had revolved so completely around the clinic. She could go home, of course, but then what?

She felt a hot current of anger rise in her. So this is where it had led! She hadn't asked to have her life turned upside down. She knew she'd made a difference to her patients. Now she had no patients. Her niece's life hung by a thread. Stride was another lost lover.

"Is this your idea of partnership, then?" she said aloud, wondering if the angels could hear her. "Where do I go now?"

But of course there was only the usual indifferent noise of the city. She cursed under her breath, repeating the words like a chant.

When she got on her bike, her plan was to go home. Maybe sleep. Or do some laundry. God knows she could use some clean laundry.

But being on the bike, being in motion, felt like a relief, an escape from her thoughts. If she was going to feel lost, she decided, she'd rather be surrounded by the unfamiliar. Feeling lost when you were at home was too unsettling.

So she stayed on the bike and took a road out of town. She got off the highway at an unfamiliar exit. And then, driving on country roads, she took turns impulsively while deliberately avoiding making a mental map.

It worked. The unfamiliarity of her surroundings, and the absence of any awareness of how to find her way back to the familiar, reconciled her inner and outer conditions. Maybe she would just go on like this, she thought. Keep driving until she found a new life. Anyway, she needed a new job now. Something practical and useful like, say, motorcycle mechanics. Motorcycles had moving parts but no second bodies. No Milgram's Knots with angels waiting on the other side to tell you about partnership. How could you partner with someone who had no address, who you would never get on the phone, who might be—and might as well be—a hallucination?

Dusk was coming on. A country crossroads up ahead boasted a rare traffic light, currently glowing red. Marti downshifted, her body surprised to realize how fast she'd been going.

At the intersection stood a gas station with convenience store. Across from it, a ramshackle roadside bar and grill.

The red light seemed to take a long time. Long enough for Marti to notice that she was hungry.

Marti dug out her sunglasses and put them on before she entered the bar and grill. She didn't really feel like noticing second bodies.

The place seemed even more welcoming when she found that it was happy hour. By the third shot of tequila her troubles were coming into the kind of perspective she wanted: distant. But she had the uneasy feeling she was being watched.

When someone slid into the seat beside her, she sighed and avoided looking, expecting a pickup line.

"Come here often?"

The cliché didn't capture her attention but the voice speaking it did.

"Dave? Jesus! What are you doing here?"

"I live near here. It's the local watering hole."

"You live—?" Marti had known Dave lived out in the country somewhere.

"What's your excuse?" Dave asked. "Following me around, are you?"

Marti felt herself blush. "No. I was trying to get lost, actually." The magic of it, that she had been running towards Dave without realizing it, made her skin prickle. Had the angels brought her here too?

"Oh dear, and now you've been found. I've just been sitting over there with some fellow barflies. I can go back and leave you alone..."

"Don't be silly," Marti said. "You can join me. I'm toasting my new direction."

"What's that?"

"I guess you haven't heard. I don't work at the clinic any more."

"What do you mean?"

Marti took off her sunglasses. "I've been fired."

Dave was still smiling, as he searched Marti's face for some sort of clue that she wasn't serious. He couldn't find one. His smile fell.

"What? When?"

"This afternoon."

"Why?"

Marti shook her head. "Oh you know. Not playing by the rules."

"Nothing new about that," said Dave.

Marti sighed. He had no idea how new things were, but she wasn't going to get into it. She looked at Dave and shook her head at the absurdity of it, bumping into him like this.

"What?" he said, not sure how to read the look.

Marti raised her glass. "A toast."

"A toast," Dave said. "What are we drinking to?"

"To finding friends in unexpected places."

Dave repeated the toast and they both knocked back their drinks.

"That's my limit," Dave said. "I'm driving."

"Oh right," Marti said. "Driving." She realized how tired she was. She started to get off the stool but her landing was shaky.

"Whoa," said Dave. "Why don't I take you home."

∞

As Dave started up the truck, Marti spoke. "What about your place?"

"My place?"

"You said it's nearby." Something about the thought of going home depressed Marti. "Have you got a guest room?"

The deer-in-headlights look on Dave's face made Marti wonder if that had been a wise suggestion. But he quickly recovered.

"Sure, yeah," he said. "I've got the kids every other weekend. Two extra bedrooms."

"I just don't feel like going home. Too depressing."

"I can understand. You should talk to a lawyer."

"A lawyer?"

"About the firing."

It felt good to be with Dave. Like a promise of normality. Maybe this was all she really needed.

She put her hand on the back of his, resting on the shift. He looked at her, and the light in his face took her by surprise. It struck her as miraculous. How could human beings have that kind of light within them?

He lifted his hand off the shift so he could grip hers, his eyes moving back and forth from the road to her eyes while he squeezed her hand. She felt their bodies trading assurances, of willingness, of trust.

The truck turned into a driveway and pulled up to an old farmhouse.

Inside, she could feel the tension. She didn't want to deal with it, didn't want to think. She put her lips against Dave's.

Dave gasped in surprise, but his lips met hers eagerly.

Soon this meeting at the boundary of their bodies wasn't enough. Marti felt her body's hunger taking over. She wanted to feel their skin meeting everywhere, wanted to completely overcome the design that had made their bodies into separate things. One of his arms was holding her, wrapped around her back, finding its way up under her shirt. The surface of Dave's fingers was firm, rough, but not harsh, the roughness waking up her skin. His other hand pressed against her left breast. Her moan seemed to resonate through his body as well as hers.

For a moment she felt like it was Stride she was joining with. She didn't fight this feeling. No matter what, it was the present moment, a moment filled with a shared joy, respite from the solitary burden she had been carrying.

She unbuttoned his shirt. The hair across his chest had the beginnings of gray in it, flecks of ash from the fires of experience. She thought about the word: chest. Her grandmother had a large old chest, where she kept special linens. Once, when still a small girl, Marti had crawled right inside it and closed the lid, hiding from her parents and a world that sometimes felt strange to her. In such a small space she could be safe, be home. The darkness surrounded her with its presence; she had never felt less alone.

Women had breasts, reaching out to give of themselves. But men's hearts were so tender, it seemed, they had to be placed safely inside a chest. It was easy for the chest to become locked, the key lost. Easy for a man to become one of those who could only take. But when Marti placed her hand in the center of Dave's chest, she knew that it wasn't locked.

For a moment, Marti felt that if she could just bury herself in this chest, she would be safe. Safe from all the uncertainty, from the hostile force that had seized Carly, from the expectations upon her as a Coil, which she didn't understand.

But no. It wasn't about protection, about hiding. It was about touch.

"You never stop thinking," Dave said.

Marti laughed. "Make me," she said.

∞

As they both surrendered to the intimacy that he had yearned for so often in her presence, Dave felt the fear that this could not last. Confronted with such a fear, he knew that men can be driven to strange actions. But Dave stood before it and decided: it does not matter. I will take this moment, this touch, this offering. I will.

Afterward, Dave felt their lovemaking had been the falling of ripe fruit. They had shared themselves, taken nothing, given everything, the kind of exchange that can happen only when the seasons have done their work: the buds, the leaves, the flowers, the bees, the fruit growing slowly in the rain and sun, drawing its flesh and sweetness up from the earth. Then there is something to bite into. For two bodies to copulate, all it takes is a willingness, a hunger. The organs involved can function perfectly well without love. Fucking can be a way to forget, to remember, to trap, to release, to punish, even to heal. We may go into the orchard, but we do not eat the fruit without love.

Here, there was love. Dave wondered when he'd last felt it, if he had ever felt it. Before, when he mated, he felt pride and possession, and a kind of protective caring wrapped around the flame of lust. And he had called that love.

While Marti slept, Dave stayed awake, looking at her. Then he closed his eyes, letting the image linger inside him, in that place where the world became an image and could last forever.

∞

Marti shivered in the chilly, late summer pre-dawn air

and pulled on a T-shirt of Dave's. She tiptoed out into the garden.

The world surrounding the house was just creeping out of its nighttime state, its forms visible but its color muted, dark blue emerging out of black. The crickets had yet to fully surrender, but their buzzing had softened. A dove, somewhere in its nest, cycled through a rhythmic call, its gentle coos mirroring her own sense of contentment. Several huge maple trees stood like sentinels, but she felt them welcoming her. Beyond on one side was a pond, densely ringed with bulrushes. Its surface was still.

As day slowly crept in, she thought that what surrounded her was poetry, not biology. As if in response to this thought, the first stirrings of a breeze rustled the leaves of the trees around her. She noticed how slowly it moved, like a wave from one tree to the next.

Marti's knees felt weak. The reordering of perception initiated by her encounter with Stride seemed to have no end.

Two arms wrapped around her. Dave pulled her against him, and his lips caressed her neck.

"This is a beautiful place," she said.

"Needs some attention."

She wondered if he was referring to himself, and turned around to look at him. He smiled.

"You're a beautiful place," he said. "Or did I tell you that already?"

She kissed him gently and he allowed her to separate from him.

"I'm thinking you might be a witch or something," Dave said lightly. He laughed at the worried look she threw him. "A good witch. I just mean everything looks really different to me this morning."

"Like how?" she asked. It suddenly struck her to wonder—if sex with Stride had transformed her so utterly, was this now an effect she would have on others? Was she the first human carrier of a current of sexually transmitted enlightenment?

Dave took her chin in his hand gently, and stroked her cheek. "Like love, I think." He looked down. "Is that too cheesy?"

"It's not cheesy," she said, but she realized she was also evading the point. It struck her that for him, the moment was all about her. But she hadn't thought about him once since getting out of bed.

∞

Back in the house, Marti phoned the hospital and asked about Carly. The news was encouraging: the girl's condition continued to slowly improve. Marti felt some relief but little comfort.

As she hung up the phone, she turned her head abruptly, as though something had called her name. But it was quiet. She was now staring at a clock sitting on the desk. Exactly 7:00.

Marti felt a twinge of guilt. She remembered the emptiness she had felt when trying to connect with Ursula the previous day, but perhaps that should be blamed on her own state of mind. With a sigh, she sat down and focused her attention inwardly.

But the garden, with the vibrant floral presence she had previously summoned with such ease, had been transformed. It wasn't so much inaccessible as darkened, wintry, barren. Nothing was growing. Marti thought about Carly's denuded second body and felt a creeping dread.

She heard her name called. For a moment she thought it was Ursula, her voice choked off and lowered by suffering, but with another repetition of her name she realized it was Dave, calling her from the kitchen.

"How do you like your eggs?' he asked, when she had come down the stairs. He had begun work on breakfast. She answered his question, and wondered if she should tell him everything. Perhaps he could even convince her that she was crazy and it would all dissipate like a dream. But something wouldn't let her. Dave watched her as she looked for something to do that would make her feel less like an open book in front of him.

The room was sunny with morning light. She heard a soft but insistent buzzing. Marti looked over to the window and saw a trapped insect driving relentlessly against the glass. She walked over to it. It was a honeybee.

She reached out, feeling an absurd impulse to caress it. Her fingers pressed against the glass just below the rotund, vibrating body, small and dark but flecked with golden light. She imagined she felt the same longing to pass through the inexplicable barrier, to be outside. The bee's frantic activity calmed, its wings stilled, and it walked across the glass to her finger.

Dave glanced over and watched as Marti, hypnotized, stared at the honeybee crawling across her hand.

"I'll be right back," she said, and walked slowly to the sliding door and was gone.

26

The bee remained perched on her hand as Marti kept walking. She kept her eyes on it as she moved, her senses heightened by the awareness that at any moment the creature could decide to sting her. But it sat placidly, and she imagined she felt its pleasure at being restored to the unconfined realm of its purpose. She expected it to fly any moment, and intended to return to the house as soon as it did.

But by the time the bee, rather abruptly, started its wings and took off, Marti could no longer see the house. The world around her was a dense weave of plant life, a fabric of green and brown shot through with occasional dazzles of other color.

A steady late-summer thrum of crickets was like an electric current sustaining the presence around her. The air was thick with scent. The cicadas had started, their song an irregular sine wave, and the whole environment seemed to be pulsing, moving toward her and then away, the space itself possessed of breath. She felt herself no longer moving through the world but moving with it, as if the bee's mode of presence had slipped inside her. The buzzing was under her skin and louder than ever.

The ground was wet with dew, and sunlight was glinting everywhere, the plants radiant, as if not merely reflecting the light but issuing it forth from within their green fibers. It entered her body; she felt it in her joints, in her sinews. As she moved she felt as though the lattice of reflected strands of light were forming patterns inside her. Behind her the sun was still close to the horizon, and the sidelong angle of its rays cast deep shadows through the trees.

The buzzing was even louder now, and then she noticed the familiar movement, the swirling clusters, radiating outward. Three wooden beehives stood here by the edge of the woods, and they weren't lights this time, but bodies, clouds of bees issuing forth toward their morning forage. She had forgotten that Dave kept bees.

She was pleased the bee had brought her here. She felt an impulse to crawl in among the hives, but decided it was an impulse best ignored. Besides, it wasn't about the bees. Like them, perhaps, she was following a scent of pollen.

She walked a little farther and then came to rest. Her focus had been on the trees, but now her intention was drawn to the ground, to a world much smaller in human scale, yet even more vast. Its scale was not something reaching upward beyond, but drawing downward, inward toward the earth.

She saw movement among layers of rich dark matter composed of years of decayed and decaying leaves. A small toad, painted in an intricate pattern in shades of brown, was wriggling its way through. It seemed to sense her at the same moment she saw it, and it froze. Its eyes were directed right at her, dark and fathomless.

Marti held her breath. The design woven into the toad's skin seemed to continue a pattern woven throughout the natural world she was standing in.

The toad's eyes were looking at her, and she felt the toad itself as an organ of perception. Its camouflaged skin was not a deception, but an expression of its unity with its surroundings. After a moment she no longer needed to look at the toad to feel that it was there, for it seemed inside her. She sensed the poignant vulnerability of its soft body, the fragile membrane of its dark skin.

Once as a child, after school, she had tagged along with a boy she liked to a pond, a hangout where he joined a bunch of his friends. The other boys immediately ridiculed her friend for having allowed a girl into their preserve. She hung back, but she was too stubborn to leave. Looking away from them, she noticed a frog slipping along the water's edge. She had surely seen one before, yet now this small creature, treading the threshold between earth and water, caught her attention in a new way. She bent over and cupped her hand around it in the water, not picking it up exactly, but gently obstructing it from moving away while she observed it, trying to feel what it was like to be that small.

She didn't notice the boy's stealthy approach, not until he was upon her and scooped the frog up in one hand, securing its legs in the other. He stared right at her for a moment with a scowling contempt, then turned to face the center of the pond. Then, dangling the frog by its hind legs, he swung his arm back and hurled the frog forcefully, out toward the center of the water. It seemed to her that the frog must have been dead by the time it left his hand, the body spinning grotesquely like a lump of skin as it arced through the air and dropped, far away, into the water like a stone. The boy turned to her once more, a smirk of triumph on his face. She felt a kind of horror she had never known in her eight years, not only at the pointless, destructive cruelty of his action, but more than that, at the revelation that such a thing was possible.

Now the other boys, inspired by their leader's example, leapt into action. A merry chase ensued, with boys plunging after frogs. The pond apparently had a lavish population of the amphibians, and they were soon being violently redistributed from its periphery to its center, launched from boyish hands with such force she thought their legs might tear off.

It was a small relief to see that the boy she liked had not joined in the massacre, but neither was he doing anything to stop it. His inaction was the last straw, and suddenly she found herself screaming at them, not least at her friend standing on the sidelines, screaming the harshest curse words she knew, with a rage she'd never known she had in her.

One or two were somewhat abashed by her tirade, but the others laughed and sneered. She imagined herself striding to the leader who had started it and striking him, feeling her fists thudding into the softness of his face, lifting and hurling him to the center of the pond. But now the tears were flowing and she knew she could not overcome him that way. She turned and fled.

Marti wondered at the vividness of a memory she hadn't recalled in years. In retrospect, the experience had been a turning point in her relationship with nature itself.

She settled her thoughts with another look at the toad, and closed her eyes. She felt a current ripple toward her. A current of what? It occurred to her that some time ago she herself had been lifted up and hurled far out into a much deeper place than she had known existed.

The sensation enveloping her took the form of a swell of gratitude, suggesting that this was the universal condition of life, properly lived: that of beneficent exchange. Metabolism, that most fundamental operation of human life processes, was nothing but an exchange. There was no such thing as a fully separate life. Gratitude was an obligation.

Yet gratitude wasn't the message, merely the opening of the door, a precondition for genuine perception. For partnership.

Movement within the air caught her attention. The bees were here, or some of them. While each was charting its own path, they formed a general drift, a flow, reminding her of the gently swirling lights that had come to her before.

She followed, and soon arrived at an opening in the woods. While, moments ago, all had been quiet, here there was a rich buzz. The goldenrod were just taller than Marti, rugged green stalks crowned with the golden efflorescence that had given them their name. Circulating among them, hovering, caressing the flowers blossom by blossom, were innumerable bees. The patch of tangled wild plants, at most a stone's throw in diameter, seemed like a bustling, populated city.

A narrow path led in among the plants, which otherwise were far too tightly packed to allow her to enter the field. It curved in toward the center. Marti moved slowly, the buzz of the honeybees rising as she did. Shortly she came to a small space, a spot among the goldenrod where the ground was covered by a much softer bed of blue chicory. It seemed like a natural hiding spot or sleeping place for an animal, and Marti felt as though she had arrived at a destination she hadn't known she was seeking.

She sank down to her knees. The soft bed invited, and she allowed her body what it wanted, which was to lie down.

The pressure of the earth against her was comforting. Perhaps gravity was just a word for the earth's love of all its progeny, its willingness to bear all and hold all close.

From this angle, the sky, blocked by the crowding plants, no longer existed. But rather than disappearing with its blue backdrop, the sun had somehow embedded itself within the earth. Against it each plant, each insect, was a sliver of darkness.

The ground was opening beneath her. She was moving again, descending a subterranean staircase, through layers of earth. Here underground, a different kind of light prevailed. A sun shone outward from within, and she felt it first deep down beneath the floor of her belly. Soil was not suffocation, but another sky above.

The light increased as some being drew closer. How strange that here underground, energy and matter had changed places. It didn't seem underground at all, but palatial, green balustrades reaching beyond her, golden crowns above.

First she saw the face, taking form out of the underground light, as if it had been there all along but camouflaged, like the toad, and carved out of living, moving, breathing, earth.

Though not exactly human, it resembled a wizened old person of indeterminate gender. The beard suggested a man, but the features were soft and feminine. Its clothing appeared to be woven from plants, matching the dark green of the goldenrod stalks, fringed with an intricate filigree. The fabric was laced with shining strands, and on the creature's head, a lattice of gold. The figure hovered on the edge of Marti's perception, but as it solidified, she saw that the clothing was actually the body.

"It took you long enough to come see us, Coil!"

The voice emanated from the creature, but its sonic texture was formed by the buzzing of the bees.

Marti felt like she was made of earth. The presence of this being was pervading her. But it was unimpressed by her sense of wonder.

"Have anything to say for yourself?"

Only now did she understand that a response was called for, and she felt a shiver of worry that, finding her lacking, he would depart. But no words came.

The Elemental being grunted, raising his arms by his side and letting them drop with exasperation.

"You do see us?" he asked. She sensed many others crowding the space behind.

"Yes! I see you."

"Well, that's a start."

She had the impression that for them, where humans were concerned, the glass was always half empty.

"What have you brought for us?"

"Brought?"

"A gift! What gift have you brought?" the being said, his appearance of impatience growing. Marti patted her pockets, trying to think if she had anything to offer, but she thought they must be as empty as her mind.

The being was looking at her hand. Marti looked down: her ring. It was a silver band, beautifully engraved, the last gift Rourke had given her. It hadn't been off her finger a dozen times in over a decade.

She pulled it off—for once it came easily—and placed it on the ground before him. He—she? them?—picked it up, his eyes shining with delight.

Then the earth Elemental was speaking to her in a volley of words she found indistinguishable.

"Wait," she interrupted. "You're speaking too fast, I can't understand."

He laughed. Strangely, his laughter, unlike his words, emanated not from the surroundings but directly from his body, a high-pitched, rocking laughter that seemed like the call of an animal.

"What's so funny?"

"Humans are humorous still. Since you are burdened with free will. Only able to think one thought at a time. So slow! Even one who should know.

"We like your gift, Coil, and we receive it! You have done well to come and ask us how—help is so rarely asked by humans now."

"Help?" she asked, confused. "I just want to give up." She doubted there was any help for it, but at least it felt good to confess her helplessness. Maybe the terrible sense of responsibility would be taken from her.

"Take my hand," he said.

The long fingers enfolded her hand with an unexpected warmth that wrapped itself around her entire being. Now his words formed inside her own mind. With the words came images.

"You would give up? There is no giving up, there is only delay. For each has a role to play.

"Look around you. Do you believe that anything has come into the world without effort? Even the daily rising and setting of the sun forever. That most ordinary cycle, which you humans can't help seeing, was begun by the incalculable effort of innumerable beings."

"I am willing to make an effort," said Marti. "I just don't understand what is expected."

"You will know when you need to! It is not only action that decides, but, in a world governed by time, where the action comes in the tides. There are things that can only be earned, at a certain point in the cycle's turn. Otherwise the entire cycle—immeasurably vast—must repeat its recital. Stride is counting on you."

"So you know Stride too. What happened to him?"

"Humpty Dumpty sat on the wall. Humpty Dumpty had a great fall." But his tone was mournful, not mocking. The image of a broken Stride pierced Marti.

"Because of me?"

"Because of the terms he himself set. Sometimes when you gamble, this is what you get."

"But will no one tell me what to do?"

"Such a demand makes no sense at all, you're the only one knows how to undo his fall."

"I'm just one person."

"You are what Stride made you. A Coil. A link. And now we are all on the brink. Now we all need to see, how well-placed was his trust in humanity."

"You aren't sure?"

"There are disagreements, you could say, about whether Stride's is the right way."

"So not everyone—not all the angels—support him? Does he have enemies? Because I think they might be after me. I might have met one of them."

"There are other agendas at play—"

"Are you saying that heaven is as screwed up as earth?"

The being laughed ruefully. "A very human question. The presence on earth of free will introduces a doubling that is difficult still. We who are closest to the earth feel the ceremony near. That which is all around you, but unseen in the dark, becomes clear. The long night is over."

"Sunrise."

"But you must set aside your doubt and your fear! They are misleading you here."

Doubt and fear. Yes. The doubt in herself. Her fear of the forces arrayed against her. But how was she to discern? Where was the boundary between doubt and reason? Between fear and necessity? Marti took a breath and let go, as best she could, of the fear of her own inadequacy. The being nodded approval before speaking again.

"The partnership that will allow earth and heaven to abide relies on your partnership with the one you knew as Stride. And now it must be rectified."

"Rectified?"

"Indeed. You have our help for this, if you wish true. But you will know what to do."

"When?" she blurted out.

But no answer came. She was alone. Her hand still tingled, but it was merely nestled in among a tangle of green. Marti was lying among the tall plants, upon, not within, the earth. She stood up; her world was as it was before, a field of goldenrod around her, the woods a short distance away. She knelt back down and looked among the plants, but couldn't reconcile what she saw there with the vision she'd just had. Her ring was nowhere to be found.

∞

She returned to the house, to smells of bacon and coffee and something baking. Dave smiled. "Did you have a nice walk?" Marti nodded.

She noticed for the first time that there had been a change in his second body. It was newly rimmed in gold, like the sun's magic hour light.

Dave pulled a tray of biscuits out of the oven and put them on the counter. "You know," he said as if reading her thoughts, "it's still happening."

"What?"

"This glow. It's kind of druggy. No, that's not it. Like a super clarity." He took her by the wrist and moved her hand. "You leave trails."

Marti took it in, letting her own fullness with the experience she'd just had subside.

"I have a lot to tell you," she said.

After he'd laid out the food, Dave sat down with her at the table. "I'm all ears."

"Soon," Marti said. "Right now, let's enjoy this amazing breakfast."

∞

Later, Marti wondered if she really would have told Dave. While they were still eating, they were interrupted by an agitated knocking.

Dave went to the door and came back a few minutes later, an awkward look on his face, leading Jim Gillespie, who wore an even more awkward, forced smile.

"I called Jim this morning," said Dave. "I wanted to know what this shit was about you getting fired. I guess he figured out from some things I said that you were here."

"I'm sorry," said Gillespie. "There's been something of a misunderstanding."

"So you'll get her job back?" Dave asked.

"I need to talk to you. In private," Gillespie said to Marti.

Marti nodded. "Okay, sure. Why don't we go outside. Dave, I'll be right back."

"No, actually," said Gillespie, "I need you to come with me."

"What? Jim, I don't work for you any more."

"I know," he said, "you must think I'm a real jerk coming here like this. But we need your help. I need your help. And then I think I can make Gansrud listen to reason, get you back with your patients where you belong."

"It seemed pretty definite, Jim. Gansrud said they're reporting me to the College."

Gillespie clung to his smile like it was his only hope.

"Things have changed," he said. "Please."

"Okay," said Marti, feeling uneasy.

"What's this all about?" Dave said.

"It's okay, Dave," Marti said. To Gillespie: "Fine. I'm coming with you."

"What? Marti? We're in the middle of breakfast!"

"I'll come back," she said, annoyed at being the object of a tug of war.

27

"This better be good," Marti said, as she settled into the front of Gillespie's black Crown Victoria. It smelled of after-shave or breath mints. As Gillespie locked the doors, she felt a sudden moment of fear. But she couldn't imagine that he was the one Harmon would send if they were intending to hurt her.

"I'm sorry," he said. "The situation is confidential."

"I still don't know what 'the situation' is."

Gillespie took a breath, as if readying for a plunge.

"Did Dr. Stefanovic tell you anything about a patient called Violet?"

Violet. It was the name on the specimen she had taken from Stef's desk. Something told Marti to play dumb.

"No."

"That's odd. Because she has asked to see you."

"To see me." Marti felt a chill.

"What do you know about Project Secure Horizon?"

"Pardon me?"

"The clinical trial, the stage two trial, that starts on Monday."

Marti remembered the meeting with the three scientists from Harmon. "Just what they told us. Why?"

"I need to remind you first, that although you no longer

officially work for us, your non-disclosure agreement is still in effect. They're really serious about that, Marti."

Marti resisted the urge to hurl some sarcasm at Gillespie and leave his car. "Okay, duly reminded," she said, mustering as much conviction as she could. Gillespie moved toward her, into her space, making the enclosed container of the car feel even smaller.

"I need your assurance," he said, "your personal assurance, that you will keep everything I am going to tell you, and anything you see today, strictly confidential. This is for your safety as much as anything."

Marti realized she was wearing her dark glasses. She took them off and looked deeply at Gillespie. Behind his confident visage there was something else, a red ribbon of fear she could see woven through his second body as if it were the only thing holding it together. Maybe it was.

"I understand, Jim," she heard herself say. "I won't disclose anything I hear and see about the project, about Harmon, any of it."

Gillespie nodded slowly, his eyes still on her, seeming to weigh whether he was sufficiently reassured, as if taking the temperature of his own fear. Marti had never sat at such close quarters with him, and she saw that the impression of youth his face gave vanished under closer inspection. It wasn't youth but a disturbing blankness, as if experience had been unable to make any marks on him.

"Good," he said, "that's good," sliding away from her, back behind the wheel. "I know it can be hard, but you'll have the satisfaction of contributing to something that is really going to make a difference to the world, positive change."

Marti tried to keep the ironic smile she felt forming from appearing on her face. You know nothing about hard, she thought, or change. "Sounds important," she said, now conscious that she had to put on an act.

"I should also tell you," Gillespie said, "that not everyone agrees with me bringing you in on this."

"Gansrud?"

"But I trust you, Marti. I don't know exactly what was going on between you and your patients, but I know that it was working. So maybe you'll appreciate what we're doing. Anyway I don't think we have a choice."

∞

For a long time they didn't speak. The car floated through the world like a sealed chamber, the leather-clad seats cushioning the road's irregularities.

"We're going to make a stop along the way. I want you to meet my wife. Have I told you about her?"

It was a strange question. They'd never had a remotely personal conversation. Marti shook her head.

"She's been ill for almost a decade."

"I'm sorry to hear that."

Gillespie looked over at her, as if it wasn't the expected response.

"What kind of illness?" Marti asked.

"I want you to examine her. I probably shouldn't say anything else, except that for the past few years, she's barely been out of bed."

Marti nodded, less and less sure of what to make of all this.

"We're almost there," he said.

∞

Hillary Gillespie was deep into the china cabinet. The plates, bowls, and utensils were stacked around her, and she was wiping them off one by one before replacing them in the cabinet.

"I don't know how long it's been since these have been cleaned," she said.

The woman was clearly well. Marti looked at her husband, expecting an explanation.

"How are you feeling today, dear?" asked Gillespie.

"I'm feeling like I'm never going to get this place clean," she said.

He gestured for her to get up. "I've brought my colleague, Dr. Powell, dear, specifically to see you."

"I don't know why," she said. She looked at Marti. "I was sick for ten years," she said. "Now that I've had my miracle and I'm out of bed, he brings me doctors."

"You saw plenty of doctors," Gillespie said.

"What was your illness?" asked Marti.

"The never agreed, did they?" Hillary said. "My husband is a doctor—you know that of course. But he couldn't tell me what was wrong with me."

"Now, dear, you know that's not true," said Gillespie. He turned to Marti. "Myalgic encephalomyelitis," he said.

"Two words for something nobody understands or can do anything about," Hillary said. "I scarcely got out of bed for five years. And now look at me."

Marti noticed the discomfort on her husband's face. "I think we can go," he said. "I just wanted the two of you to meet."

"Just a minute, Jim," Marti said. She turned back to the woman. "Hillary, do you mind if I examine you?"

"Examine me? How do you mean?"

"Actually, I just need you to sit in the chair here. I'll rest my hands on your shoulders for a bit."

Hillary snorted, continuing her efforts with the china. "What sort of examination is that?"

"I might ask you a few questions as well."

"You know, Doctor, I think I've had enough of that sort of thing. I'm not sick anymore."

"But I'd like to understand why," Marti said.

"I told you why. But fine. I'll be a patient. One last time. Then I hope you'll leave me alone."

The first thing Marti noticed as she entered into Hillary's second body was its dimness. Second bodies generated their own mysterious light. But Hillary's seemed to be shutting down. It had been cleaned out, like her china cabinet.

Marti moved down deeply into it, feeling a growing sense of unease. Normally people's second bodies, however light or dark, troubled or serene, had the teeming flux of a forest or a cloudy sky.

The residue of life and color that persisted here was in the process of being slowly eaten away by its only active component, a receding black curtain flecked with acrid foam. She knew where she had seen this before.

Corpses did not have second bodies. Hillary appeared to be on the way to being a corpse. Yet she was animate, and celebrating newfound health.

Marti descended further into the decaying space, toward what was deepest. Let it be there, she thought, please.

It was, but it wouldn't be for long. It was blackening, disappearing like a rotting foundation.

The Guardian's words came back to her. What had been knotted could be unraveled, could be untied. The black sickness was eating through Hillary's Milgram Knot.

Marti could sense the vast skein of the cosmos, of stars and atoms, of earth, air, fire, and water, the fabric that was at once physical and mysterious, to which the Knot had, until now, bound Hillary.

How could one detach from this ground of being and live? It was impossible, unless mortality was a gift from the same source as life itself.

The inner forms of Hillary's being were changing. It wasn't only that her second body was being dissolved. Her outer form meanwhile was hardening, crystallizing, turning from an inner process with an outer appearance to something fixed, like a photograph or a statue.

Mrs. Gillespie was being detached from illness, yes, but also from life. Yet, based on the interaction Marti had just had, the woman did not, in her mind, seem to recognize the process that was taking place, or at least see any problem with it. Perhaps her experience of relief at being freed from chronic illness overwhelmed all other considerations.

With that thought, Marti returned to the room. She withdrew her hands from Hillary's shoulders.

"Is that it?" the woman asked.

Marti nodded. "Thank you," she said.

"Why don't we go in the kitchen," Gillespie said. "I'll make some coffee."

∞

"I injected her nine days ago," Gillespie said. "I did it while she slept, didn't tell her anything."

"Injected her," said Marti dully.

"I told you. Project Secure Horizon." Gillespie swallowed his coffee. Marti looked down at her cup and shivered inwardly, remembering the bubbling, black liquid that had absorbed her saliva, the same substance that was absorbing Mrs. Gillespie's second body. All the horror that Marti had been holding at bay rushed toward her, a bubbling black liquid itself.

"Why would you do that?" Marti regretted blurting the words out even before the look of consternation roiled Gillespie's face.

"To help her!" he cried. "Don't you understand? Project Secure Horizon is a cure for disease. All disease."

"What?" said Marti. "No." Shaking her head.

"The flu. Chicken pox. Malaria. HIV. TB. Lyme's. God knows what else they threw at it. It won every round."

"But where did it come from? How long have they been testing it? When was it approved?"

"It's all happening really fast. Surely you can understand. Think about the implications of something like this. The end of disease! Harmon has a whole army of people working on it. The hardest thing is how exactly to monetize it, if it only requires a single dose... Anyway, we've just gotten approvals for the second stage clinical trial. I thought, why shouldn't Hillary be the first?"

"But Jim, you did it without her knowledge, let alone her informed consent!"

"Goddammit," he said, "what about my consent? Did anyone ask me if I wanted to be married to someone like that? Who went weeks without getting out of bed? Who moaned and slept and took pills and prayed and prayed some more. Who had contempt for me, because I, a doctor, couldn't help her?"

Marti nodded. She understood his pain, the pain of all those whose lives were shaped by illness. She wouldn't judge him. But she wondered what would happen when he realized that, if Hillary wasn't sick anymore, it wasn't true that she was well. To what extent was she still even Hillary? How stable was this new condition? What would happen when her second body, which had been partially eaten away, was fully gone?

She didn't dare share such questions with Gillespie. But she couldn't help ask, "And you haven't seen any other changes in her?"

"What do you mean? Of course, all sorts of changes. That's to be expected, no? She feels well, for the first time in a decade!"

She suddenly realized he needed affirmation from her if he was to move on to the next piece of the puzzle. "It's remarkable," she said.

"Isn't it? Think of it. A panacea. They don't want us to use that word. But it's going to change the face of medicine. Think of all the lives. Think of the increase in productivity." It was as if he sensed her doubts and needed to convince her.

"Astonishing," she said, and hoped she seemed merely dazed by the implications, rather than terrified by the prospect of a world full of people whose second bodies had been eaten away. She didn't understand what it would mean, but she doubted it was better than a world in which people suffered from illness.

Gillespie nodded. "Yes. That's why you needed to see this. So you can understand why what we are doing matters, even if it seems…unusual. At first, of course, I had concerns. But you know, all scientific breakthroughs came out of things that were once thought to be wrong, didn't they? Look at Galileo."

An edge of hysteria seemed to be prodding him now, the red ribbon of fear squeezing his words out as he tried to convince Marti and himself otherwise.

"But this isn't the main thing you wanted to show me," she said, worried that if she didn't move things along, she would blurt out something that would lose his trust.

"No. As I said, we need your help. But now you understand why it's so important."

∞

Back in the car, Gillespie continued his explanation.

"She—Violet—she's threatening to stop co-operating. To leave."

"I don't understand, though. Why is she central to the project?"

"I can't tell you that," said Gillespie. He looked over at her, with a gravity she hadn't seen in him before. "Trust me," he said, "you don't want to know."

But Marti did know, or thought she did.

"Harmon made a deal with her."

"Go on."

He looked at her, again that sickness of fear. "She is co-operating with us in exchange for a promise Harmon made."

"A promise to...?"

"Euthanize her."

"Euthanize—is she sick?"

"In a way. She thinks she is."

"But you're not going to."

He shook his head. "Of course not."

"Why not? It can't be a matter of ethics! I mean, you're lying to her about it."

"In the circumstances, I'll take responsibility for a white lie. But not for murder."

"Why does she want to see me?"

"She suspects we've been lying to her. She was threatening to leave. We just need another six months, then we'll have everything we need from her. She's desperate, I think, and she must have heard something about you from Dr. Stefanovic. He's the first one who saw her, you know."

Marti clenched her jaw at the further confirmation of her suspicions. The image of the ugly black bubbling specimen she had taken from Stef's desk came at her.

"So now you want me to come and lie for you."

Gillespie slammed the steering wheel. "Yes, goddammit! A lie is the smallest thing in the world! You don't think my wife's health, the health of millions of people, is worth a lie?"

His face a mottled red, Gillespie waited for her response, breathing heavily, as if he might explode any minute. She sensed the fear, and something like shame. It wasn't about something as small as one lie. It was about all the lies, about the ugly truth of what he wanted to unleash on the world, about being trapped between a worthy end and an unnatural means.

Marti regretted her comment, hoping she hadn't gone too far. Gillespie's question, it occurred to her, applied to her as well. Could she summon the same confidence in what she believed to be true? If so, he was the one she had to lie to.

"You're right," she said. "That was out of line."

Gillespie nodded, appearing ashamed of his loss of control. "Apology accepted," he said.

The car glided off the highway and into an area of large industrial parks.

28

At the gate house, a security guard checked Gillespie's ID and consulted a clipboard, then waved them through. Gillespie pulled the car into the staff parking lot. He turned off the ignition.

Marti looked at Gillespie, but he stared straight ahead and for a moment he made no move to exit the car. He took a deep breath. Finally he turned to her, flashed a forced smile, pulled something out of his pocket, and popped a breath candy into his mouth. He held the packet out to her and she took one without wanting it.

"Well," he said, "here we go."

The building was nondescript, a sprawling, bunker-like industrial complex. Marti followed Gillespie across the staff parking lot.

The entrance fronted on what looked like an office wing. An unobtrusive sign welcomed them to "Westgate Research Facility, Harmon Logistics." They passed through the door and arrived at another security point. Marti followed Gillespie in showing ID to one of the three guards on duty. He checked a monitor, nodded, and picked up a phone. "Dr. Gillespie and Dr. Powell are here," he said. Then, hanging up the phone, "Dr. Romano will be here in a few minutes."

While they waited he typed their names into a computer,

snapped photos, and printed out ID badges he attached to lanyards and handed them. The other guards alternated their attention between security monitors and this transaction, suggesting that part of their job was to observe the others.

Marti considered the dreariness of the waiting area. The only concessions to decor were some framed drawings of the undistinguished building's exterior, architectural renderings of the sort made to show clients what the finished structure would look like. It was as if to affirm that even when you were inside the building, you were outside it.

But of course, they were not really inside yet, they were on the threshold. A large set of frosted glass doors separated them from the rest of the building. After a loud buzz, one of the doors opened and a man and a woman came through.

"I'm sorry to keep you waiting," said the man, silver-haired and tired looking. He shook their hands. "I'm Dr. Romano, manager of psychological services, this is Ms. Oakland from client relations. Shall we?"

∞

The building was a maze of corridors. They passed offices, laboratories, conference rooms.

"We've given the whole of wing B, one of our residential wings, to the subject. We found she prefers to be alone, and it avoids...complications." Romano glanced at Gillespie as though he would understand the euphemism.

"Have you told her about Dr. Powell's visit?"

"Oh, yes," said Romano. "We're really glad you're here," he said to Marti. "It's going to be very reassuring for her."

They passed through the third set of fire doors. Each set required a pass-card swipe, provided by the woman, whose role seemed somewhere between escort and monitor.

"Let's go in here," Romano said, directing them into a small conference room. They sat down. The woman, Oakland, started a digital voice recorder. "Now we just need to make sure we're all on the same page. I gather Dr. Gillespie has briefed you about the situation, and you understand that our concern is to reassure the subject, that once her participation in our research trial is complete, we will be able to provide her with what she wants." He cleared his throat, reluctant to continue. "With her final exit."

Marti nodded. "Is she incapacitated?"

"No," said Romano, "as you will see she is fully mobile, has full cognition."

"So if all she wants is to die, what does she need us for? Why doesn't she just, I don't know, jump off a bridge?"

The others exchanged looks.

"I'm sorry if I'm being indelicate," Marti said. "But if you want me to be convincing, I need to understand the situation."

"Of course," said Romano, and she noticed the dark circles under his eyes. He had the look of one who was aging rapidly and prematurely. "I know it sounds, well, bizarre. But apparently, and trust me, we have verified this, the normal means of...fatality...don't seem to apply in her case."

"You're telling me she can't die?"

"I'm telling you that's what she believes. At first we were merely humoring her, assuming this was some sort of delusion. That was before her demonstration."

Romano stopped, looking down. Marti looked at the others, waiting for someone to elaborate.

"Demonstration?" she asked.

Finally, Romano nodded at Oakland. She switched on a monitor hanging on the wall, and typed on a wireless keyboard.

A video played on the monitor: grainy security camera footage. In it, Romano and two other staff members were seated across the table from a small figure. At first she was hunched over so that her face wasn't really visible. But then she looked up.

Marti recognized the face. Remembered seeing it for that one moment as she turned the lights on in the exam room she'd thought was empty, before Stef came through and closed the door.

As then, she was squinting, trying to avoid the light, while she spoke to someone off camera. The face was just as unsettling on camera, somehow lacking the subtle flickers of feeling motions that normally expressed themselves on the human visage. Like a cat, she thought.

"You're just pretending," the creature said.

"What do you mean?"

"You think I'm making this up."

"No, of course not, clearly you are quite sincere."

"You think I'm crazy."

"That's not a term we use."

Violet sneered. "No, you don't call anything by its real name, do you? You people think you are so clever."

She stood up and even on the grainy video Marti could see something terrifying in her look. Romano both on camera and in the room shrank back in his chair.

"I think that's enough for today," said the Romano in the security footage.

"You can die, though, can't you?" Violet said. "What do you think it would feel like? Do you want me to show you?" She started to push the heavy metal table that was between them aside.

Romano in the video took several steps back and pressed a buzzer on the wall. A moment later a security guard came in. "Please sit back down," Romano said to Violet, but she responded by moving toward him.

"No," she said, "I need to show you." Romano shrank back further and the guard came between them, motioning with a placatory gesture for Violet to calm down and sit. It seemed like everyone in the room was yelling at the same time, their voices distorted by the surveillance microphone or perhaps by their own panic.

For a moment Violet was frozen; at first Marti thought she was about to comply with the guard's instructions, but then the creature lunged forward with inhuman speed and grappled with the guard. The others fled the room amidst panicked shouting.

The camera zoomed in on Violet as she shoved the guard and sent him backward, dazed but still on his feet. She had something in her hand that wasn't there before, a pistol. As she raised it, the security guard lifted his hands and backed away.

But she didn't point the pistol at him. She pointed it directly at her own heart. And pulled the trigger.

The gun's explosion overloaded the audio track and made Marti and the others watching jump. Violet lurched backward, her arm flying out from the gun's recoil, her body twisting like a rag doll.

She struck the back wall of the room. But she didn't fall over. She staggered, regaining her footing, hunched over in what looked like pain, before finally standing up straight and throwing the gun down.

Oakland stopped the video and everyone was silent for a long moment.

"We examined her after," said Romano. "And examined the gun, which had been fully loaded. Powder burns on her clothing, a hole in her shirt, but no real bullet wound. Oh, we could see the point of impact, there was a nasty scar, actually, but it was disappearing as we watched. If I had been seeing it by myself I would not have believed it, but we all saw the same thing. By several hours later there was no sign of anything."

The silence in the windowless room, deep inside the antiseptic bunker, roared in Marti's ears. What she had seen was deeply disturbing, yet not entirely surprising. She realized the others were looking at her.

"So how are you going to do it?" Marti asked.

"Do it?"

"Kill her."

Romano blanched at the word. "We're working on that. But to be honest there is an argument going on about it. We've allowed her to believe that it's the entire focus of our research."

"But it's not," said Marti.

"You already know that," said Gillespie, irritated. "You understand what we're asking you to do, yes?"

"You want me to reassure her that our intentions are to fulfill her wishes."

"Can you do that? Yes or no."

Marti took a deep breath and nodded.

"I didn't hear that," said Gillespie, nodding toward the voice recorder.

"Yes."

Gillespie and Romano looked at one another, as if weighing the credibility of her answer.

"Good," said Romano. "Thank you. We realize it's a most unusual situation."

"One question, Dr. Powell," said Oakland, speaking for the first time. "Can you please disclose, what was your relationship with the subject? How does she know you?"

"I've never met her," said Marti. "As far as I know, she doesn't know me at all."

"Dr. Powell has quite a positive reputation in the Park," said Gillespie. "Our thinking is—"

"Yes, I know all that," said Oakland, cutting him off. "I was asking Dr. Powell." She was staring at Marti as if willing the truth out of her.

"What did she tell you?" Marti asked.

Romano chimed back in. "Very little. She referred to you as Dr. Marti. Said she had made a mistake and that you were the one she needed to see. Said if we didn't have you here soon she was going to leave." He raised his hands in a gesture of full disclosure, or helplessness, Marti wasn't sure which.

"Dr. Gillespie is right," said Marti. "She must have heard my name from other patients. That's what they called me."

Marti knew she needed to take control of the situation before she betrayed the extent of her doubts. "I think I understand what you need. And"—she nodded at Gillespie—"what is at stake. Any other instructions?" Her words brought a tang of curiosity and dread, but she willed her face to show only confidence.

∞

As they entered the conference room, the small figure was already sitting, waiting. Her head was down and her black hair fell forward, hiding her face.

"Violet?" said Romano. "This is Dr. Powell."

She looked up slowly. The face was exactly as Marti remembered it from that first glimpse in the exam room at the clinic, before Stef closed the door. Unmistakably aged, and yet unlined, as if untouched by experience. The eyes black, beady.

In addition to Romano, Gillespie and Oakland, there were three security guards in the room. One had come in with them, and two seemed to be Violet's escort.

"Can we be alone?" asked Marti.

"I'm not sure that's a good idea," said Romano. "We've instituted a protocol..."

"I'll be safe with you, won't I, Violet?" Marti said.

Violet nodded, a faint look of amusement at the question.

Romano looked at Oakland, who nodded slightly.

"Okay," said Romano. "But we'll watch from the other room." He gestured towards a security camera mounted on the ceiling. There was also a microphone resting on the table. "If there are any problems, just wave, we'll be in here in seconds."

"I'm sure it'll be okay," said Marti. She felt no such certainty, but she was sure that she needed to be alone with Violet.

Then the two were alone, sitting across the table from one another. Marti thought she could hear the vast building breathing.

Marti angled her body between the microphone and the camera, and then tore the audio cable away from the microphone. "I'd like to keep this conversation private. Is that alright with you?"

Violet leaned toward her and nodded, pleased.

"Good. How are they treating you here?" Marti said.

Violet gave a weak shrug of her shoulders, as though it wasn't something she could think about.

"But you wanted to see me," Marti said. "Why?"

"I think," said Violet in a normal tone of voice, then paused to clear her throat and continued in a whisper, "I think I made a mistake. I think they don't really want to help."

"I can try to answer your questions about that," said Marti. "Will you answer some questions for me?"

Violet didn't answer for a long moment. Then she said, "Maybe."

The door opened and Gillespie entered, accompanied by two guards.

"Marti," he said, "You need to hold on, there's a problem." The guard was examining the microphone.

"Get your hands off that!" Violet barked at the guard, who stopped, looked at her for a moment, then at Gillespie.

Violet smiled, a cold, intimidating leer. "There's no problem," she said.

Their fear was palpable. Both guards were looking at Gillespie, waiting for instructions, but he seemed to be frozen.

"It's okay, Jim," said Marti. "I will report after."

"But we need a recording," said Gillespie.

"Can we talk outside?"

Outside the room she tore into him. "You need to let me do this my way, if you want any results."

"It's not about your way, or my way," he said. "We're dealing with something much bigger here."

"I know what we're dealing with. I want her to feel like I'm on her side and she can tell me whatever she wants. I want to be able to give you a useful report. What about that do you not get?"

Gillespie looked over at Oakland, who was standing with arms crossed. She shook her head almost imperceptibly.

"We can't take the risk," Gillespie said to Marti.

"Fine," said Marti. "And I don't work for you any more, remember? I've wasted enough time. I'd like you to take me home."

Romano had been standing with his head leaning back against the wall, as if he were asleep. But now he spoke. "No. We'll do it your way." Oakland opened her mouth, about to argue with him. He turned to her and snapped, "I'll take responsibility."

"This is a mistake," said Oakland as Romano gestured Marti back into the room.

Marti sat back down in the chair. Violet hadn't moved.

"You can see why I don't trust them," said Violet, in a normal tone of voice. "They don't mean well."

"Oh, no, that's not true," said Marti, "not at all. They mean well. How often have they been withdrawing blood?

That's what they're doing, right?"

"Three times a day," said Violet. "More each time. They say they need more before they can help. But the help never comes."

"And help means, helping you die?"

Violet nodded.

Marti touched Violet's forearm. It was an instinctive gesture of comfort, but Marti felt all the comfort drain out of her. A terrible nausea poured into her, a black bubbling vertigo that seemed to come from inside Violet. The woman, the creature, whatever she was, had no second body.

The horror of the situation closed in on Marti. That if Harmon had its way, all of humanity would carry in its veins the blood of this living dead creature. Was this the ultimate object of humanity's quest to gain control, to free itself from nature? That it would cease to be human? Perhaps free from illness, even immortal, but no longer alive?

She knew what she had to do.

"But they won't help you die," she said.

"They won't," Violet repeated dully, a sort of question.

"Please," Marti whispered. "I want you to smile and act like I'm reassuring you. They mustn't know I've told you the truth."

Violet nodded slowly.

"The truth," said Marti, "is this: they want to keep you alive because they want your blood. They want to take and take and they will never stop."

Violet closed her eyes and turned away, but then, perhaps remembering Marti's plea to disguise her reaction, turned to her and nodded once more. Somewhere far behind the expressionless eyes, Marti could sense a burning rage.

"You must leave here, as soon as you can. But don't tell them why. Simply withdraw your consent and leave, and don't come back. Do you understand?"

Violet nodded once more, cold and implacable.

"I've answered your question truthfully," said Marti. "Now, will you answer some for me?"

"Maybe," said Violet.

"Why did you want to talk to me? How did you know who I am?"

"You're a doctor in the Park."

"That's all?"

Violet shrugged.

"What are you? Where do you come from?"

"I am nothing," said Violet. "That is all."

"Do you know Stride?" asked Marti.

"I don't know anything," said Violet.

∞

Afterward, Marti was noncommittal.

"I tried my best," she told Gillespie and the others. "I think she'll be okay now." She felt nothing about the need to lie to them in order to tell Violet the truth.

"That's good," said Gillespie, but she could see the worry in his second body. We're both worried, she realized.

29

Violet had known they were going to be angry. She still hoped that if she was sufficiently contrite, she could avoid punishment. She rehearsed her speech. She had to leave the clinic. The humans were not going to help them. They had tried to keep her locked up.

It had felt good to escape. She almost felt alive. Perhaps it was a feeling in the blood that was smeared on her body, the blood of those who had tried to stop her departure.

The door unlocked and Nerves came in, supported by Benz. Nerves couldn't stand up on her own any more.

"If it was up to me," said Nerves, "your punishment would be burial."

Violet shivered, even though Nerves' phrasing suggested that this most dire punishment would not be imposed. For her kind, burial would be a cruel parody, since being trapped underground still offered no end.

"But they weren't going to help us," Violet blurted out.

Nerves's lip curled. She reached up to Violet and grabbed a hank of her limp hair.

"Are you saying The Maker was lying?"

"No! I don't know! Maybe you misunderstood his instructions." Shut up, she told herself. This isn't going to help.

Nerves released Violet's hair and gave her a blow across

the face, hard enough to knock her down.

"Get up," said Nerves. "You're lucky. This is your lucky day."

Violet got up slowly, confused by Nerves's shift in tone.

"We've heard from The Maker."

"What?" Violet rubbed her head.

"The Maker is here. In the Park."

"I thought you said he spoke to you only, like, you know, from a burning bush or something like that."

"He is in the flesh now."

"You're not lying?"

"He knows about what you did."

"Is he angry?" asked Violet.

"He says it is part of his plan."

"What?" Violet was even more confused. "Then why did you hit me?"

"Because you didn't know that, did you? You were still disobeying me."

"Where is he then? When will he come?"

"There is something he wants from us. Someone."

Violet nodded, eager to hear more.

∞

Marti woke up suddenly. It was still dark.

She had slept poorly, troubled by dreams through which Violet's empty eyes stared out at her.

I've turned something loose, she thought. While at Westgate, she'd been preoccupied with throwing a monkey wrench into their machine. She wondered if they would actually let Violet go. Or if they would be able to stop her.

And once she was loose? I should have persisted for some answers, she thought. Then at least I would have gained something.

She brought to mind the horror of Hillary Gillespie's unraveled Milgram Knot. The horror of an individual human life coming unmoored from its own enfolded pattern of growth. Multiply that by ten, by a hundred, by a billion.

She groaned, recognizing the layers of faith required, how impossible it would be to explain this to anyone.

Marti pulled the covers over her head, wanting the thoughts to go away. But something was prickling under her skin.

Then the phone rang.

The shrill electronic bleat made her jump, and she grabbed the receiver without thinking, wanting only for it not to ring again.

"Hello?"

"You fucking bitch!"

"What?"

"Do you have any idea what you've done?" It was Gillespie. "Any idea at all?"

"Jim?"

For a long moment, all she could hear was his breathing.

"I don't know why I'm calling you. I should just leave you to them."

"Them?"

"Do you think they're going to let you get away with this? They're on their way right now. Just thought you should know. And it's your doing, not mine! The blood is not on my hands."

She heard the dial tone before she realized he'd hung up.

On their way right now. Marti stared at the phone, still in her hand, for a long moment. The floor had gone out from under her. How had she not seriously considered that Harmon's security apparatus—she felt certain it's what Gillespie was referring to—would come after her for her betrayal?

While she tried to collect her thoughts, her body was already moving. She grabbed a daypack and stuffed it with a few essentials. Then she was out the door.

On her motorcycle, she was surprised to find herself heading toward the Park. But the impulse was strong, and her relief at feeling a sense of direction was so great she decided to trust it. It was only as she entered the Park that she realized what was drawing her here.

∞

When Marti arrived outside the clinic, it was still well before opening. She was uneasy with the risk of appearing here. But she wanted to find Violet, and she sensed that Violet had returned here to the Park.

Still straddling her motorcycle, she took a breath and reached inside herself for clarity.

She felt the gentle touch on her arm while her eyes were still closed.

"Dr. Powell?" The voice radiated concern.

Marti opened her eyes. For a moment, she couldn't remember who he was. This often happened when she saw her patients in the street: a type of deep familiarity that was unattached to names.

"What are you doing here?" he asked. Marti wasn't sure how to answer. It had been her place of employment, but that wasn't why she was here. Then she remembered who this was: the father of the small child she had treated only the day before.

"How is your little girl?" Marti asked.

"You must come with me," he said, his soft voice belying the insistence of his assertion.

At first she thought he meant the girl needed help again, but he showed none of the helpless desperation she'd seen before. Then he quickly said, "The fever is gone. You gave us a miracle. But now it is my turn to help you."

He lived in one of the towers nearby. He escorted her with an arm protectively around her, doing his best to discreetly hide her face from anyone they passed. She didn't question his actions. As they rode in the elevator, he explained what had happened.

"I wake up a few hours ago," he said, struggling to find English words. "Watching my girl sleeping, for long time. I am very happy. Just seeing her sleep. So I do not know why, I turn on the television. That's when I see you. It made me worried. I went for a walk. Also to thank God for my happiness of my daughter. Not expecting to see you. But when I saw you, I knew God wanted me to help you."

His broken English left Marti wondering how much she had understood correctly. He had seen her on TV? And did he really have to bring God into it? Before she had become a Coil, she had considered herself an agnostic, which she thought of as atheism with humility. It seemed apparent that God was nowhere, except in people's thoughts. Now, it seemed that God was absolutely everywhere, and yet in some strange way, that amounted to the same thing. A mystery.

The elevator doors opened, and he guided her to his apartment.

He had told her his name, Eugenio. His wife, Sara, her eyes still sleepy, made instant coffee, offering it to Marti with such love that it seemed a refined libation.

Eugenio turned the TV on. The news channel cycled through its mixture of disasters, scandals, tragedies: stories harvested from the world, purified like a drug. And then, between the Russian oligarchs and Hollywood celebrities and suspected abusers and victims of circumstance, her photo appeared. She was "wanted for questioning in a suspected case of domestic terrorism, involving at least three deaths."

Three deaths! Marti felt her stomach heave, and for a moment she thought she would vomit. She dropped into a chair and tried to concentrate on the TV.

The story was being treated as a major news item, thanks

to the multiple narrative hooks. Terrorism. Disgrace. Murder. Secrets.

Secrets. That at least was accurate. The truth of the situation was even more explosive and disturbing than the fabricated narrative. It was as though they had to invent an illusion that was sufficiently dark to satisfy the viewers, but light enough to fly over the real threat.

A spokesman for Harmon suggested that Marti was "troubled," her strange behavior already under scrutiny.

Also shown was a photo of Violet, identified as the perpetrator of the murders, no doubt in an escape from the facility, though nothing was said about that. Viewers were warned that she should be considered "extremely dangerous."

"No," said Eugenio, "terrorista? This is a lie, no?"

Marti sighed and nodded. "Of course, Eugenio. I need to find that one, though," said Marti, indicating Violet's picture.

"Her? Who is she?" he asked.

"I think it's better if you don't know," Marti said. She got up shakily, intending to go. Again she felt a wave of nausea, and her legs went wobbly.

"Wait," said Eugenio. "Wait." He motioned emphatically, then guided her back to the threadbare couch.

He said something to his wife in a language Marti didn't know. She replied, apparently agreeing with him. She went to her bag and brought back a phone.

Phone in hand, Eugenio hesitated for a moment, then took a breath and dialed.

30

"Doctor?"

Marti awoke to Sara gently squeezing her shoulder. As she was falling asleep, she'd realized she needed to turn herself in to the authorities. But she didn't feel ready. She didn't feel ready to wake up.

She sat up, groggy. Two other men were in the room now.

"They are here to take you," said Eugenio.

"What? Where?" asked Marti.

Eugenio looked uneasily at the men. One was large and fit, muscles poured inside a battered leather jacket that was too tight to zip up. He looked around fifty, thick black hair, olive skin, and intelligent eyes. His black-skinned companion was younger, dressed incongruously in a mechanic's overalls with the name "Rick" sewn on. He was even bigger; she practically had to crane her neck to see his face. He was looking away, as if only his body was there.

"They help," Eugenio said. "Friends."

Marti thought the men did not look friendly. But she sensed only good will, in spite of their impassive faces. And a check of their second bodies showed nothing alarming.

"Please," said the one in the leather jacket, "I am Yannio. This is Pik-Lasel. You will be safe with us." He held out his hand and pulled her up off the couch.

∞

The car was an old, but spotless, BMW sedan. Pik-Lasel held open the door for her, then got in the back with her while Yannis got in the driver's seat. They explained that the blindfold was for her own protection.

Yannis scanned the radio until he found some easy listening. He played it at a soft volume while the car moved slowly, making frequent turns. She had the impression they weren't going any great distance; if they were staying in the Park, as seemed likely, the driving was merely a way to conceal their destination, since nothing in the Park was very far.

"Who else is interested in you?" Yannis asked. "Besides the police."

"What do you mean?"

He gestured into the rear view mirror. "They've been following since I picked you up."

"But not the police?"

"I don't think so. And they're staying back. Someone wants to know where you're going."

Marti wanted to take off the blindfold and look, but she thought better of it. Suddenly she felt the car make a sudden swerve and then accelerate, apparently ramping onto a freeway. The car was filled with a tense silence while Yannis continued the evasive maneuvers. Finally they pulled over and waited.

"Clear," said Yannis. "But keep your eye out for them," he said to his silent companion.

Then he resumed driving at a more relaxed pace.

∞

The blindfold only came off after they had parked, ridden up an elevator, and entered an apartment.

Marti looked around. She was in a kitchen. The blinds were drawn so one couldn't see outside. The size of the room was impossibly large for the Park, where the kitchens were invariably galley-sized, but Marti recognized certain features as typical of the buildings. It appeared that a wall had been knocked down to enlarge the kitchen. The room was intricately and artistically painted with rich colors; granite countertops and a large stainless steel stove gave the place a lavishness that was incongruous in the Park, but it had the feeling of having been done a piece at a time. A bunch of unused kitchen gadgets were cluttered in the corner. Large steel bowls of prepared food, covered in plastic wrap, were spread across one counter.

A hefty Arabic woman in her seventies, dressed in black, presented her with some tea. Yannis said, "This is Laurette," and the old woman smiled and nodded at Marti. She put a plate in front of her, piled with food. The assumption that she would be hungry was correct; Marti was ravenous. Still, for a moment she was about to refuse the food, feeling too uneasy to accept it. But Laurette motioned to her to eat.

Marti complied. The food was delicious. Laurette smiled maternally, apparently satisfied to see her food being consumed with enthusiasm.

Marti finished, indicating her gratitude. Yannis was back and now he escorted her out of the room.

She followed Yannis through the apartment. Again, while some fixtures and details suggested the Park, the layout was strange to her. It appeared someone had knocked down walls between several apartments and rebuilt them into a new, redesigned space. The decor was had a Mediterranean flavor. Walls had been papered with rich fabrics, and the place had the feel of a desert-tent interior.

Yannis brought Marti to sit in a comfortable wing chair, in a small, book-lined room. Left alone here, she took the moment to study the shelves. Many of the titles were in Arabic, but some were in English, and among those she recognized a variety on medical topics, including some out-of-date physician reference volumes. Most of the books, however, which she now realized were in at least four different languages, were works of literature.

She heard the door open. For a long moment she felt someone hovering behind her. Finally he moved into the room and came to stand in front of her, a compactly built man she guessed to be in his early fifties. He held out his hands in a gesture of greeting and she stood up. He took her hand in both of his as if she were an old friend, and she felt instantly comfortable. And yet, she saw that this was a man who could easily inspire fear. A scar ran across his face. He was largely bald, his remaining hair gray and close-cropped, emphasizing the powerful shape of his head. He wore wire-framed glasses. His eyes were blue, which seemed surprising given the dusky color of his skin. His clothing was comfortable but elegant.

His second body intrigued her. There was something majestic about it. But the power had a fearsome aspect. This was a man who had crushed weakness, in himself and in others. A man of strength.

He looked her up and down.

"So you are the doctor," he said.

"I'm Marti Powell."

"I am Qais." The name rhymed with "ice," but though he was intimidating, there was nothing cold about him.

"I know all about the good work you have been doing, helping the people in the Park. Dr. Marti, they call you. I have heard their stories."

Marti wasn't sure what she'd expected, but to be greeted as a celebrity wasn't it. She felt her anxiety soften in the presence of the man's genuine warmth.

"I am sure this does not surprise you," he said. "That people speak of you and what you have done for them."

"I encourage them not to," she said.

"You are wise," he said. "But they know they can trust me with secrets. Let's sit over here."

He led her to a couch. As they sat down, Laurette brought in some tea and placed it on a low table.

"Thank you, Auntie," said Qais.

"Now," he said, turning to Marti. "You are in trouble. I have seen the news stories. You must tell me how I can help."

Marti took a breath and weighed the offer. "Why do you want to help me?"

"I care about the people here in the Park. They have few allies. You are one. Which makes me your ally."

Marti nodded. She was studying Qais' second body as he spoke and felt reassured by what she saw.

"I'm looking for someone," she said.

"Yes, go on."

"She looks like an old woman. But she's not ordinary. An unlined face. Her hair a reddish black. Her eyes are frightening, no color in them at all. She goes by the name of Violet."

Marti couldn't tell from Qais's reaction whether he knew anything about Violet or not. He looked at her for a long moment without saying anything, then looked away.

Finally he spoke. "I would not think that you are someone who needs to be told that there are places in this world it is better not to go."

"I'm afraid it's too late for that," said Marti. She felt a momentary chill. She wondered if she was now living her whole life in those places. But she felt nothing compelling about the safer country of the past.

Qais's eyes were scrutinizing her carefully. He nodded slowly.

"They are very powerful," he said. "But perhaps you have the power to face them."

"They?"

"How much do you know about her?" Qais asked.

Marti told him what she knew about Violet, including the use Harmon had been making of her, and of the panacea they were intending to bring to market.

"This is indeed strange," said Qais. "That they would be working together with Harmon."

"What is she?" asked Marti. "And what do you mean, 'they'?"

"There are three of them in the Park," he said. "Los Olvidados. One of my men gave them that name. The Forgotten Ones."

She waited for him to continue, hoping he would tell her more.

"We do not disturb them," he said. "It is a kind of agreement. You see, it is my responsibility to know what goes on in the Park. Many people depend on me. So when the deaths started, and the police did nothing, my organization sought the cause."

"Deaths?" said Marti. "When was this?"

"About two years ago. They must have moved in then. Three of them."

He paused, looked away, something suddenly grieving him.

"I lost some men I cared very much about. Husbands and fathers. These creatures will kill without hesitation. As you also know, they cannot themselves be killed. Though it seems it is their deepest wish.

"They are strong. But with enough men, they can be overpowered. And we did that. We knew we could not kill them, but we prepared them a grave, in the basement of one of the buildings, with enough concrete to entomb them forever."

"And—?"

"I learned long ago that a powerful ally is of much greater value than a dead enemy. I made them an offer. We would not condemn them to a living death more confined and tortured than that which they already endured. They could remain in the Park. But they could not kill. Not without our permission."

He emphasized the last word, and Marti understood what was unsaid. That he would use them, when needed, for this purpose.

"Where did they come from?" asked Marti.

Qais sighed and stood up, moved to the window, and parted the heavy curtains to look out.

"We do not know their story," he said. "There is much that shares this earth with us that we do not know, though we have convinced ourselves otherwise."

Marti remembered how it felt to believe otherwise. Before the whole world seemed like an undiscovered country.

"Where I can find them?"

"If I tell you," he said, "if I have you taken there, what will you do?"

She could see he was weighing how much to help her. But for a long moment she had no answer. Then she felt words rising up in her.

"I am like them," she said. She could see he was as surprised as she by her reply. How could she compare herself to these creatures? As if answering her own question, she continued, "I'm not one of them. But I feel they have an answer: to the mystery of what I've become. Maybe I also have an answer for them. I don't understand this, but it's what I feel."

She saw a tremor of fear pass through the powerful man in front of her.

"Do you have this much courage?" he said, "to go and face them with that kind of openness?"

Was it courage, she wondered? How like foolishness

courage could look! "I don't know," she said. "I just know I have to do it."

"And what about your own legal status? How long will you be a fugitive? My protection only extends so far."

To that, she had no answer.

31

It was the most desolate spot in the Park. Marti wondered who had been the first one to decide this was a good place to abandon things. Gutted televisions, rusted tricycles, a sofa weathered down to its frame, a filing cabinet without drawers. Harmon handled garbage collection in the Park, but large objects had to be brought to a pickup station on the perimeter. Perhaps initially the objects had been randomly dropped; now they were stacked up, crowding a space that had once been a small plaza in front of a dry cleaner's and several other shops. All were now securely blanketed in plywood.

An area so devoid of human presence was an anomaly in the Park. It would have seemed a perfect location for drug dealing or other activities that preferred shadow. But Qais had explained that the spot was widely regarded as a no-man's land. Rumors of the lost ones had created an informal zone of exclusion.

To her surprise, though, here in this end-of-the-world landscape Marti sensed something alive.

Weeds were growing everywhere, forcing their way through cracks in the concrete, around the detritus. She was intrigued to notice among them large clusters of goldenrod, its vibrancy indifferent to the atmosphere of ruin. Marti chuckled at the absurdity of thinking of any plant as a weed in an environment like this. Here they were the earth reclaiming itself. Perhaps this was the appeal of the idea of the end of the world: a revelation of life's indomitable continuity.

It took a moment for her to realize why the goldenrod's presence struck her so forcefully. It was among a cluster of these plants at Dave's she had encountered the Elemental being. She took a step toward the plants and imagined that she felt something of the being's warm concern.

Yannis had dropped her off nearby, after explaining that Qais did not want Los Olvidados to know that he or his organization had anything to do with Marti finding them. That was fine with Marti, but as the car drove off she wondered if it was such a good idea. The next moment she realized she was more worried that she might not find Violet at all.

Embedded within the hoarding was a door, not immediately evident; she had been told to look for it. It had once been padlocked but the latch was smashed off. As she approached, a smell of urine assaulted her nostrils, deepening her animal unease, her sense she was trespassing.

Marti reached around the base of the door and found the latch Yannis had described. She made several tries before it opened, with a loud noise. As the door opened, Marti toppled forward and went sprawling on a filthy tile floor. Her heart was beating wildly, her vulnerable position raising her feeling of certainty that something was about to pounce.

But she was alone.

Her eyes slowly adjusted in the dark space. Narrow shafts of light, piercing through gaps in the plywood, were clouded with particles of dirt stirred up by her entrance.

Marti stood up slowly, inwardly scolding her fear. Sooner or later her presence would become known. Yannis had given her a password she was to shout on entering. Jerusalem. She formed the word with her mind, then her mouth, but withheld her voice. It wasn't fear, but a plan forming itself. She needed to summon confidence.

The ruined space, the former dry cleaner, now seemed like an underwater world. The counter remained, and a bashed-in cash register. Moisture had corroded everything. The back wall was mostly gone. The space beyond, cluttered with the mobile hanging mechanism and remains of the dry cleaning machinery, fell off into darkness.

Marti moved forward. She touched the flashlight, given to her by Yannis, in her pocket. She would wait until she really needed it.

As she secured her confidence, Marti glimpsed some trailing lights out of the corner of her eye. She turned her head toward them. They remained on the periphery of her vision, in spite of their movement, which was a curving in on themselves.

For a moment she told herself it was some sort of artifact of the darkness, but the phenomenon persisted, and Marti became aware of a heat in her chest in response to the lights. She had seen them before, but never with her eyes open. The hosts.

The lights did not illuminate the space but gave her a direction to follow, and she found that as long as she moved slowly enough they led precisely through the maze of looming machinery in the back room.

Marti's movement took her deeper into darkness. She was still silently saying the word "Jerusalem," as if ready at any moment to say it aloud. Abruptly, the lights ceased their forward movement and hovered. Marti obediently stopped and became aware that she had been approaching some sort of edge in the space before her. She looked down and saw that a few steps ahead, the floor simply disappeared.

She gasped, then held her breath. In the silence she heard

distant voices. They were raised in anger, a man's voice and a woman's voice, but she couldn't quite make out the words. Finally, something was smacked down or thrown, and angry footsteps below grew louder, moving toward her. Marti took several steps backward. The lights were gone now, and she was alone in the darkness, her own breath like a deafening wind.

"You're being childish," a voice shouted, and Marti was fairly sure it was Violet's, down below her somewhere in the darkness.

"You treat me like a child," a man's voice replied from closer to her, and she felt a current of fear rise up her spine. She wasn't sure her confidence extended beyond a confrontation with Violet, who after all owed her freedom to Marti. But the male voice was now between them, and moving closer. She heard the sound of his feet scraping on the metal, the rattle of metal against concrete. He was climbing a ladder below her and getting closer.

Marti backed against the wall, as far from the sound as she could get, hoping he would go past her. The rising footsteps drew closer. Now she wanted to flee, but it was too late. She was soaked with sweat.

She heard him clamber off the ladder mere feet away from her. For a moment it seemed he was going to pass right by her. He did go past, but then stopped. He stood for a long moment, as if debating.

Then he turned around, took a step toward her, and reached out to grab her. Marti could only see a silhouette. She couldn't bear the darkness any more. As if of its own accord, her hand yanked out the flashlight, and as the man seized hold of her she turned on the light.

One long frozen moment joined them both in horror. He was a creature like Violet, but that did not account for how familiar he looked. In spite of the pale, unlined skin, the colorless eyes, in the moment before he brought his arm up, flailing, to protect his eyes, she recognized the features.

It was Stride.

32

A moment before, she had been desperate to flee, but now she was chasing him. With a cry he fled through the door and away from the light.

Marti burst out through the plywood door right behind him. Before he'd gone more than ten steps he tripped and fell, and she was on top of him.

"Wait!" she cried, as he flailed wildly. She could feel his strength, way too much for her. The advantage of gravity would not suffice for long. She tried the password: "Jerusalem!"

Surprised, he ceased struggling. "What do you want?"

"I—I've been looking for you," she said, which was not quite right. "I've been missing you."

"Me?" he said, his lips curling skeptically. The golden light in his eyes had been replaced by a void. She saw that he'd cut his forehead when he fell, and a fluid was streaming out. Bubbly. Black.

"I'm so sorry," she said, "I'm sorry I left you."

His face betrayed no recognition, but she thought she saw a flicker of curiosity. The cut on his forehead slowly closed, like a mouth, and then was gone.

Impulsively, desperately, she leaned in and kissed him. She wanted to draw back all that had been lost, awaken within him the Stride who had loved her. If their separation had done this to him, then maybe her feeling for him, her love, could restore his light.

But it was like kissing a corpse. She shivered and pulled away.

He met the look of horror on her face with one of utter confusion, as if the act of pressing her lips to his were inexplicable, and her reaction as much so. He remained frozen there.

"I have to go," he said.

"No," she said. "Please."

He started to get up, but she grabbed hold of him. He thrashed away from her, but she held on tighter.

She didn't see what it was he hit her with, just felt the blow against her head that caused an explosion of stars. Then the ground came up toward her and Stride tore loose and was gone.

For a long moment Marti couldn't move at all, as though her mind and body had been thrown in different directions. Someone was reaching down toward her from a distance, trying to help her up. For a moment she thought it must be Stride, but as the face came more clear, she saw that it was Ursula. On her face, a look of love and concern. But then Marti opened her eyes and she was alone.

Slowly she sat up. Her ears were ringing. She tasted the salty-sweet tang of her own blood, her face was sticky with it. She tried to stand up, but her sense of balance had abandoned her, and she quickly toppled over.

A familiar green crowded her field of vision. She lay on the ground at the foot of goldenrod plants. For a moment she thought she was back at Dave's, either had never left or had returned without remembering it.

"You have courage, my pet! But you're not done yet."

"What?" Marti recognized the voice. So she was at

Dave's after all. The face was in front of her, peeking between the dark green stalks, glimmering at her through its camouflage. "Please," she said, "tell me what I can do."

"Each threshold you cross in some ways is a loss, but each new possibility brings responsibility."

"I mean Stride. He's become something horrible."

"So we'll tell you once more: you must rectify him, for sure."

"I don't know what that means."

"There's no home for the heart when flesh and spirit are apart. But no more to discuss; you must bring him to us."

Marti saw a set of great stone doors. Stride, his form made of streaming light. The light burned Marti's eyes.

"How?" she asked, but no answer came. She was alone.

Bring him to the Elemental. That was clear. "Spirit" was the Stride made of light, before—and after—he took on human form. "Flesh" was the part of him left behind, the horror she had just encountered. Which "him" did they mean?

When she sat up, she knew whom she had to go see.

∞

Dave threw down the brush and wiped his hands with turpentine. Refinishing the cabinet had been a job he was looking forward to. Working alone, in his small shop, doing things with his hands, this was his happy place.

But today he was treating it as a distraction. Maybe he should have gone into work after all.

He'd waited a whole day. He'd lain awake in bed, still believing that she would return any minute. Maybe he just needed to fall asleep first. But sleep was equally elusive.

In the morning he dragged himself out of bed but couldn't get himself to leave. What if she returned while he was gone? He knew she wouldn't show up at the clinic, and he doubted he'd be able to concentrate on the day's demands.

So he called in sick, something he almost never did. And

in a way, he was. The strange perceptual distortions that began during their lovemaking had diminished somewhat but did not disappear.

After a morning spent looking out at the driveway every few minutes, Dave decided he'd better find something to do. But now, as he forced himself to clean up his materials, he began to notice a feeling that there was something else he really needed to do. Something had woken up in him, with its own purpose.

∞

Marti rang the bell a second time and shivered as she stood on the doorstep. She felt as though something cold had entered into her when she'd kissed Stride. Her head continued to throb. She checked the handkerchief she had been holding against the cut on her forehead and was relieved to see there was no fresh blood.

After a long moment, the door opened.

"Marti!" It was Murdoch, elfin and red-haired, who'd been part of the team that rescued her. It seemed like a lifetime ago. Before Marti could say anything, Murdoch grabbed her into a tight hug.

"So you heard?" asked Murdoch.

"What? I have to talk to Ursula. What happened?"

"A stroke. A few days ago."

Marti's knees went weak, her stomach lurching up towards her throat. Murdoch helped her to the couch.

"We didn't know how to get in touch with you."

"Is she—?"

"In the hospital. Critical care. They actually can't understand how she's holding on, given the extent of the damage. I was just going to visit—her family are there but they need a break."

"I'm coming with you," Marti said.

∞

They drove in Murdoch's van.

After a while, Murdoch said, "It wasn't just some stupid stroke."

"What do you mean?"

"I mean whatever did that to Ursula wasn't just her body."

"Go on."

"You know, what happened to you when you were trying to come back to Ursula's? When Stride disappeared?"

Marti nodded.

"Okay. We knew that it was unlikely that it was just some random fucking attack. This neither. The same... thing...was behind both events."

"Oh, great. So now we have a devil, to go along with the angels?"

Murdoch smiled wanly. "I spoke with some others and learned more. We call it an Ampsy."

"Ampsy?"

"Accumulation of Mass Psychic Energy. Something happens, either a single event, or a series of events. Say a huge earthquake, or a war. It sets in motion a huge wave of human energy, generates a widespread collective reaction of fear or aversion or hatred. This energy can become a giant thing with its own consciousness, its own wants."

"A minion," said Marti.

Murdoch looked at her. "A what?"

"Never mind, go on."

"Normally, these things bounce around for a while, whipping up all sorts of shit, dread and anxiety mostly, among susceptible people. But they're inherently unstable and prone to dissipate."

"And that doesn't always happen?"

"There's another factor," said Murdoch.

"Which is?"

"The Ampsy can be a source of power. In a way, I guess it is like a devil. You've heard stories of people summoning demons, that kind of black magic shit?"

"Yes, okay. So you're telling me that's real too."

Murdoch looked at her and sighed. "Depends what you mean by 'real.' All those stories about the devil, those are allegories. It's all about power. Nowadays, we believe only in social forms of power, money, shit like that. In other times, social power only got you so much, and people wanted more. They figured out they could harness an Ampsy—entrap it—and use it for their own ends, as a kind of energy source. Leaders and non-state assholes causing wars and other terrifying shit might even deliberately create an Ampsy that can increase their own power. That's the usefulness of terror for those who wish to influence events."

Murdoch accelerated to beat a red light and swerved to avoid a left-turning truck.

"Eventually, of course, those perpetrators die. Some of them believe that they will take this power with them. But the joke's on them. Fuckheads. They thought they were using the Ampsy, but the Ampsy was using them, and it goes on."

"Forever?"

"That old magician Newton said that energy can neither be created nor destroyed, it can only be transformed. But it can be transformed. We are dealing with a particularly virulent Ampsy, pursuing a plan to undermine the Partnership. And it is not done coming for you."

Marti nodded. She'd experienced a series of reactions to Murdoch's explanation. The scale of it seemed absurd. At the clinic, she had greeted every day with a mixture of gratitude for the challenging opportunity to make a difference in her patients' lives, and a terror that she would not be up to it. But now, how could she calculate the stakes and the challenges? As she tried to grasp the situation she felt a painful ache, and then she let go. She wouldn't try to grasp it; she would let it grasp her.

33

The hospital corridors had a familiar smell, a mixture of sour and sweet, of chemicals and body fluids.

Murdoch led Marti to the critical care unit, a series of large rooms, each holding six patients, around a central station. Murdoch stopped in front of one. Through the window, the patients in their beds were barely visible amid clusters of machinery.

Time had slowed down here; it was measured out in the steady beeps of electronic monitors that offered the only sign of life. Marti took a deep breath. Events had increasingly outstripped her ability to process them.

Only one visitor was allowed at a time. Marti donned a robe and mask and entered the inner sanctum.

Ursula's face was a fragile mask beneath the apparatus that was bringing her oxygen. A welling tide of feeling roared up in Marti, too wild to name. She seemed to be persistently heading in the wrong direction. Why had she not come to see Ursula before?

She took Ursula's right hand in hers. It was cool. No, thought Marti, maybe now is the perfect moment. Maybe I can help where the machines cannot.

She moved her awareness into Ursula's second body. The descent was difficult, an entrance into a cramped space. As

Marti gained her bearings she found that the second body was distended away from Ursula's physical body, held to it by only a narrow band, like a boat that had drifted away from shore. The band was grounded to the physical body at her Milgram Knot.

If she could pull the whole thing back in, maybe it would bring Ursula back from the brink. She grabbed hold of the connecting band and began trying to pull the second body back down toward the physical. At first it seemed she might succeed. But as the two bodies drew closer, she experienced an increasing resistance, until it was beyond her strength to continue. She tried holding on, but now it was the tethered second body pulling her away with it. A primal current of fear ran through her. Her physical body reacted with panic as though she might be torn away from herself, and she let go. Ursula's second body slipped fully back to the end of its tether, which had only grown longer and more tenuous as a result of Marti's efforts.

Marti wondered if what she was attempting was a violation, an inability to let go of someone whose time had come. But she felt a renewed sense that there was a task for her here, that Ursula needed her help.

She turned her attention to the Milgram Knot, the one part of Ursula's second body that hadn't come detached. She pondered the strange geography. If Ursula was at the boundary between life and death, and the Milgram Knot, as seemed to be the case, was the connection to the realm beyond, why was Ursula's second body straining upward and away, in the opposite direction?

The Knot looked healthy, exceptionally so. It was larger than any she'd ever seen, and radiant with energy flowing from a source beyond. Marti felt a confidence growing that whatever had been demanding her help lay in this direction: through Ursula's Milgram Knot. She recalled the dreadful sensation of passing through the young patient's Knot and hesitated, daunted by the prospect of undergoing that pain again.

But as Marti felt the pull of the Knot, she let go of all resistance and allowed herself to be swept through. This time she crossed the threshold without any pain.

It still wasn't pleasant. When the roar subsided, her eyes were closed, and she heard a whispering, someone's mouth very close to her ear.

"Pay attention." Marti opened her eyes.

For a moment she was disoriented. The place was familiar, but so unexpected it couldn't register at first. Newton Hall. The steeply raked, hundred-seat classroom where she'd first taken a course taught by Stef, a course in human anatomy.

It was a place she sometimes returned to in dreams, always with a sense that she had never left. Marti had found that there are some places like that, places that change who you are, that become part of you.

Class was in session, but the other students were ghostly, and Marti quickly perceived two layers to the reality. The ghostly students of the past were being lectured to by a ghostly Stef at the front of the room. But superimposed over him was another Stef, who was more directly in front of her, speaking only to her.

"Are you listening?" he said. He repeated this several times. Marti felt as though she were emerging from a general anesthetic: it required a great deal of concentration to understand his words, but in giving her something to focus on they brought her to a wakefulness.

"Yes," she said.

"Good, because we're only covering this material once, and you can bet it's going to be on the exam."

Stef winked at her, belying the gravity of his warning,

and she felt the wink move through her, a flutter of joy at the ineffable realness of a human gesture. How much she missed Stef. But here he was.

"How are you?" It seemed a silly question to blurt at someone who was dead. Anyway, she had to be imagining this. But perhaps, she thought, imagination is also an organ of perception.

"Very busy," he said. "In a different way. Back to teaching, as you can see. I've been wanting to speak with you for some time."

"Why didn't you? I've missed you so much!"

"It wasn't possible. But each threshold you cross opens a little more space for us to communicate."

Marti felt all her doubts rise up in her.

"I don't know about all this, Stef. Carly, now Ursula, Violet's victims, all the damage. I think I'm doing more harm than good."

"It's good that you experience doubts."

"I don't know what's good any more. This thing is coming after me, and I don't want it to hurt more people."

"Don't pay attention to evil," he said. "It is part of the system. It has a role to play. Attend to the good."

But good is so weak. Stef touched her chin and tilted her face up. She felt like she was back in his study, being offered his wisdom and reassurance after a difficult day.

"May I continue?" he asked. She nodded.

"The fact that you're here means you've understood the bicameral nature of Home."

"Home."

"Of course, 'Home' is not really a technical term. But as with many things, the vernacular is so much more evocative."

As Stef continued, he began to sketch on the chalkboard. She recalled how he'd been fond of making quick diagrams while he lectured, his jacket often streaked with chalk dust.

Now he sketched two overlapping circles.

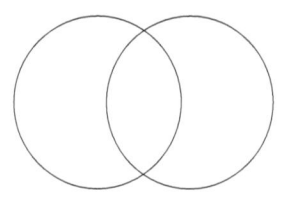

"On one side we have earth. On the other, heaven. Separated not by space, but by their condition. You might say, by time."

He shaded the center of the drawing, the place where the two circles overlapped.

"Indeed, so much separates them, we must ask, what holds them together at all?"

At the bottom intersection of the overlap he drew a smaller circle, a dot really.

"Here you have discovered the Milgram Knot, as you have named it. Where heaven and earth are joined together in each and every human embodiment. Though it connects the two realms of Home, when closed, as it almost always is, it serves as a barrier and defines the body as a closed-off space, nailed to the cross of time."

Yet she had passed through it, hadn't she? She was in the chamber of heaven, with Stef. His lecture continued.

"Here in the south"—he indicated his diagram—"the Milgram Knot. In the east, heaven. In the west, earth. The Milgram Knot is the door to evening, you could say, moving from east to west, from awareness to forgetting. But we move in a clockwise cycle." He circled the drawing lightly with his chalk. "From awareness, to forgetting, to awareness. As we come to the gate that connects the two worlds in the north. The door to morning. Cowie's Gate."

He drew another small circle that joined the two circles at the top. Marti was full of questions. Who or what was Cowie, for starters?

"One of our teachers," said Stef, as though he'd heard the question. "It seemed appropriate. You know, there are about two hundred parts of the human body named after those who identified them. Things like Batson's plexus and Brunner's glands and Wharton's duct. But there's a more important question."

"The door to morning," she said. "Sunrise. How do I get there?"

Stef nodded, pleased.

"How did you get to the south, to the Milgram Knot?"

"By descending, through the second body."

"Well, then?"

"I have to ascend? How do I do that?"

"You will have help."

"From where? I thought Stride needs my help."

Stef smiled but didn't reply. Love radiated from his smile. The classroom was insubstantial in comparison. The space, already hovering uncertainly, now telescoped inward. Stef was departing.

Marti felt a spasm of grief. To exist was to endure this constant falling away. But then the feeling inverted: Stef's presence had been more powerful, more palpable than she'd ever experienced it. And it had lived on beyond him. Perhaps grief was just the clearing away of a space for joy.

The joy came. It carried an image with it, of a pair of magnificent stone doors. A gate. She could see that what lay beyond was a rising sun. Barely discernable within the sun's light was a form. Waiting, preparing to cross over for a second time. Stride.

Though her vision could pass through the closed doors, she understood that Stride needed the gate to be opened so that he could pass through, so that his divided condition could be rectified. She tried to will the doors open, but she could find no point of contact, and her will had no effect. The gate had been opened once before, she realized, with Stef's death. Would her death be required to open it a second time?

Perhaps she would simply never return to her body. But she could already feel herself moving away, and she saw Stef's eyes flash one more time before she was pulled back to the original vision of Ursula's second body.

It was as before: the physical body trussed by the machines keeping it alive; the vibrant second body slung at a distance, but still connected. It hung like fruit on a branch. Or like a chrysalis.

Now Marti understood that Ursula was preparing, or being prepared. Was waiting for her, to help in Marti's task. She wondered how much time she had.

∞

As she approached the entrance to the desolate plaza where she had confronted the ruined version of Stride, Marti searched her mind for a plan. But life was all purpose now and no plan.

She passed through the tall weeds and imagined the laughing presence of the subterranean Elemental. She'd been in that spot once before with Stride, and she would bring him there again now.

But first she had to find him.

She was pulling back the plywood to go inside the abandoned interior when she felt an uneasy prickle race up her spine. She remembered the careful evasiveness with which Yannis had brought her here last time. This time she hadn't been careful at all, and suddenly she knew she'd been followed. A moment later she felt a heavy hand on her shoulder.

34

His face was blank but familiar: one of Gansrud's security crew. She turned and caught a quick glimpse of his second body. It wasn't chaotic like Gansrud's, but highly ordered, wrapped tightly in brackish, dark gray minions, studded at irregular intervals with a number of frightening, small black ones like festering wounds.

Gansrud and two other bulky military types were flanking him, one with a black Glock .45 trained on her, the other, scanning the surroundings, armed with a suppresser-equipped submachine gun. Gansrud glowered at her with a mixture of hostility and smugness.

"Thank you," he said, "for leading us here. You won't mind if we continue inside together?"

"Actually, I do mind. And I don't think Violet will go back with you."

"You underestimate how persuasive I can be."

"You have no idea what you are dealing with," she said.

He stepped toward her, invading her personal space, and looked her up and down with a leer before speaking again. "It seems to me that you are the one out of her depth. Three people dead so far because you. Because you did exactly the opposite of what you agreed."

Marti did her best to tamp down the mixture of rage and

shame she felt stirring. She didn't want to think about the damage Violet had done.

"In case you forget," she said, "I don't work for you any more. You fired me."

"That's true. And yet you saw fit to meddle, in a most disruptive way, in our business."

"Business. That's one word for it."

"Oh, and what do you call it? That's right, you don't go in for what we call medicine any more. You're some sort of witch doctor now."

"Witch doctor. And using the blood of an undead mutant as a vaccine? That's what you call medicine?"

Gansrud snorted. "No one's going to believe that."

"They will when I produce the evidence."

"You really are not in a good position to be making threats," he said. "Besides. Do you ever think of anyone but yourself? We have something that is going to relieve more human suffering than any product in the history of pharmacology."

"Good advertising copy," said Marti. "The truth is a little more complicated."

"You know, I hate people like you," said Gansrud. "I knew from the moment I met you that you were a problem. All people like you care about is keeping your hands clean. Do you think anything happens, any progress ever happens in this world, without someone's hands getting dirty? Well, some of us are willing to do what needs to be done."

For a moment, Marti thought he sounded exactly like Stef and the others. Declaring that suffering, failure, and even evil was an inevitable part of the system. But then it struck her that what Gansrud was saying was exactly the opposite. To Stef, to Ursula, the rightness of the action was what mattered, was the purpose of the whole system; the ends could not be controlled. To Gansrud and men like him, a determination to control the ends permitted any means at all. Marti remembered how she had disarmed him once before. She could see that his passionate anger had discomfited him.

He was staring into her eyes. She sensed him searching for her fear, needing to break her defiance, crush her power.

"I'm not afraid of you, Gansrud." She hoped it was true.

"Maybe, maybe not," he said. "You're going to help us either way. Let's go." He motioned to the others and they stepped forward. One pulled the plywood off entirely and gestured to Marti to be the first in. She stepped back.

"I don't think so."

"We're going in, with or without you. And if it's without you, there's going to be a nasty accident."

"You wouldn't dare." But she knew she was the one bluffing.

He looked at his watch. "Clinic closed for the day a half hour ago. Think how surprised they will be, how disappointed, when you're shot dead on the premises while trying to steal drugs after hours. But it will explain your bizarre behavior, your complicity in recent events. I'm giving you one more chance to work with us." He nodded toward the doorway.

She shook her head and with a quick nod from Gansrud the first guard delivered a precise blow to her head. She saw sparks and her legs went rubbery.

What happened next must have happened very fast, but to Marti it looked like a movie with missing frames. The fragments of time that remained burned themselves into her body like a series of still images.

The goon beside her taking a terrible punch to the throat.

Gansrud trying to flee as a hulking figure kicks his legs out from under him.

The guard with the submachine gun firing wildly.

The assailant turning, his face white, eyes deep black. A creature like Violet and the double of Stride, one she hasn't seen before, huge and powerful. He grunts with each bullet hit, but they don't stop him. Then the one with the gun is down.

Gansrud down, his face still recognizable, but the head behind it crushed to pulp, the red glistening and impossibly bright.

The remaining guard yanking Marti away, doggedly determined, and crashing into another one of the creatures.

Stride. He seizes her. She tries to speak but it's like a dream where you can't. Maybe it is a dream.

III

The whole world is a very narrow bridge
And the most important thing
Is not to be afraid at all.
—Rabbi Nachman of Bratzlav

35

The cloud that had beset Ursula was dispersing.

She remembered the assault now. It had come at a moment of such vulnerability, during deep meditation.

Her body, hooked up to machines, was itself like a failing machine. But much of her was otherwise occupied. The being of Ursula, the nexus of thought and feeling, the intent to be and to grow, and the mysterious harvest of a long life well lived, was on the verge not of failure but of release.

But first there was something she had to do.

∞

Marti shuddered awake. The awful images came back to her, a half-remembered dream. Her head was throbbing; she vaguely remembered being clobbered, before hell had broken loose. When she saw him sitting and looking at her, she knew she hadn't been dreaming.

Stride looked even shabbier than the last time she had seen him. No; he wasn't Stride, he was Stride's Double. Still, his features had retained their captivating beauty, his large dark eyes, the regal lines of his cheeks and nose, still visible under the urban grime that coated him like a second skin. His jet black hair was thick and matted. His hands, which were now wringing one another tensely, were as large and gracefully sculpted as before, though the nails were now long and black with dirt. His empty eyes were seemed to suck the air right out of her, and she thought she couldn't breathe.

She sat up on the grimy floor, her system still sluggish. They were in a small, windowless room. A battery-powered lantern glowed with a dismal, greenish light. The Double of Stride was on a chair opposite, looking at her blankly. He was holding something in one of his hands. She was alarmed to realize it was the Onoma Ursula had given her to wear, the amulet with his name on it. Her hand automatically went up to her throat, as if he might be holding a different one and she might still be wearing hers. But it wasn't there.

Realizing she was looking at it, he slipped the thing into his pocket. He glanced at Marti with a strange look on his face. Something like regret.

With an effort, she stood up and approached him. He got up uneasily, ready to flee. In her mind's eye she superimposed upon him the radiant Stride of angelic beauty. She was amazed at the vividness with which this image still lived in her; it seemed to have grown stronger over time. The Stride physically before her seemed affected by the image, gaining in stature and presence. Her own fear shrank. She wrapped her arms around him and pulled him to her.

To her surprise, the Double responded to her embrace, his arms enfolding her in return. Yet something was missing. Before, his embrace had been something more than human; now it was something less.

She refused to accept it. She gripped him tighter, but they lost their balance. Yet even then, she refused to let go. They fell awkwardly. He took the brunt of the impact.

She found that she was crying. All the strength had gone out of her limbs, but now he was really holding her, tears dripping off her face onto him. His form softened, and she began to feel that he really was cradling her.

Then the door opened. It was Violet.

"What are you doing?" she hissed. The Double got up quickly, frightened, and slid out the door.

"No," Marti cried. "Don't go." She turned to Violet. "I want to talk to him. To Stride."

"That's not his name," said Violet.

"Whatever you call him," said Marti. Violet didn't say anything, but stared at her for a long moment.

"I never asked you," she said, "why you came for me. Helped me."

"Because you don't belong here," said Marti. "I understand that."

"Nerves said it was some doctor in the Park that could help us. I thought it was that one."

"Stef?"

"—but it wasn't. Now we've found him, the right one."

"Help you how?"

"He's the one that made us. So he can free us."

"How do you know?"

Violet didn't like the question. She took a step toward Marti, too close. Something inside Marti cringed.

"You may be a Coil, but you're just like the other humans, aren't you? Afraid."

"I'm not."

Violet's arms shot out and she wrapped her hands around Marti's throat. She squeezed, just enough to cut off her breath. Marti clawed at Violet's hands, but they were as rigid as steel.

"You should be," Violet hissed. Then she let go.

Marti's knees were weak and for a moment she thought she might collapse.

"That is what it feels like to us," Violet said. "To be trapped here."

"And you think you've found someone to free you."

"Yes."

"Then why do you need me here?"

"Because—he wants you."

Violet pulled Marti's collar back and confirmed she was no longer wearing the Onoma. She nodded approvingly. "And now he can have you."

∞

Ursula understood that she needed to journey outward to find her purpose in the present moment. She turned her awareness away from the body, first taking care to insure that she retained a cord of connection to it.

She passed through the ceiling and then the upper layers of the hospital with little notice. She continued moving outward. As the surfaces of the physical world receded from her, there was no feeling of "up" or "down," only "in" and "out".

Swirling clouds and weather patterns arched over the curved surface of the earth, which was gradually lost to view below. But as she moved, her perception changed. It began to seem that she was moving inward, not outward; that in fact there was no outward movement possible from the appearance of the physical world of earth, that it was simply the outward surface of a vast world into which one could only move deeper.

∞

Stride held the Onoma in his hand. They had wanted it removed from the woman's body, and he had done as they told him. But now he found something compelling about it.

When he'd seen the woman the first time, he hadn't recognized her or really understood who she was. He knew she had something to do with before, and some part of him was interested. But he was also afraid.

It was good at least to be with others of his kind. Human beings were like rats in a maze, perversely pleased with their prison. Rather than rebelling, they contented themselves with preying upon one another. Nerves had told him, with her usual sour look, that "if humans ever found out about us, they'll find ways to make us suffer even more."

Nerves had been the first of them. She told him that in earlier days, she had gotten more than a little enjoyment from killing humans. Searching for the place where death hid itself in their bodies, so that maybe she could find it in herself.

She had tried to bring it to them as slowly as possible, and as painfully. The pain only lasted as long as they held on to life. So she tried to find the point just before that and prolong it, draw out their ridiculous desire to survive. Like pulling a rubber band to see how far it could be stretched before it snapped.

When it did snap, she felt a shiver of feeling, a kind of hope perhaps that some day she too might be unshackled. Afterward she felt ashamed, degraded. The stillness of their broken bodies left her hollow. It was partly because of this, she had told Stride, that she had given up killing, but also because she was afraid of getting caught.

After that she had tried to find the place in her own body where death was hiding. The practice continued with Violet and Benz. They probed with sharp implements, looking for the point that would release them. They hadn't done this to him yet, but the others' flesh had been distorted and deformed by it. The wounds always healed, but their bodies were twisted by the process. Nerves could barely even stand up any more.

She lay in front of him now, her gross form swollen on the bed, swaddled in a filthy blanket. Her face was only barely human, twisted into a hostile landscape of flesh.

"You have the amulet?"

Stride held it up, gripping it tightly. Nerves reached out

and touched it with misshapen fingers, reassuring herself, but he didn't let her take it. The symbol inscribed on it held a distant ache of familiarity, and he wanted to keep it near him. Nerves seemed satisfied just to observe and touch it.

Her face twisted into a different shape. It would have been a smile if the muscles hadn't been so damaged.

"It's time," she said to Benz, the hulking one. "Go and get him."

Benz nodded and left.

Stride felt a stirring of curiosity. It was a new feeling. "How do you know he can free us?"

Nerves looked at him with surprise. "Are you doubting me?"

He shook his head emphatically.

Normally, she would have cursed him for questioning her authority and left it at that. But maybe, he thought, the moment of anticipation was softening her.

"He is our god."

The Double shuddered. "What kind of god would make things like us?"

"Soon we will see."

"Why has he been so far away?"

"Perhaps he is ashamed. But now he will look on our faces and see that we have been loyal to him. He will be sorry for his abandonment."

"What does he want with the Coil?"

"You shouldn't think about her."

But he couldn't help it. He continued to feel the Onoma under his fingers.

He thought about something he had recently noticed about the Coil: air was moving in and out of her. It entered through her face and her body expanded to receive it, drawing it down into the center of her, where a mysterious exchange took place. Then her body released it. Within this rhythm there were irregular interruptions: now a momentary holding of breath, or a sudden, startled inhalation, or an inward clench that expelled the air more tensely. It was a kind of music, the air playing itself on the instrument of her body.

Suddenly it saddened him that he was not alive like her. He didn't want to be dead. He wanted to be alive.

When, not long after, Benz returned with a very ordinary looking man, The Double was still thinking about the Coil.

∞

Ursula was passing through layers, membranes that surrounded physical space, enclosing it like a placenta, sustaining it, providing nourishment. The beauty of colors, not fixed by pigments or other physical substance but rather moving, alive, shimmering and radiant, dazzled her. In the physical world color is a property of reflected light, but here it was an emanation. Everything she saw was a body of light. She was overwhelmed with an explosion of gratitude to the sun for its bestowal of light to the earth, piercing through the veil that otherwise kept the world in dark. Yet it was merely one of an infinite number of sources of light in the universe.

She wondered if this was all taking place in a moment, or if a hundred years had passed. The cord pulsing with light that connected to her physical body far away was still there. She took care to maintain it, the connection to the physical body which still existed and struggled to sustain its life in a space that had disappeared to her. She wondered if the image of the silver cord was an actual perception, or a mental projection. Either way, she was still anchored to time. Time was an artifact of the physical, and she had not yet relinquished her attachment.

But I am dying, she thought, there's no question about that.

The planes ahead of her, beyond that of the physical,

were infinite, and she fully perceived now that the physical plane was interwoven everywhere with and within the world beyond, so that it was shot through with infinity.

But there was a boundary line. Men and women lived inside the boundary of the physical world, the better to master it and achieve the consciousness of self that was its legacy.

Looking at it now from outside, from across the threshold, Ursula could see how full it was, like a baby come to term, how ready to explode beyond its confines. She knew what that pressure felt like. For many it felt like madness, being pressed up against a boundary they believed was the edge of existence itself, instead of merely its beginning.

From this vantage point she could see the world as a singularity, and yet the impression was one of an inconceivable vastness, the scale of manifestation demanded to meet the needs of so many beings: more than the need for food or water or air or a place to stand, all of which seemed to grow increasingly finite, but the need for experience. How rich that word seemed to her now. Experience: knowledge gained through trials.

She felt like a traveler who returns to an overlook near her home, only to realize after the long journey back that it is no longer home at all, and there can be no return. A marker of journey's end, yes, but marking it instead with a mystery: the mystery of the future, the promise and obligation of further journeys.

And then she remembered that she had a task to perform, a task that could only be undertaken by one suspended as she was between worlds. She suddenly felt the tenuousness of the connection that was holding her. She prayed that she would have enough time.

∞

The hulking Benz, who had rescued Marti from Gansrud, came into the room and nodded to Violet. She looked at Marti.

"Let's go."

"Where?"

Violet didn't answer, just motioned for Marti to go ahead and follow the tall one.

They went out the door of the small, windowless room and came out into the cavernous space where she had first sought Violet and found the Double of Stride. Violet carried the lantern. The light extended a few steps ahead, but Marti was walking into darkness.

She picked her way across the debris that littered the floor, piles of collapsed shelving units, dusty cans and boxes, some opened, others crushed. Judging by the kinds of things lying around, this must have been a large drugstore at one time.

Marti was wide awake now, a metallic tang of fear at the back of her throat. She turned back to Violet and tried asking again. "Where are we going?"

"I told you," she said. "Someone wants to speak with you." Her face was ghostly in the lantern light.

Marti took a breath. She told herself that if they'd wanted to hurt her, they would have done it already. But then there was this "someone." She pushed away the image of Gansrud's crushed skull.

In the back, a living space had been set up. It seemed more like a nest than a human habitation. Broken bits of furniture, piles of clothing, castoff debris—she noticed a pile of batteries. It was hard to tell what was in use and what was garbage.

They passed a small table with a chair next to it. Towels, crusty and blackened, littered the floor here. On the table, some tools—pliers, small hammer, nails, and what looked like surgical and dental tools. All were spattered and encrusted with clots of black.

Marti didn't realize she had stopped moving until Violet shoved her gently forward.

A few steps more and Violet had her stop while she went forward, taking the lantern with her. The hulking one had stopped, and his dead eyes were on her until the light receded with Violet and he became invisible.

Marti heard some words being spoken, and then a moment later Violet and the lantern returned.

"He'll see you," was all she said.

36

For a long moment, Marti felt like her eyes must be deceiving her. The shock wasn't the horrific creature lying in the bed. It wasn't the distressing shadow of Stride. It was the ordinary-looking man who had joined them.

"Hobbs?" She had never seen her colleague outside the clinic. How had he come to be here? Yet dimly she felt something clicking into place.

"Well, well," Dr. Hobbs said, directing his words to the creature in the bed. "Congratulations. You weren't lying."

"You knew we weren't lying or you wouldn't have come," the creature said, in a croaking voice.

Hobbs grimaced and looked sympathetically at Marti.

"I'm sorry about all this," he said. "These things lack any sense of respect. I've come to get you out of here."

Marti was still trying to wrap her head around the fact that someone from the clinic was as involved as her, more involved, with these strange creatures. For a moment she wondered if Hobbs had a twin brother. Then she realized, this was no longer Hobbs.

She remembered the sense that something had changed in him, the strange encounter she'd had with him, his interest in the Onoma. Which Stride, she could see, now held in his hand.

She took a step toward Hobbs as a counter to her fear. "What do you want with me?"

"I want to help you. I tried to help you before. That first night. Sent something to stop you from going back to him."

The revolting image of the puppet-like creature that had attacked her in the parking lot returned, but she blinked it away.

"How was that a help? Look what it did." She gestured to the Double.

"You can't blame me for them," he said. "It wasn't my idea to cross the boundary. Earth and heaven have nothing in common. They do not belong together. The Partnership, as they call it, wants to pretend otherwise. They"—he swept his hand toward the lost ones—"are the result. Admit it: your life would be much better, you would be much happier, if Stride had never come into it."

Marti asked herself if this was true. And if it was, did it matter?

"I have an offer to make," said Hobbs. "I think you'll want to hear it. You've been used by forces that care nothing for you, forces with an agenda."

"And you care for me?"

"You and much more than you."

Marti ignored his words. "But you couldn't do anything as long as I wore the Onoma." Her hand went to her neck, and she realized how vulnerable she felt without it.

"All I ask is that you hear me out. If you don't like what you hear, you will be free to go."

"What if I refuse to listen?"

The creature in the bed spoke. "Then we're the ones you should be afraid of." The hulking one stepped up and put a heavy hand on her shoulder.

"None of that," said Hobbs. "Why don't we go in the other room and talk in private?"

"Not yet," said Nerves.

"What then," Hobbs said, his obvious irritation betraying his distaste.

"You promised us," said Nerves.

"And I'll do it," he said, "when I'm ready."

Nerves narrowed her eyes. "We don't believe you. Why should we? You've left us to rot all these years. You created us, then you forgot us."

Hobbs turned to her. "Is that what you believe? You are no creation of mine. You can thank Heaven for that. You were angels. Heaven sent you here. Made these bodies for you and then discarded you."

Violet and Benz reacted with consternation and turned to Nerves. She gestured restraint.

"No," said Nerves. "We were not meant to be trapped."

"What was meant? Who isn't trapped here?"

"Humans can die," said Violet.

Hobbs snorted. "And what good is it to them? They are just as trapped as you."

"Enough," Nerves yelled, the word echoing through the desolate chamber. "Do you deny that you have the power to release us?"

Hobbs fumed for a moment. Then he spoke quietly. "Fine. One of you. One of you now. The others, after."

"You will do me first," Nerves said. "I have been here the longest."

"So be it," said Hobbs. He sat down beside her on the bed. "Any last words?" He smiled unpleasantly.

"Get it over with."

"As you wish." He put his hands on her shoulders and closed his eyes.

Marti had been trying to discern Hobbs's second body, but it was somehow cloaked.

Now, as he ministered to Nerves, she felt the energy in

the room changing. Two swirling vortices rose out and up from Hobbs's shoulder blades, opening up a negative space, a black cloud, in the air. Hobbs's physical body became limp, like an empty shell, a puppet. The cloud gave an impression of a vast emptiness compressed into an impossibly small space, creating a vacuum, a black hole. Hobbs's body was a conduit, and whatever was the persistent animating force that dwelt in Nerves was being sucked into that vacuum.

Marti remembered what Murdoch had said. This is it, she thought, the Ampsy: Accumulated Mass of Psychic Energy. She could sense the dreadful accumulation of fear.

It was over quickly. Hobbs sagged on the bed and then pulled himself back in disgust. Nerves' corpulent body had lost its form and was a mass of stinking, bubbling black decay. As Marti watched, the bubbling receded and the moisture seemed to evaporate. In moments, all that was left was a gray powder.

Benz and Violet both charged forward to look more closely. Hobbs wiped himself off. "I'll get to the rest of you later," he said, "if you still want it."

∞

When she saw the gates, Ursula understood.

The stone doors, the Onoma carved into the far side of them, were magnificent. She felt a rush of love for Stef and all his work in helping create the image.

Cowie's Gate itself needed no image. But for humans to work with it so directly was new. Humans, Ursula thought, need images to work with the invisible.

When she had helped Stef in his final act, she had not seen the doors at all. She had only met him part way, to make the return journey that he could not. Now she marveled at their beauty and intricacy, the delicacy that belied their weight and power. It made her hopeful she would be sufficient to the task of opening them. And she needed hope.

∞

The Ampsy, in Hobbs's body, felt a burning anger in the pit of the stomach. These sensations of feeling were so coarse, so unpleasant. Unbecoming of a god. He felt humiliated by the small defeat inflicted on him by Nerves. But he'd seen that they would turn against him otherwise. And while she was the one with whom he had first communicated, she was certainly the least useful for his purposes. The other three would be sufficient, once they had been returned to Harmon.

How he hated Heaven. Without Heaven, the humans would all be like Nerves, and Violet and the others. And he would be their god.

The beauty of the plan was that the humans were going to do it all themselves. At first he'd thought he wouldn't even have to take human form himself. But then the Partnership had meddled, and he had to deal with the Coil.

For a while he had even relished the challenge. But now he was starting to feel irritated by it all, irritated that he had to deal with this Marti Powell and the threat she represented.

He turned to Marti. "Dr. Powell? Shall we take a few minutes to ourselves?"

∞

"Before I hear what you have to say," Marti started, "I need you to answer some questions."

The Ampsy smiled Hobbs's crooked smile. "Go ahead."

"What happened to the real Hobbs?"

"That's a good question," he said. "I don't know exactly where they go when I push them out. But don't worry, I don't plan to do anything like that to you. The contrary."

"What about Carly? What did you do to her?"

"She was unhappy. I tried to help her."

"You used her to get to me."

"You could put it that way. But only in the sense that I

thought I could help both of you."

"Help?"

"We'll come to that. But first you must understand: unlike anyone else, I know how you feel. I am aware of how difficult things have become for you."

He was still sitting in the chair opposite her, but Marti felt him, or some part of him, creeping closer as he continued to speak.

"You have been changed. You are alone among humans. And you don't even know why."

He was looking to her for a response, but she remained stoic, though his words had struck deep into her. Hearing this truth acknowledged by another was more powerful than she wanted to admit.

"And I suppose you do know why?" she asked.

He smiled at her sadly. "No," he said, shaking his head. "What I know is: there is no 'why.' It is merely the working out of a pitiless chain of cause and effect set in motion by beings too far away to have any compassion for you here."

Marti tossed her head as if to shake him loose. "But apparently you wanted to talk to me. Was it just to express sympathy?"

"I want to offer you something. An alternative."

"No thanks," Marti said, and she stood up.

"Please," he said. "Sit down. You don't seem to realize how limited your choices are."

"My choices don't come from you," she said.

"That is correct. But let's assume that somehow you convince the creatures out there to let you go. Your life proceeds in one of two directions. In one, you renounce or fail in your mission as a Coil, you are arrested and tried and probably convicted of murder, or at least something close to it that will lead to disgrace and a long prison term."

"You can't know that."

"Alright then, public disgrace, a huge legal bill, years of appeals..."

"I get your point. But I don't intend to fail."

"So, what does the other direction, success, look like? Have you thought about that?"

Marti felt betrayed by her own silence, but she didn't know how to respond.

"I thought not. Well, it certainly involves the sacrifice of your life. You did realize that?"

"I've considered it."

"And have you thought about what you would be purchasing with your life? Have you thought about what kind of order it is, that requires human self-sacrifice like that to sustain itself?"

He stood up and paced for a moment. Marti felt the tension of his hold on her relax somewhat. The space was filling with her own doubts.

"You see my dear colleague, 'free will' is the cruelest joke ever perpetrated. The freedom of humans is far more limited than they imagine. Yet look what they have done with it!"

"So you offer something better than freedom?"

"Yes!" The Ampsy clenched his fists, his face reddening with a passion that had so far been restrained. "Not the freedom for chaos and destruction, for the ruthless vanity that has soaked the earth with blood."

He took a breath, apparently to calm himself, then sat down again.

"You cry for your niece. Will you cry for all the others? For the billions whose lives have been sacrificed on the altar of free will?"

"How are you different, then?" said Marti. "You're telling me the ends justify the means." The image of Carly rose up before her, the sucking void at her center. Marti felt her anger rising, her cheeks beginning to burn. She thought she saw, in response, a flicker of pleasure in his face. Now she took a breath, hoping the air would cool her emotions. She summoned a chill to meet his.

"What was it you did to her?" she asked. She felt another conversation going on between them at a deeper level. He was pressing closer and closer to her, and she wanted to push him back. But as she did, she realized that the chill was his—that in meeting coldness with coldness, she was losing something.

As if intuiting her thoughts, he said, "Perhaps I frighten you. But that is not a reason to pull away. The only way to knowledge is through fear. I tell you, I am here to save you, my dear colleague, if you will let me."

"You aren't Hobbs, and I'm not your colleague."

"Oh, but you are," he said, "that's the whole point. You know too much now to accept less than what I have to offer.

"Suppose you were told a story," he continued. "A story is a lie, a circle of deception. Within that circle, 'up' can be down, 'in' can be out. Humans tell stories to invent comforting lies. The hero fights bravely, defending his comrades, risking and ultimately sacrificing his life for the struggle. We cheer his accomplishment and mourn his sacrifice. But what if the cause he fights for is corrupt and malign, however earnestly he believes in it? I have seen such wars in my times near earth, such fighters, passionate and ready to sacrifice themselves for a cause they called freedom but that would in the end ensure the enslavement of others. They believed in a story!"

He leaned toward her. "What cause do you fight for? Do you even know?"

"I'm a doctor," she said. "My cause is healing."

"Or was," he said, "since you are no longer employed as a physician."

Marti shrugged. "A change of venue."

The Ampsy smiled. "There you have it. The tragedy of being human. Trapped in a story, its purpose obscure. Most people give up and just do what feels good while trying to avoid pain. Surely more is expected of a Coil."

Marti felt like she'd had enough, but these last words were too difficult to dismiss. A feeling had been gnawing at her.

She wanted to fight it. She had an impulse to stand up, but her body did not respond. She realized that he was touching her. How had she not been aware of this? His fingers were gently pressing against her ears. She knew, somehow, that she could stand up if she wanted to, even leave the room. But she didn't want to. She wanted to know more.

"What is expected of me, then?" she asked.

"You see?" he said, speaking more intimately than before. It was as if her realization that he was touching her, and her choice to remain within his grasp, had brought him much closer. "The character in the story never knows. She's merely the tool of the story. What if the story itself is evil? What if everything you think is good, everything that furthers and prolongs the story, is the source of the world's pain and disaster? That is what they expect you to serve, Marti Powell. That you will serve them."

"Who is 'them'?"

"You've seen them," he said. "Earth and all the life it holds is a small thing to them, a puddle. Earth would be better free of them."

Marti shook her head. It wasn't only his words digging inside her.

"There's love," she said.

"What about it? How much of it is there, really, in the world? Oh yes, it tries. But it is like a candle in a windstorm."

Marti took a deep breath. She could feel his coldness

deep inside her now. They weren't like this, they carried the warmth and light of the sun.

But the thought lacked conviction. The sun had gone far away, and it was night, and it was cold. If they were good, why had they gone? Gone away like all the love she had ever experienced—Rourke, Stride, Carly—it never stayed. It was true: like a candle in a windstorm.

"They ask you for too much," he said. "Don't they? To give your life, to bring about their plan. Their plan has failed! The earth is a slaughterhouse! Do you not know history?"

Marti found it difficult to speak. "And what do you want?"

He smiled. "I want to give you the life you deserve. The life you should have had."

She wanted to protest. But her thoughts were far away, and he was so close.

Without intending to she was holding her breath, resting in the hollow between in-breath and out-breath. She hadn't been aware of how oppressed she had been, how troubled, by the deep tensions that consumed her. Becoming a Coil had not freed her from anything, it had only expanded the scope of her doubts and uncertainty, deepened her loneliness and pain.

"I want to take you home."

His words were no longer outside her, mere sound vibrations disturbing the air, agitating sensitive membranes within her ears. They were being spoken somewhere deep inside her, and they crashed down into her like bombs through a forest canopy.

"Home" exploded last and loudest. Images poured out of it.

First, her own images of home. The apartment they'd moved out of before her second birthday. It was a cascade of bright images: a lamp, a rug, a cat, a bedspread, most of all her parents' faces. The house where she'd grown up, on the edge of a suburb that backed onto a ravine. The privacy of her bedroom and the secret places out back, the dining room table where the family convened, the couch in front of the TV. These memories opened up with a vividness she had never experienced.

The rhythmic caress of water against the beach, sun baking salt into her skin, sand shifting under her as she sat up, naked.

For a moment Marti was disoriented. She looked around. Behind her, against the hillside, was the palapa, the open-walled hut she and Rourke had been sleeping in.

Rourke. She knew that she had gone away from him. Or he had gone away. And she had taken a long journey. But now she was back.

She heard whistling. She recognized it and got up. She felt like it really had been a long time since she'd seen him, though she couldn't have been lying there on the beach for more than an hour.

The palapa was much larger than she remembered. Rourke was in the open-air kitchen, preparing a lunch from fresh seafood. He smiled when she came close but held up his hands, slick from the sea creatures, in warning. She wanted to kiss him so badly.

He wiped his hands off. "I knew you'd come back, babe," he said. He put one hand against the base of her neck and drew her close.

"Listen, I've got the best idea. Let's just stay here. Forever."

Marti felt a swell of joy. Forever.

It was what she wanted. Wasn't it?

Of course, Marti thought, why wouldn't I? But something was tugging uneasily at her awareness, like a cold gleam in the sunlight.

"Don't you want to?" he asked.

"Forever is a long time."

"No," he said. "It's beyond time."

How she wanted to surrender to him. But something held her back. She looked at the pile of fish and shellfish he had been cleaning. A beautiful meal, fresh from the ocean. It reminded her of a meal she'd had long ago, on a beach in Mexico, with Rourke. Two eras were clashing inside her.

"I want to kiss you," he said.

Yet something held her back. Something in her refused to let her go to him. She turned to face it, to try to cut herself loose, but as she did, she realized what it was telling her: that she was not seeing things as they were. She felt this was wrong, but she could not dismiss it, and she affirmed an intention to understand what this brink was.

As she did, suddenly her body shuddered, releasing the carbon dioxide her lungs had been holding. The vision disappeared with it. As she gulped air in, she plunged into a terrifying darkness. No: a terrifying darkness plunged into her. It invaded every cell, every passageway inside her. She tried to open her eyes, but they were open, the center of her vision obscured by a black cloud. It wasn't darkness as a void of light, but as an active presence, which her inner senses had mistaken for light.

A face appeared at the center of that blackness.

At first she thought it was Rourke, and she called his name.

But Rourke was gone. It was Hobbs's face. She saw through it to something beneath, something she yearned for. This disembodiment of the face into a transparent mask only made it more real to her, more familiar. It seemed as familiar as any face she had ever seen, more so.

She remembered, as a child, the daily ritual at nursery school when, after interminable hours in a world without parents, the mothers, and some fathers, would arrive to take their children home. She remembered clearly the feeling when her own mother appeared, as though her mother's face were a key that perfectly fit a lock inside her, swinging open a door of love.

Now she couldn't even remember her mother's face, or any other face. There was only the face before her.

Some part of her was saying this was wrong. She wanted to move her body, but she felt pinned. His hands were still on her ears, but that wasn't the main thing. He had reached right inside her.

His face came closer to hers.

"I am your home," he said. "No one, nothing else, can offer you that. Come home to me."

As Marti gazed at his face, she felt it too was a key, fitting a lock inside her. But what lay behind the door wasn't love. She observed this from far off, as though it were too late to make a difference.

What was behind the door he was unlocking? Release, she thought. Some caged bird in her wanted to fly free, to fly away, fly home.

The thought filled her with excitement. What was there to hold her here? Oppressive duty, sorrow, loneliness?

Yet she wanted another moment to reflect. A small, distant voice was saying to wait, that if that bird was released, it would be a loss from which she would never recover. That evil was something right at the wrong time.

Marti's body spit out the word as if of its own accord: "Wait."

Hobbs's face froze as if on command. A shadow of anger crossed it.

"No," she said. "No. This isn't what I want."

As she spoke the words, her sense of what was taking place inverted. Darkness and light returned to their original places. Weariness and grief rushed into her body as air filled her lungs. The pain was overwhelming.

She felt herself falling and she realized that the Ampsy, who had been holding her body up, had dropped her as if she had become too hot to touch.

On the floor, her body wracked with shudders, Marti's breath began to return. She realized she had been crying, could feel her face was smeared with mucus. She rolled over. She saw the Ampsy looking down at her and on his face a look of fear and surprise, as if he had encountered something unexpected and troubling.

She felt as though she had just re-entered the earth's atmosphere from the far reaches of space. There, she had been weightless and transparent. Now the planet itself bore down on her, crushing her to its bosom with paralyzing force. She was being exiled to a hostile atmosphere. She didn't want this; she wanted to go home. Why had she come back?

The Ampsy held out his hand, but she pushed it away.

"What do you want?" Marti asked hoarsely. "What do you want with me?"

"I wanted to help you," he said.

Marti sat up and wiped her face. Her head ached terribly.

"You want to help me with a delusion?"

The Ampsy laughed. "You surprise me, Coil. I thought it would be easier for you to understand. Your niece understood better than you. Do you really believe what you just experienced was a delusion?" He gestured to the room around them. "How then is this not a delusion? Merely because the perception of it is shared by others?"

He waved away his own argument with apparent disgust. "I didn't bring you here to debate." He extended his hand to Marti, who was still sitting on the floor. She avoided it, getting herself up and sitting in the chair.

"What I offer was made from your own wish, your own happiness."

"No thanks," she said, without even thinking about it.

"Reconsider!"

Marti could feel his will bearing down on her. She felt hers profoundly weakened.

He reached out again to place his hands on her ears. She suddenly felt a roar of righteous anger. She welcomed it, welcomed its certainty, let its power course through her and bring her fully back to life. She smacked away his hands and stood up.

"How dare you," she shouted at him, the words pouring out without thought. "What do you think I am? Another lost teenaged girl?"

He responded with equal ferocity. "What do you know of what I did? Of what I do?" With lightning speed, he grabbed her by the back of her neck and drew her close to his face.

"You may have powers that ordinary humans do not, but your body is human. I've offered something the so-called Partnership who toy with your life will not. Do you think they will protect you? They will sacrifice you! There is no protection! Life, for many, is a hell of pain. And yours might yet be so. Do not refuse me!"

As he spoke, she felt a cold sting radiate out from her neck where he touched her. Marti was paralyzed, couldn't breathe, all her senses on fire. She wanted only for it to stop.

After what felt like hours but was only a few seconds, he withdrew the pain but continued to hold her up. Her body shuddered, her legs had turned to jelly. Relief flooded her. For the first time she felt a tenderness toward him.

"It's a form of closeness, isn't it?" he said. "This giving and receiving of pain. Human beings have found much intimacy that way. I offered you the greatest happiness you've ever imagined. You refused it. I want you to remember that. What happens now is your choice."

"No," she said. Hatred flared in her like a fire. Hatred at all those who blamed their victims. How good the hatred felt.

She could feel the Ampsy responding, connecting with it, with the current of her hatred. It was opening her wide to him, hatred giving him purchase on her.

Noticing the Ampsy's response abruptly detached her from her hatred, and she saw what it was: a promise of immediate relief, a means to throw off pain.

Marti groaned. She would have to accept the pain, of the loss of Rourke, and maybe of Carly, of Ursula, of the imperfect small life she had lost when Stride came into it.

More, she had to enter directly into the pain, because, somehow, that was where the love and the real power lay. She felt herself reddening with the intensity of it, felt the pain swelling her heart. And her heart said that a pain fully borne, and fully forgiven, need never be experienced again.

But she could not free herself from the creature using Hobbs's body. He was inside her now, and she could feel his thoughts.

∞

He had never been very patient, and his latest human vehicle had made things worse. This Hobbs had apparently been an unpleasant fellow.

For all the unpleasantness, it was, he reminded himself, a useful skill, this taking on of a human body. He could thank the Viscount for teaching him how. It had been his first encounter with that peculiar mixture of vanity and despair, the dissatisfaction that led men to long for inhuman power.

Soon now the black fluids of the fallen ones would, thanks to Harmon's efforts, flow through the rivers of the human body. The absurd Partnership brought to a close.

Then he and the earth would together be free, free of Heaven, free of the whole tragic undertaking.

He had hold of her Knot now. When he tore it out, the Coil would be finished.

A moment earlier it had seemed like she was his. Her doubt and then her hatred were openings to him; now she was meeting him with something else. But the love would be too little, too late.

∞

As Ursula pressed against the great stone doors, her energy wavered, unequal to the challenge of their implacable weight. The connection to her physical body was weakening.

Not yet, she thought. Let me complete this task.

37

Marti felt herself disappearing. The hatred and the doubt and the fear were gone. She felt a wistful sadness, a regret at her failure, and a vague sense of disbelief, as if destiny had been usurped. Her thoughts went to Stride, a final yearning, a call of love and awakening.

Hobbs' face filled her vision. Beyond it was the coldness of the black light, of a place that refused change and growth.

"Let her go!" Marti heard the words at a great distance. It did not seem like they had anything to do with her. Again: "Let her go."

She heard a sickening, wet sound, and the vision of Hobbs' face tore open and disappeared, leaving only his body, now gone limp. The Onoma was dangling before her. Stride was standing behind Hobbs, a look of intense concentration on his face. Hobbs' arms dropped to his sides, his crumpled body held up by a sharp-ended metal pole that Stride had driven right through him, the Onoma wrapped around it.

Marti fell shakily to her knees and watched as a raging black miasma rushed out from the ruptured container of Hobbs's body. It swirled around the human form several times before being sucked upward in a vicious stream, up through the ceiling, and then it was gone.

Stride let Hobbs's body drop. It was collapsing into decay already. He retrieved the Onoma, wiping it off carefully, and kneeled down in front of Marti. His face wore a puzzled look, as though his execution of Hobbs had surprised him as much as her.

He held up the Onoma. "What is this? What is it doing to me?"

The word that came to Marti was "healing." Stride had broken into two parts. One was in heaven, one was on earth. But she hesitated to say it. Instead she asked, "What are you feeling?"

"Like I am on fire."

An ache rose in Marti at the words. "That is what you did to me," she said. "Try to remember."

She took his cold hand and wrapped it between hers. This is what she had come for, and it was all that mattered. She felt a swell of love for him, the whole of him, the light and dark of him, the broken and healed, lost and found, past and future. Looming over her at Ursula's, his great wings beating, filling her with a light that had transformed her, turning her life inside out.

It's me that is broken, she thought. She leaned on him to help herself stand.

Checking her body, she seemed whole. But one thing she had learned as a doctor was that the bodily effects of an assault were often the least significant, the easiest to treat and the quickest to heal. Sense of self, security, and personal power can bruise and break as well. The body itself was a home.

The body was a home. The truth of this washed over her gently, offering succor to her sense of exile. No home was permanent; this was perhaps the most difficult truth to accept. The body certainly wasn't permanent. But the body is a home.

"I couldn't let him hurt you," Stride said, almost apologetically.

She nodded. "We have to get out of here."

"Where is the door to morning?"

"The door to—?" Had she heard him right? He repeated himself and held out the Onoma, as if indicating it had the answer to her question. She pushed it toward him. "You keep it."

Marti didn't hear Violet enter the room. But there was no missing the inhuman howl of outrage.

"What have you done to him?"

Benz came in behind her, his face twisted as he bent over the broken remains of Hobbs.

Violet turned toward Marti, her face swollen in rage. "He was going to help us!"

Benz launched himself at Marti, grabbed her hair in one hand, her shoulder in the other. Stride charged at Benz, but Benz swung Marti around and used her as a shield. He elbowed Stride with great force and sent him sprawling.

Benz looked to Violet for direction, ready to snap Marti's neck.

"I can help you," said Marti. She blurted the words without thinking.

Violet stepped over to her and looked her in the eyes. "You are lying."

"No," said Marti. "I've always told you the truth. And I'm your only hope now."

"Go ahead then. Help us."

"First, let me go."

Violet gestured to Benz and he released Marti.

Marti rubbed her shoulder, felt a bruise forming. "You have to wait here for me," she said. "Stride must come first."

"Take all of us with you!" said Violet.

"No," said Marti, "it's too dangerous. They're looking

for me, remember? And you know what they'll do if they find you again."

Violet motioned toward the hulking creature beside her. "Benz will protect you. I can too."

Marti shook her head. "I can't have anyone else hurt."

But Violet wasn't to be deterred, and there was no more time to argue.

∞

As they moved together through the darkness, Marti wondered if she'd spoken the truth. Because she had no idea what to do. But she knew where they had to go.

The Elemental's invitation resounded in her mind. "You must bring him to us."

As they approached the exit, Marti's body came to a standstill, gripped by a sense of dread. An image of Gansrud and the three other men came back to her. Their broken bodies were just beyond the exit and it was a sight she did not want to revisit.

The three Lost Ones realized she had fallen behind and stopped.

In the silence, Marti heard the sound of several vehicles pulling up outside and then boots hitting the ground. Apparently authorities of some sort had somehow been alerted to the bloody remains of Gansrud and the others.

"Is there another way out?" Marti asked.

Violet nodded and pointed. Only when they were moving in the new direction did Marti realize it was taking them away from the goldenrod domain of the Elemental.

38

Dave's empty bed seemed unwilling to provide rest. On the second night of Marti's absence, he got up and walked outside. The moon was almost full, and it lit the way as he wandered past the cut grass and into the woods at the back of the yard.

Where was Marti?

Soon he could no longer see the lights of his house, and his body stopped moving of its own accord. Dave sat down on the ground. The earth was soft with pine needles. He wondered how many layers, how many seasons of needles had been dropped here. He could feel the fecund, receptive medium of their decay.

Suddenly Dave felt surrounded, overwhelmed by life, as if in the night things were freed from the isolated separateness of their forms, the cloak of darkness revealing that they were, after all, one thing, one living, growing, entity.

He couldn't explain why these sensations were bringing him closer to Marti, but he felt they were. He lay back on the ground and felt at home, though he'd never been to this spot before.

Tiredness rolled in on Dave like a fog. Just before falling asleep he thought that Marti was there, joined with him on the soft bed of pine needles.

∞

Marti watched for the car. They had found their way out from the bowels of the ruined stores to a different corner of the Park.

Violet and Benz crouched in the shadows. Stride stood guard, keeping his eye on the nighttime wanderers that floated through the neighborhood, all with the aura of either predator or prey. Marti listened for any sign of the boots she'd heard dismount where the bodies were. She briefly thought that maybe the intruders had gone and they could return to the patch of goldenrod. But she didn't want to take the chance.

She was startled when Stride put his arm gently on her shoulder. She turned and gave him a long look.

Briefly she thought about fleeing with him from Violet and Benz. But as much as she wanted to attend to him, she knew that if she left them at large, it was only a matter of time before they ended up back in the hands of Project Secure Horizon.

So when the car arrived, she knew she had to take them with her. Yannis got out from behind the wheel.

"Thank you for coming," said Marti. She turned to the others. "Let's go."

Yannis looked at "Los Olvidados" uneasily, then at Marti.

"It's okay," said Marti. "I want them to. They need our help."

With a sigh, Yannis pulled a blanket over the backseat and motioned them in. Benz couldn't fit in the back. Marti saw Yannis wince as the giant squeezed himself into the front passenger seat. In the back, Stride sat between Violet and Marti.

As Yannis eased the car back onto the road, Marti gave him directions. She was glad to be sitting next to Stride. She reached for his hand and found that he was still holding the amulet. She could feel its subtle warmth penetrating him.

"Where are you taking us?" Stride asked.

"To a friend's place," said Marti.

"Your friend will help us?" Violet said.

Marti nodded. "There's something there that can. I think."

Violet looked over at her. "You think?"

∞

As Yannis pulled up with long driveway, Marti looked for the words she would say to Dave. She wished she'd told him the whole story.

She hoped he would be away, though it was still too early for work. When they arrived at the end of his driveway, his truck was parked there. Her anxiety about Dave distracted her from her anxiety about what they had come here to do, and whether there was any chance it would work.

They climbed out of the car. Marti hugged Yannis.

"That's twice you've saved my ass. Thank Qais for me too."

"I just hope you know what you're doing," he said, gesturing to Violet and Benz.

"Me too."

"Enough chatter," said Violet. "Let's get this going."

∞

While Dave had slept on a bed of decomposing tree matter, his dreams had been vivid and strange. At first he felt himself being drawn down, as if he too were slowly settling into formlessness. Here, death was part of an infinite cycle of growth, and on the cusp between waking and sleeping, he briefly imagined that he was dying. A part of him shrank from the prospect with horror and urged him to flee back to the house, turn on all the lights, drive away the dark, soft, moist descent. He thought about what he would leave behind, if his body were to be cast off here like a dead leaf.

Normally, sleeping was a blackness, lit up by occasional sparks of dreaming, little of which he remembered in the morning. Here on the bed of earth, there was no blackness. He felt a rumbling far beneath him. The rich humus below him was merely a crust. The dreams had not reached him yet, but they were below that crust.

They wanted to enter him. That is why he had come here, to receive the dreams. His body held a billion portals between the particles of his physical form, and it required only his consent for them to open.

Yet that consent required a peculiar kind of effort, something feminine. Dave had loved many women, most of them young and beautiful. He loved their curving softness, the way he penetrated them with his hardness, and not only in the obvious, sexual ways. For in these penetrations his own hardness was softened, turned to water, released.

But no woman was present, and he was being asked to soften of his own accord, to soften and be penetrated himself.

∞

The shed had once been a small barn, but now Dave used it as a lockup for garden implements and other storage.

"You'll be safe in here," said Marti. "Until I'm ready." She wasn't sure what would make her ready, but she felt certain she needed to be alone with Stride to do what needed to be done.

Violet narrowed her eyes. "How do we know you'll come back?"

"You don't trust very well, do you? I'm in a lot of trouble because of you. If not for me, you'd still be locked up with Harmon."

"I'm starting to think that wouldn't be so bad," said Violet, but without much conviction. She looked at Benz, who was looking at her impassively. "Don't be too long."

"I'll be back as soon as things are ready. And if anyone else comes along—it's Dave, he's a friend—don't hurt him."

Violet looked askance at yet another demand, but then nodded her consent.

Once they were inside, Marti closed the door and shoved a piece of wood through the latch to make sure it was securely locked.

She turned to Stride. "Okay. There's something—someone—we have to meet."

39

Dave had awakened some hours before. His throat was dryer than it had ever been, and his body ached from lying on the ground.

The morning's beauty surrounded him. How could something that happened with such an unvarying rhythm, the turning of night to day, seem so unexpected? It was as if he had been deposited on another planet, where the nights lasted for ten years, and the morning was a magnificent festival. The sun glinted through the trees, its rays everywhere refracted through droplets of dew. Dave too was covered in dew, and without thinking he began to lick it off of the backs of his hands and forearms. He wanted to relieve the dryness afflicting his throat, but he found himself imagining he was imbibing a magical elixir.

Had the world always been this beautiful, and he had never noticed? It was the kind of beauty that harrowed away all the trivia and distraction and demanded that you live as though your chaotic, imperfect life held the same potential.

Dave stood up and stretched, the movement releasing stiffness from his joints and opening more space in him. He looked down at his palms and something caught his attention. He was perturbed to see the pale glow had returned. At first he thought this was a trick of the light. But he stepped aside into the shade of a great tree and the light remained, now a little more noticeable in the surrounding shadow.

His hands were emitting a soft, phosphorescent glow. He moved them around, and the light trailed slightly.

The image brought him quickly back several nights, to the one spent with Marti, their bodies finding purchase in one another. He remembered, as his pleasure had climbed inside a rhythm of movement that enwrapped them both, glimpsing trails of light coming off her.

He tried to dismiss the fanciful image. It was one thing to be pining for a woman who may now have ditched him, another to imagine she was some sort of alchemical source of light. He wrapped his arms around himself and curled up. Maybe he could fall back to sleep.

∞

As they arrived at the woods, Marti felt a relief that they hadn't run into Dave. But she also felt bad about it. Maybe he should be part of this.

The notion made her think of Ursula. She kept having the sensation that Ursula was beside her.

As they moved into the woods, the Double trailed behind her uneasily. He looked up at the trees and seemed frightened. "What is this place?"

Marti looked back to him. He was like a child—a waif, abandoned and unsocialized. But in spite of his weakness, something was changing him already. As they walked she felt the will that had been growing in her, the intention to heal Stride. Only now did she fully understand: he needed her. She had been so preoccupied for so long by her own loss and longing. Sunrise depended on her. She didn't understand exactly what that meant, only that her doubt had finally exhausted itself. She would heal Stride.

The Double was waiting for an answer. "We're almost there," she said.

"Where?"

No longer caught up in her uncertainty about whether this would work, she realized she'd been treating him like luggage. Now she willed herself to look at him with the love and devotion she felt toward Stride. She touched the Double's chin and lifted his head up so that their eyes could meet. She summoned, from some mysterious place, a reassuring care.

Something in him responded. His eyes gained focus. She took his hand and together they began to move forward again. Marti didn't have to think about the directions.

They reached the field of goldenrod, and Marti guided the Double in to the hollow at its center, where she had lain down and met the Elemental.

∞

Ursula had expended much of her remaining strength against the doors. And she had succeeded.

The gate was open. But Ursula's eyes were closed. She stood at this most awesome of thresholds, earth behind her, heaven before her, the extravagance of light on her face, warming her with a love of which the sun's glow had been but a faint reminder.

Then she opened her eyes. Ursula saw that through the gate, the great body of light was preoccupied with a singular task. A being was coming forth from it.

It wasn't exactly a birth, but a separation, a leaving home to embark on a journey, a phase in an endlessly repeating cycle. But perhaps birth is always just that.

She found herself willing the being toward her. She felt she was meeting a presence that had been close by for her whole life, yet always just outside of perception. As though her life had been shaped by an orbit around this being, her own personal sun, a pattern she could no more perceive than she could perceive the orbit of the earth itself. Yet as surely as she felt and saw day turn to night, she had felt the glow of its rays rise and fall within her as, day by day and year by year, she had drawn closer and then moved farther away, in a spiraling rhythm. Now what had been inside her was outside, before her, and she felt fully permeated by its emanation of love and wisdom.

Ursula felt her connection to her body, to life, growing ever more tenuous. When it expired, she knew that she would slip across the threshold and the doors would close. She was ready to let go. She wanted nothing more than to dissolve into this feeling of joy, to surrender finally and fully the bonds that tied her to her dying body. She looked down at the silver cord and saw that it was becoming pale and brittle. She didn't have much longer. But she had not completed her task. And she couldn't do it alone. She was waiting for something. For someone. To meet her, as she had met Stef. She knew who it was, of course. This was the task she and Marti had been preparing for. But where was Marti?

She couldn't wait much longer.

∞

The Double lay on the ground. A new feeling was coming over him. The ground, which had felt so hard and alien to him, seemed to be softening. For the first time it was not indifferent to his physical form, but rather welcomed it. That was good; flesh was of the earth, or should be.

He sank down into it.

Marti was sitting beside him, and her worried look relaxed when she saw his demeanor change. Abruptly she closed her eyes, as if in response to something inward commanding attention. She stayed like that for a long time.

Marti opened her eyes and looked at him. "I have to leave you here," she said. He was surprised at the panic he felt, and then it quickly subsided and he felt ready to be left alone.

She touched his hand, and it was as if he were being touched for the first time. For the first time he was not locked in a room alone. Someone was here with him. She would come back, he simply had to trust and accept that. That feeling unsettled him as well; he had been living in an eternal present, in which anything absent was absent forever.

Even when she left, he felt something linger, as if in leaving she was also coming toward him.

40

Walking away from the tangled mass of goldenrod that concealed the Double, Marti was hoping something would call her back. It seemed to her that every time she finally accepted something, she was then asked to give it up.

She hadn't seen the Elemental, but she had heard its bubbling voice. It had told her to go away, that she needed to place physical distance between herself and the Double, and that there was something else she needed to do. But it gave her no clue as to what!

A strong impulse drew her toward Dave's house. As she walked, she fought back anxiety.

Dave's house was silent. But Marti felt his presence. Something compelled her upstairs to his bedroom, a quiet hope that she'd find him there and crawl in under the covers with him and pretend she had never left. Forget words and let their bodies communicate in an older language.

But the bed was empty, and ship-shape, like everything else in the house.

Ursula appeared in her thoughts and she realized it must be the appointed time when they'd been having their daily meeting. But then she reminded herself of Ursula's condition, and that she'd been unable to connect inwardly with her. She decided to see what she could learn through more ordinary means.

It wasn't until she got off the phone with the hospital that she realized she'd convinced herself that the news would be good, that Ursula would have begun to heal from the stroke. But that was not what they said. She identified herself as Ursula's family physician, and learned that Ursula was in a coma, her condition extremely fragile. She could go at any time.

Marti resisted the familiar impulse to tabulate her losses. She refused to dismiss her original feeling: that Ursula, vital and engaged, was somewhere nearby.

"I'm with you, Ursula," she thought.

She felt, from somewhere beyond her, a sympathetic response roll back toward her. It did not feel like the emanation of a woman near extinction, weak and helpless in a hospital bed.

And then she realized that Ursula was with her. How foolish she had been! The discovery that Ursula was in a coma explained why she'd been unable to be in communion with her for some time. But that was then.

She sat down on Dave's bed and closed her eyes.

The image of Ursula's garden came so fast it was as though she was simply receiving it. As always, the roses were the anchor. Their vividness increased with her attention. For the first time she could even smell them. As the intoxicating fragrance entered her, she turned and saw that Ursula was in the garden and waiting for her.

The woman's beauty made Marti gasp. It struck her that what appeared as aging in the physical world, with a loss of the physical perfection of youth, must in the hidden, inner dimensions be a gradual attainment of perfection. Ursula's hair was swirling as though she were underwater, her body now fully permeated by the grandeur of color Marti had previously observed in her second body. Perhaps, Marti mused, the second body was the body we were creating for the next world.

But was Ursula dead? A pulsing umbilical cable suggested she was still attached to her physical body.

Ursula reached out her hand and Marti took it. She felt only a moment's hesitation, remembering stories in which unwary sailors were tempted to an underwater world in which a single day cost ten years of earth life. But Marti knew that Ursula was no greedy spirit. They had work to do together.

"No matter what," said Ursula, "hold on."

As soon as Marti nodded agreement, their bodies began to rise. Marti had the impression of moving through water, of a buoyancy drawing her upward.

She reached the surface. Instinctively Marti gasped for oxygen, though she didn't really need it. But her mouth filled with something thick and granular. What they had arrived at was not air.

Soil. Above the water was a thick blanket of earth. She could no longer see Ursula but the other woman's hand still held Marti's firmly. They climbed upward. Unlike the water, the earth resisted them. Marti found that she could claw her way forward, keeping her eyes and mouth closed. Where at first the sensation had been suffocating, now she felt held and massaged as she moved.

The next layer they passed through was fire, though for Marti it was more as if the fire was conflagrating through her, searing away and cauterizing. What she felt wasn't physical pain—perhaps the earth caked on them protected their skin—but a heightened sensation that was in its own way almost unendurable.

Finally she managed to pull herself through. And was dazzled.

Marti felt as if she had lived her life on a dark plain, and for the first time the illumination of day had arrived. The hemispheres of earth and sky were equally transparent, equally solid. The space was filled with moving glints of light.

Earth was in the distance now; she couldn't tell if she was above it looking down, or inside it looking up. Normal geometry didn't seem to apply. The earth appeared not as the familiar blue-green marble, hanging in a void of space. It was instead a vast, trembling sphere of movement. Marti thought of a beating heart, an organ formed by enfolded, interpenetrating layers of being. She might have been inside a great body.

She felt Ursula's patience as she let Marti take in what surrounded them and the earth. It was like a sky with a thousand suns, each one a different color and character. Gradually her inner organs of perception adjusted. Each of these bodies of light was a base station or matrix for innumerable smaller bodies, varied in size and shape, flooding toward the membranes that surrounded the physical world. At the same time a similar procession was returning to its source from the other side.

She had noticed these as glints of light, and understood what they were in the moment before Ursula communicated the word.

"Angels."

Refreshed from their sojourn back within the vast heavenly body from which they had just emanated, they streamed down and outward toward their work in the physical world. This close to their source they appeared as undefined pulses of light, but she turned back and saw that as they moved through the membranes toward the physical world, their forms became more defined. They remained nonphysical, but they nevertheless took on elements of human appearance as if in sympathy.

Marti tried with her vision to follow a single one. As it slipped through the one membrane and then the next, its form became more defined, with wings of light reaching out behind, and a shimmering face radiating compassion and concern. Then she lost it among the mass.

The next voice that formed words in her mind was not Ursula's: "Each is called forth by a purpose, you know."

Marti felt him behind her, but she continued to watch the angels' descent. She could almost glimpse the purposes before her as she concentrated on each angel. Purposes of healing. Of growth. Of enormous obstacles to be overcome. Each purpose was a destiny, and the sum of those purposes was the world. A world in which no one was alone.

And Marti was not alone, had never been alone.

"And what is my purpose?" she asked.

∞

The Ampsy, driven out of Hobbs's body by the Double's brutal disruption of its physical integrity, had been badly diminished by the attack, much of its vitality lost.

But it lost none of its intent. It could still put a stop to the Coil and to the Partnership.

If it couldn't expand, maybe it could compress itself. Something tiny enough, with sufficient density, could do great damage.

It searched for the Coil. Among the shabby gray twinklings of humanity, she was not hard to spot. She was asleep in a bed. And to the Ampsy's delight, she was not wearing the Onoma.

∞

Even before she turned, Marti knew it was Stride, or whatever his original name was—the unutterable name inscribed on the Onoma, one of the names that had resonated matter into being.

His form was not physical, not yet. His boundaries were

indistinct, powerful wings pulsing upward behind him, the light that formed him streaming across the great threshold. She felt it brushing through her, reawakening an ecstasy she had not forgotten but that could not be captured in memory. Her happiness at the reunion only anticipated his return to physical form.

He stood at the threshold, surrounded by great stone pillars. No, she saw, they were doors. Cowie's Gate.

She felt her hand squeezed. Ursula was still beside her, their hands clasped together. Now Marti saw that they were each surrounded by layered sheaths, made of the same stuff as the membranes surrounding the physical earth, like spacesuits, sustaining their connection to life. But Ursula's was thinning, worn almost through in places, and as Marti watched it tore open like a popped balloon and vanished.

Marti felt a bittersweet ache. She nodded at Ursula, and in return felt a delicate, flowing caress. A cascade of rose petals enveloped her.

Then Ursula, facing her still, was crossing backward over the threshold of Cowie's Gate. She and Stride bowed their heads to one another tenderly.

At the last moment Ursula turned away to face her new beginning.

∞

Ursula had not noticed the moment when the cord broke. She hadn't felt any sudden interruptions, but rather a gradual separation. The grace that had permitted her to remain in between two worlds was now strained, and soon she would need to go in one direction or the other. Ursula wanted it to be the direction of growth, and she knew that wasn't back to her body. She could cage herself there for an indeterminate time, as many did, lying in institutions not fully alive yet not dead, trying to gain the condition of freedom, or accomplish the task, or let go of the fear, that would allow them to move on. But Ursula already felt that freedom, felt her task complete.

It was only now that she had completed her work with Marti, and felt the joy of what had been accomplished, that she could even think about her own state of being. This is what we live—and die—for, she thought, for a task so great that we can forget about ourselves. It's like a painting; while she was applying the paint to canvas it belonged to her, was an extension of her being. But once complete, it went into the world. All the work, the experiences, the suffering and struggle of our lives, was like a painting, a boat we were filling with stores to send off into the unknown.

When she looked down and saw that she no longer had the living connection to her body, she felt a moment of terror. She thought of Hansel and Gretel when they realized their trail of breadcrumbs had been eaten by birds.

But the terror dissipated almost immediately; it had been a reflex, something from the past that had no more meaning. At the other end of the breadcrumb trail had been her home, her body. If she had imagined a return before, it now seemed absurd, though as soon as she had thought of it her body lay before her. It was wrapped in a thicket of tubes and machines, and she floated by the ceiling watching as two nurses unplugged it from the flatlined monitors. There was nothing for her here except to say thank you and goodbye. But that wasn't something one could do in a moment, not after eighty years.

∞

Marti and Stride stood on opposite sides of the threshold. She saw now, for all the power of his form, how diminished he must be. The great wings were there, but barely moving. He was surrounded by a retinue of hosts, bearing him up, too weak to be here on his own. She reached out her hands and there was a long moment's hesitation, during which she sensed the hosts scanning her intention, seeking reassurance.

Then he took her hands.

The world across the threshold suddenly exploded in Marti's perception, a world of pure movement and light, as intricate and layered as the richest biotic community, quite similar in its patterns. It radiated towards her as feeling, and the feeling was inviting. How right it suddenly seemed to her, that joy and peace have a home. It would be the easiest thing now to simply slip across, to join Stride in his world. But instead she stood firm where she was.

His breath was moving into her, as light, and the strength of her embodiment was moving into him, a conversation between spirit and matter. It reminded her that she was here to give something. He needed her, and if she allowed herself to slip across the gate, she would have failed. Marti sighed. This inexplicable choreography of surrender and affirmation had no end. But the renewed intention opened out a deeper layer of perception. What before had been a belief now became a certain experience: Stride needed her.

He had passed through this gate before, she knew, but that knowledge did nothing to diminish the fearsomeness of it. And his weakened condition made it more perilous, uncertain. Marti felt the weight of his previous descents to earth, the sacrifices that had now almost broken him. She concentrated herself and began to draw him towards her.

As she did, she felt the pressure of a membrane, stretched across the threshold, resisting his entry.

It isn't going to work, Marti thought. She drew him further towards her. The membrane only stretched, until he was fully lodged within it and it clung tightly to his form.

Then, finally, something snapped.

He broke through, now wrapped in the membranous substance. Before, he had been pure light and beyond any of the refraction or diminution known as color; now he seemed to have put on a coat of many colors. Each was a feeling: joy, longing, sorrow, desire, ecstasy, despair. Where before he had been pure love and wisdom, now he had submitted to the infinite gradations of sensation, feeling, and desire that cloak and give love and wisdom form, however imperfect.

She sensed a massive trembling in the angel. It was not a loss of innocence; rather, the willingness to take up a burden, a sweetness and suffering that had been known, and would be known again. She wondered if that's what it was like for all beings on the threshold of life.

The hosts that were supporting Stride stayed with him as he passed through the membrane, unaffected by the passage. Now she supported him as well. They were moving down from heaven to earth, yes, but it was also a movement outward, as though heaven were, paradoxically, deep within the earth.

Another membrane blocked Stride's progress, this one thicker, more opaque. Marti slipped through it easily, feeling it merge momentarily with her own membranous sheath. But again it resisted penetration by her angelic companion. She held on to midwife him as he began to press his way into this resistance.

She redoubled her will and slowly he entered fully into the membrane, enveloped by it. She could feel that it was painful. The pain of birth was not only the stretching and opening of flesh, but the pain of the moment before surrender. Finally he broke through.

The spectrum of color and feeling that defined his form had now taken on movement. If the first membrane had brought the animal processes of feeling, this second conferred the autonomous, impersonal processes that sustained human existence: metabolism, breath, circulation.

Stride now had something much closer to a human form,

yet without an actual physical body. In the movement Marti could for the first time discern a face. It was as if the face had always been there, but was now growing perceptible. The features were tight with concentration. Then a breath poured into him. He looked at her, smiled, and nodded.

One last membrane remained, that which separated them from the physical earth itself. It loomed before them. Its surface was pulsating with life, patterns of nourishment and exchange sweeping across its surface like thunderstorms across a lake.

∞

Lying on the bed in Dave's room, Marti's body continued to breathe deeply. Dust motes floated through the air on invisible currents. Among them was something that wasn't a dust mote, and wasn't floating aimlessly. Soon enough it reached the proximity it wanted. The next inhale drew it deep into Marti's nasal cavity.

The seizure began moments later. No one was in the room to see Marti's body convulse, her jaw clench and teeth grind, her limbs contort. And Marti herself was completely unaware of her own body.

∞

Thoughts were not new to the Double, but the sensation of life was. He felt the earth teeming below him.

He made a wish. It wasn't the wish the others had taught him, the wish to die. He wished to live. He wished for the teeming circulation he felt below the ground to awaken within him.

Sometimes a wish arrives as the whisper of destiny. He felt a star shining over him, very far away, and in its distant light shone the valor and necessity of his wish.

He lay near the base of a giant maple tree. Perhaps the wish was here in the life he felt, the life of this great being, a concentration of energy and matter accumulated over the long pulse of time, its roots reaching deep below him, even as far as the branches reached up. As his senses expanded in both directions, he felt that the tree served a purpose beyond that of its own growth and reproduction. Other kinds of beings moved along its pathways, its roots and branches; it was a kind of roadway.

Come to me, he willed them.

He closed his eyes, sensing their shyness. He wanted to make the invitation in the best way possible. Then came tiny pinpricks on his skin that awakened him to sensation. He'd thought maybe he would go to sleep and be changed. The change was coming, but not the sleep.

∞

Marti and Stride were preparing to press through the final membrane to the physical earth when it happened.

The sheath surrounding her tore open. She was thrust out of it, as if naked, into a storm blowing in every direction at once. Stride clung to her, wrapping his body around her as she felt herself begin to disperse, halfway between heaven and earth.

She had retained, throughout her journey, a dim awareness of her physical body lying in Dave's bed. But now this awareness was gone. She had been cut loose.

They floated like this for a long moment, and Marti saw that they were drifting back towards Cowie's Gate, the force of her own will towards earth aborted.

"What happened?" She didn't need to speak the words for Stride to hear her.

He looked at her with deep tenderness. "Something has happened to your physical body."

"I've died." She meant to ask it as a question, but it came out as a statement. Stride neither affirmed nor contradicted her.

So this is it, thought Marti. Her heart filled with the

presence of all those she would never see again. The sadness she felt was tinged with a fierce gratitude for their love, and within that love a regret for all the ways she had let her loved ones down.

The aching, bittersweet yearning swelled in her. This is what dying is, then, she thought. Something far too big for your physical body, growing inside until it explodes you out of this world into one that is expansive enough to hold you now.

She looked toward the earth and was overwhelmed by a tenderness that felt like goodbye. It was a realization of the gifts given her, even in the most hard-pressed moments of her life: the gift of experience itself. How had she not seen this?

Marti looked down and saw that her definition was beginning to slip away. She pressed her hand against the membrane to see if it would still be possible for her to bring Stride through. The tip of her finger poked through, and the end vanished in a whiff of smoke. She could no longer cross over.

"I'm sorry." She'd been thinking only about her own death. What about him? In his weakened condition, would he survive this? And what price would earth pay for her failure?

She closed her eyes, trying to hold the moment back, wanting to be with him for a little longer.

When she opened them, she saw that they were on the grand plain where he had taken her after their lovemaking.

Now he was more beautiful than she had previously seen or imagined. The lineaments of his human form were visible, but shaped out of light. It wasn't an imitation of something physical, but rather its prototype. The prototype of a man. Twin helixes of light swirled out from his shoulders—or were they coming toward him?—pulsing as if breathing in and out.

Below them was the translucent arc of the earth's horizon. Not the earth of nations and material, not the fixed earth of prisons and dynasties, but the living orb, the singular manifestation of a yearning too vast for comprehension. The rising sun was setting this earth's thick cloak of darkness afire with light. Sunrise.

The vision dispersed and they were back where they had been, huddled together, drifting back from the final membrane to earth. Why, she wondered, why show me the vision of what I have failed to attain? There would be no Sunrise.

But the thought that came towards her was, No, the possibility remains, I haven't failed yet. She must allow herself no doubts. She summoned all of her will, a whole lifetime of yearning. She gripped on to Stride, and felt him quicken beneath her hold, ready himself. And then, every fiber of her being straining, she drove them towards the final membrane.

41

Darkness swept over Marti. From the vast space of joy she was sucked into a void, every part of her imploding, crushed. The pain was a searing nightmare that wiped out every other reality. She recognized it from her passages through the Milgram Knot, only this time it wasn't ending.

Then something in her burst open and fire roared into her. No, not fire. Oxygen, burning her from within.

A face loomed over her: determined brow, deep worry in the eyes.

Strong hands slammed her chest down against the bed. She gasped, gulped air, coughed, tears and mucus smearing her face.

She tried to speak but couldn't find her voice.

Dave, registering that she was alive, stopped compressing her chest. He let out a sob. He scooped Marti into his arms, words forming through his sobs.

"You came back. You came back."

After a few moments he released her. Marti was just beginning to understand that she wasn't dead, she was alive.

Alive.

Then Marti felt the pain. It was behind her forehead, the kernel of something cold. The thing was lodged inside her, in a sinus or some other cavity of her skull.

With a flash of horror she sensed the familiarity of its energy. The Ampsy. It was no longer in Hobbs. It was in her.

Marti took a deep breath. She dismissed the impulse of panic, of flight, and directed her attention toward her fear, toward the dark kernel.

It shrank from her but she persisted. She recognized the cold, bubbling void, the black miasma that had swallowed Carly and had almost swallowed her. She had escaped from the inside of it, but now it was inside her, like a tumor. The thought brought another tug of fear, but she pressed through it and moved even closer.

Now she saw that the dark cloak, like a clenched fist, concealed something within it. She remembered the sense of release that the Ampsy had held out to her as bait, and wondered if that was what the being itself needed.

She began to peel back the clenched blackness. Stop, some part of her thought. It was like opening a casket that might contain everything she'd ever feared. And yet there was something poignantly, desperately, human about it, as if each person were nothing more than a space closed around a terrifying mystery. What had the angels been doing to her but opening her up like she too was a clenched fist?

The thing resisted with all its being. But she was stronger now. To Marti's astonishment, as it began to open, a burst of light rayed forth, then another. The light, no longer trapped, blazed in her eyes, as warm and giving as any she had ever felt.

With a violent flutter that felt like a beating of wings, the light departed completely, leaving behind only a dry, empty husk.

"Can you talk?" Dave was still facing her.

"I think so," she said. Her voice shaky.

"You weren't breathing. I thought for sure it was too late."

Marti nodded and looked around, only one thought now. "Where's Stride?"

"What?"

"Stride."

"Is that a person?"

"I can't have left him behind!" Had things somehow gotten reversed? Stride sent back across the Gate and her down to earth? She felt a terrible dread, that after everything she was separated from him once again.

"Calm down. You need to—"

"No." Marti pushed Dave's hands away. Panic seized her and she tried to sit up. But her stomach flopped over and the floor rushed up towards her. Dave grabbed her as she almost fell over, and laid her back down on the bed.

"I'm going to take you to the hospital."

She shook her head. "Please. Not yet."

Something was different about her body.

It was in her heart, her back, her groin, her hands, everywhere. Something pressing down on her, a weight.

She was sweating. Not from exertion but as if from the application of heat. She shivered; the air was chilly against her hot skin. She was disturbed to realize that she must have a very high fever.

Using all her strength, Marti managed to sit up in spite of how nauseous it made her feel.

"Lie down," said Dave.

"I have to go to him," she said. "He's out in the woods."

Again she experienced the sensation that she was carrying something. And her body was fighting it. Illness was an antagonistic response. She felt her mind beginning to dissociate, another symptom of a high fever. The light coming in through the window made her squint. Her eyes burned. She closed them and turned her attention inward, determined to meet whatever it was without resistance.

Her body felt too dense, too tightly packed to carry this weight. She tried to spread herself out, and felt the first moment of relief. She breathed deeply and undertook that most exquisite and difficult act of will: the voiding of itself into surrender. She repeated the inward gesture over and over again, struggling to communicate it throughout her body cell by cell.

She encountered pockets of resistance. But with the weight bearing down on her, she found more and more strength. She imagined surrender as a gushing stream of water that dislodged the tough kernels of scar tissue, painful memories, self-righteous attachments, all the strange and bitter stuff that clogged her inner byways.

"You need to be looked at."

"Dave, please trust me."

She looked at him with all the certainty she could muster, and she saw his anxiety subside. In turn his eyes carried Marti the final steps back into the unresisted present moment. Dave touched her cheek gently and nodded.

For a while she remained still and did nothing, nothing but breathe. Breathing seemed in the moment like something magnificent, each breath binding her to life.

Then Marti pulled herself to the edge of bed. Her body felt no less strange. Something more was still inside her, something that was not her, but she no longer felt that it would destroy her. In the expanded space that they shared, she felt her perception beginning to focus. It wasn't outward sensory perception, but an inner sensing, and what had moments ago felt alien and hostile now began to fill her with a familiar joy and comfort.

She moved again and felt an immediate vertigo that wiped away the joyful sensations, but when she stilled herself they returned. Now she knew what the presence was. Not what: who.

∞

At first, Marti thought he had left. She was sure she had returned to the right spot, with the thick community of goldenrod and the great maple tree as the marker, but as she approached she saw no human form nearby.

Movement had been difficult. At first each step had set off a bout of nausea and disorientation. Gradually she got a handle on it, using her breath to restore equilibrium at each moment of stillness, and establishing a slow, continuous movement that her state could bear.

She was certain now that she was carrying Stride within her. The full spectrum of him, his vastness somehow sufficiently compressed for her to carry it within her own being.

Finally she saw the Double.

It looked like he had become part of the forest floor, part of its tapestry of growth and decay.

His clothes lay in a pile beside him. But his body appeared to have been claimed by the elements.

What she saw had the suggestion of a biological process, but one taking place at an impossible speed. A crust was forming over his body, apparently of its own accord, foaming and then hardening in place.

"Good Lord!" Dave was right behind her, his hand over his mouth in horror. Marti raised her hand and waved him back.

She kept focusing on the Double as she drew closer, and she felt her vision penetrate through the veil of the merely physical.

She saw the beings that were working on him. They combined glimmer and shadow in a way that marked them out as separate from the physical realm, not subject to reflection of light and so not visible to the outer senses.

Their bodies were tiny, round, hairy, and elastic; at first she thought they had no faces, then it seemed like they were all face. Their industry was prodigious. They were allowing themselves to be seen, and perhaps that was important to their purpose, but they paid her no attention.

They were moving in and out of him like worms, opening him up as if he were lifeless, compacted soil. She thought it should be an image of horror, but it was not. At least she felt no revulsion; rather, she felt wonder. They were moving so quickly it was hard for her to remain focused on any individual, and she kept getting drawn back to a sense of the overall movement.

They were not eating; on the contrary, they were bringing nourishment. It was as if they needed to move through every cell in his body, and in moving through it they changed it. A cocoon was forming progressively around him. He was already more than half covered when she arrived, and as she watched, his body disappeared from view.

As her vision of the phenomenon deepened, she saw that the tiny creatures were moving as part of a single entity; they were the appendages of something. Tracing back to their source, she saw the smiling face of the earth-being that had invited her to bring the Double here. He was inviting her again now, inviting her, without words, to come closer to him.

After her near-total separation from the earth, his embrace was a homecoming. It felt good to bring her body to a position of rest, and on the firmness of the earth. The teeming Elemental creatures were vibrating beside her. It was a sensation she had encountered before, particularly as a child in the woods near the subdivision where she had grown up. She'd never seen anything extraordinary, but amid the rocks and trees, the leaves decaying into the soil, the chatter of squirrels and the sun glinting through the canopy, there pulsed a rich sensation that made her feel more alive, made time stretch out like a wide plain, instead of the narrow tunnel she felt herself pressed into so often. The roar of traffic on the suburban road could be heard, though, and seemed to declare that this biotic community was an oversight that would eventually be replaced with a purely manufactured environment—as it was.

Closing her eyes now reaffirmed the familiarity of these Elementals that had been known to her before only as a kind of joy in nature. Before, she had believed such feelings were simply a mysterious, human response to a world with no conscious properties of its own, a living factory of raw material ready and waiting to be harvested. Now she understood that they were the perception of life by life.

Her body lay alongside the Double's, and for the first time the nausea subsided. The heat had not receded, and she felt even more of it beside her. The furious movement that had enshrouded the Double thrummed against her skin, and she began to feel goose bumps rising on her in those places. The sensation continued to move across her like a slow wave, and then following on from it a deeper prickling, and behind that an ache. The Elementals were moving through her body now, and began to work her into the cocoon with him.

Marti felt as she imagined a planet might feel. The activity across her surface was at once tremendous and distant. At her center her heart swelled, its rhythm anchoring not one body but two. She tried to hold both bodies in awareness, and gradually felt that her being was a link. At one end, Stride's body, at the other, Stride's spirit. She was the narrow bridge. The sun was rising across the canyon. Marti could feel the force of it now; the doorway had opened wide and would not be closed.

∞

The strange hallucinatory edge that had tinged Dave's perception since making love to Marti had now begun to puncture a hole in reality. It wasn't only the bizarre phantasm unfolding before him on the ground, nor Marti's trance-like consent to enter into an embrace with it. It was the strange twilight quality of the vision.

His mind told him to grab Marti, drag her away from here, but his body was rooted to the spot.

∞

Marti opened her eyes but saw nothing, only a diffuse, veiled light. Perhaps this was how the caterpillar felt as it began to dissolve. Now it was the familiar visible world that had become pure feeling, the earth below them and the sky above, while here she could see everything that had been hidden. She thought she must then be on the distant shore of death, a place where light and dark change places.

But she was not alone. Stride was here with her, both outside and inside.

She turned to him and what she saw was a readiness to receive her. Her love for him took the form of a great rushing as the immeasurable constellation of being that had rooted in her from Ursula poured from her depths to the surface and moved toward him like a river toward the sea.

Within the movement there was an indescribable ache. Her being was curled around another, carrying it within her, and now she had to let go. She knew she couldn't hold it forever, but as the movement between them built she suddenly felt an urge to resist. It was too big, it would tear her apart inside. As her resistance tightened the ache turned to a searing pain.

And then, in the distance, she heard someone calling her name.

It was Dave.

Not yet, she thought.

She felt certain that if she wanted, she could go to him. She could back away from this threshold. She knew that if she crossed it, she might not come back. It was yet another choice.

It was as if this choice had been preparing itself all along.

Dave was calling her, calling her to a life of companionship, of shared rhythm. A life of comfort and security in the world that could be seen and predicted. But, she realized, there were no such assurances. A life with Dave was as great a mystery as what lay across the threshold with Stride. These thoughts had taken place in a moment of suspension. She let out a groan from deep inside her: this was the choice she had to make once more, the choice to let go of all assurances.

The ache as she let go had both pain and pleasure in it. She allowed all of her being to move toward that sensation, and as she did she felt her limbs joining with Stride's.

Their bodies came together, lifted up into the rush of spirit. It was like tears or laughter, it was a joy beyond anything Marti had felt before. The joy of homecoming after long exile, she thought, homecoming to the beloved, in the beloved. It had been accomplished.

All stories end with this, she thought, with reunion. Those that don't are not truly endings, but recognition of what humans had learned in the loneliness of isolation: that reunions were not easy to attain, that endings did not come until the traveler had persisted across the threshold.

She still had no idea where this was leading, except that it was leading home, though not a home she had ever been to before. She felt herself tossed between a wave rushing toward shore, and an undertow pulling her back toward the center of the ocean. She could feel people standing on shore, waiting for her, but she couldn't reach them. Once more she felt herself sucked away, and she lost all resistance. She would not make it to shore.

Then she felt a hand in hers, and it was pulling her upward, out of the surf, and then she was in Dave's arms. He held her.

"Marti?"

"I'm here."

"You're okay? I don't understand what's going on."

She gently separated from him and touched her body, surprised by the familiarity of its form, everything that made it ordinary and everything that distinguished it. It was no older or younger, no more or less blemished. She ached as though she had been slammed back into herself a little too roughly. But she was glad to be back.

"Who is that?" Dave said.

Marti turned to see Stride, still lying on the ground, but the cocoon was gone.

He seemed to be asleep. His eyes moved rapidly under their lids, his limbs trembled slightly. He had changed again; his body, which had been so dense, had now been filled by the light she had carried to him. Before, he had been devoid of a second body; now she couldn't entirely tell where the flesh left off and the light began. She touched his skin, still not quite believing they were here together. Alive.

Perhaps he was now the same as when she had first met him; her ability to perceive beyond the physical had not yet awoken then—it was he who had awakened it, and then disappeared. She had longed for his return, another lost lover. He had first entered her through the opening of her sex, but now she had entered him in return, an intercourse of the heart, something much larger than sex. Perhaps he'd had to go away and return precisely to make this possible. To make Sunrise possible.

She saw that his eyes were open. "We came back," she said.

"Yes," said Stride. "Sometimes, through sacrifice, and through love"—here he looked at Dave, who was hanging back, a look of confused astonishment on his face—"a new possibility opens."

Stride turned to her now and reached out. She could hold him now, could feel the pressure of his flesh, the aliveness of her skin against his. But his wings were there too, made not of flesh, but great arcs of light that enfolded them both as they embraced.

"Marti?" Dave's voice pulled her back. Confronted with this strange intimacy between her and Stride, he looked hurt.

Marti separated from Stride, motioning him to wait, and moved towards Dave.

She saw the movement when was still about ten feet away. She tried to shout something at him, but her voice froze in her throat. Or maybe Violet was simply moving too fast.

Dave's hurt look changed to one of sickening surprise as Violet pulled him back by the hair and cuffed him brutally on the head. His knees buckled. She shoved his staggering body toward Benz, who scooped him up. She pointed an accusing finger at Marti.

"You left us!"

Marti found her voice. "No! I had to do this first."

"And we are always last," Violet said. "And the end never comes."

She turned away and motioned to Benz, Dave limp in the giant's arms. "Kill him," she said.

"No." It was Stride. He stepped forward and Violet now registered his presence.

Violet took a step towards him, her legs suddenly wobbling.

"You," she said, and fell to her knees in front of him. Benz, astonishment on his dull features, released Dave and likewise dropped down.

Marti rushed to Dave. He had lost consciousness, and she listened for his breath. Reassured that he was still alive, she cradled his head in her lap and prepared to defend him with her life if necessary.

But the others now paid no attention to her. Stride took

several steps toward Violet and Benz, who were both kneeling in front of him, their faces upturned, trembling.

As Stride moved, Marti saw that he was not, as she had assumed, undergoing a process of embodiment, of concentration into a human form. Rather, the familiar physical form was being absorbed into the swirling currents of light that now permeated it, funneling with increasing power through the great "wings."

Violet nodded, as if he had been speaking to her, then stood up to meet him. When they were an arm's length apart, the expansive star-like body that permeated Stride now encompassed Violet as well, like a flame leaping from one piece of wood to the next. Marti didn't notice Benz stand up, but a moment later he had joined the other two, the three bodies now fully and equally absorbed into the angel. In the light, Marti could see their faces release the torment of their twisted separateness.

This was what he'd had to come back for, she realized. He had returned only to retrieve what had been left behind. They were part of the angel, just as much as the Double Stride, the residue of previous descents, and now the angel was making himself whole.

Marti felt the tears running down her face. The angel turned towards her, the individualities of Stride, Violet and Benz now merging into a single face of such expressive depth and beauty that she gasped.

If the feeling that flowed towards her had been expressed in words, the words would have been, "thank you."

The light was warming her face like the rising sun. She knew he was going to return to heaven now, but she felt no grief, because heaven was right here, right now. The distance had been in her, and now the distance had been worn away by love and by surrender. There was a deeper together always waiting for recognition.

Marti willed every particle of her being to open and receive the blessing of this awareness. It was a kind of marriage, a deed, an event she felt inscribe itself on some indissoluble layer of being. Soon, time would resume its ineluctable flow, but this infinite moment was the deeper reality.

The angel continued to radiate gratitude towards her, the contours of his being spread far beyond. Particles of light were shedding from his periphery, the tiny spiraling lights of the hosts. She could feel him receiving the affirmation that was swelling in her heart, and then he seemed to nod. The outer edges of the light body turned inwards, wrapping around his center like a cloak, and then suddenly he began to disperse outward into a billion tightly clustered particles of light.

They swirled in a wide arc, their glimmering light gradually subsiding, until they had fully become substance.

Bees.

Their movement continued as the swarm swirled towards a resting place on the branch of a tree.

Stride and the Doubles were gone. The angel had returned to Heaven. No, Marti realized. It was not a retreat. Heaven had come much closer.

Dave groaned and moved, rubbing his head. "What happened?" he said. He tried to sit up, but fell back immediately, holding his head.

"Ugh, who was driving the car that hit me?"

Marti caressed his check. "Hey," she said, "go easy."

He looked up at her and his eyes lit up, as if he had just realized that she was here with him. He reached out and stroked her cheek reciprocally. His fingers caught the moisture of her tears.

"You're crying," he said.

"I'm happy to see you," she said, back in the embrace of time. Stride was no longer in view, but he was not gone.

She nodded towards the swarm, hanging placidly in a giant cluster on a branch.

Dave blinked, followed her gaze, trying to focus.

"Shit. One of the hives swarmed?"

"I think it's a new one," said Marti.

42

"As a gardener, you're a really good doctor."

Marti looked back over the row she'd just weeded. She'd been paying attention, but she could see now that plenty of weeds remained between the tomato plants.

"I'm sorry." She sighed.

"No, really," said Mr. Boujeyeh, smiling. "Is this the best use to make of your time?"

"It's only once a week," she said. "It helps me to put my hands in the ground sometimes. I can't see patients all day, every day..."

Three young girls ran up to Boujeyeh. One held up a small carrot, its orange so bright it seemed on fire, dirt still clinging to the tiny hairs that fringed it.

"You said we should pick these, but Henni says they're too small," one of them said.

As she watched the old man follow the girls to the row of carrots and patiently offer guidance, Marti stood up, stretched, and looked around her.

After barely a year, it was already hard to believe the community gardens hadn't always been here. This one was the second. The first, mostly flowers, had been established as forage for the bees, after Dave had agreed to move his hives in to the Park.

They hadn't even had permission when they started. The first garden had been made on one of the Park's patches of bare ground, earth so hard it needed to be worked for days, turned and broken, before it could be seeded. Rhea, who still worked as receptionist at the clinic, had gotten involved, bringing garden tools and bags of compost to dig into the sleeping soil. Each day brought more participants, and soon a second garden was started.

The second one was in a perfect, sunny spot, out of the way of foot traffic, except that the soil had been long ago covered with a layer of concrete. Soon a team of young teenage boys, glad to be breaking something up and to be able to strip their shirts off in front of the girls, were smashing away with sledge hammers and peeling the concrete skin off the earth.

Marti passed by every day and saw the change happening. Not only that flowers and vegetables were being grown, but that people were regaining agency over their lives.

She was the one who'd gotten the ball rolling by urging Dave to move his bees to the Park the previous winter, in response to the kind of inexplicable impulse she now obeyed without question. But she'd had no idea that it would lead here, and that so many skills, whether gardening or leadership or simply hard work on behalf of the community, would be uncovered.

Marti stood and stretched. Maybe Boujeyeh was right. She wasn't cut out for this. But perhaps that was the point of life. All a practice, a learning. The afternoon sun glinted on the plants, and Marti smiled at the beings that surrounded her.

There were the humans, and the others. It seemed that a human being was just a point in a vast intermingling of worlds. A bridge. A coil.

Still, it was easy to escape notice of them. Their movement—at least from the human point of view it seemed like movement—was constant, even when she sensed they were hovering in one spot. But more and more for her their presence was a simple reality. And for others too.

People who visited the Park were astonished at the gardens, the vigor and fecundity that seemed to be springing out of this nowhere of a place. The color and fragrance of the flowers, the size and flavor of the vegetables, even things that weren't in their ideal climate zone. But Marti wasn't surprised. What she saw was the fruit of partnership. A hint of what was possible.

"Dr. Powell?"

Marti glanced behind her. In the Park she was generally known as "Dr. Marti." She'd had had her fill of journalists and others with questions. The journalists had subsided some time ago, but she remained on her guard.

"If you're here to help with the garden," she said, "I'm not the one to talk to."

"No, it's not that. They said I'd find you here. My name is Adam Dennison." He held out his hand.

Marti turned around and looked at him. No, she sensed, he wasn't a journalist. He was small, in his early thirties, carrying a full backpack with a bedroll. She felt like she'd seen him before, but couldn't place him.

Marti took his hand and then realized that hers were covered in dirt. "Sorry about that."

"That's okay."

Adam was travelling by himself, but he wasn't alone.

His second body was suffused with a deep, dark blue light threaded with golden fire. The colors, as they always were, were unique, expressing the distinctiveness of the Partnership. The man was now sharing his second body with the source of that light—another, much larger being. "Guardian" no longer seemed like the right word. Partner. The partnership of angel and human, formed out of love, was that of wisdom and will.

It was a condition she'd never seen in anyone before the day she'd rectified Stride. Perhaps the possibility had always existed and the limitation had been hers, had been one of perception. But over the past months she had seen it in more and more people. In some cases, she watched while the transformation took place over a short period of days, as something opened in a patient. Sunrise.

And it hit her, what every schoolchild knows, yet remains unreflected in our language and perhaps unrecognized in our perception: even in that most everyday cosmic event, it wasn't the sun, the constant, radiant sun, that rose. It was the earth that turned to receive its light.

Marti moved into the next row of tomato plants. "If you want to talk to me, you need to help me weed." He put down his pack and followed her dutifully as she knelt down.

"Really, I just wanted to thank you," he said.

"For what?" she asked, surprised. He glanced around to see if anyone else was in earshot. They were alone.

"Project Secure Horizon," he said.

Marti stopped weeding. "How do you know about that?'

"I work for Harmon. Well, I used to, before I quit."

"A fellow ex-employee."

"I was a lab manager. Some of us knew—but, it just seemed all wrong. There has to be a limit to the ends justifying the means. But no one really could stop it. Well, none of us even tried. I still don't understand that."

"Until Gansrud..." The image of his broken body made her shiver.

"Not exactly. Yes, a lot of shit came out after his sudden death." The look on Marti's face brought him up short. "Oh, but of course, I don't have to tell you that. You were exonerated as a result."

Marti felt uneasy. "But Project Secure Horizon is dead."

"Oh, yes. No question about that. It happened apparently in an instant. We still had a huge supply of the stuff when we lost the donor. But a little while later, right after Gansrud's death, every vial in every box went inactive. Overnight. That's why the whole thing fell apart, so that when the authorities came in, they thought it had all been a hoax. But I know it wasn't."

Marti already understood that when the angel had reclaimed Violet and Benz from their imprisonment on Earth, somehow the residue of Violet's body, which Harmon had made into the panacea serum, had disappeared as well. But it felt good to hear about it. She realized she had stopped weeding, and turned back to the job.

"Do you mind if I ask you something?" he said.

"Go ahead."

"Why don't you fight to get your license back? Go back to work at the clinic? Everyone knows you were railroaded."

Marti wondered how to answer. The security recordings had cleared her, and all the charges against her had been dropped, but the truth remained that no medical clinic was ready for the kind of work she did. Anyway, she had become quite fond of the new office, even if her practice, which relied on whatever donations her generally impoverished patients could make, was economically precarious.

"Why don't you go back to work at Harmon?" she asked.

He smiled and nodded. "Point taken."

"So what will you do now?"

He shrugged. "I'm enjoying figuring it out as I go along. I seem to know what to do when it's time. And then I do it."

Marti smiled. In its simplicity, it was as good an account she'd heard as any. Without further words, Adam swept her into a brief goodbye hug.

When Dave arrived a moment later, apparently coming straight from the clinic, she passed the hug on to him. She never got tired of basking in Dave's second body, a landscape of coral and turquoise, where she had first recognized the effects of Sunrise.

"It's not your shift today," she said.

"I just wanted to see you."

"You saw me at breakfast, and I'll be there for supper."

"That's too long to wait!" He kissed her.

Marti laughed.

Dave went to check on the hives. Marti watched him, feeling grateful. A bunch of laughing children ran by. She looked back at the row she'd been weeding. It seemed like she'd barely made a difference. She sighed.

Marti knelt down and sank her hands into the soil.

ACKNOWLEDGEMENTS

Places: New York, Toronto, Paris, Hornby Island, Kolkata, Istanbul, Toronto again, Claremont (ON), Rural Karnakata, Amsterdam, Toronto Finally.

The time of writing this book also involved some unexpected (isn't it always?) underworld travelling. I made it through thanks to the love and support of too many people to name here. But a few were particularly important to the development of this work:

Helpful readings were given by Philip Shepherd, Amanda Hale, Shandi Mitchell, Geneviève Appleton, Harriet Friedmann, Judith Weisman, David Buchbinder, Lisa Taylor (I will write another book to hear more of those squeals of delight), and, beyond the call of duty, Gale Zoe Garnett. Sat Kaur Khalsa always helped me see what was in front of me. Alexis Gargagliano provided editing, and Marie-Lynn Hammond copy editing. Anne Ngan and Sue Peehl provided places to work. Ellen Levine challenged me to make it better. Shawn Watson and Melissa Kajpust's excitement about the project in a different medium really got it going.

My first reader, Elyse Pomeranz, was a close companion on the journey that finds expression in this book. That it is "for" her was not decided after the fact, but was a reality from the first word.

ABOUT THE AUTHOR

Mortal Coil is Amnon Buchbinder's first novel. His previous book, *The Way of the Screenwriter* was published in 2005 by House of Anansi Press. He has directed two theatrically-released feature films: *The Fishing Trip* (1998) and *Whole New Thing* (2005), which screened at over a hundred international film festivals, winning a dozen best-film awards. Working in the film and television industry he has written and rewritten numerous screenplays in funded development, and taught professional screenwriting workshops in a dozen countries. He has been a curator and film programmer for organizations including the Vancouver and Toronto International Film Festivals. His third feature film, the docu-myth *Travelling Medicine Show*, will be released in 2015, and he is currently writing and directing the web-based interactive documentary *Biology of Story* exploring "story as a living thing." He is an Associate Professor and former Chair of the Department of Film in the School of the Arts, Media, Performance & Design at York University. He divides his time between Toronto and Hornby Island, BC. Even more information at www.amnon.ca.

Made in the USA
San Bernardino, CA
02 July 2015